THE MISTS OF
MANITTOO

THE MISTS OF MANITTOO

Lois Swann

CHARLES SCRIBNER'S SONS/NEW YORK

Copyright © 1976 Lois Swann

Library of Congress Cataloging in Publication Data
Swann, Lois.   Mists of Manittoo.
  I. Title.
PZ4.S9715Mi [PS3569.W258] 813'.5'4   76–2387
ISBN 0–684–14585–5

1 3 5 7 9 11 13 15 17 19 H/C 20 18 16 14 12 10 8 6 4 2

Printed in the United States of America

I wish to acknowledge my great debt to
MARK LANDAU KASDAN
and TERRENCE GARTH SWANN
for their encouragement and enlightened
criticism during the writing of this book,
and for Mr. Kasdan's knowledgeable and
devoted help in obtaining and maintaining
my research materials.

Author's Note

I wrote this story in response
to whispers from my own memory
of characters and events I
may have known 200 years ago.

Chapter 1

Southeast of Boston, in the year 1746, in the crescent of farmland fronting Buzzards Bay, late summer heat lay moist and
stifling, permeating even the ground. The clanging in the harbor overlooking Martha's Vineyard and the Elizabeth Islands
was silenced. The shipbuilders and sailors, merchants, and tran-
sient population had given up all activity and retreated to the
dank coolness of the public houses, giving their throats over to
the mercies of the local ale and cider.

Three miles inland, where the hilly land was undisturbed by
commerce, the farms lay in exhaustion. The crows that nestled
in the church steeple for shelter in the winter sought out the
shadows of its small bell portico this day and declined to pester
the fields of corn and wheat, beans and peas, bursting their
borders toward the coming harvest.

The farms near Buzzards Bay were small and as productive
as the tenants who worked them, but farther in, on the heights
and sloping fields, the plantations were vast and prosperous
seats of old families brought by the ships of the early adventurers who had filled the land with business and religion and their
progeny.

Buzzards Bay, fifty miles from Boston, the vital spot of the
New England anatomy, was an ideal spot for nurturing the
more independent sons and daughters of the first English settlers. This section was settled by those not acceptable in the
Puritan scheme of things, those followers of John Cotton who
moved to Cape Cod to escape the slights of their Anglican
townsmen. One by one they bargained for the land with the
Indians across the Bay. They cleared trees and built fences and
traditions which fostered security for independent thought in
religion and politics. The isolated settlement granted, as a
bonus, exclusion from the bickerings, wars, and religious ex-
cesses that plagued the rest of the Massachusetts Bay Colony.

Insular and complacent, the residents of Buzzards Bay occupied themselves with building the productivity of their farms,

adding to their stretches of seacoast property, and devising new ways to garner the rarest of commodities, money. They were content to leave pretensions to European civilization to the close-knit members of Boston society.

In the southwest of this fertile place was the village of Sweetwood. Fringed by fragrant pines and a forest of juniper, sassafras, maple, and birch, Sweetwood was surrounded by a remnant of Indians from the Great War between English yeomen farmers and allied woodland tribes under Metacom, or King Philip, as his adversaries called him. The descendants of the families who had followed Philip and had avoided exile after his defeat peopled the deeper woods.

Gone was the dominance of their ways and their mastery of the coast, but by agreement they were left on their own in back of the wall of trees to parcel out the salt and clear rivers and to allocate the forest for hunting. Some tribes were sustaining and even increasing their numbers, decimated after their near victory over the English almost one hundred years before. Yet farm and forest were two countries of two differing peoples who never touched except when money and goods drifted between white and red hands.

Near this forest lay a huge triangle of settled farmland. In the unabating heat of this mid-September afternoon, the fields and meadows refracted the bluish light in visible waves, and nothing stirred in the white houses, scattered to the points of the triangle. The cattle stood fascinated by the unearthly brightness and the pressure of the warmth they could almost lean against.

The northern property belonged to Gilbert Worth, who had come from England twenty years before with plenty of money, great ideals, and no religious scruples. His wife, Hanna, was sister to Charles Dowland.

Charles, owner of the western and largest part, was head of one of the oldest Presbyterian families in the region. His only daughter, Elizabeth, a girl of seventeen, was engaged to their minister, Annanias Hudson, who farmed the eastern portion while looking after a widespread church membership.

Hudson was a Boston man, of a family of civic leaders, and he had served the farmers for a decade, monkishly alone. His farm and house adjoined the church, which was fitted out by the

2

Elders with floorboards and mahogany side chairs. He had not asked for, nor did he get, a fireplace in the fifty-year-old structure. Annanias Hudson's goals did not center on unnecessary comfort. Regard for his bride-to-be, however, had nudged into being improvements of his well-scrubbed home.

The end of the month would close his long period of waiting for his marriage to Elizabeth Dowland. The people prayed among themselves that his coming happiness would temper his zeal, turning ruthless in his rooting of their faults. Now thirty-four, he had been an impressive model of strength and virtue among them, patiently waiting seven years while Dowland's daughter ripened to a marriageable age.

After the civil ceremony, the local families would come to the lawns of the old Dowland farm in the October sun and share their minister's victory with a spread of food and bowls filled with a ruby mixture of sugar and the juice pressed from the native cranberries.

Most of the people who would come had had a stake in the preparations. The men had pitched in on refinements of the manse, and the women and girls had worked on the quilts.

There were thirteen of these, the final one for the bridal bed. Prue Hanson and her mother had taken the lead, filling gray satin with goosedown, securing the batting with tiny white ribbons to complement the bright red-and-yellow ship motif.

Elizabeth gave them a free hand at the bees, not having her heart in the preparations. But her mother, Mary, glowed at the quilting parties, serving with grace the puddings, breads, and cold meats the ladies brought along. These gatherings were the culmination of her hopes, planning, and prayers, brightening the disappointments of her middle years.

* * * *

Reverend Hudson was spending this unbearable afternoon making rounds of sick calls. By two o'clock he had reached only his second stop.

Prudence Hanson was not well. Her recurring melancholy disturbed her parents, and Hudson visited to read and speak to her and to enjoy her mother's cooking.

With the lack of breeze in the Hansons' large kitchen, even the

3

cool cider they sipped gave no relief, and Hudson reminisced about his days in Cambridge, finding it easier to dwell on past successes than to address himself to the present battleground on such a day.

Miles away his betrothed wife, Elizabeth, had crossed her father's steaming meadow to the house of her Uncle and Aunt Worth. Nothing kept her from these visits. She went daily, except on the Sabbath, to sew in their sitting room.

Together this childless pair had made a remarkable house, planned around the land it was set on. Built toward the southern light, it made a rambling arc around an ancient cherry tree which filled the house with fragrance and color from spring through autumn.

Elizabeth and Hanna had sewn the heavy hanging that blocked the winter draught from the large, widely envied sitting room window, scaled seven feet square. They embroidered thousands of white blossoms and tiny pink birds into deep green wool to simulate the tree wintering out of doors.

Charles Dowland considered the house a folly and a waste of engineering skill, but he never interfered. His brother-in-law, Gilbert, who had studied in Paris, had a French influence and was, in Charles' mind, beyond the common sense of typical Sweetwood residents.

Gilbert Worth still struggled after two decades in the New World to keep his knowledge current. He sat in the afternoons with Elizabeth and his wife, making music on his harp, revealing European arts and letters to them.

After basking in this atmosphere of exploration and aesthetic pleasure, Elizabeth had developed a loathing for the life she was expected to undertake in the hollow of land that belonged to Annanias Hudson. These afternoons would soon come to an end for Beth, as she was known, and in the heat she was unable to concentrate on the little tucks she was sewing into the high bodice of her wedding gown.

She sat at her aunt's feet and watched her uncle as he made notes in his diary. Beth considered his small, lithe form, fair coloring, and fine-featured face and exulted for Hanna that she had found a man of so many gifts and such physical appeal in this quiet village. His collar was thrown open, revealing his throat.

"Annanias will never open his collar in the parlor."

"Did you speak, Beth?" Hanna stopped fanning them both.

The girl closed her eyes and saw her betrothed husband. Broad of body, considered tall at ten inches over five feet, he was gaining flesh with each passing year. His flattish face and pale eyes were a forbidding wall to her. Although she had sought to understand him and become his friend, she did not know how she would manage to be a wife to him and bear him children, when her interests and inclinations were only beginning to open to her most private self.

"The clergy have need to be formal, pet. Doesn't mean Hudson wouldn't like to throw his bands out the window." Gil Worth looked up from his work and regarded his niece.

She bore the mark of the Dowlands, who differed in looks from their other English neighbors. In the family mold Beth was slender and handsome, with a sway of importance in her movements belying her small size, causing more interest than she knew simply by appearing in the family pew in church.

Gil saw her neck, in exquisite balance with her spare, shapely face, and the brown of her eyes and hair, underlaid with henna, as a reproduction of Titian women. This connection with the artist's bright auburn trademark was founded not on chance but by the facts of the Dowland family tree.

At the time of the family's original emigration in the mid-1600s, the traits of a Corsican bride were introduced to the English palette. The mixture had imparted to future generations large, dark eyes and an elegance of body.

Gil smiled to himself, for this vivid presence was a point of division, he was sure, between Beth and her mother. Mary was the product of austere prosperity and simple tastes. Mrs. Dowland's love of fine porcelain was her most amenable weakness, in Gil's eyes.

Beth was a changeling from another land, and Gil was afraid of her sometimes, for she was almost commonly frank and perceptive about her poor prospects in the life her parents had outlined for her. Gilbert Worth felt her goodness and cast of beauty were wasted on the provincials of Buzzards Bay.

He closed his diary, his heart heavy to see that Elizabeth disguised her tears with sweat, continually wiping her face with her handkerchief.

"The summer will not end, will it, Beth."

"I hope it never does, Uncle Gil. A pity, the calendar changes though the heat remains."

Hanna petted Beth's hair. "Sweet, we would do anything to see you happier."

Elizabeth buried her face against her knees. "Aunt Hanna, I am a lost cause. Do not bother more about me!"

"No, no! Come up here by me." Hanna assisted her niece onto the settee, and Elizabeth pressed her face against the silk, staining it with sweat.

"It is as if I died and let my empty shell walk about."

Gil pulled a stool in front of the women. "Is there not a saving grace in him, Beth? He loves you, and is provident, and can think and talk very well."

"I am so tired of hearing his virtues! What of my own? I will suffocate from his obsession! That is not loving of him.

"Oh, Uncle Gil, forgive me. I should not speak against my duty. It is like slandering my father. But in four weeks Annanias will not be obliged to talk more, but be allowed to touch me! How will I endure it?" She gripped her uncle hard and hid her face against his neck. "Is not a wedding to bring a couple joy? Tell me, while I am brave enough to ask, is not a woman to feel comfortable and giving? What happens if this is not so? Doth she die of hurt? Can she live, year after year, in that shame?"

Hanna bit down on her folded fan, and Gil was left to soothe them both through the sudden upheaval of the quiet afternoon.

"Child Beth, listen. Listen now. I will brave your father's objections once again and try to talk your way out of it. I promise nothing, but I have known Charles Dowland even longer than thee, dear Beth. He was ever fair when I came, a stranger, to ask for Hanna's hand."

"Think thee he will relent, with the town hanging garlands from the window boxes and Mother smiling again as if this wedding were her own?"

"I offer no false hopes, but I will try! If your papa insists you marry Hudson, why, I will have the fellow up here, and have a talk with him, and put him straight on how to make you glad."

"Oh! My God!" It was half a prayer. "If only I could die before!"

6

Gil hopped up before his niece could cry again and took a velvet box out of a table drawer. "No more of that! Look at this, look at this. Hanna and I were supposed to wait until the day, but who's to say a girl cannot have a peek at her wedding gifts."

"As the legend has it," Hanna ventured, "the wedding is waylaid, whose gift is not delayed."

"Then by all means!" Elizabeth brightened. She found a silver vial cradled in the box.

"Lift it out," Gil encouraged. "Hanna and I have had a jolly time getting this thing made up for you in Boston. Look underneath. That's the man who fashioned it."

"But Gil designed it for you, sweet."

"It will serve you so much better than land or lace." Gil could not resist this appeal to his niece's sensible nature.

The cylinder was fitted at each end with tiny hinges. When Elizabeth lifted one cap, a silver thimble tumbled into her lap. She slipped it on her finger, a perfect fit, its circumference wreathed in tiny gold ivy leaves. She slid open the other end of the case and saw, housed in blue velvet, five gold needles in graduated sizes, with silver eyes and points.

"Why! It is a brooch, as well! Uncle Gil, it is the finest thing I have ever seen. How I thank thee both for thy love!"

Tears welled up in her eyes again, and Beth made a sudden exit from the room and out the kitchen door, taking the path she usually walked home.

Chapter 2

Beth moved painfully down the road, not knowing where she could go to find solace from the heat and her anxieties. She passed Matthew, her uncle's black houseman, whose freedom had been bought by the Worths. He was lying in the grass, his face half-covered by the news sheet. She did not see him and could not know he heard when she began to weep.

Beth usually turned off the dirt road at that point and climbed the gradual slope, where after a walk she could see her father seated in his study, watching for her and working at his desk.

Suddenly fleet, Beth made a run for the line of trees and entered the forest. It was as hot underneath the pines as on the path but the cool green light was some relief. She struggled along, kicking aside the carpet of sweet-smelling needles, passing places that she recognized from searches she had made for wild berries and balsam at harvest time with Matthew and her friends. But she went deeper than she had on these festive hunts.

She was angry and thirsty and walked unconscious of her surroundings until the foliage began to change. Laurel hedges and sassafras, wild onions and groves of birch, replaced the pines. Large trees thinned, opening into meadows. She surprised a flock of wrens and was entangled by them as they flew down and away in confusion.

Many times the twisting of her ankle, her disturbance of little creatures, and her inability to find fresh water taught her that she could not move any more comfortably in the grand and quiet spaces under the trees than she could in Annanias' closely shuttered house.

Calmer, exhausted by thirst, Beth sat and backed against a tree on the heels of her hands. She gashed her palm on a hidden stone and sucked the blood which sprang from the cut. She hardly noticed the beginnings of a little breeze combing lightly through the treetops from the northeast.

In her thoughts the day was warm, late May of nearly three years before. It was a time of celebration in addition to the annual picnic after the planting. An era was ending.

The edict permitting the routing of Indians for bounty, stemming from the ugliness of war to the north, had been retracted. Never popular in Sweetwood, its cancellation was also welcomed as a sign that poachers and adventurers would be leaving the out towns, and all were happy.

The bright image of her brother, Henry, running in a pack of eight-year-olds, swished by in her memory. This present day's real heat brought back the flush of embarrassment that had shown when the amiable son of the Poores, friends who traveled with her aunt and uncle, had asked her to dance at a party Worth had given. To dance was an experience not allowed her.

But at that young age Beth was already used to denying her desires, knowing she had been promised, that there had been exchanges of signed contracts. She was bound to marry a different sort of man, behind whose façade of geniality Elizabeth saw the unbending will of a stagnant personality, a man without moral courage who held sway over the consciences of everyone she knew.

Of course Annanias had interfered, tucked Beth's arm under his, and Stephen Poore had turned away, his neck red under the tail of his fine white wig.

A headache brought her to the present, and now she noticed the breeze was heavy and wet. Still, she wanted more time. Instead of going home she went farther into the woods.

There was sufficient light under the trees, and now clouded sky, for Beth to collect fragrant branches for her mother. It soothed Beth to select the slender kindling piece by piece as an apology for her lateness. The sweetness of the juniper and other trees had given the village its name, and she could smell the perfumed smoke that would rise that night with her family's evening prayer.

But directions blended, and when she realized that she wanted to start back, she did not know how to go. Even the wind, growing out of the breeze, seemed lost and began to bend the thinner branches back, whirling the leaves in circles.

The terrain changed. The trees grew closer together and it was dim near the ground. The sun that had been so strong was shrouded in a sky suddenly gone dark. As she made her way along the soft earth, Beth felt close to her brother, Henry, and wondered if from his coffin he could detect her misery as she

9

walked alone. Almost two years before he had died of the pneumonia that infected all the Bay. Hope had died with him at Dowland Farm.

Henry was the only son and the last in direct line from Peter, the original emigrant. Everyone had loved Henry. He was quick and lively and possessed marvelous skill with his hands. It was expected he would make a good farmer with his early ability. After his short day of work, his favorite thing was to sit in the back field with a pocketful of pencils and his book of paper, drawing ever more proficient pictures of the things that grew around him. Grass, grain, trees, and crawling animals held him fascinated for hours. He liked his sister to sit with him and often charmed her into holding some wriggling creature for a portrait. Some people said he should be apprenticed to a painter in Boston, but Charles Dowland could not lose him to such a life, and now the boy so cherished was forever gone.

Beth found a cache of strawberries she knew the Indians called "hearts" and ate a quantity to cool her thirst. She removed her apron and combined the fruit with the burden of sticks in one large bundle. Her hair lifted up from the fringes of her bonnet against the strengthening wind, and she grew even more anxious about the time. Milking was over. Her mother and father would have eaten, thinking she had stayed at the Worths' to dodge the heat. They would go over later in the cart to fetch her. It had happened before.

It would be a painful journey for her father, ill since Henry's death with a sickness he had been controlling for many years. Gradually his bones warped and he could neither walk nor sit a horse. Accepting their slow-moving ox for a vehicle, he oversaw the fields, traveled to church, and went to Wareham market on its back. The neighbors applauded his show of ingenuity and widened the local roads at narrow places so he could travel unbothered by faster conveyances.

In his worsening condition Charles Dowland, with strong concurrence from his wife, added to the dowry that Beth would bring to Hudson. He signed away three hundred acres more before the wedding would take place.

Within a year of the Maytime picnic, Beth watched the laborers carry away the low stone fences between pastures, permitting Hudson's cows to graze on wider meadows, fattening for the wedding feast.

This new bond was celebrated at a private tea and Beth still remembered the sunset that filled the sitting room as they talked politely over cakes. The subject of the wedding date was broached, everyone still wearing black for Henry. Beth's mother suggested autumn. Beth would be seventeen and the sewing of her linens, so long in progress, could easily be finished by that time. The daughter pleaded for a longer wait, saying she was not yet joyful with Henry's death so recent, and left abruptly.

Annanias' dog, Princess, barred Beth's way with snarls at the kitchen door, and the girl went for a bone, with the meat still clinging, to buy her passage outside.

Hudson was piqued at more delay, and Mary Dowland mollified him while Charles sat still, gathering strength to follow his daughter to the field he knew she would visit.

Mounted on the ox, he found her curled like a worm in the gathering darkness.

"What does this mean, Elizabeth?"

"Do you love me, Father?"

"Everyone has been searching for you."

"Tear the papers, Father!"

"Tear? You are upset, dear. Tear?" He could not grasp her intention.

"I will marry no one. That is my wish. I shall never marry."

Her father reached his gnarled hand down to her. "Perhaps, Beth, thy mother should be with thee now."

"I do not think I am afraid of marriage, Father."

"Are you not?"

Twilight mushroomed into darkness before Elizabeth spoke again. "Father, dear, will you not release me? I can name half a dozen others more suited to this man. Girls with wealth behind them! He could not object. Why, Prudence Hanson is most fond of him and I cannot do this thing."

"Beth! That is enough. This match is your salvation. Hudson will be your mentor and your guide when I am gone. Is he not a good man? Would I trust you to him if he were not? His beliefs are sound. If you do your duty and live your life by his side . . ."

Beth turned her face toward him and he could not continue.

Finally he said softly, "Then you are afraid."

"We simply are not suited!"

"Is there another, sweet girl?"

Beth wished she could say yes. "None."

"Then, my dear . . . with your brother gone from us, this land will be some distant cousin's seat if I do not fix it on you somehow."

"My life for the land?"

"Do you know what it would be, unmarried, living as an unwanted guest where once you were the mistress?" He reached for her cold hand and kept her next to him as the ox moved toward the barn. "You are loved by Annanias. Look how he has waited and prepared a place for you in his home. There will, at least, be charity between you, and that alone can stand you through the days that will come. Give yourself another year. Eighteen is late enough. I do not feel strong."

Even now, one year after they had exchanged those words, a chill spread through her body, as much from recollection as from the wind which tore at the trees around her. The stifling afternoon had yielded to new weather and the first good rain in weeks would come. Beth took the apron and held it to her chest as the wind caught in her dress. She hurried through the falling dark to try to find a path. She judged the sudden cooling and heard the cracks of thunder as no ordinary rain. This would be a gale, and boats would fly loose from their moorings, flitting white above the towns on high water, dancing out to sea, then crashing onto beaches from Plymouth to Provincetown.

In a thicket, with wild sounds about her, Beth dropped to her knees, praying forgiveness for the worry she would cause, knowing a dry bed would not be hers that night. She lay trembling on the apron as rain came.

She endured the hardness of the drops, was coated with the mud they made, and experienced a deadening of body as time passed. Wet and wind, defeating her resistance, stirred one central thought, her only light in the noisy blackness.

Henry lay beneath the earth that she must walk. And al-

12

though she was alive, it was the ghost of her brother's frustrated future that marked each succeeding step on the path her father had laid out for her. But the memory of Henry, her small confidant, guiltless in this mapping of her life, settled over her like a cloak, and at last, toward the middle of the night, she refused to care. Disregarding the screaming storm, she drifted into sleep.

Chapter 3

Beth's own shivering awakened her. She moved wet leaves away from her eyes with her wrist, her fingers too stiff with damp and cold to move. The sun's glare made her smile. She nearly chuckled aloud as she tried to stand, shivers rumbling through her like departing thunder. As she straightened, she sucked in her breath at the spectacle of newly stripped branches drizzling their sparkling residue of moisture on the fallen leaves below.

The girl rubbed her hands and tried to move forward. No thought came except how to manage the cold, wet, clinging hem of her dress which tangled around her ankles as she tried to move. No matter how she pulled and gathered the full skirt it coiled itself around her legs like rough rope, rubbing as she walked.

The freshness of the air, the golden light, the new perspectives through the trees whose leaves had been prematurely torn away, would have delighted her senses the day before. But it was the fact of her own survival that formed the faint smile that kept reappearing on her lips. Unprotected, unseen, perhaps unmissed, she had survived the night exposed and had awakened in freedom. The pleasure of self-sufficiency warmed her and she sought fresh water with an assurance that had not been hers the day before.

Beth held her skirt up to her knees, removed her ruined shoes, and stopped to judge the direction of the breeze. She was momentarily alarmed by the thought that there might be large animals going to water as well. Preoccupied the day before, she had not admitted this other peril into her mind. She listened. All sound was distilled into the drumming of the drops from the trees. She dragged along with the cumbersome skirt, then stopped again. There was a fluid noise like the pattering of the drops, but more constant, rushing. The ground rose sharply in front of her into a hill with trees thickest at the ridge. Since she had seen no stream on level land, Beth had no choice but to scale the hill.

14

Wind-caused tears skidded across her cheeks as she used her hands to aid her ascent. She was surprised by cranberry bushes spread thickly along the spine of the hill so uncannily neat they looked laid out by hand. Then she raised her eyes from the bushes, down a gradual slope heavy with birch, and saw the river.

Sparkling, swift, blue in the early light, the river revealed to Elizabeth the thrill of Englishmen of over a century before who had come upon such American wonders daily in their searches for a safe, inland harbor.

Her exultation at the speed and beauty of the river, determinedly following its path to the sea, dulled to resentment when she considered the strictures of her own life. Her direction had been sealed before she felt the need to determine her own future. Shivering in the light wind, Beth formed her confidence into a resolve.

There would be no going back and no apologies. There would be no wedding. She would refuse to submit her body to the whims of a man she hated and her mind to his sullen intelligence. She would walk away along the bank of the river. Surely her parents would relent at such a protest.

She glanced back for a last look at the sodden, twisted woods and grew sick in her stomach. Below her, fanned into an arc as if arranged by a landscape painter, were the foreshortened figures of her Uncle Gil, Annanias, Matthew, and one other man she did not recognize. Her eyes wound around wistfully to the river, and she choked back sobs over her near escape. The embroidered quilts, the pewter service, the hundred tucks in her dove-colored dress, glinted in the bright points of the water as the wind blew against its flow.

Strength returned. "My apron!" Moving fast, yet careful to stay low, not breaking any branches, Beth backtracked, determined not to be found. She must have time to think and to make them understand her.

"Annanias' dog must be here too. Smelling about. What a blessing the rain! All scent washed away, foot marks blown over!"

Her plan born whole, she felt her way, on hands and knees, under and around faint landmarks to get at the apron. She would have to climb the hill again and stay in front of the wind until they gave up.

She saw it, a tangled mass of cloth and brambles. She damned her complacency of the previous evening, allowing her to fill the apron with such unwieldy stuff. She struggled to untie the wet strings to empty it, failed, and started tearing the branches out, ripping the cloth, looking up and back and to the sides for the dog the searchers must have brought. Princess would be ahead of her master where the scents were fresh. Shreds of fabric clung to the freed branches so she gathered the whole burden up again.

A low growl froze her. The wind had brought the sound. The dog could not have the scent yet. Looking all places and seeing nothing, Beth fled through an open glade that led back toward the hill.

A ring of high bushes separated her from the incline. She crawled through them, clutching the bundle with one arm, her ankles and legs bleeding from the rubbing of the ice cold hem. In her intensity she did not hear the noise she made as she forced herself into open ground. She burst into an area of tall, leafy trees which rose with the land and felt, at once, she was not alone. The shadowy area was a blackish green and her eyes adjusted slowly.

She perceived, as she stood very still, the figure of a tall person looking at her quietly from between two dark, spiraling trees. She moved forward several steps to be sure. It was a man. She looked far up into his face and beheld the countenance, handsomely shaped and calm, looking with large, dark eyes. His hair reflected blue what little light there was, the breeze lifting long strands from his shoulders.

Beth could not at first accept as real the presence of the man just ten feet from her. She was sunken into sudden peace, the absence of any threat, and moved no farther. It was his eyes that changed and his mouth that slid into a smile and he who moved toward her with the Indian's greeting.

"Cowaunkamish."

Beth was stirred by his deep intonation of the most formal salutation, "My service to thee." She lifted her miserable skirt slightly to make as graceful a curtsy as she could, knowing no suitable reply.

16

She quaked with chill as she stared up at the man, but his attention was riveted high over her head and behind her. She noted his long doeskin cloak strung back from his shoulders and the small breeches. These were his only garments. His bowcase, a rolled blanket, and quantities of rope were hung about his person, blending gracefully with his figure.

Raucous barking assaulted Beth's absorption, and desperation at her lost running time contorted her face. She bolted toward the hill grasping the ragged apron.

The Indian lunged for her and held her. He motioned with his fingers to be silent, guided her firmly to the muddy mound between the trees, and pushed her down. He drew his blanket off and open and Beth was covered.

She burrowed out enough to watch for the dog she knew was coming. Submitting to the Indian with total trust, although she had questioned his reality minutes before, seemed utterly sensible as she scanned the bushes.

She watched the man walk to the spot where she had broken through the undergrowth. He was as relaxed as an Englishman standing near his hearth. He felt for a knife-shaped stone in a belt at his hip. In the next instant the hurrahs of the human hunters joined the hysterical baying of Princess as she came hurtling through the broken bushes toward the climax of the morning's hunt. Drunk with success, her heavy body passed the Indian, her nose reading only the sharp signal that had evaded her so long. She reached the blanket, screaming out her victory, then whirled on the alien scent that tainted her achievement. She bared her teeth to the gums, judging the distance between herself and the interloper.

The man raised his left arm in front of his chest, baiting her, and the dog ran directly at him, hurling her body upwards toward the temptation. The Indian never moved until the last moment. Reaching like a cat clawing a fly, he seized the dog's tongue just before her jaws closed on his flesh.

Princess fell to the ground, gurgling and slashing, strangled for air, and as the undergrowth began to snap under the boots of the men, she rolled back her yellow eyes and died. The Indian was upon her with his knife, holding her foaming muzzle, slitting the bitch's throat. He wiped his blade on the ground and

17

replaced it in its sling. He took hold of something underneath the flap of skin.

Beth watched the muscles of his back and shoulder thicken and slide as he gave a mighty pull, eviscerating the animal in one stroke. Beth saw no more. There were impressions of rifle cracks and excited voices, a heavy weight dropping on the blanket which covered her, a rush of cold air and patches of sky as she was borne along, quickly, high off the ground.

She came to consciousness lying on her stomach at the bank of the river, retching, a bronze hand supporting her chin and another restraining her forehead. There was a gush of cold water and her stomach came under control. The Indian washed her face with his hand, then stood.

"Peeyaush, netop." He pointed to the northwest.

As Beth stood to see what he was showing her, she raised her hands to her hair and looked down the expanse of her filthy clothes and saw her legs bare and bleeding. All went black again.

When she opened her eyes the smooth face was next to hers and a warm hand rubbed each wrist. Beth's eyes glazed over with fever and in a small voice she said her only Indian phrase, the ancient English greeting, "What cheer, netop?"

Chapter 4

The Indian swung Beth up in his arms again, after washing the dog's entrails in the river, and walked north in the cool air, stained gold by the September sun. He never slowed his pace nor seemed burdened by the English girl's weight. When the river wound away and the land rose sharply, he stopped.

He wrapped his torn cloak around her, took some parched cornmeal from a basket at his back, and made a portion of gruel with water in his cupped palm. He fed the girl with a carved spoon, unhurriedly, and ate some himself.

Beth watched him as he tidied up his bundles and prepared to travel again. She tried to rise, but weakness and the sharp angle of the land unbalanced her and she crumpled onto her side and watched the river as it flowed away from them. Unable to move, Beth passed many minutes simply looking at the water, listening to its rustle along the bank. Never in her memory had she been idle at this hour. Each day was busy with the chores of living that had changed from a way of survival into the art of colonial life. She felt it strange that she did not fear the man who had carried her away from what she had known into this new world.

The Indian approached and squatted at her side, thinking. Her fever was firmly established now, and little puffs from his tobacco pipe made her drowsy with its sweet scent. In the abstraction of her fever, Beth was unguarded and openly returned the man's candid look.

His uncovered body, his marvelous endurance, his grace and calm, encircled her perceptions. While he had carried her Beth had become aware of her own skin where it touched him. There had been a tiny moment of regret as he set her gently down to prepare their meal.

A shriek interrupted their silent exchange and they turned to watch a herring gull light at the edge of the river to rest. The gray bird was far afield, turned aside from its usual course by the force of the storm. It strutted before its audience, then gave in to fatigue and plumped down on the coarse grass near the water's edge.

The man laughed and took Beth's hand cordially.

"Kayaskwa, kayaskwa."

"Think thee the gull and I are alike?"

The man gave no sign that he understood her words but placed her hand at her side and repeated quietly, "Kayaskwa."

They left the gull at the river and continued to climb. She slept in his arms but woke to the renewed sound of rushing water and saw a slimmer branch of the same river cutting through a wooded area. Pines, maples, birch, chestnuts, were crowded together wound around with girdles of firethorn bearing fat, ripening berries. The hills seemed to vie with one another for a view of the river and at the meeting of two of these rises, forming a plateau, they stopped.

The man sat Beth against the trunk of a tree and disappeared into a round hut covered with fiber mats and bark. After a short interval he emerged wearing dark doeskin leggings and moccasins, stood Beth on her feet, and, supporting her, led her toward the door. Crouching to the level of the shingled door the Indian backed in first, holding Beth's hands.

"Peeyaush, Kayaskwa!"

The Indian guided her to a pile of fresh-looking mats near the center of the high room and helped her to kneel on them. But she slid forward, away from his supporting hands, to rest her aching head. The man reached for a basket half his arm's length across and drew out a white broadcloth shirt cut in the Indian fashion, many times washed and worn. He sat Beth up and removed her wet sewing purse and placed it in an empty basket. He slipped the shirt over her head. Exhausted, she lay down again, her eyes glassy and her face flushed. The man groaned at her discomfort and unbuttoned her light dress and camisole, working them down her body and legs, covering her with the shirt as he went. Beth tried to help with her muddy things but sank down with a cry, caressing the clean shirt.

As she lay on this strange bed, covered with a heavy blanket, she watched the man busy himself in her behalf. He worked with close concentration and speed but without strain. He made up a fire with an old fire drill, opened the flap of matting in the roof for the smoke, and hung a birchwood cauldron over two stakes pounded into the dirt floor. He went out to fill a large birch bucket with fresh water, poured some off into the kettle over a thick bunch of dark green dandelion leaves, and sat near Beth as it began to heat. He moistened her lips and made a cold wet compress for her face with his hands. Beth tried to speak, but only inarticulate noises slid from her. The Indian held a long straight finger to his lips, turned, and went out.

Beth awoke during the night, impressions of her surroundings heightened by her sickness. She regretted her weakness from the fever. She wanted to get up and run her hands over the mats which formed the inner walls and settle in her mind the meaning of their painted black-and-red figures. She wished she could stir the brew in the birch cauldron, now giving off a tangy steam, and explore the back of the hut where odd-shaped skins hung in various stages of being dressed. She marveled at the quantity of baskets, the uniformity of weave, and the variety of their sizes and shapes, each serving some exact purpose.

The fire was very low, filling the core of the room with amber light, allowing the far walls to remain darkly private. The Indian lay against the east wall in view of the door. Lost in the blackness, his presence seemed as ethereal as it had been in the wood many hours before. His face was averted and Beth could not tell if he slept or rested. She looked in wonder at his relaxed hands and his body. She wondered if others of his family and tribe were as beautifully formed.

The only Indian she had known was Jack, the town cobbler, and he was very different from the man who lay fifteen feet from her.

He had worked all day to succor her, a stranger, a trespasser. Not once had he abashed her with questions about her wild appearance or her reasons for being afraid. Natural warmth and courtesy flowed through all his actions. Never had he flustered her when his eyes met hers. That she had not been kidnapped was certain. Whatever his words meant they carried the sound of helpful guidance, not persuasion or menace.

"Kayaskwa." She formed his word silently with her lips. The gull. He had called her Sea Gull. She realized then he would not even ask her English name.

21

Beth placed the Indian's age at thirty. He was in his thirty-second summer. His skin was the glowing color of the room and the sight of his thigh slanted upwards, touched by the firelight, caused her palms to ache. His legs were muscled, yet supple, without hair, strong and graceful like the rest of his body. His face, especially, inspired Beth with the wish to touch. The places under his eyes, divided by the long, straight nose, arched very slightly at the bridge, appealed to her. Mystery hovered in the shadows beneath the high bones of his cheeks, and to touch those places seemed to Beth the way to knowledge of his whole self.

Beth's fever flooded her with discomfort. At her sigh the man rose to full height and walked to her side. He removed the birch cauldron from its cradle and tasted the contents with his finger. He dipped a polished wooden bowl into the broth and began to feed her a pale yellow liquid with the spoon Beth remembered from their earlier meal. It was bitter but soothing, and Beth took all he would give her. He seemed pleased at her receptiveness, and when the bowl was almost empty he stopped.

He held the spoon with his left hand and stroked the form of the animal carved into its handle, showing her the many grooves that represented the fur and bushy tail of a fox. He pointed to the well-wrought features showing even the nostrils.

"Wonqussis!"

"It is a fox. Wonqussis is fox?" Beth reached for the spoon and drew back, surprised at the sharpness of the tip of the animal's nose. She wondered if he used it for a pick or a little spear. Her hand dropped to her side with fatigue and the Indian took up the spoon again.

"Wakwa," he whispered. "Wakwa! Wonqussis!"

"Wakwa?" She tried to focus on what he was teaching her.

Patiently he repeated the two words again. Beth reached for the spoon and her arm seemed pale and sickly in the dark red room. She touched the smooth bowl and asked in his words, "Wakwa?"

The Indian moved her fingers along the handle to the face of the carving and repeated, "Wakwa," and after a short wait, "wonqussis."

"Fox and wonqussis are the same? Wakwa is fox, too?"

He did not respond to her English but placed the spoon on the floor and touched both his cheeks with his hands and said earnestly, "Wakwa!"

Beth pulled herself up on her elbow. "Thou art Wakwa! Thou art the fox! A special fox." Tears filled her eyes. "Now may I thank thee, Wakwa!" She turned onto her stomach and hid her face.

The man named Wakwa became busy again removing the boiled dandelion leaves from the kettle, throwing them onto the fire. The sweet scent of burning wood circled about them. He approached with a fresh bucket of water and while Beth continued to cry began to wash the blood from her legs and ankles, carefully covering her and wrapping her tightly when he finished. He swabbed her wrists and fingers and the back of her neck. Then he turned her over and wiped all her face with the last corner of the linen cloth.

While she rested quietly he began to pull burrs and other matter gently from her hair, which was dark from sweat and stiff with mud.

Beth lay very still, her gratitude growing. He had observed and tenderly addressed himself to everything. She thought her hair would have to be cut to remove the burrs and be jagged for months as had happened occasionally at home with her mother and father. But Wakwa, seeing her unhappiness, sat with his legs crossed one over the other, unknotting and spreading the strands, picking out the dried and thorny matter as if no other pastime could have contented him more, as outside the moon reached its zenith and the trees chattered in the silver night.

Chapter 5

Dawn was bright and warm but it remained dark inside the hut. Wakwa had been out for water and wood and was collecting smooth, round stones from the river when Beth awoke. Her skin was slick with sweat and her mat smelled stale. Everything was in place, the fire hissing and popping. The one new object in Beth's view was a deep pottery vessel. She studied it for a time, its purpose gradually becoming evident as she stared. What great consideration the Indian showed, leaving her the chamber pot! Almost obediently, she relieved herself and dragged the pot across the floor, in spurts of strength, to clear it away. The fresh air outside the hut door started violent shivers through her body and she huddled back under her fetid blanket.

She tried hard to understand why the sweat ran off her when she felt cooler than the day before. She longed for more of the yellow soup but the cauldron lay on its side against the wall empty and dry. She hoped Wakwa would return but shrank at the thought of being near him in her condition.

Fantasies of entertaining him at tea dressed in a gown of brown velvet, made with wide sleeves against the civil regulations, occupied her for a time. Then she slipped completely from her surroundings. She walked again with her dead brother in his field, telling him about the things she had seen and known since the night of the storm. She laughed and spoke aloud and grew disturbed that she could not get close to him nor touch his woolen coat. When she complained about this a gentle hand slipped into hers. Holding it in both her own she fell into a sound sleep.

Wakwa approached the hut with his heavy burden of stones and heard the English girl in animated conversation. He went silently through the opening with his hand on his knife. Relief and dismay at what he found prompted him to hurry his tasks.

He heated the stones and placed them around Beth's body after rewrapping her tightly in the blanket. He was free with firewood and tightened the flaps of birch bark to protect the girl

from draught. He ate corn, tossed some sassafras into boiling water, and drank tea as the hours drifted by. Mostly he sat at the side of the girl he called Kayaskwa and held her hand when she reached out in need. When he lay down on his mat at night he was weary.

Beth woke first, as night changed into cloudy day, and she pushed some wood into the fire. She was astonished that she had been living for two days in the darkness of an Indian hut, sleeping near a stranger, a man, an Indian man. He had not offered her the slightest incivility, yet her own father might have difficulty in believing that some devilish rite had not been performed over her as she lay asleep.

Beth began to see it as a measure of the barbarity of her own people that Wakwa's charity and chastity would be considered an absurd impossibility. A few years before it would have been unthinkable for Wakwa to have helped her. The Indians in Buzzards Bay had not been hotly persecuted during the time of the bounty on scalps, but she remembered the whispers about the young militia man who had attacked a Mashpee just within his land rights, killed him, and paraded the scalp through the small towns on his way to collect his one hundred pieces of eight from the magistrate. There had been no repetition of such an atrocity, since the Buzzards Bay towns were determined to stay out of the troubles of the English and the French and were content to keep the good will of their well-contained native population.

Beth wondered if Wakwa had known any of the families hunted out and scalped for money. She herself was invading his territory although it did not seem to concern him. Again she remembered the day when the yellowed provision paper, passed before she was born, was torn off the door of the church. Sunday after Sunday she had passed the quaint printing.

> "For encouragement to prosecute the Indian enemy and rebels, and to prevent their skulking and lying in wait in and about the frontier and out towns—that the following rewards be allowed and paid out of the public treasury, to any company, troop, party, or person singly, who shall kill or take . . ."

25

Beth reviewed the words she had unwittingly memorized, gleaning for the first time their harshness, their righteousness. Perhaps the sight of the red man sleeping nearby prompted her latent sympathy, but the common ambitions of her contemporaries for snug lives with this or that young farmer, and even the Calvinist theme, had never caught fire in her heart. She recognized shame in the phrase, "paid out of the public treasury," for the colony admittedly devoted to God had turned the expediencies of war into the general practice and the general guilt.

The god Beth prayed to was different from what he appeared to be in the Sabbath readings. For Beth he was a being of unity and warmth who caused all things to grow, cows to calve, people to couple and to nurse their sick through dreary nights. That Jehovah smiled on this hut was never in doubt for Elizabeth Dowland. She concluded that her duty to herself and even to those in Sweetwood was to keep her disposition free of servitude. How to heal the wounds this would cause remained an abiding trouble to her.

When Wakwa opened his eyes he found the sick girl in a sober frame of mind.

"Good morrow, Wakwa," Beth greeted his clearing gaze.

The man sat up and pushed back his hair, grayed with ash. "Cowaunkamish, Kayaskwa."

With the glaring fire between them Beth could not decipher the expression in his eyes. Finally he made the effort to pull himself up. He squatted near her and held his palm to Beth's forehead to satisfy himself that her fever had broken.

Without a word he prepared their food. He opened a new basket of corn and ladled some into his kettle. He handed Beth a pestle and a large bowl of fresh strawberries.

"Wuttahimneash." He offered her a berry to taste.

She repeated, "wuttahimneash," in a whisper as she bruised the garnet-colored fruit into a pulp.

They ate silently of the corn boiled with spring water and berries. She was hungry and finished her bowl of sweet porridge.

"Wuttahimneash!" She smiled at him.

Wakwa acknowledged her effort with a look. Then he got up, knotted his hair into two intricate braids, and hung his rope and other equipment around himself.

"Npunnowwaumen." He gestured to his accoutrements and the outdoors. He glanced back at his torn cloak on his way out but made his exit without it.

Beth sat confused. He was so preoccupied. Perhaps, since there was no common language between them, it was his way of telling her that her presence had become a hindrance. Certainly it had. He had cared for her more tenderly for two days than she had ever been cared for at home by her mother. She felt that if he were a hunter he must be much behind in his work. She began to look about for things to do to express her thankfulness. If he required her to leave she would be all the better prepared.

Wakwa walked northeast into the forest. A hunter and trapper, he also performed more complex services for his sachim. He had been about the business of repairing the rain damage to his traps when he found the English girl and had not been to his own town since he rescued her from the dog and its masters. Although there was no rush to bring food home to the otan, Wakwa was ill at ease when he left his traps too long unattended.

After a brisk run in the gray woods he came to the first trap. Wind had intertwined the big loop of rope into the branches of the tree above. The action of unraveling the knots brought back the first night with Kayaskwa when he had removed the burrs from her thick hair.

Making a slip knot of proper tension, he draped the loop from a bough and secreted the end on the ground. He spread some acorns across the hidden noose to tempt a deer. He traveled to several other traps, knowing their locations with minute exactness, and was able to find the ropes without much trouble. He set most of them to catch deer, still the basic support of native life even though many things had changed for his people since the English had established themselves on his shores one hundred years before.

Looking at the sky, while he ate some meal, he decided to cut back to the river to check a trap of which he was especially hopeful. It was near the head of the bright stream which passed by the tanning hut. The delay of two days because of the white girl's helpless condition concerned him. He was conscientious, not as relaxed as his hunting companion, Awepu, who lived

27

without the expense of too much effort, yet proficiently enough to make a pleasant partner.

Wakwa stood at the trap, angered by the sight before him. A doe had come to drink. As the rivulet of water streamed dully by in the overclouded afternoon, Wakwa was thankful he was alone. It would have been embarrassing to have had Awepu witness this carelessness. Because he had neglected the trap, the doe had not had her neck broken but was caught by her hind feet. She had torn down much of the surrounding foliage trying to free herself. Some small meat eater had had its hunting done for it and made the easy kill. A pack of fox or a pair of wolves had dined well.

It was bloody work turning the half-eaten carcass, and disengaging the feet of the once beautiful doe from the knots sickened him. He fought off flies, trying to save as much of the skin as possible.

While Wakwa cut at the tawny hide, Kayaskwa came to mind again. When he caught sight of her on the slope the morning after the rain, she had been a hunted thing. As she stood at the crest of the hill he had had the desire to climb after her to help her. Her hair, stiff with mud, stood out from her head like the skirts of the Englishwomen. Her features, straight and handsome in profile, surprised him with their softness when he saw her face to face. He grew further upset with himself. He had left her alone, not yet well, lost in the miles of forest she found frightening to traverse. She had relaxed under his care and he did not want her to lose trust in his help. Her story was probably easy to discover although she offered no explanation.

It was clear that she was fleeing her people. If silence were the right of the fugitive, the obligation of the one who harbored her was to help her keep, not break, it. Because of this etiquette he felt correct concealing his knowledge of English from her. It was also his keen desire not to intimidate the girl. He did not wish her to run farther. He would simply cure her illness, enabling her to decide what her path would be.

Wakwa left the flesh, although in colder weather he would have taken some portions. Instead he took stones from the stream and tied them into some rope. Draping this delicately from the tree overhead, he duplicated the traps he had fixed

earlier, looking forward to some profit from his failure. He knew the wolves would be back and the sunnuckhig trap would help him avenge his lost catch.

His thoughts were not on the new pelts he would have to cure nor on the trading house as he made his way with his burdens toward a large wooden structure. He was hurrying, unsure Kayaskwa would be at the hut and he wanted to make her well.

He had built the house himself for a comfortable lodge when he went on big drives with others, sometimes a score of men together. European tools were expensive, so, using arm and hand measurements and the ancient methods of obtaining lumber, he had produced tight corners and stout expanses. Below the house a bridge spanning a narrows still stood, built by his father twenty years before.

Wakwa swept aside a door of beautifully painted matting, took a basket, and tossed in supplies he would need at the hut. He took a fresh blanket, some new mats, small pieces of finished doeskin, sinew, sewing quills, some clean linen shirts, and a fire drill. He went outside and dug close to the house and lifted out a deep basket filled with little jars of dried fruit. Then he bounded down the hill, uncovered his canoe, secured his parcels in it, and sped the three miles downriver to Kayaskwa.

Wakwa declined to use the clean blanket, although he felt chilled by the dark air, and regretted leaving his cloak behind. He was cheered when he saw a thick spiral of smoke from the hut joining the gray sky.

He did not return to her immediately but made his way to a small room carved out of the side of the hill a little way north of the hut. From the store of wood inside he made a hot fire on the boulders in the middle of the floor and placed a green alder branch and a vessel of water close by. He stepped outside to wait. When the stones glowed with heat he snuffed the flames and left for the tanning hut.

Wakwa touched the clothes and mats still damp from washing which the girl had spread in front of the door to dry. He carefully made a path through them and called her name in his smooth voice before entering.

Within, all was the same and all changed. He found her sitting far from the door against the north wall. Her face shocked him with its pallor. There were bluish circles under her eyes, but a warm smile broke over her face and she took his outstretched hand.

Wakwa's eyes roamed the inside of the hut. The earthen floor had been swept with a pine bough and the ashes removed from the fire and water sprinkled over the whole so the floor had dried clean and smooth. He saw a myriad of small decorative stones around the fire, circling the flames like a coin. The baskets were in place and two bowls were set out. His cloak was folded neatly into a basket. The muscles of Wakwa's face twisted and he bowed his head. He longed to speak to her, to know her.

Beth trembled looking at him, understanding why the Dutch called the Indians "wilden." In disarray from his occupations, his skin was sweated and dirty and there were dark red stains under his nails. He smelled strongly of smoke and blood. Yet when he took her hand she felt lighthearted.

"Keen! Keen!" His eyes glistened as he wrapped her in the soiled blanket and carried her through the door.

When they arrived at the room in the hill, Wakwa dropped his small apron and Beth's blanket without putting her down.

"Wakwa?" Beth realized through her fear that he had taken care to keep his nakedness from her.

"Pesuponk, Kayaskwa." He calmly sat her on the warm floor and supported her back with his side.

Soon sweat began to slip off her face and arms, and her shirt was soaked through. Beth turned her face to his. Little drops slid from his forehead into the corners of his eyes, down the dark places of his face, joining the wetness of his neck.

"Wakwa!"

He threw the green alder branch and a few drops of water onto the hot stones and inhaled the aromatic steam given off.

"Pesuponk, Kayaskwa." Patiently he reassured her, teaching her in his words that the experience he was introducing her to was simply that of sweating. Not distracted, as he had been in the morning, Wakwa was glad to pay close attention to her pronunciation as she learned, relaxed, and even smiled.

Wakwa loosened his hair and shook his head in satisfaction. Beth looked away to lessen the pain which mounted inside herself at the beauty of his steaming face lit by the glow of the hot rocks. She lay down, hardly able to breathe in the heavy air.

30

Wakwa gathered her tightly in his arms, reached for their things outside the door and broke into a run. Beth screamed from shock at the change of temperature as Wakwa rushed down to the river. Struggling, shouting objections in her own language, Beth became almost too much for him to hold. He waded unsteadily into the fast-flowing water, not acknowledging her protests, and submerged them both to the neck. She was nearly pulled from his arms by the quick current and her foolish struggling.

"Kayaskwa!" he said gruffly and pushed a handful of his hair into her hand.

He used long, powerful strokes with one arm while Beth grappled for balance. He laughed at her and swam downriver. Beth imitated the kick of his feet, holding his hair so tightly she pulled his head around to her. The Indian turned like a fish and submerged, coming to the surface smiling with pleasure as he progressed strongly against the current back to the place where he had left their coverings. Beth was moving more rhythmically, and her body turned warm with the strenuous activity.

Wakwa scooped her, dripping wet, out of the river, wrapped her in the old blanket, and taking a longer, less steep route to the warm hut began to consider what else he could do to prepare her for the parting which must come. He stood her facing the fire and dressed himself in doeskin leggings and a shirt, shook out a clean shirt for her, and discreetly went out.

Beth was dressed and sorting things from the new basket when Wakwa returned carrying two fish. While they grilled, he kept himself occupied bringing in the mats and clothes, hanging them over the tanning pole, aware that the mist ascending from the river would soon grow into rain.

He watched the girl from his mat as she finished arranging the supplies. Her body's thickness from front to back was hardly half his hand's length. He had come to know through his care of her that her breasts, hung low, were softly rounded near their bottoms like teardrops, giving her a free, boyish appearance in the loose shirt. Her skin, which did not crease like other European faces he had seen, had taken on a healthy peach hue since their swim. She coughed but he could see she would be better.

Beth felt strong after the violent sweating and swimming. Clean and renewed, she licked her fingers with enthusiasm

31

when they ate the sweet fish. They shared the dried berries and drank sassafras tea from great wooden cups. Their silence had become their bond.

A gentle rain began tapping leaves outside and Wakwa laid on more wood. He brought her the newly washed mats and clean blanket and made up a bed for her.

But she handed him the basket with his folded cloak and sat at his feet. He looked from the basket to her expectant face, then slowly pulled the garment out. He stood with it at full length. The tear had been near the shoulder and he had thought his cloak permanently spoiled. Now a wonderful embroidery spread on the soft skin. Stemming in red silk from the shoulder to the middle of the back was an arching limb of a leafless tree. A network of tiny branches shot out and around the main one. Near the hem a corresponding branch in miniature arched upward toward the first.

Wakwa was amazed. He took her hand and turned it over and over as if to see what magic it possessed to produce such work. He put the cloak on and stood motionless so she could evaluate her work. Then he hung it, tapestry-like, from an arched long pole so that he could regard it from his mat.

Beth brought out the silver case, which had remained tight and dry through the storm, with her little sack of threads and half-finished embroidery, partially spoiled by water. He admired each separate thing and laughingly produced his own sewing equipment. Beth examined the quill and sinew and required him to show her how to use them.

That evening Wakwa cut for her a pair of doeskin shoes he called "mockussinchass" and stockings, too. He also presented her with a carved comb and they both tried to pull it through the knots that persisted in her hair.

When they lay down at evening's end Wakwa raised a chant in a full, sweet voice which dropped low and climbed high. Beth was moved and her happier face rested on her hand as she lay curled, waiting for sleep.

32

Chapter 6

Wakwa rose during the night to build up the fire. The brief rain had left the air unseasonably cold. Kayaskwa was sleeping her first healthy sleep since her entry into the forest. Wakwa would have liked to have been up preparing for the day of business he had planned, but he would not disturb the resting girl.

Instead of his planned trip to Wareham he wished he could spend the day with Kayaskwa, walking under the trees and showing her the small secrets that gave life in the forest its joy. But she could not walk abroad in an old shirt with cool weather coming on. She had need of cloth and comfort. He felt her progress could slip if she became discouraged by unnecessary hardship.

He took up the mockussinchass and sewed in the bright light of the fire. It was a job for old men, but all knew the art of living, and Wakwa made a neat job of joining the pieces of skin together. The shoes, cut high over the ankles like boots, were made with a double thickness of sole to keep her feet dryer and warmer. An idea came to him and he rummaged in a basket of finished furs, coming up with two strips of gray fox with the paws intact. He sewed these around the tops of the shoes, hoping the fur closures would give her pleasure. That would do until he finished her stockings or perhaps, he grinned, until she did.

Looking at her as he worked, Wakwa considered her poise during the days since the big rain. Her movements were refined and unhurried, stemming, he thought, from a life of quiet and security. Her hands were strong with work, but not roughened like those of a common laboring girl. He could not conceive of her plucking geese in the streets like the ordinary white girls, spring and autumn. He did not think she had run away for an offense against a master or a town. Rather, he thought, the wild look in her eyes was lit by some offense done to her, some onerous circumstance that weighed down her natural sweet spirits. His desire began to grow that she not end her exile but

33

remain in the woodland, walking the paths that could unwind from within herself.

As darkness yielded to gray he placed the slender shoes close to her mat and laid out things for their meal. He went out for water and wood in the cold morning and dipped his face into the stream, washed his body, and ran his hands through his hair. While the samp of fruit and corn bubbled in the cauldron he wrapped an old red band around his head. He called and she awoke, startled at the sight of him in readiness to leave.

Wakwa slit the downstream waters in his canoe as the morning lit the clouds in shades of bloody red above him. When he knew he was out of sight of the hill where the girl stood watching him, he removed the cloak she had wrapped around him, to avoid questions in town. His long hair blew back, catching in the collar of the good shirt he wore into the English towns under his jacket of skin. He had on leggings and beaded shoes and wore his knife and arrow case. His waist was wound around with heavy lengths of shell money, both wampum and sukauhock, the white and the black.

Wakwa made the run of a mile after securing his canoe and entered the streets of Wareham at the height of the morning trade. His stomach always tightened at the sight of these small men in their waistcoats or jerkins, their busy hands framed in lace, figuring and counting, scurrying after prices and bargains, telling and reading the news from sheets.

But he had friends here and enjoyed immensely the stores of imported treasures in iron and glass, housewares and English cloth and commodities, and jars and tins of savory stuffs. He avoided trade with the smaller places, realizing they had the greater need to use him for their profit. It was in the open and bigger markets that Wakwa made himself welcome. The volume of trade was no longer great enough in the area for merchants to send traders into the woods regularly. Therefore Wakwa made sure the furs he brought with him were always top quality. He helped the traders increase their supply of furs for foreign merchants, recommending other trappers to them, determining what was in demand and trying to supply it. His day was usually passed pleasantly and without hurry.

Today Wakwa made his entry into the town with one purpose: to buy fine cloth for Kayaskwa so she might be free to walk which way she would.

He ducked under a canopy belonging to two town Indians who bought fish from the Mashpee and sold it fresh to American colonials. Each day they made a giant pot of chowder and served it for a few cents a bowl to passersby until the kettle was dry.

Wakwa moved directly through the shop and out the back door to the landing that faced one of the piers. The old woman came outside to him with affectionate greetings and a disposition to hear any news he had of the Ninnuock, as the Indians called themselves among one another. He whispered a message in her ear and she waddled to the front of the shop and talked to her husband. He judged his clientele with a shrewd eye and called out in his own tongue to his son to go fetch Kirke's agent for Wakwa.

Wakwa was impatient sitting in the sun. He kept away from Kirke's trading house this day for he did not wish to meet too many people; in fact, he did not wish to get involved with Englishmen at all. He ate the chowder the old woman brought and questioned her about the news, but there was nothing in the wind about any missing girl. The sweat began to drip into his headband and he handed back the bowl with instructions that Kirke's man should wait. Then he was out on the street again, his curiosity piqued.

Pure Massachusetts Indians were tall as a group, but Wakwa, standing at least four inches over six feet, was, in his native dress, a sight to behold as he moved through the crowded marketplace, very much above the heads of the settlers. Newcomers always looked after him and the woman was rare who did not steal a glance at his retreating figure. He had been accepted as "that tall Indian."

He walked to the tool manufactory and bargained for a light-weight iron hoe. He turned back toward the fish market, his wampum belt disagreeably lightened.

"Indian!"

Wakwa whirled, his head high in indignation. But it was Kirke's man, waving, laughing, and pushing his way over to him, grasping him in warm greeting.

"What cheer, wetomp?"

"Asco wequassunnummis! Askuttaaquompsin?" Wakwa nearly lifted the slight, graying man in his excitement.

"I am very well, very well. Asnpaumpmauntam." Kirke's agent rattled on in both their tongues, while the people who moved aside for the pair wondered at his hearty manner with the imposing Indian. The agent's ascetic, pock-marked face, unchangeably somber with its thin beaked nose, his fine dark clothes, and plain but exquisite linen were a startling contrast to the natural grandeur of his friend.

At the back of the fish shop the old woman strained under the heavy basket of furs which she placed at the agent's feet. She came again, with a bowl of chowder for the Englishman, and Wakwa watched him while he ate politely and eyed the basket.

"Aspaumpmauntam committamus?" the agent for the London merchant ventured.

Wakwa glanced at the hoe and said quietly, "My wife doth well, I thank thee, Dire." Wakwa's English was cleanly pronounced and quaint of usage.

"Ah, Silent Fox! You have stayed away and stayed away. I nearly came after you."

They both laughed at this.

Dire continued to tease. "You have been out hunting the black fox again, eh!"

"Doubt not, I have come close! Someday I will bring thee the tip of his tail."

Dire quieted. "I believe you will." Straightening his neckcloth as he gathered himself for trading, he said, "Fox, I have renewed demand for beaver! Beaver, beaver, and more beaver! Britishers are wearing muffs again. Young buck, too, is needed. My profit is down and you'll get twenty pence per pound for deer hide and that price is holding fast all the way south. Have you these?"

"Dire Locke, thee asks much. Soon I will show thee the few things I have brought. There are some doe among them, but it is true I have several buckskins still hanging, done to an especial softness only for you. One, with the hair on, I may not give up!"

"You should get your asking price, and more, my friend!" Poor Locke was beside himself at the thought of a skin so fine Silent Fox would not trade it. "What is it? What would you like, then, that I can supply you?"

36

"I would you bring to me, within an hour's time, both wool and linen. Twelve yards fine black wool, warm, yet fine to touch. Twelve yards, as well, of red. But this should be stout and firm and without yellow threads. More a brown-red like unto blood. Some bleached linen and some natural."

"Domestic or Irish?" Locke readied his chalk and pocket slate.

"French."

"French!" Locke wrote.

"Some thin stuffs too, brown or gray and light-colored, that would go close to the skin, and one thing more. I wish something else, excellent, that I would not know of, would make a present even for an English lady."

"Ha! There is an important council coming soon makes you court some hapless official through his wife? Or perhaps you would honor Tame Deer? You must bring me home with you again, I did so enjoy my stay."

Wakwa would not reply.

"And this is all? Why did you not come to Kirke's with this to have your pick of stock? Are you not well-treated? I should have taken you to Boston for goods to dress a queen!"

"Wetomp! My dear friend! This day belongs not to me but to those who need me. I would I did not have to bring thee hence and away from thy work. But it is best I not be seen trading for these things."

"Great God, Fox! You are sorely pressed. I never thought I would see you so."

"I am not pressed now, but may be," Wakwa hinted with a good-natured smile. Then he dropped the cover from the basket.

Before he would lower his eyes to examine the contents, Dire Locke said sternly, "Let nothing happen to you or yours, Silent Fox, that I could prevent. I am helpless myself but have the ear of every blackguard and gentleman for a thousand miles on this coast. That you know very well. Do not let me hear you have been too proud to call upon me, your old friend!"

Then Dire Locke took out the furs and skins one at a time and appraised them. There were fifteen glossy martins among the doe, beaver, red fox, otter, and mink. He was especially excited when he discovered the skin of a wildcat, the light brown hairs shimmering at the tips with silver.

"If I could afford to be a gentleman, I would look no further and say, 'Take the rest back with you.' I am ashamed to take this many beautiful beaver for what you wish of me. Oh! Wakwa! They are excellent. Good and dark . . . good sheen, not a red hair among them! Where do you find cat in these times?"

"We shall hunt him together someday!"

"You pry at my secret desires. Mayhap, friend, when Thomas Kirke gives me a day's rest."

"Perhaps you will gain that day of rest when he sees these. Wetomp. For the House of Kirke." Wakwa pulled two matched beaver pelts from his coat. Dense, very nearly black, each one had a broad brown stripe down its back.

Dire Locke groaned as first he gazed, then touched, and finally took the furs into his own hands. His blue eyes went hot at the possibilities of such prizes in trade and prestige.

"These I take to London, next summer, myself! No one else shall touch them until I deliver them personally into Kirke's hands." As he moved off he called, "I sleep with them between times!"

Wakwa laughed. He always saved the best for Locke, who was truly a friend and never tried to cheat him of the value of his goods, never offered him rum before the trade, and always rated his wampum as high as ten-pound sterling for a single wide belt. There had been times when Locke had supplied, gratis, or on credit, wheat and corn and other services when Wakwa's folk had been in difficulty over land rights. It made Wakwa happy to give Dire the opportunity to ingratiate himself to Kirke with the unusual furs. With little favors such as this Wakwa had helped make himself an indispensable link between the great trading company and the most valuable of the thinning woodland goods.

Wakwa spent the next hour buying food and some little things for Kayaskwa that he thought would lift her spirits. He chose a box of English soap that smelled to him like the wild violets that dotted the forest in the spring. He resisted a retort to the shopkeeper's wife who remarked under her breath as she pocketed his money, "Can't figure this one out at all. Neither where he got his sterling nor what he means to do with the soap!"

He bought sweet butter and a tin of milk from a farmer, read what notices he could find about the marketplace, and casually passed close by the church that stood white and straight at the water's edge. Apparently Kayaskwa was more like the sea gull than he had imagined. She had blown inland and not caused a ripple of concern. When he returned to the fishery he bought six dozen small clams from the old couple and sat calmly in the afternoon sunshine waiting for Locke.

Dire came and tipped the messengers who had carried the parcels and were to take away the furs, so he might stay alone with Wakwa while he evaluated his purchases.

Wakwa approved the wool. The colors and textures were much to his liking. The French linen was very fine and there were both brown and gray in the cotton goods. He delighted in the discovery of some peach-colored watered silk, considering it to be a good omen, the color pink a sign of happy expectation among his people. But he was anxious to see the special gift he had left to Dire's discretion.

Locke put a plush bag in Wakwa's arms and drew the cloth out for him himself.

"Wunnegan! Wunnegan! So beautiful, Dire!"

It was buff cotton cloth woven so finely it was like silk to the touch. Within the weave was a scattering of tiny English rose buds, shaded from dark brown to white. To complement this Locke included a width of sky-blue satin and a bundle of personally selected trims and fastenings. Wakwa embraced his friend, supremely content with their bargain.

Embarrassed, Locke jibed, "The Welsh crone who wove these fifteen yards gave up the ghost with the effort, so it is the only stuff like it on this earth. I would certainly like to meet the lady who is to receive it!"

Wakwa chuckled. "I shall keep her well away from thee, Dire. I know thy reputation! I myself know not even her name, but this will fill her big sad heart with joy."

"You surprise me, Silent Fox! You can never lecture me again about my forays among the ladies, and you a married man!"

"It is no woman but a poor broken bird this cloth shall bind."

"There it is again. You are genial, yet you frighten me. An Englishwoman, this?"

"She seems to be."

"Seems?"

39

"Never have we spoken. I found her alone, much frightened. Have you heard in the town of such a person missing?"

"Missing person?" Dire stood in confusion. "If she is English and you . . . you keep her with you . . . Abraham! Your head of hair is doomed!"

"There is a law?"

"Who needs a law? You are red-skinned and she is white, sunna matta? I think Virginia has a law. Carolina has a law. Perhaps Massachusetts Bay has a law. I must look into it for you."

"There has been no offense of any kind of law! She lies ill and I refrain from asking even her name lest she fear I, too, hunt her. How can I return her where she would not go, and worse while she is still sick?"

Dire Locke fitted himself into a small corner of the steps and said miserably, "You Indians are so damnably moral. And who believes it but me? Don't you feel the white wolf breathing at your neck? Open season on Silent Fox, over some poor waif. Look out for your hide, friend. There are bastards who love this sort of thing."

"Dire, thy name suits thee. Do not worry about Silent Fox. He will teach thee to trust in waiting and watching and holding aside judgment. You only must help me find who she is."

"I will do that." Locke reached up to Wakwa's shoulder and rubbed the soft skin of the fringed coat. "What makes you think I am anxious about you, you scruffy Indian? Although, who will bring me parti-colored beaver and white panther if they hang you on the common? Be back within eight days for news. I am gone south then, and after that, Scotland, where I always get led straight to the Devil."

As a final gesture Dire Locke gave Wakwa a wooden box, made of pale English ash, which opened outward into a progressively bigger square by means of tiny hinges.

"The latest thing for cutting and sewing on in Europe, good fellow. It can be carried anywhere. Even into the woods. That is from the House of Kirke to the lodge of Silent Fox."

Wakwa stood amazed.

Chapter 7

The morning after the great storm which broke the back of that hot summer, the father of Elizabeth Dowland sat behind his desk in his study. Sunlight blared through the window from where he studied his wet meadows and planted fields strewn with debris. He had been there since dawn, after a sleepless night.

Charles Dowland sat low in his chair, his crippled legs curled against one another. His hands shook slightly as he rubbed the knobs of bone that formed with his progressing illness. He had been a handsome man, fair-skinned and dark-haired with straight features and large brown eyes. Although he was just over fifty, the mental and bodily pain he had endured over the last few years had whitened his hair and crosshatched his face with lines.

He waited in the maple wood room for his brother-in-law, Gilbert Worth, and Annanias Hudson with the cobbler's assistant, the town Indian, Jack. It grated on Dowland that his daughter should have disappeared after a visit to the Worths. He felt his sister, Hanna, was over-tolerant of Gil's freethinking. Without children, the Worths seemed a pair of doves, delving in frivolities and too-fine living. The aesthetic appeal of their house seemed sensual and unnecessary. They worked long, arduous hours in the service of people unsuitable to their propriety— prisoners, slaves, orphans, derelict sailors—and all took advantage of their sympathies and their money. But Charles, too, had begun to depend on Gilbert Worth for innumerable kindnesses during the last two invalid years. This morning he bowed gratefully under his indebtedness to a man he knew he could trust.

"Nothing?" Mary Dowland entered the room, prim in dark gray.

"I have sent Sam over to Gil. It begins. I keep expecting to see her come walking over the hill with her apron full of things from the wood."

"You did not sleep, Charles?"

"And thee?"

"I have prayed. I have prayed for strength. Charles, do you know I believe this to be the final blow! I do not hope ever to see her again. The Lord puts us through a continual wasteland these past few years and I pray not to resent it, but I do, I do."

"Mary, dear! You are making a great deal of this too soon. Any number of things may have happened. She might come in at any moment. I have sat here retracing the steps she may have made between the afternoon and the time the rain came."

"Oh, Charles."

"How far could she have gotten? Gil's black says he is sure he saw Beth walking down the cart road toward the tree line, midafternoon. But he did not actually see her all the way to the forest and so might she not have doubled back and walked to a friend's house by caprice, planning to be home by milking? She was stranded and will come marching in here in a few minutes and get a round scolding out of all of this!"

"I do not believe you."

"Do you think it right you should discourage me? I cannot move as it is! We must pull ourselves up a bit. She is not inconsiderate. She has been dutiful. Loving. She shall come or be found!"

"Dost think she would like to be found?"

The husband and wife sat in silence waiting for the search party.

At the same time, Gil Worth paced near the great cherry tree, impatient at having to wait for Charles' prearranged signal to start for Hudson's house and roust out the minister. He kicked rain-felled leaves aside with a high, shining boot.

Ready to ride when Beth was first known missing, he was forced to defer to the violence of the storm and remain at home, readying his saddle pistols. The hard wind which cleaned the sky of rain came in morning dark, and so he relented and slept two hours from exhaustion.

The Dowlands' farmhand found him whipping the mud into foam.

Worth let his horse warm up to the slippery run, not immediately racing him on the way to Hudson's. Gil was no woodsman, but the elegant riding of his youth had toughened with his residence in New England.

42

Half afraid to find her, he kept a sharp look out for Beth, some scrap of clothing, her pouch, or the silver case he had given her the day before. Packs of dogs often roamed the farmlands in the dark hours, returning home meek and mild for their morning meals. When Gil heard them on their romps he thanked the Power above he was not outside. That his niece had been exposed to their ferocious wanderings dictated he hold his mount in.

He descended the sloping field that intersected his land and Dowland's and looked at the white church steeple at its eastern extremity.

"Mr. Hudson!" The bay spun to a halt and Gil shouted for the clergyman without dismounting.

The minister emerged from his barn carrying several freshly sawed pine boards. "Good morrow, neighbor. God be with you." Hudson felt affable in the early sunshine.

"Take horse, Mr. Hudson! Your father-in-law requires you!"

"I had thought to get a good start on the new room this morning before my rounds, but there is always something. You see why I shall never finish before the wedding!"

Gil Worth dismounted. "Let those go, Hudson." He took hold of the boards at one end. "Unless you come, and quickly, there may be little incentive to finish whatever improvements you are about. My niece is missing."

Hudson clung to the boards, dumbfounded.

"Listen hard, and listen fast. She came to us as she does every afternoon to sew. She left during that sultry heat and we thought she had gone home by her usual path. She has not been here?"

"She doth never visit me. Did you not know?"

"Her parents thought she had stayed with us to supper, but when the hour grew late they came in the cart to fetch her and, of course, she was not with us. What has happened I do not know but I like it ill since Beth is hardly given to whimsies of this kind. Charles wishes you to bring your dog, and I would say . . . your gun."

"My gun?" Hudson stood with sweat forming in the folds of skin under his eyes. His body sagged and his curly brown hair shook with his trembling.

The small rush of pity that overcame Gil subsided when the

minister spoke. "I knew something would happen. It all seemed too smooth. I was beginning to be happy."

"Get your coat on, sir!" Gil snarled at Hudson's whining. "I start without you!" He galloped up the long hill to the clatter of the boards as they struck the ground.

The first search was made. Gil, Matthew, Hudson, and Jack, the town Indian, left for the woods. The dog was made to sniff Beth's clothes and, although Princess was enthusiastic about the hunt, the wind and rain had gone against this kind of search. By nine o'clock neither dog nor men had found anything but the wreckage of dismembered branches. Then the dog caught a hint of something near the hill fronting the river. Minutes later they nearly walked over her corpse.

"Bear!" said the discouraged men, and they started back to reorganize their rescue team.

Jack said nothing when they came upon the carcass. He observed the place of struggle and the neat slit in the dog's throat and belly. He found the flattened mound of earth under the trees and a partial print of a naked foot. Jack walked behind the others on the way back to Dowland's farm, cogitating about how to extend his morning's earnings into an even larger reward.

They all gathered in the study, weary, wet, and dirty, surprised they had not found the girl.

"Why, Annanias, do not be discouraged. We have only begun." Charles' face showed his own fatigue.

"Mr. Dowland, I have this day a great loss."

"I'll get you a new dog, Hudson." Gil glowered.

"Gil!" Mary was shocked.

"It is all right, Mother Dowland. I am used to his gentle abuse. I was about to say that I have lost both my betrothed wife and the feeling of Divine protection which has carried me through all the loneliness of my existence until this day. But I will also say, if he would have it, that Princess was the best hunting dog in all New England and it will take years to find and train another. And then, she was good company."

"Fitting company." Worth walked away slashing at his boot with his crop.

"Gil, this must stop!" Charles scolded.

"You must see, Charles, I came not to bicker with this priest here, and we waste time talking about his excellent hunter who hath mistaken a bear for your little girl and got its throat slit in the bargain!"

"Entrails gone, too," Hudson intoned.

Gil turned back briefly in disgust, then kept up his pressure on his brother-in-law. "I say we need help from people who know what they are doing in that damnable woods and we are not the men for the task."

"Perhaps, perhaps. Jack, what did you find?"

"No sign I saw of a girl."

"And what of the dog?"

"A bear may have come, or something else," Jack hedged.

"What else?"

Mary interrupted. "Bears, Indians, dogs! What does it matter! Something has taken my Beth and you all stand about and quarrel like women at a bee! Yea, I have never seen women act this way. Call in the magistrate! Rouse the farmers! Comb the docks! Do something!"

Jack had gained time to rephrase his answer to Dowland.

"You are wise." He nodded toward Mary and took Gil in with his glance. "It will be a good thing to talk to the near village of the Indians. They know each leaf of this forest. Live within a few hours' run of here, less, maybe. I borrow a horse? I can find them. I not so good at running as used to be. Town life . . . I will tell them you would come among them seeking their aid."

"If you find these Indians I shall give you the saddle. Find my daughter and you shall have the horse to keep as well."

"You are generous, brother, but I make no claim on you. I gladly do all for nothing. My day without wages is my only worry."

"Find her." Gil slipped a gold piece into Jack's hand.

Jack the cobbler fixed his dark eyes on Gil. "It is the truth we found not one sign she walked in the forest. This may bring you all hope."

Mary looked at him with some gratitude, but Hudson broke in.

"Jack has some sense. I say she never went into the wood. She could have been picked up on the road! Some rude carter or sailor breezing in as they do in the hot weather to invade the fields with their bottles of liquor."

"My child!" Mary stared in horror out of the window.

Gil rushed to her since Charles could not, but Charles spoke to her softly from his chair to comfort her. Then he said, "You are tired, Mary. We are, as well. Send Priscilla in with tea and take some yourself in your room. We shall finish here soon and I will come and tell you what our course will be."

She obeyed him without question.

Dowland turned on the minister. "Young man, you are my spiritual counselor, true, but do you think you are in your church making sermons of a Sunday morn? This is thy mother-to-be and you give her such a fright? Do you not know we have all thought the same from the first? I have broken my strength this morning in that cart just for this purpose. And you to be Beth's husband!"

Hudson said nothing, realizing his mistake. The decision was reached to let Jack begin again in the wood. Annanias was to ask each minister within a fifty-mile radius to make discreet inquiries, hoping to avoid the embarrassments of a public search. Gil would contact all the departing ships and check quietly in the surrounding towns.

After they were all gone, Charles Dowland put his head down on the smooth wood of his desk and thought how peaceful it would be to walk out of his house in the company of his dead children, holding their hands and talking with them as had been his habit long ago.

Chapter 8

In times past, before the great war between the English settlers and the Indians under Philip, the second son of Massasoit, the Ninnuock roamed in lordly stewardship over the land. From high, windy summer heights to snug winter valleys they wandered for survival in the expanses of blue hills for which their word was Massachusetts. They followed the firewood, the game, and the southwest light for the corn.

In the years after defeat, due to intervention by the English king and his soldiers from across the sea, the remnants of the Massachusetts tribes were bound into reduced domains where they could move but little. By the end of the seventeenth century this scattering of people lived free yet constricted, avoiding as far as possible conflict over the sensitive borders and dealings with white poachers. For this reason the strip of land sweeping northward from Fall River in a tight crescent, studded by the palisades which harbored sentimental Philip at his death, was the permanent home of several stocks of Indians.

One of the more obscure tribes, the ancient Massachuseuck, clung to their foreshortened lands and a vestige of tribal individuality in the vicinity of the Sweetwood plantation. The lodge of Silent Fox stood on the high western bank overlooking the Twisting River in a town of about two hundred fifty people.

Silent Fox, or Wakwa, was nephew to the sachim, Waban, and his father still sat in the council of the sagamores, aiding Waban with inter-tribal affairs and communications between the Indians and the white farmers. Wakwa had been born to Pequawus and the sister of the sachim and was brought up close to his father when the mother died, a youthful victim of woodland life. It was from this background that Wakwa developed solitary habits and a serious outlook.

He had been selected by his uncle to be spokesman for the tribe, to help maintain Massachuseuck unity and prosperity, as well as to act as liaison between the Indians and the strong little governments of the white towns. There was conjecture that

New England would break someday from old England, and the Indians did not wish their position to be further jeopardized in the expected conflict between the colonials and their foreign king.

This arrangement of his affairs suited Wakwa, whose father had taught him to read in his own tongue and in English from a well-preserved Eliot Bible. Eliot's book, a unique, bilingual achievement, had survived King Philip's War and the disastrous exile on Deer Island and had come into the non-Christian hands of Pequawus from the widow of the man who had used it to pray before his murder by a white trapper. The other legacy Wakwa possessed was the obsidian knife with which he had so smoothly disemboweled Reverend Hudson's dog. This weapon had been kept through migration, subjugation, war, and peace and was the best and most enduring tool Wakwa had. He could skin a deer with it in a quarter of an hour, half the time of his steel blade, and come away with a perfect job.

In the otan, as a boy and a young man, he had always been agreeable, good at games, and a skillful gambler. He was popular with the young maidens, and under the proper forms of the Ninnuock had had relations with many young women, but never returned frequently to one girl or formed clear attachments that would lead to marriage. His independence upset Pequawus, who was anxious for Wakwa to father children. The older man always used as his example Wakwa's gregarious cousin, Awepu, who had married after several fevered courtships and had sired four children while Wakwa lived alone in his hunting district or with his father in the otan.

Wakwa and his father were closely bound to a family who had absorbed them into their household at the death of Wakwa's mother. The warm friendship continued after Pequawus and his son again set up their own lodge. This family had a daughter a few years older than Wakwa, who from shyness and quietness had not married and was still living with her parents at the age of thirty. It was thought a great waste of her beauty and goodness. But her wishes were respected and she remained alone.

It was a natural thing that Wakwa and his childhood friend, Tame Deer, so often seen together in close conversation, drifted together and were wed. Their courtship, composed and comfortable, was disappointing to the bright maidens who had all hoped to interest the tall and handsome nephew of Waban. Wakwa's father was mightily pleased with the match and made much of the wedding exchanges, offering a strand of blue wampum to Tame Deer's mother, showing his acceptance and magnanimity with the precious gift.

For his bride Wakwa built a large bark house with two fires and an extra room for storing meat and furs. After their union he grew to enjoy domestic warmth and was a generous provider. Tame Deer listened with intelligence to the experiences he encountered in his work, brought in good harvests of corn, kept stocks of dried foods plentiful, and painted the fine mats she made with much finesse. They entertained generously, and often an overflow of guests from their uncle's home would stay days, sometimes weeks, in their lodge.

Within a year Tame Deer presented her husband with a daughter whom they called Sequan, for the spring. Wakwa loved this child with boundless tenderness and was seen carrying her about the town in his arms as much as Tame Deer carried her on her back.

Following custom, and being uninvited, Wakwa did not approach the bed of his wife from early in her pregnancy through the normal time for nursing the child. For eighteen months Wakwa lived without knowledge of Tame Deer, who retreated into her former shyness, keeping him in abeyance, neither giving up her nursing nor accepting her husband back. They talked of pulling apart but Wakwa, who did not want to be separated from Sequan nor hasty with his wife in what he felt was a time of sickness for her, made the decision to wait. Failing improvement, an amicable divorce would have to be arranged.

Wakwa strode into this home after his hasty trade in Buzzards Bay. He left most of his parcels in the canoe, bringing only the new hoe and about forty clams for his uncle's household. His lodge was quiet, the fires low for such a cool day.

Tame Deer came from the far room, surprised to see him. Her greeting was warmer than usual and Wakwa touched her face.

"Where is Sequan? It is so quiet in here!"

"She is sleeping at my mother's house, Wakwa. There has been great excitement here today."

"But why does she sleep with your mother?" Wakwa walked from room to room in disappointment. "The serving girl is gone, too!"

"Mother thought I could use some rest."

Wakwa looked at her carefully, missing his mother-in-law's elaborate scheme to leave Tame Deer free. "You look in good health, Qunneke."

Although supplied with the best materials and furs, Tame Deer usually dressed modestly. But this afternoon she wore braids twisted with wampum, a new chemise of dark blue silk twill, and a beaver skin skirt slit to her thigh on one side.

"Oh! Locke asked after you today."

"So, you have been there! All these days? Everyone has been asking for you, especially this morning, and of course, I did not . . . There are things I wanted from the town."

"I went on a whim."

Tame Deer served him a bowl of hot stew made of onions, deermeat, herbs, and potatoes.

"I've brought you a hoe." Wakwa accepted the meal.

"A hoe?"

Wakwa smiled. "It will help with the harvest, which may be early this year. I could come with you if you like."

"Wakwa, that is good of you, but without the corn the girl would have little to do. I take care of Sequan and we do the corn together."

"It was not the corn I was thinking of." The man sighed and paid more attention to his food. "Well, it is here and you should use it. A fine price they got out of me, too. But it is strong and not too heavy and will last. The meat is good. You cooked it?"

"Yes, dear Wakwa." Tame Deer grew upset, seeing habitual error in her refusal of his kind offer to assist her, remembering how pleasantly they had once worked alongside one another.

Wakwa filled the silence, eating with enthusiasm after having done without meat for four days. The wife stood looking at the hoe. Wakwa felt sorry for her and put down his bowl and came behind her.

"My wife?"

"It is pretty!"

"Is it so?"

Tame Deer walked away and looked down at the floor mat. "Are you happy to see me, dear wife?"

She shook her head affirmatively. There were tears in her eyes. Wakwa stood close once again. He looked down at her tall, rounded form. Her skin was a creamy tan, her black eyes small and bright. Wakwa saw Kayaskwa's face, gaunt white with the sunken eyes, for just a moment.

Tame Deer's quiet voice erased the vision. "I do not wish to disturb you. Finish your meat."

"It can wait."

"It will be cold!"

"Look at me?"

Tame Deer did not lift her eyes. Her husband stepped directly in front of her and grasped her shoulders firmly.

"I have not complained to thee, have I, my wife? You know it is for you to say. You are most loving."

At this Tame Deer let her head sink down on his chest. "I hoped things would go better between us, Wakwa. Perhaps they can again."

Wakwa kissed the black hair that fringed her forehead. Tame Deer stood deathly still.

"Sequan tried to comb her own hair today!"

"Shall I ask thee, then, wife? Do look at me!" he whispered.

"I cannot." She stood motionless, her head against his chest, and heard his heart's beating quicken.

"Why? Do I dazzle you, Qunneke?" Wakwa's laugh was short and sharp. But he wrapped his arms around her and rocked her as he would Sequan if she had been crying. "Come, come. Lie thou with me again. I will warm thee. Oh! How I long to see thee smile again!" he pleaded.

Her reply was silence.

"I hold you against me, but you are far away." The man let his hand slip from behind her neck and softly stroked her breast.

"You were far from me this morning, when I had to make excuses to your uncle."

Wakwa suddenly withdrew his hand and Tame Deer fled across the room near to the hoe. The husband stood alone in the center of the hall, tight-lipped, snorting out little breaths. When he was calmer he marched across the floor to the bowl of stew.

51

It was cold, and the liquid dripped from his lip, staining his white shirt. He threw the bone into the bowl and pressed his closed eyes with his knuckles.

"Tell me then. Why could the sachim not live the morning without me?"

"He wished you to talk to some men. They were white men, an Indian, and one black-white man."

Wakwa looked up.

"They came about a missing maiden, lost the night of the rain."

"What should I say that my uncle could not?" Wakwa's shirt was wet with sweat.

"Why, her father's farm borders on your hunting bounds! They had good reason to seek you! Her father is Charles Dowland of the old family, a man of substance."

Wakwa was lost in thought, incredulous at his own stupidity. Why had he imagined that Kayaskwa had come from some far place into his woods? Yet, was it natural she would walk out her back door and become lost, bruised, and hysterical? What had they done to her on that peaceful farm that had made her as he had found her? Why should Dowland, a silent man he had seen from far away at the great council two years before, drive his daughter, distraught, into the forest?

"Did you see this Dowland?" Wakwa was up, straightening himself for leaving.

"No. He is a very sick man. He can get about only on the back of an ox! Can you believe that? Charles Dowland says that if his Elizabeth be found by us he will become a true friend of the Massachuseuck and give us the yield of his southwest acres for three summers hence!"

"All that corn would rot! Who gave such a message?"

Tame Deer watched him closely. "Waban spoke with the girl's uncle who lives next to the Dowland farm. Waban did his best, not having you there."

Wakwa glared at her.

"This uncle brought us many, many bushels of the finest apples I have ever seen. Corn as well. He said the girl was to be wed within the month."

"Wed!" Wakwa went weak with surprise. "Came he to invite us?" he said acidly.

52

"Wakwa! She is to marry their holy man who has offered to teach English to him who brings her back. He would give us books as well."

"I must rush out and find her then!" Wakwa spat.

"That is just what Waban wishes you to do! Your uncle said to this Englishman that if she had been in the forest you would have found her already."

"He is right!" Wakwa stared bitterly at his wife. He turned toward the doorway with his basket of clams, but looked back in an afterthought. "What was the holy man like?"

"He did not come."

"I see. Too holy to search for his bride."

"Wakwa Manunnappu! I am not much of a wife to you but I am always your friend. Your sachim says if she is found there will be great security and ease for the people. More than that! You would be raised in his favor for this service, in white men's eyes, too. They would trust you in the councils. It will bring you closer to the design your own father has made for you. Waban wants you to find the maid. You see, she is much loved."

"It would seem so." He turned and left her.

Wakwa was fuming. All day he had roamed up and down the streets of Wareham like an English goat when all the news he sought awaited him on the lips of his wife. How fortunate he had brought back the hoe. Being away, he had not lied to Kayaskwa's relatives. Not Kayaskwa, but Elizabeth! How the name suited her. He knew he would not have lied. He would have told them everything and had some bad moments with all these old men over why he had kept her himself and had not tried to return her. Yet he had acted in good faith. But what did English-Americans know about good faith? Wakwa's hopes for her unhappy spirit were lost now that they had found her.

Pequawus, the Gray Fox, met Wakwa half running toward his uncle's house. Pequawus was alarmed at the look on his son's face.

"Dear son!"

"Father!" Wakwa managed to embrace his father for a moment.

The older man, tall and graying, was beginning to stoop at the shoulders.

"What has happened, Wakwa?"

"What has happened here? Where is Waban? I must talk with him."

"He sleeps."

"He sleeps!"

"He has looked forward to seeing you since dawn, my son."

"So my wife has told me. Am I the only one in this town with eyes? Where is Awepu that he cannot help his sachim if I take a notion to go and buy a hoe?"

"He searches, Wakwa. He and four others have gone to your bounds to look about the traps and the river until the white men are satisfied."

Wakwa could not move. They had been out all day. They must have found her. What a mess he had made. How would it look to Kayaskwa's uncle to find his niece wearing new mockussinchass, cooking over a hut fire.

"Do not be so upset, Wakwa. It is a small thing. That land is Awepu's as it is yours. You do not have to find the girl. We've lived without Dowland's corn up until today."

"Father, you are still the wisest man in the town. Tell that to your brother-in-law when you give him these clams. My wife is not so easily convinced."

"Ah! That is it. You are angry with Tame Deer. I cannot believe it."

"I am nearly at an end of things with her, father. Expect no grandsons from me. Be sure to give those clams to Waban when he wakes. I'm off!"

"Wakwa, how can you leave me like that? What do you mean? Are you separating from her?"

"Do not forget the clams."

"Not even one for me?"

"One!"

"There is a big gaming in ten days. The harvest comes in early. Will you come?"

"If you will have me." Then he was gone.

Chapter 9

After Beth could no longer tell Wakwa's canoe from the shadows and light bouncing on the river, she went back to the hut. Her new shoes fit excellently and she felt warm enough to consider going into the forest to look for balsam.

Every autumn, at home, she made up the gray-green needles into little bags and placed them in closets and drawers to sweeten the rooms during the months of keeping the house closed in winter. Over the years the aroma had pervaded the floors and walls.

Today she thought about the smells in the hut that were a new mixture of staleness and sweetness, some baskets containing acrid-smelling cakes of stuff that did not seem edible and others brimming with savory onions and wild herbs. She emerged wearing the clean blanket like an Arab, fastened at her shoulder with her brooch.

Maples were scarring with red and yellow, and oak leaves swooned down, the first victims of the coming cold. But the sun was bright and Beth's spirits were even as she began her search for the proper pines, using the stream as her landmark. Her only company was a little bird with a colorful crest who called to her in a cocksure way as she filled her basket.

Beth spoke to it lightly and walked back toward the river, as much to see about a new group of trees as to be close to thoughts of the figure with the blowing hair and shining paddle, hurrying southward in the dawn.

She renewed the pledge she had made to break the hold Annanias had on her. So many girls were fascinated by her prospects with Hudson—his lineage, his prestige, his intelligence, his attentiveness, shown in the new windows of purple glass he had ordered from England to please her.

Prudence Hanson, so prominent at the quilting bees, hoped openly that Beth would break off her engagement, seeing Beth's lack of mutual compassion with the minister, feeling she could fill the gaps in Beth's affection for Hudson. Now Beth did not know if he loved her or simply sought his victory over her stubbornness.

Freedom was what she had wanted four short days ago, but the ache she felt at Wakwa's parting still crouched in the bottom of her and would not let her forget his eyes or the strength of his arms, or his silken movements as he swam in the river after the sweating. She began to wonder if he understood the few words of English she had spoken to him. They did not seem to need speech for understanding, and Beth was content with quiet.

It was then she heard the bark of dogs from the boat and saw her Uncle Gil climb out in the company of a tall, thin Indian.

"Elizabeth Dowland!" Gilbert Worth's deep voice rang out along the rocky height.

She ran to the hut, hid her basket near some larger ones, checking for signs of her presence. She fled up the hill to the sweathouse as voices grew nearer and louder. There was no light in the charred room, and she was grateful to Providence that her uncle had left the dogs in the boat. Perhaps they needed Wakwa's express permission to bring dogs into his hunting area. Perhaps they were coming not to look but to talk, to ask Wakwa questions, to enlist him in the search. They must have slim hopes of finding her if he had not.

She could hear very little when she was inside. It was a dark world apart, a cocoon, a womb of privacy. If they searched from the doorway she would be safe in the darkness. If they entered she would be discovered. Beth climbed into the center of the pile of stones, blackening her skin and coverings with the soot that lay thick, not realizing the camouflage she was making as she wriggled down against the hard surfaces.

After a long wait the spot of light in the doorway was blocked and Gil called out, "Beth! Beth! Beth." The third call was soft and hopeless.

She held onto her resolve, wishing it were Hudson and not Gilbert Worth she had to ignore. She heard the tip of his long gun clattering across the rocks. The noise and her sorrow at not being able to run to him and explain, to see understanding and sympathy break over his face, brought her hands against her ears.

56

"We've need of the torch or the dogs, Awepu."

"Nux, netop. If you wish. Enter whilst I am gone. Pesuponk is a small place."

Beth did not feel her constriction, wedged between the boulders. She was all consciousness instead, listening to the tap of metal on stone, her uncle exploring the cave like a blind man. How to heal his heartbreak if he found her willfully rejecting him brought a cry into her throat. There it stayed as Gil's discouraged voice addressed himself.

"She's not here." He walked around the center stones, his eyes adjusting to the darkness. "No need for that, Awepu." The Indian flashed a burning branch around the room. "I see without the torch she is not here." The uncle jabbed the butt of the gun against the center stone. It slipped, and he never knew it was Beth's hip that supported it in its new position.

"You are sad, netop. Do not be. I will talk with my kinsman. He must return shortly. If she is to be found, he will find her. The group to follow will look deeper about."

"Yes. Yes. I believe that," Gil humored Awepu.

The light popped back in its place and their voices blended and faded as they descended the hill. Beth heard her uncle talking about such sweathouses in the north countries of Europe. She covered her face and lay concealed with her remorse, waiting the second party, whom she did not hear pass by with the dogs.

Chapter 10

Wakwa was less nervous once back in his canoe. The morning which had begun with so much promise had stretched into a wasteland of mistaken judgments and frustrations. He doubted he could rectify the great error he had made not returning Kayaskwa before he had come to know her. He felt whole in her presence, and the loneliness which had become a point of pride with him was dispelled when he thought of her. Desire gave impetus to his paddle and drove his hope high that if the girl had been spared him, there was some possibility of annexing her to himself with honor.

He roped the heavy parcels of cloth to his back and wore the cloak with its red embroidery over his shoulder against the wind. He carried the food basket which he had dragged in the water to keep fresh, groping his way up the steep hill with the afterglow of the sunset at his back.

There was no smoke from the hut and his heart sank. He called her name and no one appeared. He entered. The place was dark, cold, and empty. He pierced the black with the sound of her name and came into the open.

So, the thing had been done. He drew off his belts of wampum and threw them against the wall of the hut, cursing and wiping his eyes with the back of his hand. The wind rose and flattened his tears against his face. He was ashamed to be crying when he needed all his poise to find where they had taken her. Reason returned and he sat heavily on the dirt.

If they had come this way in the early morning they would have found her and been back at the camp by the time he had come home to Tame Deer. No one had seen Awepu since he left with her uncle. They searched for her still.

He saw her hidden in the forest, swallowed in the mass of blowing trees with the darkness licking at her, hearing the cries of the wolf with the frost at his back. Wakwa did not see how her spirit or her body could withstand a second night of such horror. He walked slowly toward the stream, crossed it, and

entered the ring of trees. He came to a standstill. He crossed back, picking up his pace. As he passed in front of the hut he tore off the red band which was tight on his temples and his hair billowed back in the growing wind and he ascended the hill to look for her down along the bank of the river. That was where she was heading the first morning. Away from the trees that frightened her, toward the bright water.

Wakwa thought of their night in the sweathouse and the run to the water, her fear and her conquering of fear as she pulled on his hair to stay afloat.

The memory and his unsatisfied need to know where she was aroused him and he stirred beneath his apron. Remembering her slender body wrapped only in the wet shirt, her face small and rosy in the glow of the stones, he grew full and stood miserable in the cold, pushing back the pain of not pouring into her the wealth of his feelings. He began to shiver and the sweathouse formed into a shape in his mind. Gradually, slowly, his passion subsided and he stood calmed with a new hope before him.

He started to climb the hill, then broke into a scrambling run, grappling with the rocks and tall grass, calling her name. The wind pushed the sound back in his face and he shouted again and again, "Kayaskwa! Kayaskwa!"

With the wind which carried the sound and bent it in its courses and dissolved it in its speed, Wakwa moved sure of his instinct.

"Kayaskwa!" he screamed repeatedly.

He neared the flat of the hill and saw movement in the dark mouth of the cave. A small, featureless form opened its arms for a moment and started to come toward him.

He called her again and, black as the sky behind her, she was suddenly within his reach and he closed her against his body, her head pressed against him in his crossed arms.

There they stood while the darkness grew thick and a warm spot formed at the place where they touched.

Chapter 11

The body of the girl was cold as stone and Wakwa led her back to the tanning hut, full of fear she would be sick again. They fell into their familiar silence, knowing everything and nothing about one another.

Beth was more content than he, having made her decisive step when she did not respond to her uncle's call. That Wakwa had found her and was glad she was there filled her with peace. The solution to how they could continue to live closely in their state of increasing affection would not take shape in her mind. Tomorrow they must somehow speak. Tonight she was safe with him.

"Mauataunamutta," he said, mending the fire.

She helped him bring the dry sticks, seeing well in the blackness, accustomed to it since morning. She closed her eyes to the leaping light and shivered as the center of the room began to heat.

Wakwa came to her and rubbed her hands and she looked at him. She gasped, seeing his doeskin coat marked with black across the front and his hands becoming dirty with the soot of her own.

She felt her face and saw that all she wore or touched was smeared and rubbed with black. Wakwa found a little mirror and showed her her face. She was shocked at how wild she appeared, the whites of her eyes contrasting with her filthy skin. She gave a hearty laugh, relieving a day of anxiety. Trying to stop, she looked at her face and roared again, and Wakwa was entranced.

For the first time she was happy. Her laughter subsided, then bubbled up and Wakwa, seated crosslegged, delightedly called her "kihtuckquaw," seeing her as a full-blown woman still caught in girlish good spirits.

She sat near him, all smiles, and apologized in English for this new inconvenience she had caused him. He reached a long arm behind her and pulled his basket over to them. As his arm came

60

close the smile faded from her face because the decision she was putting off until the next day began to press her. She stared into the fire while he rummaged through the basket, then she reached out and took both his hands into her own.

"There now, it is done. Wakwa, do you know the joy it gives me to be with you? If you understood my speech I could tell you why I can no longer stay. You have made me live again. You do not know but I was content to die several days ago. Now I would live! But I cannot take of your kindness more. I take and give nothing! On the morrow I shall leave you. Understand, please, dear Wakwa, dear friend!" She looked into the man's eyes, hoping he would read the light in her own.

"Nowautam, Kayaskwa. . . . I understand." He looked down at her hands holding his.

Flooded with the import of his words, she held tighter to his lean fingers.

"I understand . . . Elizabeth!"

"You know that too?" Feeling a slight betrayal, she let go of his hands and turned slightly away at the height of her warmth for him.

Now he sought her hands and held her palms together, pressing them hard between his own.

"Knowst not why I did not speak? Nor was it two hours past I knew thy name!" He kissed every part of her black and dirty hands, still touching as if poised for prayer. "I shall not touch thee more, for well I know thy creed and customs which to me at this moment are most bitter."

Grateful and disappointed, she rested her forehead on her arms.

"Did we need words when I found you? See you not how I would have driven you back with words? Elizabeth?"

"Yes!" Two thin streams of tears made a white path down each cheek. "How beautiful your speech! You were very right, dear Fox. How can I leave you on the morrow and how stay?"

"And where would you go? It is I who go from here—tonight. I wish that you grow strong and free here under the trees. I shall tend you from afar and teach you the ways that will let you laugh again. I would not persuade you to any course."

"You are kind, yet do you know what I have done this day?

I have let slip my home and all my folk. My dear uncle was close to me as you are now and I spoke not! I must learn to be alone. Wakwa, you understand these words?"

"Yea, my gull, I understand." He caressed her hands as he released them.

"May I not know about you? You know of me."

"I knew all before I reached this house with thee, when first I called thee 'Kayaskwa.' That you were tormented and should not be, that courage and sorrow filled your heart until you began to drown of them." He stood up and moved into the shadows. "Now I know you are soon to wed."

"That I will not!"

"And that thy father is great among his people and holds the deed to many acres."

"That is naught to me! For pity I agreed to wed but now I disobey and leave my father, even in his illness."

"That I cannot understand! What is it they do to you that you seek refuge under the trees and come under my care?"

"Such care! And I have done nothing to help you."

He came to her again. "Do not talk of that. You fill me too with joy. Even were it not so I would have helped you." He took her hand and stroked the palm lightly with his fingertips. "I will tell thee of myself when and how I can tell thee without pain. Now we must eat and care for thee again. You are always in need of washing!"

They laughed together and Wakwa brought out the wooden box of soap. She held it as if it would break, and he was happy in his soul to see her admire the small, greenish cakes and revel in the light scent of flowers they gave off. He poured warm water into a big wooden bowl and left two bucketsful for rinsing. He went out into the cold to open the clams.

Soon she was at the door with the buckets. "You have brought clams! If only we had milk I would make you a grand chowder, Wakwa."

He refilled the buckets. "There it is and guard thee against scalding it. I doubt you have ever cooked in birchwood."

He washed the shells and stacked and stored them near the house. "Kayaskwa, may I come?"

"Do, Fox. Can that matter after all we have been through?"

"Ah! Now all is changed. I would not give offense. You are well enough to help yourself." He found her waiting near the low door with a glow in her eyes. "You smell of flowers and your skin doth shine, but you are sore in need of help with your hair!"

They boiled more water and he showed her how to put in herbs and leave them until they made a tea of proper darkness. He knelt her down and rubbed a dry clay into her hair over her disbelieving protests and rinsed it through with the cooled liquor. He helped her dry the long strands which reached the low point of her back and washed himself and his hair with the clay and the tea. He changed into buckskins and gave her the last shirt and supervised the fire and her use of the cauldron while she combined their provisions into an English chowder. They talked as they ate, with as much enjoyment as they had kept silence during their first days together.

"If your uncle be sachim, are you then a prince?"

"You are ambitious for me?"

"I only want to know it right!"

"I am close to Waban, but a prince I am not. That is an English word! Waban works to guide the people. He marries them, buries them, punishes those who offend, and exalts those who deserve it. He watches like the eagle for the smoke of disturbance. He chose me to be his emissary, to speak for him. I do not wish to rule. I see not the need to enlarge myself when I can be free, in my own way, alone. I am large enough as it is!"

"How busy you must be, hunting and walking such long distances for your lord."

"My tasks so close to my heart make the time, as you say, stretch before me like a meadow. Poor Awepu, who hunts by my side and begins to travel with me, suffers. He would rather sit and let the deer walk up to him and eat of the fringe of his coat as take the deer and eat it."

The girl laughed, recognizing the name from the morning. "He seemed very friendly to my uncle and though he brought a light neither of them saw me. Do you know, Fox, I felt protected by the glare of that light? It was as if they were blinded by it and could not sense my presence as well as they could in the dark."

"Elizabeth, it is the same with my name. Wakwa is the old

word for the fox, before wonqussis, before pequawus, who is my father. My name, Wakwa, is for the black fox whom men stalk at night and come so near they see him at the brightness of dawn, but never is he caught. We say Wakwa is protected by the light of Manit. I believe this. I felt his warmth around me like a coat when I went to seek my name in the heart of the woods as a youth."

"But were you not called something until then?"

"Manunnappu."

"Manunn . . ."

"Manunnappu . . . he is quiet . . . still . . . careful. . . . I do not know the proper English word."

"Discreet, perhaps?"

"Perhaps. Wakwa Manunnappu. Thus white men call me Silent Fox."

They circumvented what was really in their hearts and spoke of hunting and trade and places they had seen. Wakwa kept away from talk of home or wife or child but listened avidly to her description of her life on the farm and mystified her when his eyes dimmed as he learned of her young brother's death, understanding now all she had moaned in her delirium. When the meal was finished he spread out her mat and placed the square package bound in muslin on it.

She refused it, ashamed to receive more of him, and he turned away, upset.

"Wakwa! Never would I give you pain. It is a long habit among us to refuse kindness."

"When you were ill you received it openly."

"I will do it, then, when in health. You shall see."

Wakwa looked at her, really seeing her for the first time as she felt the cloth lovingly. She was healed and clean and becoming happy. The hair he had first seen as nearly as black as his own was revealed as many rich shades of brown, casting little halos of bright colors in the waves that curled like new leaves. He watched her move and hold each piece as she wondered what to make of the cloth.

"What lovely shiny tabby! I have never worn pink before."

It was then he gave her Locke's special gift of the cutting board and the rosebud cotton. Elizabeth, overwhelmed, sat stroking the fine cloth.

"The most precious of these is thy friendship, Wakwa." She put the fabric reverently aside and came to him. "What do you need? I will make you something fine."

"They are all for thee."

"But why did you not let me have some skins you have hanging about this place? This were a costly gift."

"I found you an Englishwoman and English you shall always be. How can you be free if you cannot walk away from here without shame?"

"I go not away."

Disregarding her remark, he showed her how to use his stone blade, cutting through an edge of the wool like butter. They worked the cutting board together, and then she lay on her mat, exhausted.

He sang in a deep voice that night, calling out to Manitto, elongating the syllables of the deity's name in chant so that as his voice died away after minutes of singing he had said his god's name only once.

During his song Beth crept from her mat to put the cloth next to her. Wakwa covered her with his cloak, tucking her in like a wayward child.

He saw her through the fire from his mat. One of her hands lay on the cloth. All the rest was the glowing abundance of her hair and the line of her body under the cloak.

"Kayaskwa!" he called softly, hopefully.

But she was asleep and without a parting word he rolled his mat and left.

Chapter 12

There were not many hours left until dawn when Wakwa pushed aside the mat and entered his own lodge. The fires lit the big rooms and in the center of the house lay Tame Deer, sleeping with Sequan at her breast. Tame Deer was bared above the waist and the little child wore no clothing this night. Wakwa thought it a lovely sight to see their soft bodies resting one upon the other, molded comfortably into one form.

He stooped and drew his daughter to himself, holding her loosely so she would not wake. But she stirred and saw him, uttering, "Nosh!" She lifted her round arms about his neck and fell back to sleep.

Tame Deer awoke and watched her husband place their child on her little raised bed of mats. He groaned with fatigue as he lay down beside his wife.

"Dearest, are you angry still?" Qunneke asked.

Wakwa did not look at her or raise his head as he spoke. "I worry for you but I do not hold your actions against you."

"I have decided what I will do."

"I am tired. Let it wait."

"Let it wait! How long will you wait? You have waited too long already."

"Qunneke, you are without pity. I need to sleep."

"But I have thought and thought all day and have come to my decision!"

Wakwa sat up grimly, barely keeping his eyes open.

"You will make an old man of me before the night is over! What is it?"

"That is it! You are young. You are too young for me. We are back to what we were. We are just friends again."

"Qunneke!"

"I feel done and complete. I feel indecent being the wife of a man like you. When I see you come in the door I cannot believe you are my husband."

"Qunneke, why are you saying these things? It is so very late."

"That you may sleep in peace and with a wife who deserves you. I go to my mother's when the sun is up, and always you will be welcome to come and stay and be with Sequan. But never seek me more as thy wife, for I have lost all hope for myself. I am the one who has become old this day."

Wakwa was not moved. "That is fine! You know another man would have beaten you well for this afternoon. But I did not. I have not for the flight of eighteen moons. More! It has been since you conceived! You despise my patience, yet you say we are forever friends. In a short time I will have need of all my good friends." He took her head between his trembling hands. "I have been patient and now it is your time to wait. Here you will stay until I bid you go!" He released her. "Two things I would have of you. They are hard to ask for I love thee still. I bid thee keep thy milk no matter what your family and all the cackling bitches say. The other is, breathe not a word of our troubles to anyone."

A look came over her face and she turned, abashed, and stared into the fire.

"Especially say nothing more to your mother. I may need your help in some way soon."

"Anything! What is it?"

"I do not know what it may be. I need you for a little while at my side." He let his face fall into his hands, and a crying, bitter and loud, took hold of him, so against his nature was it to manipulate another human being. "I would have had you to-day. . . . I like not saying such things to my dear wife, dear friend."

"You are beautiful, Wakwa!"

"Then you do look at me!" Wakwa sank down onto his side with his arms across his face, and his wife could not tell if he slept.

Chapter 13

Dark wood creaked underfoot as Gilbert Worth climbed the narrow staircase to his brother-in-law's bedchamber. The upper hall was still as a tunnel. Gil looked back to the bottom of the steps, wishing he did not have to see his brother-in-law with such a lack of news. A pink-cushioned chair was caught in a circle of sun from the first-story window.

"So, you have come, Gil! I owe you much."

"Charles. You talk as if the search were over! How do you feel?"

"Like an idiot. A fool. If I did not have Mary I think I would be a madman now, for these legs."

"There is hope, Charles, in that we found not a sign. Not a shred of evidence she ever went into the forest. We have been to the Rhode Island shore, down Fall River, north and west and east of the Twisting River for fifty miles. The Indians, all of them were most helpful. While I slept the second night they kept up the search. We were invited into their lodges to look, every one! They have sent runners to interior places, and the hunters look for her daily on their rounds. I have learned so much! Old Waban is most sympathetic toward you."

"Not a sign . . . six days. What did they make of Hudson's dog?" Charles asked blankly.

"Some fools talked of spirits and others assured me that bear come down from the hills every fall to fatten up. That is how the natives nab them before their harvest feast. Waban said it could have been an animal, possibly wolves. Oh Jesus, Charles! I cannot dwell on that!" Gil gouged the floor with his heel.

"What do you think?" Charles persisted.

"I cannot tell. I do know they resent dogs on their grounds."

"It were not a bear."

"Yes, Charles! I feel she lives. I simply could not find her."

"True. We cannot find her. I have lost hope. Over Hudson's objections I have called in Cooper—and the selectmen." Charles rejected Gil's attempt to interrupt. "They have combed the ponds and streams and shot off guns above the salt rivers where they come down to the sea. That will take a few days more. Today, six-month notices are posted every town an hundred miles north and south of Boston." Charles handed Gil a copy of the paper. "There is nothing to do but wait for nothing." He fought tears.

Gil pounced. "Wherefore does the priest object? Does he think his fellow pastors shall find her tied in ribbons, waiting in the pew of some church?"

"You two do not get on."

"What does that matter? The whole point is he does not get on well with anyone, least of all your poor daughter! Has it occurred to you this is why she is gone from us? She walked out of my house and I feel a responsibility for it! She left very sad and it is not your sister nor myself who put her in that mood. Who is he not to call the magistrate!"

"Gil. You are tired."

"Yes! I am! I have slept on the damnable ground for four nights, I have been freezing and eating dry corn and half-roasted squirrels, all the time growing more amazed that you have been so taken in! If that dear girl still lives you could get her back, you know. If she has thrown over her everlasting obligations to you, Mary, and that belly full of wind, you might get her back by canceling the whole marriage contract. Think of it! You might still be in time!"

The brothers-in-law looked hard at each other.

"Gil, you are an impulsive man. I think as you do. She is either with Henry—dead—or has left us of her own will." The father grew a little cold. "Not having children of your own you cannot realize what a burden the nursing of their souls can be. I have agonized here while you were out looking. I see clearly that if she has left the path of her duty I must not follow her example. She must be brought back to it! Can you not see that if I broadcast the news that she may do just as she pleases with the lives and hearts of so many, she could never take her place in this house? She has lived here a dear and beloved and good child. But she has become willful on this one subject since Henry died. Nor does she like the notion of taking property with her to her husband. She rebels against an hundred years of toil. On a stickler's point! This is pride. If you saw her mother suffer you would know it. I know my girl better than you think."

"Brother Charles, I am not quarreling with you. . . . Truly. I do believe you do your best. But do you realize how much she resembles yourself?"

Charles overlooked the remark, but his voice softened. "Gil, there is a new will. If she does not return within two years' time, the land here is yours, save the three hundred Hudson should have had at their marriage. You may do your will with the house and farm. Tell the Massachuseuck they may have this year's southwest corn yield for their troubles, since they value that exposure so much. I do so wish to die!"

Gil caught this remark at the door, and although pity welled up in him he said with the tenseness before tears at the back of his throat, "Duty, Charles."

Chapter 14

While Wakwa devoted himself to preparations for the fall feast, the corn was delivered from Dowland's farm. He brought Beth the news as she sat sewing in the sun.

"I have great guilt accepting this gift when I know you are safe here."

"Then do not eat of it." She surprised him with her hardness.

"My own guilt is shared by themselves, I think."

Wakwa declined to press her for her justification and found her in a milder mood the next morning.

"I could take these in for trade but it is more fitting you should have them, Kayaskwa. They robbed me of a doe the day I found you." He dropped two black wolf skins in front of her where she sat with the sachim-bird and worked on the cloth.

Beth learned the use of the acrid-smelling cakes as Wakwa rubbed oil into the hides with them to preserve and close the pores of the skins. He showed her how to gather pennyroyal for tea and how to preserve the fruits and chestnuts that had ripened on the trees. He watched her adjusting to the loneliness imposed by her decision and admired the clothing she created, never showing her how charmed he was by her fluttering brown dress and her sensitive face framed by a puffy white bonnet.

While Awepu and Wakwa were occupied bringing in rabbit, partridge, wild turkeys, and deer and setting up lattices in the stream, making a reservoir of fresh fish to be picked out just prior to the feast, Beth thought and sewed.

She designed clothes for herself that would suit her outdoor life yet not sacrifice the current modesty. In fact, the linen shirts she made, caught close about the throat, were more practical around a fire than the lower-necked gowns she was used to. In place of frills and trims she substituted painstaking stitches and hidden seams. Ties replaced buttons for convenience and speed, making graceful complements to the original tailoring. For special wear she began work on a full-length skirt of black wool to be worn unhooped, but, cut in a circle and deftly gathered, it would hang attractively full. She invented a waistband which would allow her to simply wrap the skirt around her waist and lined the garment with the rosebud cotton. She could not resist an underskirt of the same buff material and squandered two afternoons over its tiers of ruffles. She started a new camisole from the tabby silk and a gray apron, with capacious pockets, which was fancifully bunched into a pouffe at the back.

Aside from her personal things, Beth's two special projects were an ivy-embroidered shirt of the snowy linen and a warm greatcoat for Wakwa. Her design for this took shape and re-formed every day as she listed all the qualities the coat must have to be worthy of such a wearer. She must learn to work the wolf fur into sleeves and to devise a moisture-proof exterior for a lining of red wool.

By her eleventh night in the forest she was strong, rapt in her work, and grimly attached to her resistance to her parents' will.

Wakwa came in with a basket of new apples just as she was lying down to sleep. He nodded a greeting and sat on his own mat, peeling an apple with a small steel knife.

"What do you do?" Beth ventured behind him.

"I pare."

"To what purpose do you pare?"

"This apple has a worm. It will not do. Will you get me another from my basket?"

"These are orchard apples!"

"Your uncle's." He contemplated the shiny green fruit with some pink showing near the stem.

"You think me hard, Wakwa, for not returning. Yet what choice have I?"

"Elizabeth, I think you much abused. Strange, your people's marriage customs."

"Few make matches as soon as mine. Why do you press the flesh?"

"To make a face. Sit by me! Can you not go to them and ask to break this written bond? I have thought much of your father these past days."

"I as well. And my mother, too."

"I have no mother. Is it sweet?"

"Nearly always. I have felt she loves me. But they would hold me to the contract if I went back. I am sure of that and I cannot think of losing . . . this. Why make a hole?"

"It will be a place for the neck." He handed her the peeled apple face and went for string.

"I see! It is a poppet."

"Poppet! Now there is an English word. A maze, thy tongue."

"Do you not like the English, Wakwa?"

"I respect the English. Such strength cannot be denied. Many I like, some love."

"Is it for me? The poppet?"

"Would like one for thine own?" He hung the first apple face behind the fire to dry.

"Do you know, Wakwa, I know nothing about you."

He began to peel another apple. "Kayaskwa, go please to my flat basket and bring me the corn husks you shall find."

"Wakwa, I am not yet free, for someday I must comfort my family again. How can I tell when that will be if I cannot know about you? It is important that I know."

He looked into her face and pressed deep eyes into the apple and squeezed its round bottom into a pointed chin as if he were sculpting her image into the fruit.

"Why do you not do as your parents wish?"

"Wakwa!"

"Answer, Elizabeth."

"Ah, yes, m'lord, Silent Fox! I will spin you a tale past believing." She struck back at him with the story of her troubles, her anger building against his lack of sympathy. "On the day I was ten I was denied my childhood. My father came to me and took my hand and told me that that night I would greet the man who was to be my husband. To him I must be true, always and forever. With him I would lie and of him conceive children and by his side rest my bones when I passed from life! And I accepted this, for mother and father were my world . . . and Henry." Tears started and Wakwa would have stopped her but she spun away from him. "This man I listened to each Sabbath. At first I was in awe and then admired him for getting up in the church with such conceits of language! All the girls did love his curling hair, which to me always smelled like lamb. This Annanias, circled 'round me at dinners and occasions—I have memories of him with pen in hand, signing, signing, evermore, agreements with my father. When I grew older and did look kindly at others, he was always at my elbow, keeping off the flies from his choice confection! After Henry died he sought to fill my brother's place in my heart and, more, he stole my mother's love."

"Still, parents who love do not force their own children to suffer!" Wakwa gingerly came near, wary of her excitement.

But the girl did not hear and her face assumed the fear he had seen the first morning in the wood. "The two of them saw my hesitation, and after Papa fell so sick he could no longer walk Annanias and mother made sure of three hundred acres more and set a date for the marriage. I pushed it back a year, and that time is spent in several weeks. Then he will take me to his house and despoil all my self-respect with his massy face close up to mine!"

"Kayaskwa! No more!" Wakwa was furious.

She looked at him and recognized him. "Shall I go back, Wakwa? Denied my childhood and ever, ever, my womanhood? Each day he grows more adamant in meeting and shouts much more than prays, and the people fear him and whisper he has bolted his orders and starts a church of his own. . . ."

"Enough!" Wakwa cradled her head in his large hands, but her eyes began to dart with different lights.

"There are places, Wakwa, you and I have never seen, where stone cathedrals reach the sky, where music by an hundred players is heard each night in special parks, and rooms are filled with precious paintings of the great, and machines to make men fly stand incomplete! Yet I must bed with a man I fear or sin against the world! Is it fair a woman hath no choice to pick her way or even be alone if she so choose?"

"And do you choose to be alone?" Wakwa held her arms and she could not break away.

"Now that I know you . . . I cannot."

The skin of his face drew back. "Then bear another burden, my sweet bird."

He took her to himself and they stood as they had by the river and he softly said, "Elizabeth, I have a wife."

"And the poppet for the child?" She wrapped her arms more tightly around him.

"Just so."

Beth leaned back to see his face, and he pulled her down to sit. He took the husks in his hands that were never still. Carefully, as he plaited, he explained his friendship and marriage to Tame Deer. He never stopped his braiding and overlapping of the straw-like pieces, and arms and a torso appeared.

"Qunneke would leave me now, that I might wed again."

"How may you wed again?"

"In these parts, Elizabeth, an Indian maiden doth ask the man she favors to come to her in bed. If they are happy they marry, or if not she seeks another and another until she finds a partner that she loves and doth love her. By different ceremonies tribe to tribe the couple bind themselves into sacred constancy and so stay married forever like the swan. Yet they may part if trouble come between them. It is only sense. Partings do not happen often; couples are so companionable after so much looking!"

She caught the humor and smiled.

"This is where I am with my Qunneke. She would have us part as friends and I see Sequan anytime I would."

"What a blow for Sequan to be removed from her first home and a father such as you!"

Amazed by her understanding, Wakwa hurried on. "I am what we call 'winnaytue.' That means a rich man. Indeed, I am rich, favored by Manitto for my relation to the sachim and for my work for him and the very strength that lets me hunt. I provide much meat to the town and thus can freely ask to wed another woman. I could have both wives if I please, or if Tame Deer prefer, let her go. But two wives, you see, or three or four bring wealth to the Ninnuock. More corn and babes and I have only to add another fire to my house! I have known a man with two wives. He was very happy." Wakwa dropped his work. "Can you see it happen that I keep two wives or even gain you for my only one? How could I bring a girl like you to such a life? And if Qunneke heal in her mind someday, and has already left me, both she and Sequan will be bitter against me."

"Harder still to lose her ground to an English girl," Beth whispered. "She would be mortified in her soul again."

"I had not thought of that."

Beth reached over and pulled the body of the doll out of Wakwa's hands and examined it while she spoke.

75

"Teach me, then, your ways. I do accept her and your baby, too. And I will try to be their sister." Beth looked into his dark eyes. "But do not let me go."

"You would do that? Elizabeth!" Wakwa rose and paced, then lay back on his mat, defeated. He saw the bend of the long poles and closed his eyes. "How shall we do it?" His voice was thick with sorrow. "Shall I don my fur cap and send the groomsmen to your father to propose a new match over the yoke he hath already laid on thee? Shall I present him with a strand of wampum for my recommendation? Or take you here and now, and live with you, hiding in these woods? Should I leave my sachim and renounce the charge he has given me, and we live, like bears in their den, apart from all the world? Elizabeth Dowland!"

Beth went to her own mat and closed her eyes, enduring the wait for his decision with a dark pain all through her middle. When she opened them again it was day.

Chapter 15

The day before the Taquonk feast, Wakwa came up from his canoe when the sun was at its noon height. He was weighted down with raw deerskins and went straight to the hut. Kayaskwa was not inside and he dropped the bloody skins in a pile and waded through dry leaves to find her.

He heard the carol of her sachim-bird and his worry subsided as her own voice joined in, "The rain is over and gone, and gone, and winter is hard. . . ." The rest was lost in the scraping of the withered leaves which mounted to Wakwa's calves as he pushed through.

He was near enough to see her under some pines, her thin shoulders bent over her work. She pricked at a piece of white cloth with her gold needle. She repeated her words to the bird as if she would teach him English, but her face dimmed and her singing stopped. Only her white hand and the needle moved.

She was serene, as he loved to see her, coaxing shapes out of the cloth he had brought her. She seemed part of the thicket, an alignment of angles and softness, so self-contained and clean he could not approach.

He became conscious of the stench of his own body and left her without a sound. He went back to his work, rinsing and scraping and rubbing the skins, removing the hair from most of them. He hung them and walked up the hill with the firewheel and clean leggings and breeches.

The afternoon began to cool and Beth moved to a clearing to catch the last of the fall sun. She was struggling to finish the ivy embroidery on the front lappet of Wakwa's shirt. She did not expect him to keep her alone in the forest after the feast. If he would not have her stay, she had resolved to find a place to live where she could support herself by her sewing. If she continued in hiding from her parents she had no hope for work even as a servant in another house. In her mind's eye she saw Wakwa's back as he would finally leave. Just then she smelled lobelia smoke from his pipe, and he appeared with a spherical sack strung over his shoulder. His wet hair, his relaxed movements, and his clean skin told her he had been at the sweathouse purging his body for the feast.

"You overdo, Kayaskwa!" He half knelt at her side, his upper body naked except for a wide band of polished copper high on each arm. He placed the soft bundle on top of her sewing and sat back comfortably.

Thoughts of separation dissolved in laughter as she discovered the bag was filled with bright wild turkey feathers.

"What a clever bag this is!" She restuffed it. "Perfect for my sewing. Don't you see how dry everything would always be?"

"It is the stomach of your friend the dog."

The shape became suddenly familiar and she jumped back with a disgusted scream. "I thought to have seen the last of that horrible thing you did!"

Now Wakwa laughed and picked up the bag.

"I knew you would not like it. Take the feathers for yourself, the bag is for my mother-in-law."

"You should have higher regard for her than that!"

"You have said it is a clever bag. So it is! She will use it to keep acorns in."

"Why doth she keep acorns?"

"Dost not know? We eat them. Bark as well."

"Thee eat acorns and bark!"

"When we are hungry in winter such things taste quite savory boiled in water. They fill the stomach."

"But you hunt and fish and save your corn! Wherefore are the people hungry enough to eat wood?"

"When we must leave our homes in midwinter against our wish if we have lost a piece of land to the English, or if the deer do not come to the traps because the poachers have shot them first, or for one of the many reasons the forest herself doth give, we tear the bark like bears and taste of it as if it were succulent meat."

"Wakwa, have you been hungry though you are rich?"

"I am rich in what you coatmen have left to me. Can two hundred fifty souls be fed from the money I carry about my waist? Shall I eat while the rest starve?"

"But our lofts are full of wheat! It is a wonder you do not come and take it!"

Wakwa drew on his pipe and said nothing. He broke their long glance and lay back on his blanket over the thicknesses of colored leaves.

"You would discourage me," she deduced.

"You are subtle as your governor. It would do me good to have you by my side at the next great court. You might teach me to understand his thoughts, not only the words he saith."

"You have met with the governor?"

"Many times."

"Is it thrilling?"

"Perhaps he is thrilled to entertain me."

"What would I wear to such a meeting! You would have to buy me silk and even velvet, and I should have to powder my hair and would be so nervous I could not think how to say hello."

Wakwa groaned and turned onto his stomach, burrowing into the soft mattress of leaves. "I could never have you as my wife! You would dissipate my money with your velvets and your satins, never doing a thing but to sit and sew your gowns and stare into the glass. I would be reduced to my apron in the Boston streets and you in your dresses would lead me by a strand of wampum."

"Have you, then, thought, Wakwa?"

"I have only sweated." He caressed the blanket.

"When you were alone in that hot room, you did not think of me?"

"Without companions to share the hour, I smoked. Smoked and sweated and did not think. Now I lie here in the sun. Ah! The wonder of the sun. I feel its warmth and there is no need to think."

"How can you not think?"

"Winter will take my sun away and I shall freeze in the river and not lie warm and sleepy after my swim."

She refused to answer him.

"Ha!" He tangled his fingers into his loose hair. "I become English. Instead of enjoying my sun and the sweetness of lying here, I worry about winter and snow."

He lay quiet now, obviously thinking. He did not hear Beth move close. She bent suddenly and kissed the small of his back, clean and warm and ruddy in the red light of the sun.

Wakwa cursed his fingers, knotted too tightly into his hair to grab hold of her. She looked down at him in his confusion, her cheeks blown pink by the fall wind. He made a little howl and cradled her in his arms as he had on the day he found her. He brought her to the door of the hut and stood her up.

With infinite care he untied and removed her bonnet, and all her hair tumbled onto her shoulders in great loops. He filled the bonnet with the feathers, tied it to her wrist, and said, "Tomorrow, when the moon is there, we talk."

Backing slowly away, with the limp sack in his hand, he motioned his farewell.

Chapter 16

Fires already glowed in the center of the otan when the sun climbed out of the clouds. Soon the roasting of the meat would begin. Children began to appear, some dressed finely in furs, others naked. They played in the tall grass behind the houses, keeping out of their parents' way.

Wakwa's lodge was stirring too. Today the serving girl dressed Sequan, and Tame Deer tended to her husband. But Sequan was giving the maid trouble, running away, wriggling out of her quill-decorated dress, shaking her head, resisting the tight braids.

Wakwa caught her between his knees and kissed her, growling like a bear.

"Paukunnawaw is so hungry for a little maid who will not stand still." He chewed her flushed cheeks. "Qunneke, have you ever seen such a face for kissing! She is like a squirrel with his cheeks stuffed with food."

Tame Deer was unhappy about the jostling. "Stay still, squirrel, and I will let you wear paint today. Some on each cheek." With the tip of a feather, Tame Deer drew a single stripe of red high across the bridge of Wakwa's nose, extending it from cheekbone to cheekbone. "Sequan! Be still! There will be no paint today if you do not let us get finished."

She tied a short wide belt of black beads around her husband's forehead and decorated the knot at back with dark green feathers from a drake. Wakwa finished himself with leggings, a painted doeskin cape, and silver arm bands. Then he pushed the mat aside and stepped into the morning.

"We thank thee, thank thee, thank thee for the corn!" The single voice of the chanting powwaw wailed his invocation to the great southwest god, giver of the corn and keeper of all good souls. The young men moved their bodies up and down, dancing their adoration in a circle. The powwaw, restored for the day to his traditional prominence, led the great ceremony of life that kept his people together in difficult times.

81

From his place behind his uncle, Wakwa experienced a vibration within at the warmth of his bond with the many hundreds from up and down the river who had come for the joy of the Taquonk feast. Being what he was, he knew more clearly than they that enactment of their beliefs might soon be a memory.

The women's dance came with no other music than their voices, their graceful motions forming pictures of the constellations. Wakwa's eyes found Tame Deer dancing among the rest. It seemed to him she looked this day as she had years ago when he first began to regard her as more than his sister. Barefoot, she wore a deeply fringed doeskin skirt topped by a bodice of gray fox, her naked arms wound with silver bracelets.

The sachim's second son danced for all the people and met their cries of "Cowequetummus!" with small gifts, clothing, and knives, things valuable to the poor ones among them.

The tribes mingled on the plain and the women passed trays of meat and little girls brought fruit and water as the sun climbed higher.

The gambling arbor, twenty feet high, hung with stores of money which shaded its interior, was ready. Wakwa fingered the shiny cylindrical fossil he and all men carried to these occasions for luck. The English had dubbed these bits of belemnite "thunderbolts" for their shape and "crystals" for their magical purpose. Wakwa did not mind thinking of the token in that way. He was eager for the central play.

But the preliminary tosses to select two main antagonists from among the many towns present began only after Waban made supplication to several gods to aid the players in their judgment and skill. Wakwa's and the town of Black Earth were chosen, and the elimination began among the best gamblers of each to choose the final antagonists. Again spirits were beseeched and the pairs of painted plumstones cast into trays.

When Wakwa's stones showed matching symbols, he rubbed his hands with oil, working them until they were warm, drying them while he waited for the betting with an older man from Black Earth to begin. Cordial introductions and preliminary prayers whetted their ambitions. Surrounded by orderly rows of their partisans, the two men began the play.

Waban watched Wakwa closely, admiring the coolness of his

betting and the confidence with which he placed valuables in jeopardy. Yet he never gambled to the point of hurting his family. He had the advantage of staking from the abundance of his possessions and personal services and never felt embarrassed in defeat.

But today was not Wakwa's day for losing and the crowd was afire with his string of winnings.

"Wakwa, you are just like me! A child of the spirit of the wind to the marrow of your bones!" Waban laughed with youthful memories, playing on the meaning of his own name.

Wakwa was more jubilant with every toss of the plumstones, and his opponent struggled against him. The man from Black Earth lost more and his betting grew wilder. He had long ago lost his stores of wampum and black money. To regain them he put up his house and two servants. Wakwa saw him suffering, but admired him for not withdrawing or whining over his losses. The stones were tossed.

The judge sang out, "Black Earth has lost all!"

The man from the otan to the west started to sweat. He poured a gourdful of water over his face. "I have nothing more to gamble, young man. Only my wife and daughter are left to me. Perhaps I could turn the horrors of this day around if you would visit my dwelling." He laughed, embarrassed. "In fact, it is now yours. Come, and meet my daughter. That is really a fine idea, don't you think? I should at least have a strand of wampum of you if you liked her well enough to wed." The man guffawed.

"Your jest is out of order. Make your bet or retire." Wakwa grew wary.

"I cannot see how you or she could mind! She has a comely face."

"Leave play."

"Then I am your slave! I will have her brought here. She is very pretty."

"You dishonor yourself, old man."

The playhouse buzzed with the visitor's scandalous attempt to salvage a scrap of success.

Waban was disgusted. "Let the gaming stop! Brother, be satisfied with losing and grateful you are not beaten in the camp for staking your daughter!"

"Massachuseuck!" the desperate man from Black Earth mocked.

"Stand!" Wakwa towered over his gambling partner. The man rose. "See you not you spoil our game? Are you a fool to insult my uncle, the sachim, and in his own dominion? Are you blind like a bear that you cannot see the trouble you cause, extending far beyond the day of this feast? In place of your daughter shall we call forth the sachim of Black Earth to see if he will defend your conduct? No. Not even a man like you would risk that. For if my uncle does not whip you certainly your sachim would. The stakes shall be this, neighbor. If I win the toss you shall take all that I have already won back with you to Black Earth. All except your money which I do like well." And rubbing his plumstones in his palms he shouted, "As for your daughter, even if I win, tell her I shall come to her with a strand of your black money that she may seek a husband in a more fitting fashion!"

The puttuckquapuonk was alive with dissension. If Wakwa won he would lose. No one knew who to pull for. But Wakwa felt success in having diverted them all from the disgraceful wager and removing all complaints from the Black Earth man. No one could hear the judge in the shouting that followed the cast of the plumstones. But the happy tears of the foolish father as he swore never to touch plumstones again told them Wakwa had won. The visitor stood to yield his place to someone else and Wakwa walked him to the side.

"Never again gamble with the life of your innocent girl. You do not know the havoc it would raise within her soul!" Silent Fox laid the belt of sukauhock around the man's shoulders and rejoined his uncle.

"I am tired after that, nephew. Take me home."

They walked in the late afternoon breeze, Waban's guard moving in a discreet circle around them, out of hearing.

"You almost had your problem solved for you. You should have taken up the last bet."

"Waban! And what do you know of my problems? Has Qunneke come to you? I have strictly forbidden her to mention this to anyone."

"Contrary to your habit, you give yourself away, my nephew.

It was not your wife at all, but your faithful father who worries over you who told me, since you do not seem to have a care for yourself."

Wakwa fumed.

Waban patted his arm. "Do not be angry. Truly, it is time we spoke. I have a need for heirs myself."

"You have your sons!"

"Ha! One has been debauched in the city and I do not see him save when his belly cries out in winter. This is the older. The other one is fine at dancing and fathering daughters, although I do love them all. There will be no one for the people to follow soon. It comes down to you. See to a son, Wakwa."

"My life is not as easy as it may look, my Sachim."

"I think you are mistaken somewhere in your treatment of your wife." The old man stopped, the feathers in his hunter's headdress winding out behind him on the wind. "She may not need the kindness that you show her but a stronger hand! There is, at last, a time when you must prevail in these things. If she were mine, I'd chase her well around the lodge and you would see her fall into my arms and be big within the month."

"How can you say this, knowing the woman!" Wakwa lost his self-possession. "More, you tell me I am weak! I am close to giving you a great surprise that will make all your chasing seem like child's play!" Furious with himself for slipping with his secret, he apologized to his uncle. "I beg pardon for my bad temper."

"Never mind your diplomacy. Have you then met a new wife? You would marry again? It would be most fitting! I would be pleased and not surprised, and I do never think you weak but overpatient."

Wakwa would not answer.

"She is from another town?"

"She is, indeed!"

"A vain man chooses a woman less than himself. But you always seek out loveliness. She is beautiful?" The sachim's old eyes glistened.

"As a star is beautiful, she is beautiful."

"And you have known her and agree?"

"I have not known her, no."

"There you are again! You never will beget sons in this wise! Be quick. If all the commotion a second wife will bring you in the town does not agree with you, why, marry as the common folk. Go into the forest! But do not hesitate any longer. I am feeling very old. We can greet her with the baby on her back."

"Cuquenamish, Sachim!" Wakwa bent to the old man and stroked his shoulders, according to the custom of the Ninnuock, as two swans circled in the golden light.

Chapter 17

Four hours before midnight the moon floated in a black sky at the place Wakwa had pointed to as the mark of time for their meeting. Beth stood ready in the cold just outside the door of the hut and watched the forest begin to light with silver.

She had sewn far into the previous night and all of that day and now wore a simple long cloak of unlined red wool modeled, from its pointed hood to the flow of its sleeves and the containment of its hem, on the pictures of cloistered French priests she had seen in her uncle's library. The dusting of mist over the water drew her attention, and she was excited that her senses had come alive enough to know a little of what Wakwa knew about the world they lived in. She heard the soft disturbance of the water's steady rhythm as Wakwa turned his canoe into the bank, and she was not surprised when he appeared on the palisade.

She was frightened when he stood close to her. She saw the dark line painted across his face, his immensity in his jacket of bear fur, his hair fanning out from under a martin cap that added to his height.

"Peeyaush, Kayaskwa! Come hither!" The dark forest itself seemed to growl the invitation.

She followed him to his canoe, and he sat behind her, paddling upriver through the mist. They passed the silent bulk of the hunting house and turned up a narrow inlet with very little current. Wakwa's strong strokes did not lessen, and they sped through the trees that came up to the bank. Eyes of small animals darted in the grayed light, and all the fear Beth had known the night she had wandered through the rain, alone, clung like a cat to her back. She trembled and Wakwa put up his paddle to steady her with his hands on her shoulders. She turned to him.

But he said, "Look ahead, Kayaskwa."

There were no longer any trees. They had come to a wide, still place, the mouth of a vast circular pond that extended a mile in every direction. The moon pierced the night sky and saw itself in the placid water. Mist clung to the edges of the pond and newly risen stars shone over its clear middle, hot lights in the cold air.

The woman and the man sat one behind the other, studying the pearly vision, when slowly a large white bird coursed out of the mist to the pond's glassy center. The swan's mate followed her swiftly, circling her, making a ring of water around her as they swam. They grew still and the cob faced his mate, dipping his head far into the water, bringing up a silver spray when it emerged. The pen imitated his action and again the cob circled around her. Briefly their breasts and beaks met, forming a sinuous heart. The cob stroked the neck of his love with his neck. The pen smoothed her feathers and floated a little away.

For a long time the viewers sat motionless in the nearly freezing night. Imperceptibly the pond became dotted with the forms of other swans silently blending behind one another into one, then swimming on into their several selves. A large cob came from another direction and swam near to the dominion of the original pair. The night air was rent, suddenly, with the throaty scream of the first huge trumpeter as he arched his wings and sped toward the invader, his breast brazenly raised before him. He lunged repeatedly at the intruder, who persisted for a while but finally spread his wings and flew off in fear, passing close over the canoe.

Beth was astounded at his size, the spread of the wings reaching farther than the length of the boat, blanketing the sky from view. All the pond came alive with the metallic screech of the swans and the air sang with the beat of wings as others nervously rose, then resettled. The affronted cob pecked at a few dun-colored birds before returning to the side of his mate, who was preparing to sleep just inside the ring of silvery mist. In rapture, they rested their heads across each other's necks and slipped back behind a covering of reeds, leaving the water undisturbed and the pond in icy solitude.

Beth turned her hooded head and saw Wakwa, who sat aloof at the back of the canoe, staring at the far bank which he could not see. The girl, too, looked toward the shore out of view and at that moment knew the answers to all the questions she had about his life, his ways, and his being. She saw him, one, no different from, part of the earth and water and sky which formed his domain. Prince-like, he was the servant of every force that moved the creatures of the forest to live their cycle. He was a thousand years behind the existence she had left and was unchangeably the future of the place that had given him life. She knew at once the land into which she had been born: virginal, yet complete; open, yet guarded by the Ninnuock who loved her but did not waste her.

And the English girl gave way to the pull to go back in time, joining the future of the red earth of the place, putting aside the artifices and inventions of the civilization which had wounded her. Her torment of past weeks was dissipated, as was the moon's light in the mist, and she not only loved Silent Fox, but became of her will and understanding part with him of his realm.

They moved swiftly now through the trees and out into the river, in haste before the cold. The moon was on its way to setting and they hurried up the bank, stiff and ungainly from the long coldness they had undergone on the water.

He took her up through the woods and in the dimming light stopped her and looked at her face, seeing within her eyes the change he had yearned for. She had made the leap into the center of his existence and his fingers fluttered down over her hood, touching her face, feeling on the surface of her skin the vibration of the change that had occurred within her.

He whispered, "Thou art Manittoo!" then slipped past her, walking swiftly ahead of her to the hut.

"Can you spend one more night alone?" he asked her as he built the fire high and made her some tea. "Tomorrow I will come for thee and will decide our course."

She slept very little and awaited day.

Chapter 18

Wakwa rose late the next morning from a sleep which did not come to him until early dawn. He had struggled with the many-sided problem of keeping Elizabeth honorably as his bride. He had no delusions about her family's blessing their union. In over one hundred years of close living, the mixture of English blood with the Ninnuock had been pointedly rare. He weighed all the advantages against the disadvantages and fell to sleep unhappy.

He ate silently, Tame Deer having sent Sequan to her mother's so Wakwa could rest as long as he desired. The town was still full of visitors, and feasting would continue for three or four days, but now it was quiet.

Tame Deer addressed her husband for the first time since the previous morning. "Does this Elizabeth have fair hair?"

Wakwa choked on his food as he fumbled with the bowl of meal. He put it firmly down on the floor and looked at his wife.

"For a man who says nothing of his affairs to a living being, least of all himself, I must be as easy to see through as water! First the sachim explains to me the method of seeding you with sons and now you . . . you lay waste all the torture of these weeks in two words!" He leaned close to her, hurting her chin with the anxious grasp of his hand. "How did you know I had found her?"

"I knew when you did not find her! I knew when first I saw her men in the camp. I knew it when you desired me and when you bade me keep my milk. Do you have her at the hut? Does she carry your child already?" This last was said with concern, not rancor.

"Qunneke, do you think me a fool on top of everything else? I found her almost mad and near to death. You must think me brainless as a beaver! Would I turn an animal over to his mother in such condition? I kept her and I healed her that she might be strong to face her troubles. Do I turn a bird with a broken wing out into the forest until it is mended?"

Tame Deer was mystified. "The maid is surrounded by a

90

family that is saddened at her loss! The man who spoke for her crippled father was upright and gentle in his speech, although I could not understand his English words. How do you take it upon yourself to cure her? Let her people nurse her. You will bring about much anger. After all, Wakwa, my husband, you are a man and she is a woman."

"It is clear to me you know not the customs of these people. And I spoke no word to her until the night of the day her uncle searched with Awepu. She is as much a maiden now as when she entered the wood! Qunneke, this girl, with all her possessions, is more a slave than any serving maid who has washed the paint from your face." Then he explained the story Beth had told him about the contract of her marriage. "These civilized people place great weight on owning, as you well know. Gold, land, and, I begin to think, even the women that they love. There is no choice when the two are connected. She shall go to the holy man like a keg of powder or a pail of salt in exchange for his feeding her and keeping her safe! The same fate awaits her daughter should she have one."

"If the priest knows she cannot love him, why does he insist on her as his wife? Can he not simply purchase ground from her father?"

Wakwa stared at his hands.

"Doth she have yellow hair?"

"Qunneke! Why do you persist in this! She hath not yellow hair but a wondrous shade of brown, deep and glossy as the chestnut, and it changes with the light so I would swear I have seen green and blue dancing there as well!"

"I would have had some yellow hair of her, just to touch. I found her uncle's beautiful to see."

Wakwa went wild. "Do not bring her uncle into this, Qunneke! I am torn already about what to say to him and to my own."

"You love her then?"

"I must say that I do."

"I have known that too. Never have I seen your eyes lit as they have been for this whole harvest."

He began to protest.

"Shhh. Wakwa. It is all right. Even when I watched you as a

youth growing up, no girl you stayed around held your desire. I have seen happiness in your eyes with myself but never the burning that lies within them now. Perhaps I have known that all along. From the beginning. Perhaps that is where our trouble lies. But you must have her for your wife and I will leave. For if she inspires you in such a way and yet is so good, then you should have her, for there is no man like you."

"Qunneke. Never have you said such things to me before!"

"As you see it is my loss."

"Not loss, no. Why, she accepts you! Sequan as well. And she has promised to be your sister and live under our ways."

"I congratulate you, husband, on this bride! She is welcome in my house. I cannot speak to her in words, but I will do all I can to make this a home for her. She needs a home, not a cave to hide in."

"I would trust you with that task, Qunneke, above any person. You and home are one for me."

"Never have you said such a thing to me before!" She smiled, repeating his sentiment, and said as he took her hand, "This holy man . . . can he harm us?"

Wakwa's finger traced the smooth edges of her nails. "His power lies with his tongue. I could match it."

The woman took her hand away and held it to her stomach. The life-pulse in her throat worked with her misgivings. She stared over his shoulder at the long specter of thwarted red-white dealings, then questioned, "Is the maid all that you think her to be? Does she leave her father easily?"

"With great difficulty. But she is different from the rest. She seeks things closed off from her life. She is no mouse. She is a brave bird."

"Then go. Do what you must to win her." Qunneke based her courage on his judgment.

He stood, abstractedly, moving toward the baskets, trying to piece together suitable clothes for the day. "I am going. But not to wed. I return her to her father."

"You!" Tame Deer threw her hands up in exasperation. "Why do you love to torture your poor self? Do you know, I think you have the brain of a beaver after all!"

He shied away from her scolding and fumbled in his basket for a jacket. "I do this that she may not be tortured."

92

"You will serve her up to the priest like a deer cut into stew! You will feed her to a man who has licked his chops over her since she was but a few winters older than Sequan!"

"Manit! Qunneke!" he profaned in tremolo. "I shall not drop her like a gnawed bone! I will go to them and make them see. I will free her!"

"You are not afraid of the farmer. You can talk the priest to dumbness." The wife was gentler. "What is it? Fear you Elizabeth will grow tired of her new ways? That she will turn away from you . . . too?"

"Matta. Not Elizabeth."

"Is it the town? Sequan? Is it me?" She watched Wakwa pour fresh water into a bowl. "I am in your way! Let me go!"

"There would be no need yet, even were I to keep her."

"Shall I hide? When all were well you could come to bring me home."

He felt comfort from their deep tie reaching across the room to him. He dipped one hand into the washing bowl as if to cool the instrument that would give Elizabeth back to her family.

"Qunneke, I could stop Elizabeth where she is." He spoke in a collected tone, sharing insights he had admitted to himself unwillingly during the night. "The wonder of her is mine for only saying yes to keeping her. She has such love for this portion of earth on which we stand. But even she does not know how far her eyes see past me, the forest, the ocean, to places born into her as the river was born into us.

"She will excel in the gold houses of high white men as she would have excelled with us, making simple strawberry bread. To get her this chance, I have only to defeat this other man who wants her more than his own soul." Wakwa's misery formed into a smile.

Tame Deer helped her husband prepare for his mission as she had helped him on so many lesser ones. Her heart was heavy for his loss and she scrubbed him as if he were to be a bridegroom that day. She trimmed his hair to an even length below his shoulder blades and washed it. He refused paint but consented to put on the cream-colored doeskin he had finished soft as cloth for his wedding almost three years before. The sleeves were outlined with fringe that fell two feet and were encrusted with rows of black money mixed with figures of white. His leggings matched the color of the coat and the small apron was worked in patterns of wampum and sukauhock. Tame Deer wound his belt of wampum around his head for a band and it hung, shining, to his heels. Its value in sterling had never been estimated, but based on his dealings with Dire Locke, Wakwa was confident that it could pay his passage to London and back with a year's high living in between. The wife brought him his arrows and was upset at not finding the knife.

"She has it to cut clothes."

Tame Deer could make no sense out of the details that escaped her husband.

She stood back to look at him. "You do dazzle me, Wakwa."

"I apologize for those words, my wife."

"No. It is true. I shall have your evening meal hot, as you like it, and be waiting with it."

A tremor passed through him and he did not reply. There was nothing left for him to do but go to Elizabeth.

He cautioned Tame Deer as he went out. "Tell not even the grass about this. I will refuse the reward for returning her, without my uncle's knowledge. It rankles so to bring her home."

Chapter 19

Elizabeth Dowland, too, prepared for Wakwa's coming as if for their wedding. When she was clean she dipped her face into the stream many times to bring color to her cheeks. She rejected the idea of her bonnet, not wishing to hide her hair from him, and made three slender braids at each temple, binding them in loops above each ear, using the rosebud cotton for her ribbons. For the first time she wore the delicate peach-colored underclothes and the ruffled underslip with the lined black skirt. She tucked in the white linen blouse and, careful of its flowing sleeves, cast fragrant sticks on the fire with a heap of balsam, filling the close air with the scent she loved.

.Alone in the tidy hut, she thought of the swans and their artful affection. She found it impossible to relax on her first holiday since Wakwa brought her the cloth. Impatient by midafternoon, she reached for her red cloak to go and look for him by the river.

She turned toward the low door and he was there, just inside. Beth uttered a sound and stared at the splendor of his costume and the grace with which he wore it. He was beautiful, exceeding even the swans in poise and strength and color. Wakwa's perfections vied so masterfully with her own that Beth forgot about affecting him with loveliness and experienced the piercing delight at the quick of herself that she had often felt for him in his absence. For the first time her desire for him and his nearness were almost irresistible and she fought to keep her self-possession, the habits of self-denial rooting her to where she stood.

"Hawunshech, Kayaskwa."

She was mystified at the new word.

"Farewell, I say to you, my gull."

Her neck and face grew red but she did not move or speak.

"I bring you now to your father and will speak in your behalf to lift your burden."

"You are grown cautious since last night." She answered in

momentary cruelty and whirled away. Without turning to him she apologized in a softened voice. "I did not wish to give you pain, sir, I am much the weaker of us two."

And the word *sir* cut into him more deeply than her first response.

"When would I see you again?" Her throat pained her.

"My dear friend, I cannot tell."

She kept her back to him as her face twisted with the tears she tried to hold back. Quietly they slipped down, and almost unseeing she walked to the back of the hut and reached for the little brown wool bag she had carried with her when she had come.

"Have a care for your deerskins when I am gone. There shall be no one to kill the lice in the hut." She hid herself in one of the hanging skins like a child in a blowing curtain and cried in an ugly voice, "I will be going. I will be going."

Ready, she looked for him at the door, but found him hunched on the pile of wood he had put in for her several days before. The heels of his hands were pressed hard into his eyes and the muscles close under his skin trembled so that his limbs seemed to shake.

And, in her memory, Beth saw again the muscles slide in his back as he ripped at the dog who had been a threat to her in the wood and she made a stand in front of him.

"I had made a plan!" she began. "That we should have wed here in the hut with all your Gods and my own, alone, as witnesses, and later, when you wished, announce our life. I will come then and live as do the Ninnuock. I know how I must inconvenience you, you being in the limelight of your tribe." She waited and watched his face, then hurried on in a quieter tone. "If you went to my father now, I cannot think you would win approval were you the pharaoh himself! Just so you were a simple farmer with an English face." She cried again a bit. "Wakwa, listen! Listen thou to me! I know I am but a girl to you, though I am all of seventeen. Indeed, before a month is out you may add a year to that! I am not frivolous nor filled with vain desire. At this moment I do wish I were like others and would rush to you and trap you in my arms. I am no temptress but a simple woman who doth desire to be your wife! You are nearly twice my age and have gained knowledge and wisdom of all kinds that I have not. Yet think you, Wakwa, my poor father will pursue me without mercy? Think what the accomplished fact of our union would mean to him! How better to break the bond with Hudson than simply break it? I will leave their law and their protection—yea, their love—until he acquiesce, for surely I would die if I wed another."

"I have reasoned all this out myself," Wakwa moaned, "and now you lay open the decision I had firmly taken! It is for your sake that I return you, for to marry me would be to join your sacred English blood to the savage, yes, the heathen as your people say, and they would damn and hound you until the very love we have should wither!"

"You do then love me?"

Wakwa looked at her as if she had blasphemed.

"You have never said it." She smiled frankly.

He saw her dressed so sleekly, her hair arranged in a blending of both their styles, and he searched her small, handsome face. He was in agony now, split between their differences and their affection, his duty to his people and his care for her happiness. All the control of the past weeks must dictate their proper course.

"I torture you, I see, and for love of you shall do anything you wish, but do not tremble so! Methought a savage did not show emotion." And again, she smiled.

Wakwa sought her eyes. There was no change in them since the moonlit night. He saw no romance but a dedication that made herself one with him though he should never touch her.

"It hurts to see you suffer, so I must go." Her voice was husky. "But I will walk out of here alone. I could not bear to see you turn away after leaving me with them." She knelt to him and ran her hands along the inside of his thighs covered by the soft leggings, saying sadly, "Do not tremble so!"

He touched the fantastic braiding of her hair with admiration, then stood and lifted her up in one movement, holding her under her arms, pressing his lips against the hollow of her throat until she could not breathe. He lifted her higher still, and she wrapped her arms about his hair. Wakwa nestled his face against her tender breasts and kissed them through the linen blouse.

"Let these clothes, then, be our wedding raiment!" She removed the great white belt from his forehead.

He placed her gently on her feet and slowly wrapped the

heavy band of beads around her wrist and lower arm. He picked her up and brought her to her mat, then laid her down and placed the wampum belt at her feet. He removed his jacket and leggings and moccasins and sat near her as she had first seen him, dressed only in the small apron. He leaned down to her and kissed her.

"You hold back nothing!" Wakwa pulled the little ties that held her white shirt closed and kissed the length of her throat as it was revealed. He undid the sleeves and camisole and pulled down on them, seeing openly the whiteness of her skin, and held her softly against himself for many minutes. He could do nothing with the skirt, so involved was the tieing, and Beth stood to remove it, opening it from the side.

"Madness to put that cloth inside!" Wakwa said, horrified at how she had squandered it where no one could see.

"Do we not all hide what is most precious?"

"And so I have hidden thee these many days."

She lay back and looked away from him and did not see the tremors of panic passing through his eyes.

"It is not much, Elizabeth! We are together now."

"Wakwa! Oh! I am not afraid." She sat up and wrapped her arms around him. "I simply would not offend thee by a question. I know not the ways of your people . . . yea, I know not the ways of my own."

"Ask what you will, but do you see how words keep us apart? That is why I finally spoke to you, for if I must rely on only looks and touches we would have come to this pass many days ago!"

"It is not that I would ask."

"What then?"

"I love yourself and I would see you. Without this." Beth gingerly touched the front of the beaded apron.

"Ah! Then you would discover all mysteries in one day. We are so close, at times, I do forget you are not Ninnuock. This is normal to see, for clothes and coverings are not necessary to us."

Wakwa took both her hands and touched them to the string which was about his waist and down the several knots to where it ended at his buttocks.

"Pull on it then for I would know thee now."

She pulled on the cord and Wakwa threw aside the apron and sat and watched her face as she looked at the arching stalk of the phallus and then met his gaze. He laid her down and as he did he kissed her body many times, and with the fingers she had watched so often at heavy work caressed with gentleness her legs and stomach, resting at last on the mound of maidenhair.

"Ah! Elizabeth!"

"None, none has ever said my name the way you do! I am known by all as Beth but hereafter I am . . . oh! Do say my name again!"

And he said, "Elizabeth!" and came between her legs and entered a little way into her. There he stayed and kissed without hurry the round bottoms of her breasts.

She reached for his thighs and thought of her first night in the hut as she had watched him resting in the firelight and she suddenly went warm.

The man pressed a little on the maidenhead, thrilled to feel it there.

"Fox! I cannot believe!"

"Oh! You must, you must!" Feeling her hold back, although before she had been warm and free, he spoke to put her at her ease and still excite her, and as he did he felt that most wonderful of touches as the membrane thinned and yielded to his pushing phallus.

"Uppeshau!" he breathed.

"What say you?" the whisper of the unknown word replacing fear with wonder.

"Elizabeth! Ah! Right now you are the flower and that word to us doth mean, 'to burst forth into bloom'!"

And before he had finished saying this the void that had been within her and had gone so long untended was filled, and she was flooded with the man. As she looked up at him he bent his head to her and she no longer saw, obscured from light, encircled by the curtain of his long black hair.

He moved within her and she saw with other eyes as the coolness that was there warmed to the touch of his striving phallus.

Slowly, slowly, he moved, gentle to the last, until great throbs rolled all through his long frame. He lay still across her warm body and she wondered what she had done to be so honored as to have knowledge of this man. She wondered, too, how his weight seemed so fitting on top of her and why it did not crush her as she lay so still and small.

Wakwa raised up on his arms and surprised her with a hard, relentless kiss upon her mouth.

"I cannot express myself in English! To know you . . . to be within you . . . is to be . . . ah! . . . touohkomuk. . . . I mean to say you are . . . the forest, as we call it, place of solitude, a wilderness. I have at last found warmth in such great aloneness. Oh! Kayaskwa!" He looked concerned and his back stiffened.

Elizabeth felt him grow within her and was glad, glad beyond all happiness she had known, glad in her soul, and glad for her body. He arched back and away from her and she reached up to his face and touched, at last, with tender fingers the dark expanse beneath the bones of his cheeks. She adored the smoothness of his hairless skin and held her hands gently against his cheeks as he strove harder this time. Gradually other sensations awoke within the girl, making her tremble from her center outward as he had done minutes before.

There was nothing between them anymore, and his flesh and hers blended with the pushing and waning of his body embraced in a warm circle, knowing no limit but a sharing of the hot skin and blending of soft rises and muscular pressures.

A clear, high cry escaped the man as his floating seed was released. Then he rolled onto his back, staying within her, and rested with his hands measuring the long curve of her smooth buttocks.

And so they lay as the light outside changed from gold to pink, violet to black. And they slept at last, all struggle quelled and longing surfeited.

When the night grew dark Tame Deer took Wakwa's portion off the fire and dug a hole behind her house. She poured the meat into the ground and buried it, although such waste the night before would have shocked her. She closed the mat across her entryway and lay down to sleep, alone, wondering about the second wife and how it all would be.

* * * *

Wakwa and Elizabeth spent the next day in the sun near the stream that ran through the trees reflecting the golden leaves above. They were bound comfortably in silence, their sudden satisfaction fresh within them. Wakwa sat crosslegged while Elizabeth napped with her head in his lap. The afternoon cooled and he woke her with a little kiss.

"Do you know how sweet I find your breath?" she asked.

"How sweet?"

"Why, when you speak or kiss me I think it fresh as wind or grass or flowers."

"It is because I do not eat bread with my meat as do you English!" He laughed. "And lately I do not eat at all." He took her into the woods and pointed to the good herbs and showed her what was not to touch.

"Take me to the hut, Wakwa!"

"You are tired, Kayaskwa." He lifted her up to carry her back.

"No, Fox, I am not!"

He stopped in his path. "You always overdo! I shall harm thee if I know thee again so soon. Rest thyself."

She wrapped her arms around his neck and pressed her head against him. "You know that is not so. How can you not?"

Wakwa chuckled. "There is tomorrow, little bird. And I would like someday that you be well enough to make my morning meal. I fear you are indulged."

"But I do wish you so!" She sought his lips.

"Are all the English girls like you?" He avoided her.

"You are only fortunate."

He kissed her in his arms then, with the evening wind picking up around them, dry leaves crackling like fire overhead.

She stopped on the path as she followed him home.

"Is it wrong of me to want you so?"

"Why should it be wrong to love, Kayaskwa?"

"But our love is other things as well."

He confronted her. "You think too much in the afternoons, Elizabeth. What other thing is love? This is the root of all friendship in a married pair."

"Then there is English in you, Wakwa! I see you give this thought as well. And further . . . if you do not share her bed, how come you to keep faith with your wife?"

"My first wife!"

Elizabeth went red. "Again I ask too much."

Wakwa took her arm and walked by her side on the narrow path, more English, Beth thought, than Indian.

"Kayaskwa, Tame Deer was as a sister to me long before she was my wife. Our friendship has another wellspring. Nor is it clear to me I will keep faith with her."

"Wakwa! I would not push her out!"

"Innocent you are, Elizabeth. It is because of you she remains my wife and tends my field. It would be half the year for me to arrange with the sachim to divorce and marry again. It is not permitted to put aside a wife unless there is good reason. I have reason but have waited too long, considering you and how you came to be here. With her in my lodge is the only way I see for you and me to be connected! All will depend on what your father says. If he comes to solemnize the marriage of you as my one wife, I shall put her away and not regret."

"Father! I had quite forgot that side on this lovely day. What would he think if he knew what I would do with you?"

"You cannot think of him and me in the same moment."

"It is only he thinks me afraid."

"What is it you would do?"

"I know not exactly. To love you better each time you come to me."

"Elizabeth, there are no rules to follow nor things forbidden when an act comes out of love."

"Then I will make your breakfast and your supper too, but do not think to get away from me tomorrow!"

They were in the hut. Beth repaired the fire and laid out the bowls and spoons. Wakwa was busy untangling a fishing net.

"What will you go for?" she asked.

"Can you cook uppaquontup?"

"What is that, I pray?"

"A most dainty dish of bass heads—the brains and fat are sweet as marrow."

"But of course! I did not recognize the Indian name. Mother doth bake some every Wednesday night."

Wakwa stopped straightening the fibers and stared at her.

"I would rather have some boiled beef with peas beside!" Her laughter gave her lie away.

102

"Pah!" The man went out to fish.

* * * *

As usual, Wakwa rose first, before sunrise. He had slept on his own mat and came across the room to look at his bride before going into the cold for fresh water.

According to his people's custom she lay unclothed. Wakwa smiled at her young face turned toward the fire and gazed at the spare but womanly body, the full soft thighs flowing from the widespread bones of her hips.

He yawned and stretched with his legs apart, his hands clasped behind his head, the bucket hanging against his back. Studying the sky through the smoke hole, he flexed the muscles of his upper body, his taut stomach caving in under his ribs. He looked down as he relaxed and saw his young wife looking up at him.

She greeted him with a kiss on the arch of his foot. The bucket came down against his side.

"Elizabeth?"

Without answering him she continued to kiss his strong smooth leg, slowly rising to her knees, her hands spread open on the floor. Her kisses wound ever upward, serpentine, around his leg, with the heat of little leaping sparks, and she came underneath his body through the opening of his legs.

She did not see his upturned eyes as she moved under him holding his thighs with the palms of her hands, gently pressing her lips against the soft, full hang of the sac between his legs. She continued frontward, never ceasing the light pressures of her lips, and turned her own body to face his and kissed the stiffening rise of his erect penis. Her light, hot caresses held Wakwa in suspension. He did not change his position nor seem to breathe at all. She reached his hand and took the bucket from him, holding his hips as she kissed his stomach, covering his skin with the warm touches of her mouth.

She could not see his eyes as he looked up toward the high roof, rapt in the flattery of her desire and affection. He did not interrupt her wandering over his body, but rocked back in delight when her tongue touched the tip of the phallus and he buried his fingers in her hair. He looked down at her upturned face, still soft from sleep.

She spoke to him. "How perfect you are!"

He knelt low to her, still holding her face between his hands. "And thou!"

"Good morrow, dearest."

Wakwa answered with a slow and lingering kiss upon her mouth. He touched her back up and down with the sensitive tips of his long fingers and slipped his hand, for a moment, between the circumferences of her buttocks.

She lay back on the unmatted floor and, crouching low, Wakwa tenderly kissed the soft opening of her body, then lay next to her on his back.

Never had the girl known a feeling of such goodness as he gave her with that kiss. Fear and shame, anxiety and loneliness, were floated away on the warm breath of that caress, and she came to sit upon him and bent to kiss his face.

But the calm and pride that always rested there in his expression had given place to illumined pleasure, and directing her buttocks with his hand he swiftly pushed his phallus into the newly opened vault of her. Supporting her willowy body with his thighs, they joined themselves again.

When at last Wakwa slipped from within her Elizabeth moaned in a new kind of loneliness more painful than any she had known. "I am bereft of half myself at thy leaving!"

But the man closed his eyes and she was left to wait the time of the next rising of his body into hers.

* * * *

They spent the days walking in the woods and near the river, Beth learning to see the life that was around her. Wakwa did not hunt or fish, and they ate concoctions of maple sugar and cranberries and always the corn boiled and sweetened with fruit. They worked in the evenings making the strong rope which Wakwa used for trapping. Beth was quick to learn how to wind it tight, and it pleased Wakwa to see how she fit into his way of life. When her hands were raw from work and her cheeks burned from wind, Wakwa waded into the stream and returned with fish. They ate the flesh and he ground the bones into powder with the pestle. He mixed this with oil and covered her reddened skin with the paste. When she rinsed it off her skin was soft and renewed.

On the fifth day after Wakwa had taken Elizabeth as his wife they sat in front of a fire of a few sticks in the sun which was no longer warm, finishing the poppet for Sequan. Each day Wakwa had molded the apple with his fingers to retain the features he had shaped there. Today it was ready to be connected to the corn husk body with a neck carved out of pine.

"I shall convince them." Wakwa spoke half to himself.

"You look quite an Indian just now!"

"They must put some store in happiness."

"Yesterday and the day before you were simply my dear love, Wakwa. And now I perceive that I am in league with an Indian."

"I shall tell them that our union will be important as a force to bind the farmers with the Ninnuock, that they will see men listen to my words because of you, and that you will help me understand and bargain for secure agreements between our peoples."

"The poppet doth need hair, my love. She looks somewhat like a rotten egg with eyes."

"Can you not be serious! You distract me!"

"A thousand pardons, Silent Fox! Here, take off a lock of my hair. No, not straight across. From here. That's all! I will sew it to a cap and Sequan can learn to tie it on. When she wishes to have an Indian doll she may slip off the hair."

Wakwa sat still watching his young wife sew with quick, sure fingers on a gown for the toy. She would not listen to him. She slipped away from his attempts to prepare for the visit to her father which must come.

"What is it that drives English people away from one another?" He waited for an answer but she sat abstracted, a strand of thread between her teeth, stopped in the act of breaking it.

Wakwa leaned across and snapped the thread.

"You did not know I am an Indian? You thought me an Englishman disguised, hiding in the forest?"

"My love, that is myself."

"Then to keep you from always being hidden must I not speak to your father who holds your life in balance?"

"You are very sharp at leading me where my thoughts would not dwell. I see how you are effective at your councils."

He smiled vaguely at the compliment.

She took up the toy again. "I saw you first as a creature like a bird between those trees and then I learned you were a person. And after that, a man, and then my husband. But now I am surprised to see you are an Indian dressed in skins, eating at your fire, talking of councils, trading, and trapping, and wearing your money, and I am left amazed."

"It is you who lead me away from my thought. And the poppet, as you call it, now doth look like a rotten egg with eyes and hair!"

"What is the difference between us, Wakwa, that makes this visit with my father so difficult? Though you are the most handsome suitor I could have conjured for myself!"

"Handsome." He flashed his smile. "That attribute has led me many times into the mouth of the devil and I fear his jaws have shut around me now!"

"You are proud! That is for me to say! How do you call yourself such a thing?"

"I do see it every morning in the glass." His eyes twinkled.

"Were you a Christian you would be whipped for such flaunting of your beauty."

"Yes! You name one difference between our peoples. Whipped for truth and rewarded for lies. White men act against the stream of things."

She frowned, considering each word he said.

"Would you not be praised for going home to this man, Annanias, when all know how you hate him?"

She had no answer.

"This is not the only difference. We are a castrated race because of gold, little wife."

"No!" She balked at this.

"But yes. Now you see into what you have married. It is very simple. An hundred years ago when first the ships came across from England, my fathers denied all gold in payment for our lands. They knew from within that land is not to sell. But your fathers insisted we take something that they might plant their own seeds in the virgin earth. Ninnuock chose to receive that which was most valuable to them, beads of glass and bits of shells and bones of fishes. Gold has not more value, I think, than these, but it is the money of a more powerful race and it is to the tune of gold that your most sober judges dance. If the Narragansett and the Wampanoag had accepted gold we would now be growing instead of diminishing. We were cut off from our old ways and from thoughts of new, from cities of our own and from places to plant and trade what was valuable to us. We had not even knowledge of silver when I am sure across the sea it lined the gutters with your pigs!" Wakwa's face darkened with his passion. "We are bled and palsied now and are moved and shifted and fenced off from our land. The fence! The wall! We make walls only to defend us from our enemies. The English build them to stop the passage of their friends so that a stinking cow may wander undisturbed! I cannot understand this, but I try. I try. I am like this arrow pointing ever to a goal . . . to bind the open wound of our amputated life so that the parts may grow together and be stronger. Perhaps to blend the red and white. Perhaps to build stronger fences of our own."

"Would you then leave this life? You could live a great man in the town."

"Dream not, Elizabeth! What would I aspire to? Clean dung out of stables, apprentice to a carpenter? Shine boots, perhaps, in the public houses?"

"Stop!"

"Then you see the differences without asking. You are well aware how you coatmen look upon my doeskins and my feathers."

"But you are a great man."

"In the forest I am great and also small. I have mastery and am subject to the greatest laws."

"But you are rich!"

"In freedom I am rich. You may count all the sterling and beads in the world for naught!"

"But you are wise and worthy."

"In your eyes and to my own blood. To common English I am scavenger and heathen, wild and impotent!"

"I am ashamed. I am filled with shame. I am a spoiled babe and most unworthy. Oh, Fox, I do so fear now what may be said or even done if you go to Sweetwood to my father."

"My fear is double yours since I must go!"

"I am shamed with what may happen. Some indignity, some insult that may be said in their anguish over me. And I am ashamed in myself, even now! Oh, how can you love me?"

Wakwa stood over her. His countenance was not his own but angles of dark skin stretched over the bones of his face.

"And with all this shame how can you love? Stand you up!" He undid the cord of his small apron and threw it back among the leaves.

Beth looked away from his body.

He lifted her skirt and underskirt and fumbled with the strings of her drawers.

"It is a mighty wonder white men ever multiply with impediments like these." He did not smile as he said this for he was out of himself, seeing not himself nor her but all around them both toward his purpose.

Beth was surprised she did not run away from fright, and the armholes of her blouse showed wet. She was even more surprised that she was open to him as he lifted her right there and leaned his back against the arching maple for support and took her, standing, straining, in the cold.

He seemed desperate that she feel every nuance of his movements, although his hands were tender as he held her underneath. He reached the quick of her at last and in that instant Beth could feel she was no longer herself alone, or Charles Dowland's daughter, but a woman, all women, and the man who did this not the savage, but a man, all men. This must be the prime connection in life's circle. Her girlhood left her and she held him as she screamed the new responsibility's inception.

He dropped her to her feet and kissed her mouth and said, "Such is the bride of Silent Fox!"

The beauty of his eyes and the angles of his face were his own.

He kicked out the fire and they went off together to the room in the hill to sweat, their affection fused into a marriage by the heat of his act. This time she could regard his body and he could look at her without offense.

When she was limp with sweating he helped her stand and warned her to run quickly. He raced ahead and left her squawking in the cold like a chicken. She ran after him, throwing her clothes at the roots of a tree, and splashed into the freezing water on her belly. His arms wound around her and he took her to the middle, again giving her his hair to hold.

They came safely home and dressed and ate and slept like creatures born of gods, called by the Ninnuock, Manittoo.

* * * *

Beth awoke uncomfortable with itching. She was dotted with red splotches from insect bites. She drew her brown dress over her head and put the bonnet on to keep her hair dry when she washed in the stream. She put a log into the failing fire and left the hut quietly, shutting the door behind her.

She was determined to make a filling meal for Wakwa this morning. They ate when they were hungry and as much as they pleased and seldom wasted their supplies that way. But with the new rope finished, Wakwa would start to hunt and go for fish at night, downriver. It was time she assumed her place in his house.

She found his small apron half-buried by dark red leaves from the afternoon before and went to the stream. As she turned back toward the hut with her brimming bucket Wakwa stood in her path.

"Oh!" Water spilled onto her skirt. "Such surprises do become habit with you! You might at least have said hello!" She handed him his breeches. "Came you after these? Not that they will keep you warm. Oh, do put something on."

"I did come to look for thee, having no interest in dressing just now."

"Will you lie about forever? Is it not time to hunt?" A grin escaped her. "I wish to have some skins. You are right about my clothes. They are unsuitable. I would make some trousers right away!"

"Elizabeth. Thou art learning quickly how to be a wife." Wakwa took the bucket. "Trousers! Women do not wear such things. Aiee!" He examined the backs of her hands, covered with bites.

She scratched her neck against her shoulder. He bent her head forward and saw the marks.

"You are bitten! Come and take this off. I perceive you meant to hide this from me. Are there many more?" He hurried her to the hut.

"There is nothing to be done about it. I will not let you see. You would better spend your time killing the rats I found hidden in that filthy basket."

"Remove your dress without delay. I must put on some paste. What cheer, netop? My lady doth not like thy company,

109

good fellow. Make haste to leave for she would have you dead!"

"Wakwa, do not touch it, oh!"

"And is the Dowland farm unvisited by vermin? Have you never seen a little rat?"

"We do not fondle them but catch them in a trap. What a scourge they are with such a tail. Oh! Put them out."

"You are very right. I would not like to find one in the morning meal." Wakwa threw them into the woods and burned the basket. He washed his hands carefully and made a paste of fine cornmeal and water and approached Elizabeth's dark corner.

"Woskehhuwaen! Spoiler! You disfigure yourself." Gently he patted the paste where the spots sprang blood where she had scratched.

"I said you should not see."

"This day we move from here. The hut is infested."

"All today? What of your hunting? And the skins?"

"The traps must wait. You see, the hut itself must go. I should not be curing lice atop the skins."

"I shall be a help to you, dear Wakwa. You must teach me how to carry. Your women do."

"Never shall you lift or carry, Kayaskwa."

"But I must!"

"You are not made for it. These shoulders so thin and back so fine would bend and break under unfamiliar loads. Never shall you carry."

"Of what use am I to you?"

"It would be a mighty favor to your husband if you could carry but yourself and this, perhaps." Wakwa whistled and reached his hand out to the sachim-bird who flew down to him and pecked his finger. "I have done back here, where else doth it itch?"

"There is a place here, on my breast."

"We cannot let that be!" Wakwa rubbed the spot and yielded to the softness of her body.

She did not object or remind him of his other duties when he desired her.

They were familiar now, and comfortable and afterward were warm and filled with energy.

"Wash now, I must do the paste again. But if I do, I think we will never leave today!"

**** **** ****

Flames marked the death of the hut. They left, mid-afternoon, Wakwa leading her overland to the wooden lodge above the river. She cajoled him into letting her carry her own cloth and clothes. The little sachim-bird chose to sit on top of Wakwa's head, making him an animated crown.

The man was laden with mats and baskets, carrying some things by a strap of leather bound around his forehead. He did not grumble under this novel chore, but he missed Qunneke and the maid. He was more interested in finding, stripping, and setting poles for a new tanning hut.

When Elizabeth saw the house, so high and long, unused and cold, she was upset.

"I pray you, take us back! This place makes me shiver in my soul. The ceiling is so high it will surely fill with shadows. I will be far too lonely when you are gone."

She slipped back out and looked hopelessly down the path they had just come. Wakwa escorted her in again.

"The spirits here but need warming, little wife. And you are safer from beasts, for wolves and moose and even bears play all about us. The walls make not the home, my beauty." He showed her through the lofty rooms.

"If you will make a door, Wakwa, I shall try."

He stooped to kiss her throat and she gazed over his head.

"Do you know, I see a tapestry already, draping down from beam to floor across this big hall! Shall I make it covered with pines and flying birds? Oh! Do go into Wareham for blue and green. My threads are also low."

He shook his head and moved away to get his arrow case.

"You look like a potentate in here, my Silent Fox. At last you are not cramped and I may watch your lovely movements as you walk."

"Enough! I am going for a deer and will not be trapped myself in all the honey that you speak to me."

Wakwa planned to take meat to his uncle, having been absent from the town for six days. Elizabeth was invited to come and

111

followed in his steps, declining to ask questions, not wishing to distract him.

She was collecting wild onions twenty yards from him when a doe startled her in the thicket. The doe, so large to Elizabeth, was startled too and froze. Then Elizabeth saw a flash of tail as the deer fled. The earth was jarred with the crash of the animal's body against the ground, her skull opened by Wakwa's arrow.

Elizabeth dropped the onions in horror.

Silent Fox came toward his English wife. "Come and let us see the kill." He held her around her shoulders and moved her toward the deer.

"But she was so beautiful!"

"And we must eat. And wear her skin. And she will never die because she lives in us and gives us warmth. Pick up the onions. You shall make a stew, Elizabeth."

She stared at the glossy hair of the doe raised in the afternoon breeze. "First teach me to shoot."

Again Wakwa kissed her, happy with her giving nature. He helped her hold the bow, much too large and heavy for her. After forcing off several arrows she stood back, alone, and aimed at the dead deer.

"Close!"

"It is enough for now, Kayaskwa. I am happy that you missed, for as you see the skin is perfect as I have shot her."

On the way to the house Wakwa changed his mind about the doe. He would take her whole to Waban. He dressed for council in breechcloth and leggings, decorated his loose hair with a cloth band and a rope of down, and rubbed walnut oil onto his neck and shoulders and chest. He ran the distance to his canoe and paddled back upriver near to their new dwelling. He lugged the deer on his shoulders and took the descent to the water crouched under its weight.

"If you would raise them in a pasture and kill them at your will you could avoid much labor."

"You have the makings of a shrew, Elizabeth. Or how is it said . . . a prophet! When the moon is there I shall return."

Chapter 20

Wakwa pulled the canoe onto land. Then he made a wild call again and again over the sound of the river, signaling his pleasant victory to his kinsmen. In only moments he saw Awepu and Pequawus coming down the slope from the otan.

"My son! It is good to feel your arms around me."

Wakwa embraced Awepu too. "Awepu, we must tend the traps. I feel this will be a season of great bounty. As you see this doe has fallen at my feet in the canoe!"

Wakwa could hardly contain his good spirits as he carried the doe's carcass to the sachim's lodge. But his father was wary.

"What is it you have done for these past seven days? You have lost a fortune not being at the gaming. Even Awepu has been winning. Your uncle missed you greatly at the closing of the feast. He has some plans for you, and when I asked your wife where you were she said to me, 'Is he not freeborn? I do expect him any time.'"

"A resourceful woman, my Qunneke. My Father, when we see the sachim you will know all, for I shall tell this story only once."

Wakwa called outside the sachimmaacommock for entrance, and Waban came to greet them himself, his long gray hair tinged pink in the sunset.

The men sat around the fire in Waban's private room and sipped cool water from Waban's oak burl cups. Waban offered Wakwa his pipe, encouraging him to begin.

He began. "I have news which will please you and trouble you, my Sachim, my Uncle. My own consideration of my acts during this Taquonk has been deep as the leaves that have fallen into thick mats in the forest. Now I wander as in a night, beautiful, but dimly lit with silver light, which is cold and lonely unless I bare my soul to you, Waban, and to my father and to my dear friend."

"Wakwa! You try our patience." Pequawus was worried.

"You shall have it, Father!" Smoke from the pipe curled

around his face, softening Wakwa's expression in a fragrant haze. "I have taken under common law a second wife whom I do love past any living thing." Wakwa saw his father's head snap up and his back go erect. "She does feel the same for me and will graciously accept Tame Deer and my daughter so that she might not cause them sadness. As you well know, Sachim, my first wife has not received me as husband for some time." Wakwa waited.

The older men said nothing but gregarious Awepu showed his feelings.

"Old friend, I wish you as many children as I have myself! How pleased I am you have found a generous woman! Why did you not bring her here with you?"

Wakwa looked only at his uncle. "She is Elizabeth, daughter of Charles Dowland, the maiden absent from her home."

Pequawus lowered his head. Awepu sat very still, blinking back the thoughts crowding his mind.

"I glean she is a maiden no more?" Waban's relaxed demeanor was unchanged.

"My ruler, you speak truth."

"Pequawus, be not sad." Waban passed the pipe to him. "You see how your son is always quick to follow my advice? It was the last time I spoke to him I bade him do this very thing."

"You advised? . . ." Pequawus' mind sped past the gap in his understanding and settled into memories. "Should I be happy? Why is it I feel as I did the last time I saw my wife go into the woods to gather?"

Wakwa reached for the pipe impatiently. "What think you of my action?"

Waban engaged his glance. "I think at last you have gambled far too high! It is not a plumstone you have cast upon the forest floor but the life of a woman, a white woman, a New English woman prized highly by her folk and bound to wed another!" Waban inhaled the gentle smoke of the tobacco Wakwa always supplied him. "She does return you your affection, nephew?"

Wakwa looked down for the first time. "She would have no other." He faced his uncle. "This is no ordinary person, but one who bends to breaking to understand and is always giving of her spirit. She might have been born into us! Such sweetness and such strength I have never found combined in one human heart."

114

"Yet she has broken with her family and her ways?" Waban exhaled his doubts with smoke.

"Who in this room would have the courage to do that? I went to take her home, although my own heart was breaking, and she at last agreed to go and sacrifice herself to this priest to whom she has been promised, as we would a slave, since she was a girl. This she would have done out of care for me. It did seem more manly for me to claim her. I have stayed by her side these six or seven days. I am grateful, Uncle, you do care if she is happy. It seems not to matter to her own. She would live as Ninnuock. This must I tell her father."

"I envy you not that! Nephew, you do not understand these foreign people. They look calm as a pond and gentle as the mourning dove, but I have found they are hard within, all stomach, no heart. You need my help. I will come with you, if you wish, or entertain this farmer Dowland here. We will take her in, but go carefully. Wakwa Manunnappu, I need you sorely. More than you need this marriage."

Pequawus cut into his son's reply to Waban. "I told you, brother-in-law, that we would be living without Charles Dowland's corn. We have reaped his harvest now!"

The conversation broke open with questions and surmises about Dowland's character. Relying on the family's long history of unobtrusive prosperity on their American plantation, the strength and tact shown after the war, and the safety of Wakwa's own borders and Charles' own statements in Buzzards Bay records about respecting those borders, they determined how to deal with him.

They selected delegates to go to Sweetwood to prepare the Dowlands for Wakwa's coming.

"Son, be sure Awepu and Mosq go well-armed, but you carry nothing. Not even your knife. I would have you back from them untouched."

"My Father, they will not cut me down!"

Wakwa left the sachim's house elated. He laughed out loud with a fantasy of placid sonship with Charles Dowland, happy together at the feast Waban would hold to solemnize the union between their peoples. With his face lit by such reflections, Wakwa hailed his neighbors and turned into the door of his own lodge.

"My prayers are answered, you are safe!"

"Qunneke." He held his wife close. "A long silence you have kept. I am more grateful than you can know."

Their child came between them, reaching for her father, and Wakwa swung her up to kiss her.

"I have been in the forest, baby Sequan. See what I have brought you!" He pulled the doll from his basket.

His child looked wonderingly at it and very slowly and shyly touched the shiny blue dress with her small hand. The father knew she had never seen any clothing like it.

"It is a poppet!" Wakwa laughed at a memory.

"Popy!" Sequan attempted the word.

"Good, little, very good. Nosh made part of it. That is what took him so long in the woods. The dress and hair and hat are from the hands of someone who lives in the forest. She is a shining creature changed from a white swan into a woman by Manit."

The servant put down her cooking spoon and circled around them trying to view the doll. She stood close behind her master and he turned sharply to her with a message for his father to come and stay the night.

"Qunneke, send her away in the morning. I do not like her face and she listens better than a rabbit."

"Should we not wait, Wakwa? Soon I may not be managing this house. I see you have changed your mind about Elizabeth."

"Do as I say. I do not like her work. Elizabeth already makes me better rope than she who was brought up to it." He softened. "Fear not you will be sent away as well. I have come just now from the sachim. He offers help and counsel. Soon I will go to her father."

Tame Deer touched the doll's fringe of rich brown hair. "Do not tell them about me."

"I will not. At first. I would stake my life Dowland will neither take his daughter back nor persecute her if she stay. She is no longer the same as when she left him."

Qunneke trembled and said in a husky voice, "Seek the help of her uncle, Wakwa. The one with the golden hair. Awepu says that he was very warm."

"I do not think it is their way but I will ask . . . if only to please

116

you. If I meet success I shall have a lock of him! Dear wife, do you fancy just the hair, or him?"

Tame Deer smiled and cried at the same time.

While Wakwa held Sequan, Tame Deer fed him, and their daughter fell asleep in his arms holding tightly to her apple doll.

Chapter 21

Even alone, Elizabeth was not afraid. There was peace in the wooden hall where she sat in a rectangle of moonlight after an evening of sweeping and putting their baskets in convenient places. She was mistress of the place, thinking about light and shadows and night colors which filled the house.

There were so many inspirations she wished to reproduce in cloth if she could make the time. She thought if she could take a bit of the beauty of this quiet hour and sew it into something tangible for her family they would be glad she had found harmony.

She heard Wakwa's light step and rose to greet him outside the door.

"Shining creature!" Wakwa looked at her. "Hardly can I touch you! You may float away on the moonbeam!"

"Never shall I float anywhere away from you. I am very real and ever will bother you with my presence." She laughed at him. "Your poetry doth speak a measure of success."

He took her in. "You build a fine fire, Kayaskwa. The sachim says I may make an Indian of you." He enjoyed her closeness at that moment. "I am cold. I went almost naked to the town."

"But for the grease you put on I would let you wear this to warm you. It is my wedding gift to you." She produced the ivy-embroidered shirt.

"Your gift was yourself, forever, but this is very grand! There is great perfection in your work. That is how I like to make my traps."

"May I come and see sometime?"

"Tomorrow, early. There is much for me to do to prepare for the going to your father. I shall wear this shirt that he may see you are well and do love me. What is this leaf?"

"Cannot you tell? Let me see! Perhaps it is not rendered clear enough!"

"Elizabeth, be calm. I only do not know its name, but I have seen this leaf twining around the chimneys in Boston and one much like it just outside the door."

118

"English ivy, Silent Fox."

She drifted to sleep discussing the quilting frame to be built. Before light she was restless and disturbed Wakwa by her unconscious moans.

Troubled that she was having bad dreams at the start of their new life, he forced himself up, restored the fire, made some tea, and mixed a new bowl of cornmeal paste for the red marks that were showing through on her skin.

She grunted, drew her knees up against her chest, and put one hand between her legs. Wakwa watched her closely.

She opened her eyes. "You frightened me!"

"And so you did me. You have been dreaming, Kayaskwa?"

"Not a dream the whole night." She grimaced and sat up. There was a stain of blood on the shirt.

"Kayaskwa!"

"I do apologize! Oh, what a way to begin a day. Do not be so worried. It is but my monthly sickness." She curled up again. "I was hoping it would not come. I am sorry to make such a spectacle. I am usually very tidy."

"Are you sure that this is all this is? Such a quantity of blood! I think you must be ill! Why, you sweat and have been moaning half the night."

"Sorry. Sorry. I have the cramp. It will soon go away. I must get up. Please do not stare at me."

Wakwa walked away nervously. "I may not hunt this morning, either. I must build you a shelter."

She grunted again. "I feel so ugly, all grainy with that paste, all spotted and bleeding. You will think me an English cow."

"How do you make light of your condition? I am beside myself just to see you! I do not know how to help you."

"Wakwa, dearest, . . . does not Tame Deer fall this way each month? I cannot think you would go on this way having been a married man."

He came to her with some tea. "Never like this. I have never seen any woman with such pains and there is blood even on the mat!"

"I will be up and clean it soon."

"With Qunneke and most Ninnuock women, I have heard, it is a matter of little blood and they are back from the shelter and merry within a few days."

"Then they are blessed, or healthier than I. I go on sometimes for nine days and change my cloths many times. What do you mean, a shelter? Am I cast out because I have this show twelve times a year?"

"You cannot live within, Elizabeth."

"I will not abide it! It is no great thing. I do promise you that I am very clean about it, as I said."

"Your sickness makes you uncordial, wife. It is not I alone who decree this. It is custom."

"Custom!"

"My love, I cannot touch you while you bleed."

"Oh! Such revelations at this early hour. Now I have an headache." She smiled at him. "So, you truly are the lost tribe of the Jews. I had always thought Cotton Mather quite a bag of wind. He must have passed by one of your female huts and made his deduction." She curled tight again and could not speak.

"There is something else wrong! I have never heard such moans with a woman's sickness." Wakwa approached her again.

"Oh! Then I am up! It will not last, I say, but now it is here and so are you and you must bear up a bit!" She shook where she stood bent over. "I have enough to do trying to find the soap."

Wakwa filed through her things to help her, thrown off his guard by their first difficulty together. She passed by, located the box immediately, and began to boil water. The sight of her limping about in the red-smeared shirt, doing the necessary things to rectify her inconvenience, weakened his adherence to the code he revered. He held her close and kissed her head, pushing himself to action forbidden by tradition.

"I am hideous!" She cringed away from his embrace. "Must you really put me out? It is a quarter of a month."

"It doth sound very long that way." He smiled. "I know you have done all the bending up until now. Somehow we shall combine our customs to make our living smooth. Pardon please my clumsy speech today."

* * * *

Wakwa was stripping twigs from saplings he was preparing as long poles for the wetuomemese when she brought him his breakfast.

She sat on a flat stone warmed by the sun and sighed, "That makes it better!"

Wakwa stopped work. "I should not even eat in your presence but you and I, we will make exception, nux?"

"Nux."

"What happens on the farm when you are like this?"

Elizabeth could not understand why he found her condition so remarkable. He was immovable about the matter of the hut. It was a first frightening step back for her. She was weighed by the more primal culture and foresaw a necessary loss of her former sense of herself. Wakwa's hands shaking her knees called her from her reverie.

"Oh! I go about my work."

He was up, driving the thin poles deep into the ground. He made a disapproving noise as he pushed down on the wood.

"Mother heats up a brick and I lie with it a while like that. But the work must be done. I rise and keep myself clean, milk morning and evening, spin, bring Father his noon meal in the fields, go to my aunt's to sew, and do all the ordinary things that I do until it is time to listen to Father read the evening prayer, for, after all, does not work give dignity to ourselves?"

"I say the person lends dignity to the work."

"But that would mean, would it not, that the work itself were not necessary?"

Wakwa would not debate with her. "I also know it is kinder to thyself to rest when thy body needs comfort."

They were at another stalemate but she saw his point. It annoyed her that she could always see his point. But she no longer fought the idea of the small hut and tried to help him as he bent the pole, pushing the free end into the dirt, forming an arch.

"Women do not help with poles. I will teach you in a while to place the mats for the walls and roof."

"I see I will never make a Christian of you."

"Not if I am to have you for a wife!" He grinned devilishly.

Beth felt close to him again and was docile when he established the time for his meeting with her father for after she was free of the small hut.

She packed up a basket and crawled on hands and knees through the low door of the finished shelter.

Chapter 22

Elizabeth lived alone in the wetuomemese and Wakwa went north with Awepu and the other men to work on a new fishing weir near the fall of the river.

She thought constantly about the courage it would take for Wakwa to face her father and toyed with the idea of going along. She took a square of undyed linen and began embroidering a message for her family. When she tried to date it she realized she no longer lived under a system of clocks. She and Wakwa existed in a network of events, causes, and effects, the effects causing new events. The month of the fall of the leaf, three sleeps since her husband parted for the north. She knew from her short experience that his return, scheduled according to the light on the fifth day, would be exact. She could be certain the hot meal she would ready for him would be eaten before it was cold.

She mapped out the days that had passed with a stick in the dirt. She discovered that a few miles away it was the nineteenth of October. The day of her wedding to Annanias was past, the threat was over, the contract broken. She was free.

Her flow lessened and she was impatient for it to stop. The urge to touch Wakwa's face, to be seen by his eyes, to feel him within her body, grew strong.

At the appointed time Wakwa was there, wild, darkened, and happy from the tasks that yielded him his satisfaction. But she remained in the wetuomemese while he met the hunters at the sweating room. He would rest in his own town overnight and go to trade in Wareham the next day.

She cut a jacket of beaver fur and sewed it with the heaviest of her gold needles. She rested and tried to give herself the relaxation Wakwa had spoken of.

The elation she knew in the task of pulling down the female hut and roving in the fresh air was evidence not of dislike but of her willingness to convert to a different habit. Her very bleeding was recognized and rendered important because of the days she was required to spend apart and incapacitated. Her sharing in the life pattern was special and specialized. Her return home to Wakwa would bring, each month, reborn appreciation.

She luxuriated in hot water and the violet-scented soap and took the stone knife, as she had seen Wakwa do with a doeskin, and passed it over her legs and armpits, delighting in the new feeling of smoothness. She dressed in the clothes she had worn the day he took her as his wife, but left her clean hair free. Wearing her monk's cloak and carrying her basket, she went to collect sweet kindling.

She walked for a while and came upon some flattened grass that had been swirled around and around by the body of some heavy animal which had slept in this soft bed and was wandering now like herself. She started back at sunset, sounds from the trees crossing above her, and one of her uncle's songs came out in a hum, then broke into words.

    " 'Trolly lolly lolly lo,
        Sing trolly lolly lo!
        My love is to the greenwood gone,
        Now after I will go. . . .' "

The song floated away as her eyes rested on the face of Silent Fox.

He held her and kissed her. "You are a vision!"

They never broke that embrace, but lay together on the wealth of dry leaves as the sky was shot through with purple and the sun slipped down among the western trees. She was alive inside, unconscious of their movements, feeling only the deepness of his reach into her. Numberless times he touched her depth, and the strong sounds of her perfect pleasure careened against the bark of the trees and grew in the quiet time of early night.

They came shivering home, laid the kindling on the fire, and ate a stew Tame Deer had made in the town.

Wakwa ran his hand up her leg. "What have you done while I was away?"

She answered his surface question. "I did not like hair on me anymore. You have none."

"I shall miss it. It was soft like the feathers of your sachim-bird. I will have to get you a blade. Think not you are going to use my mighty knife to this purpose. It would as soon cut off your leg as the hair!"

Elizabeth went to look for her embroidery. "I will show you how I otherwise spent my time."

"First, I have something for you." He handed her a parcel.

Beth unwrapped a small wooden box from a large piece of printed paper. Her face changed as she read of herself, described as "a young female person missing, loved and honored daughter of Charles Dowland, lost or abducted from the flock of Annanias Hudson, Sweetwood. One thousand pounds offered for information reuniting her to her family." She threw it into the fire and watched it burn.

"I daresay they won't give you a thousand pounds for the information you will bring to them! When go you?"

"The second day from this, Elizabeth."

"You seem exceeding calm!"

"I must seem so."

"Do you know what you will say to Papa?"

"We must think of something more for me to bring that they may know I truly have you with me." Wakwa circled around her question.

"Can you read this, Wakwa?" She brought him the square of linen.

"Printed letters I can read but this is only a brown silk snake to my eyes."

"Then I shall teach you how to read and write these little snakes when all this marriage fuss is settled. It will push you ahead in your work."

Wakwa sat with her on her mat. "I begin to see as the days go by how awesome are your people and why they live possessed of land where Ninnuock once roamed free. Never do you rest! Most clear is your goal! Most intricate your art with these letters!" He bent his body down where he sat crosslegged and hid his face. "Teach me then."

She traced along the silken script with her hand guiding his, reading aloud as they progressed across the cloth.

"Elizabeth Mary Dowland . . . Bride of Silent Fox . . . eighth day of Taquonk . . . time of falling leaves . . . seventeen hundred forty-six . . . in happiness."

124

Beth opened her silver case, withdrew a needle, and pinned the face of the cloth through the word *happiness*. In the firelight the golden needle gave the word sparkle.

"Take it to them, Fox, with my love."

"It is more the challenge of an arrow!"

"I shall go with you. You will not know how to tell them."

The man's face was tense. "Wife, I offered to take you many days ago. It did not seem a happy prospect to you then."

Beth looked away, seeing how she had hurt him.

"I expect I am skilled enough to speak my thoughts honestly to an honest man. Never again make my fear grow larger than my hope!"

Beth was ashamed. "Pardon. Pardon." But she had the temerity to ask, "What is it you will say, Wakwa?"

"I shall simply tell your father I have taken, forever, his most precious achievement, his child, and I would have him bless me for it."

The young wife went for the knife and cut a piece of her hair from underneath, as long as her arm. She tied the top with a scrap from her old, torn dress and bound her ribbons of the rosebud cloth around the bottom end. She coiled the hair into the embroidery and gave it, neatly folded, to her husband.

"Neither Dire Locke nor I meant to bestir you so," Wakwa said as he opened the box that had been wrapped in the reward notice. "My friend from Kirke's has great concern for me. He left the paper with what is in this box. Look at his happier gift." Wakwa pulled a long string of tiny shells from a velvet bag. "This is Indian money, Kayaskwa, Dire sent it all the way from Williamsburg. I will give it to your mother. It is very old. I have been looking for a suitable strand since you became mine and there it was, waiting for me." Wakwa wrapped the rope of shells around Elizabeth's waist and it trailed down the folds of her skirt onto the floor. "How he understands! One thousand shells on this circle. A shell for a pound."

Elizabeth examined the shiny shells, shaking her head in worry.

"Also he included sharp Virginia tobacco for Waban. If all white men were like Locke there would be no trouble about you and me, sunna matta? You see how the shells are matched, the pink spreading equally from their centers? Not polished or shaped in any way?"

"Oh, dear! They are truly beautiful, but must you offer Mama the bride price?"

"Is that how white men say it? Bride price? It sounds as if I would buy you like a basket of clams. It is a mark, woman! A sign that shows my high regard for you. To say that of this precious offering to your mother!"

"What of her reaction to them, though they be ever so beautiful and valuable and thoughtful?"

"Hah! How will she be hesitant to receive a string of shells when she has bartered for a son-in-law with you yourself and her very land!"

Elizabeth sat quietly at his feet while he smoked, then knocked the ashes from his pipe and watched over him until he was asleep.

Chapter 23

Charles Dowland had never known a better autumn for the beauty of the weather. But today he began his examination of the harvested fields wrapped in his long coat lined with woolly sheepskin, feeling the hollow warnings of premature snow. He straddled the ox almost gladly in the melancholy noon, relishing his discomfort, knowing he would soon be confined to his desk and chair, a man without a body. In other times, when Charles looked across this field at this time of day, he could see his daughter, Beth, carrying him his midday meal.

The ox rebelled against standing still and Charles repaid the pain of the jostling with a blow on its muzzle. This task of surveying, once filled with satisfaction, was now a vacant exercise since Elizabeth's disappearance. Charles turned away from the place where she would have been coming over the hill with the tray and saw two tall gray shapes entering his property line from the road.

Even from that distance he knew by the sway of their garments that they were Indians. He urged the ox toward them, spurring his speed with a broad leather belt, and the beast obeyed.

Dowland greeted them first, taking in their unusually large display of bead money and their fur caps. "What cheer, netompauog!"

They nodded to one another, appreciating the correctness of his plural greeting. The taller man extended his arm, wary of the ox.

"Our service to you, brother. You are Charles Dowland?"

"I am. You speak my tongue well!"

Awepu, who had rehearsed this scene many times with Wakwa, was proud of his instant success. "This man does not speak or understand, but I myself speak, yes."

"Nux." Dowland, alert to any possibilities for information, fought to master his excitement, not daring to offend his awesome visitors with direct questions.

"It is good of you to try at our speech." Awepu relaxed.

Charles' patience thinned. "Never has this farm been honored before by a visit from our native brothers. Come you from a long way off?"

"Father, you and I are made of one soil. I am Awepu, man of the Massachuseuck from the town across the Twisting River, west. This man is Mosq, the Bear."

Charles studied the quiet man, shorter than Awepu and broad as a barrel, holding a pair of wild turkeys freshly caught and killed. Charles Dowland tried again to direct Awepu to the point of his visit.

"My brother-in-law, Gilbert, told me of your vigor in the search for my child."

Awepu looked long at the Englishman's gnarled hands and twisted legs. "Myself walked the forest with Gilbert Worth. It was a friendly time but we did not find her for whom we searched. I am called a good hunter."

Charles, disappointed, fought for control.

"Did not the corn arrive, as was promised? I much appreciate your effort in our behalf. She were a good girl who has vanished from our home."

Awepu waited, separating Dowland's rapid sentences in his mind, trying to connect his questions with the message he had ready.

Charles gave in. "Have you news of her? Have you seen anything? Have you found my daughter!"

Again Awepu waited, concerned about saying too much, spoiling Wakwa's chances to deal with this man, or simply misunderstanding. He licked his lips with his mental effort.

Charles Dowland lowered his eyes, sudden hope ebbing.

Awepu waited to speak until the man looked up. "We have come this day on a sacred and important errand. I prepare the way for a great man who would come for discourse about thine Elizabeth. . . ."

"Then she lives?" Poor Charles' eyes lit again and he gripped the fat neck of the ox so hard that it snorted, surprising the Indians, who quickly moved back a few paces.

"The man for whom we speak is Wakwa Manunnappu, to the English, Silent Fox." Awepu regained his composure and dropped his official tone. He moved forward in his friendly way. "Father, this is the man who teaches me your tongue!"

There was no response.

Awepu stood his ground and pronounced the delegate's speech with all his energy to make the white man understand the full importance of this visit.

"Silent Fox is nephew to Waban, wise and generous sachim of the Massachuseuck. He is a good man. I never saw him in any wrongdoing. I can only say that he is a good man and can do everything. He is an expert hunter and builder. He speaks for his people at councils great and small and comes among the English, often, in the cities. This is he who seeks discourse with you!"

The inflection of this speech reminded Charles of prayerful readings in the church on Sunday. He questioned more gently. "Does your man know of my daughter? If she lives?"

Awepu considered his answer. "She lives."

"The Lord is just!" Dowland covered his face with his hand.

Awepu was shocked at its deformity and wondered about the justice of the white man's god if he could strike this good father with such an affliction. He pitied the man sprawled across the back of the ox, struggling for composure.

"You are welcomed into the domain of the Ninnuock by the sachim."

"Will I see her at the town?"

"She dwells not among our people."

"Then where?"

Awepu left him to his mystification.

"Does this nephew of the sachim wish to discuss the reward? It is posted in the cities the terms I shall give. One thousand pounds. It matters not if the finder be an Indian! Does he wish more?"

"Silent Fox comes not after money."

Charles was troubled by Awepu's statement. "What terms would he have?"

"He wishes your brother, Worth, attend the council and that it be held where you will feel most content." Awepu pointed to the ox. "Your means to travel is well-known." The etiquette of a native suitor to make his appeal to the uncle of his intended bride, rather than to her father, was implicit in Awepu's request.

"Yes! Yes! As he wishes." Had Charles known the Indian courtship custom his reply would not have been so eager. "Have this man come to me, here, as soon as he will, my brother-in-law and I await him. She doth live, you say? Is she well?"

But Awepu raised his long arm to the sky, now shedding slim drops of rain. "Tomorrow, at the fullness of the sun." He nodded to Mosq.

Mosq gave his catch of birds to Dowland.

"My salutations to the sachim!" Charles watched the pair disappear the way they had come. If it were not for the brilliantly feathered turkeys, he could have convinced himself he had dreamed the whole experience.

Charles could hardly contain his joy when he called Mary from her work and pushed the turkeys into her arms. But she was wary, concerned more with the details of the coming meeting than with speculation about the credibility of the Indians' message.

"We must tell Annanias right away. He should be there!"

"This spokesman does not want the whole village present," Charles resisted. "He comes to talk business to me. And to Gilbert. I shall still handle my affairs, Mary!"

"This is not only your affair! Annanias would have been Beth's husband by now if she were not absent. She is Annanias' business as well. Cannot you see how angry he will be if you slight him? What has her uncle to do with it?"

"This Silent Fox asked especially for her uncle and he shall have him. And I grow as weary of Annanias' moods as Gil. I can see Mr. Hudson negotiating with Waban's nephew, departing into the Scriptures and confusing the issue, whatever that may be, with some angry phrase! I know very little about talking to Indians, but I would guess that thinking before I speak will not hurt."

"He loves her, Charles. Naturally he is sensitive."

"I love her too, as doth our brother, Gil. Tell Annanias she lives if it will bring the two of you comfort. I will see him tomorrow evening, but do not dare suggest that he come here earlier, for I refuse to be bothered with his sensitivities when I have so much else to think about!"

130

Chapter 24

Gilbert Worth was tantalized by Awepu's phrase about the "great man who would come for discourse. . . ." He was encouraged about his niece and formulated a dozen theories why the sachim's nephew wanted to talk. The most logical was that she had wandered into their village and was somehow incapacitated. Perhaps the spokesman wanted to clarify that her condition, if it were ill, was not their doing. But it was the man he had narrowly missed seeing the day of his search in their territory who engaged his mind.

"Hanna dearest, will you fetch me some boots? Matthew has my things laid out for either the opera or a funeral." Gil rejected a pair of black satin pumps. "This is neither, Ana. It is a business meeting, a discussion, a council, discourse!" Gil stamped out a dance in his new golden brown riding boots.

"Gil! You must control your fascination for the natives and think of Beth and be some use to Charles." She brought him his pistol case.

"That is a mite martial!" Gil buckled on his favorite sword instead, an efficient saber heavy near the hilt, tapering to lethal thinness toward the tip. "Damnable thing! I hope all the sterling silver at my hip will take this spokesman's mind off the purpose of wearing such a thing. Perhaps he will think it mere decoration."

Gil arrived at Dowland Farm at half past ten and was surprised by Mary's uncustomary bustling as she oversaw the roasting of the turkeys and the preparations of the house.

"Sister Mary, you are in better spirits than I have seen for a long time. But you should rest. Be calm. You may need all your strength. None of us knows what today's meeting brings."

"Wild though they may be, Gilbert, these men have been kind to you and if it would get my Beth back home I would scrub their filthy smoke holes with my own hands."

"Have you ever seen an Indian house, Mary?"

"No, thank God!"

Gil paced the downstairs rooms, guarding the windows,

watching the meadows for the visitors. "I wish Awepu had given the exact time. What does it mean, 'at the fullness of the sun'?"

"And what should we make of it if the day were cloudy?"

"I think, Mary, we must adapt us somewhat to their ways. After all, these Indians are helping us. How is Charles today?"

"I do not think he slept last night."

"You do not know?"

"We have not spoken this past day," Mary said blankly. "Through the door I heard the pages of his Bible turning, turning, and not stopping. As if he could not find a place for his eyes to rest."

Gil stopped behind Charles' high-backed chair.

"'I am not at ease, nor am I quiet,
Nor am I at rest; for trouble keeps coming.'"

"You amaze me, Gil. I did not know you kept up your Bible."

"I have it up there, Mary, with the rest of the poetry!" Gil tapped his head. "What will you wear, sister?"

"Why, Gil!"

"It would be a courtesy to them if you chose something a bit fine."

"If you think it right. Send Sam up to help with Charles, it is nearly noon. I have never known him to sleep past dawn." From halfway up the steps she said, "The best I have is the new one for the wedding."

Gil Worth continued to pace to the tick of the clock. He circled the dark oak table, spread to its full length, but could not picture the conduct of the dinner Mary had planned with such guests at her board. At last his gleaming boots stood still in the center of the main room, his brown wool clothes and green silk waistcoat lit in a beam of sun. He stood motionless, his fine fingers lost in his light, unwigged hair.

* * * *

The Indians came in sight of the white clapboard house standing at the top of a swell in the land. Wakwa was accompanied by a guard of three, Awepu leading, Mosq and a young captain, White Cat, protectively behind. Their pace increased as the sun spread noon light over the cedar roof shingles. Awepu had led them by the road southeast of Dowland's property, since it was politic that they approach the house from the front. Wakwa watched him walking confidently ahead, fully armed with knife and arrows and his smallish bow, his prized English bayonet and his carved club, decorated with pheasant feathers, swinging casually at his side. Wakwa loathed putting this man, with a large family dependent on him, in danger. Awepu laughed and called his weapons proud display.

"You are too tall, dear kinsman, and will frighten your wife's folk before you open your mouth. I wear weapons to make you look more docile."

Mosq and White Cat broke the silence now and again, both considering their inclusion in the party a great honor. Neither spoke English, but after his previous day's meeting with Dowland, Mosq judged the possibility of violence unlikely. In his opinion this was strictly an attempt to skin the deer after it was roasted.

Wakwa, protected front and rear, turned his gambler's thunderbolt, his good luck piece, over and over in his cold hand, thinking of the Bible and Annanias Hudson. He saw Elizabeth's flushed face as she sent him off in his beautiful deerskins, arranging the great wampum belt across his chest, securing it at his shoulders from where it hung to his calves, broadening his impressive figure. She tied a band of black beads around his forehead as his Indian wife had done for him weeks ago.

"I do not need all this finery, Kayaskwa!" he had objected. "My name and the shirt you have made me should impress them with my substance and sobriety."

Elizabeth insisted on the fringed jacket.

He teased through his nervousness. "I would not wear it out. It should rightly be saved for my weddings!"

"Save it for such a purpose and you shall find it cut up for long pole ties." Elizabeth pulled his white collar out over the soft jacket and spread the lappet open to reveal his neck and throat.

The tears she left on his coat still showed in three dark spots on his breast.

White Cat separated from the group and ran to the western trees close to the house as a sentry. Pequawus had insisted on some protection for his son outside Dowland's house as well.

Any sign of trouble would be relayed by White Cat to the tribe.

Wakwa felt his stomach go hard when they reached the door. What a thing, the doors of the English! More menacing than a wartime barricade, they opened stiffly and closed with a noise, staring from the houses with dumb challenge.

"Should I call them out?" Awepu murmured.

"You rap upon the door!" Wakwa caught Awepu's fist as it neared the wood. "Softly, dear friend."

Wakwa resumed his place and Awepu knocked twice, gently in slow succession.

Gil was brought to himself with a rush, and the young serving maid who had been needlessly dusting the shining barometer stared at him with wide eyes.

"They are only men, Priscilla. You shall do well."

The girl opened the door, and beyond her white cap Worth saw the face of Silent Fox. Whatever the initial greetings were between Priscilla and the other Indians, Gil never heard. Gripped by the beauty and intentness of that face, Gilbert Worth began to think about his niece.

The tallest man bent to enter and stood with his party at the periphery of the room in a semicircle of wild splendor.

Gil moved from the hot center of the room at Awepu's friendly greeting. He nodded in response to his introduction to Mosq and looked up into Wakwa's clear eyes.

"My regrets, Silent Fox, that my wife's brother, Charles Dowland, is not down to greet you. Movement is slow for him these days. I am Gilbert Worth."

The low-ceilinged room was so stifling to him, Wakwa could not gesture the greeting so becoming to his people in the forest. Instead, he shook the hand of Elizabeth's uncle, letting a smile loose at the sight of Worth's wiry gold hair and moustache.

Worth turned to the housemaid, who stood hesitating a little way off. "Priscilla, tell your mistress her guests have arrived."

"It is your special presence I appreciate, Gilbert Worth." Wakwa appraised the small, elegant figure of the Englishman and found him striking.

"I am honored to comply with your request!" Gil's excitement grew but he continued to be formal. "My brother-in-law would speak with you in his study. May I lead the way?"

Wakwa bent again as they entered an even smaller room. The walls, beautifully wrought of polished maple, the small fireplace, its heat barely reaching the center of the room, the few finely made chairs, and the desk in line with the north window gave Wakwa immediate respect for the man who ordered his life in this stoic privacy. The fragrance and silence of the house also impressed themselves on him as the men arranged themselves around the room in tolerable quiet.

Wakwa felt sympathy for the Dowlands in losing Elizabeth's lively grace to him, and saw her in the room for a moment in his mind's eye, the sun lighting the rich colors of her hair. He turned to the wall of pictures.

"Who are these, brother?"

"They are the ancestors of my niece." The men exchanged a long look. "Come close to see. Brother!"

"It is she!" came to Wakwa's lips. But he controlled his words. "This young woman is different from the others." Wakwa had chosen the double wedding portrait of Peter Dowland and his wife.

"Quite. You have come at once to the heart of the family secret, Silent Fox."

"She was not English?"

"How could you know that?"

"French, perhaps?"

"Do not let the master of this house hear you say it!"

"Forgive me." Wakwa saw his candor as a diplomatic error. "I have come to know hostility runs as long and deep between you and the French as between us and the Iroquois."

"For myself, I have no argument with any man." Gil struggled to remain aloof. "Angelica was born in another century on an island between the kingdoms of Italy and France. It mitigates the sting. The place is called Corsica."

"I know it not," Wakwa admitted. "But is not Italy a place where people believe that our mother earth is round?"

Gil caught the humor and laughed freely.

"And is there not a city called Rome in this place which sent the soldiers who killed the son of your god?"

"You have it right." Gil looked hard at the young Indian. "Angelica is not talked of among the Dowlands. She refused to leave her land or her family to board ship for this shore with her husband and son."

"There is great courage in the face," Wakwa said, engrossed in the painting.

"She died of not eating because of a broken heart, the story goes."

Knowing then that Worth sensed some of the truth about Elizabeth, Wakwa said stiffly, "The story is misread. I did perceive warmer waters behind the blue of her eyes."

But Worth relaxed, willing to stand corrected, content to parry in the midday with a man with a mind for words.

A shuffling was heard, and Wakwa stepped quickly to his place near the desk. The door was pushed open by a strong young man moving a chair with flat runners bound in cloth across the polished floor. Charles Dowland sat in the center of his study.

Charles made a small attempt to offer his hand to his tall guest at their introduction, but Wakwa sensed Dowland's hesitation because of the hand's deformity and simply bowed his head in a gesture of respect.

The long fringe of his costume and the weighty money belt swung forward as his body moved, and he felt the white man's eyes register the costly ornamentation of his jacket.

Dowland spoke. "I understand you are a relation of your prince and from what I know of your people and from what I see, you are a prince yourself."

Wakwa remained in congenial silence, willing for the moment to command Dowland's respect even with this foreign title.

Charles' eyes swept over Wakwa's armed companions. "You do me honor coming to me during this time of trouble. You must have many affairs of importance to look after."

"The news I bear is of the first importance to us both." Wakwa's voice was deep and full of feeling. He waited while Dowland gave a direction to the boy.

"You find me, Silent Fox, in a weakened state of body. It is easier these days to talk and think from behind my desk." The servant settled Charles at the desk and left.

"I remember you as you were!" Wakwa chanced a sincere flattery. "You have borne much pain in those two years."

"Do I know you? I would remember!"

Wakwa threw his head back with a flash of a smile. "I must have been sitting! It was at the great council of the swearing of peace between all the Massachusetts tribes and Governor Clinton. I noted you because they said our boundaries did touch."

"We are truly neighbors then! Sit! Sit! Be comfortable. That was a most confusing day to me. So many people."

Wakwa remained standing. Charles rescued them from silence.

"May I explain why I have asked my wife to remain away from this room for a little while? I know not the nature of your news and I would tell her gently if it is not good. She has borne much since those days as well."

Wakwa took courage. He had seen more warmth from Elizabeth's father than from her much-touted uncle.

Quiet settled on the room and Awepu moved forward with the velvet bag in the palm of his hand.

"It is for me to say, Awepu!" Wakwa intercepted the delegate's speech. "Mr. Dowland, before I speak of your lost daughter, I ask you two things."

Dowland liked this direct approach. "What do you want?"

"First, that you remember the agreement which was made with Governor Clinton of New York two years ago. Did not the southern tribes of what you are pleased to call New England agree to concur with the Six Nations, keeping neutral from the war between the French and the English to the north?"

"They did."

"Has there been any violation of this agreement in two years?"

"No agreement between the New England commissioners and yourselves has ever been violated."

" 'Fathers: You are a great people and we are a small one.' I repeat what was said that day to refresh your memory. 'We will do what you desire and we hope you will take care that no harm come to us.' As a people would you say we have been honest?"

"I would. Yes. You desire some special protection from me in exchange for your information? Have white men violated their agreement?"

Wakwa did not respond to this direct question. "The second thing I would have you remember is this. I have a part with the

137

Scatacooks and many other tribes in keeping alive this peace. I myself travel many months alone and with my kinsman, Awepu, for the sachim because my word is valued and my mind and speech clear. I have many friends among the English."

"I appreciate a man of your gifts sparing time to talk to me, but what has this got to do with my daughter's disappearance?"

"I wish only that you consider what I will say to you comes from the open heart of an honest man."

Dowland grew uncomfortable. "I cannot judge thy honesty." He traced the features of Wakwa's face. "I see only you are a man to be remarked, no matter where you are from or where you would go. I must believe anything you tell me for, indeed, it will be more than I now know about my lost girl. I hope you are straightforward, for I must trust your word."

Wakwa stood immobile. Dowland had evaded the beguiling trap planned and set so carefully. If they could converse as moral equals the Englishman would have to accept Wakwa's actions and deal only with their consequences. But Wakwa had been made to feel like an unknown voice, a stranger on their joint soil without importance above mere information. Sounds from the kitchen distracted him for a moment and his eyes took in the portrait of Angelica and the face of Gilbert Worth.

Wakwa looked back at Charles and said softly, "Elizabeth, your daughter, whom you esteem greatly, has become in righteousness my beloved wife."

Charles Dowland sat stunned and looked into the Indian's face with hard eyes. "This is your news? I do not believe you."

"But you must. It is the truth."

"Truth! You come with great to-do about your honesty and tell me you have outright stole my only daughter!"

At the word *stole* Wakwa shook but did not back down nor move his eyes from the white-haired man.

Charles clawed at the smooth desk top, aching to rise. "Gilbert! Do something!"

"I listen, Charles."

Passions were steadied by Gil's response and Wakwa addressed Elizabeth's father in a quiet voice again.

"If you will hear all I have to say you may see my action in a different light. I have not stolen but accepted. The difference

138

between our peoples did make me think her past your giving."

"How do you mean she is your wife?" A half-hope lit Charles' face.

"Under common custom of the Ninnuock, my wife. All and everything that word doth signify in both our tongues. By the blessing of her spirit and her person she has been mine, and I her own."

A sob escaped Dowland, but his manner quickly changed.

"Then your saintly face does cover up a black heart! How did you find it in you to trample on the virtue of my sweet daughter, an English girl!"

"Never was it so."

"Don't tell me she would have this happen!"

Wakwa came closer to the desk as he opened up the story, walking lightly to and fro like an impatient animal, his lofty body nearly touching the low ceiling. "She did desire this to happen as much as I myself. May I tell you, please . . . I found her sick and maddened and much in need of care. I thought her hunted and brought her to a quiet place that she might mend. I did all that could be done to heal her wounds and calm her fever that she was filled with from the rain."

"You had found her then, at the beginning, and did not bring her home!"

"I did think she had a right to decide her own actions. She surely was not happy where she was."

"How do you presume!"

Ignoring opportunity for argument with Dowland, Wakwa included Worth in his glance. "It was only after I thought she had been taken on the day of search, while I was far away in the harbor, that I knew how deep was my care for her. Until this time I had not even spoken to her! I did struggle against my feelings for some time and saw to it from afar that she grew strong enough to know her mind."

"Silent Fox!" Gilbert Worth, sallow from anxiety, broke in. "If my niece was so well-nurtured and whole in her mind as you say, why, why, did she not seek to contact us who have loved her for so long?"

"Much has she suffered over love of you and all her family but said to me from the first she never would return and would be

miserably alone rather than wedded to this priest she fears."
Wakwa continued his plea for understanding through a sharp
exchange of looks between the brothers-in-law. "Even then
would I have brought her back to you that I might intercede in
her behalf, knowing I could never have her doing this."

"And why did you not do it?" Dowland demanded.

Wakwa stopped in his tracks and looked down at the sheen of
the polished floorboards. "She was so against it!"

"You were easily persuaded by the ramblings of a child."
Dowland grew antagonistic.

But Wakwa refused to be drawn into an argument with the
father of his wife. "It were no child that you have promised to
marry to your minister. She hath been preparing as a woman for
many years, I think. She sought for us to break your contract by
deed and end the threat or evermore be lost, one to the other.
She signed away your high regard, her customs, and your law
and fled to me and mine which did seem gentler to the sweetness
of her nature."

"How convenient for you both."

"It is not convenient!" Wakwa shouted, giving way. "Not in
the least convenient! I stand to lose all I have worked to gain for
my sachim and our forlorn people. If this marriage is not honored she and I would lose our happiness and her children be
scorned among the Christians. My word would no longer be
honored in the cities and I would be divested of my power to
spend my effort for the good of my people."

"Then why did you go and do this thing if you appreciate the
difficulties." Dowland was cool as a knife.

"I tell you she would not hear it! She is strong both in understanding and in love. How should I refuse her?"

"By the Lord God!" Charles, with mighty effort, pulled himself up out of his chair, supporting his full weight on the desk
top with his clenched fists and shaking arms. "In one moment
you have told me my daughter deserts her creed and family and
seeks you out like some common Jezebel!"

"You twist what I have said! Never was she that!" Wakwa,
wild, grasped at his hip for his missing knife and bent toward
Charles Dowland's face, the glare of Gil's unsheathed sword
abetting his anger. Awepu and Mosq rushed tight against their

140

lord's sides. "All is my responsibility. I acted the part of a man, not an old woman, in refusing to condemn her to the life of slavery you would force her to endure! Does her happiness mean nothing to you?"

Charles fell back into his chair and looked away, unable to face the rage in Wakwa's eyes.

Without mercy Wakwa ground his point home. "To an Indian marriage is more sacred than to couple people to preserve a name or land! I could not see her spirit crushed when she had so recently found kindness for herself. Is it not more honorable in her to be a wife to a man she loves?"

"Indian! The command of God doth read, 'Thou shalt honor thy father and thy mother.' How can she do this and still belong to you?"

"Old man, she does belong only to herself. And do you not see how she honors you? She has the grace to love me and understand me, a person different from herself. She comes to know the land and does not fight it anymore. Is it not also your rule that you love your neighbors as yourselves? I have read your book closely. Without love for herself she would live with this other man as chattel! She honors you by her strength and perseverance and her honesty. You taught her these and she has taught me to accept what is unchangeable."

At this Dowland slumped onto the desk, his head resting on his hands. Gil sheathed his sword and Wakwa's guards relaxed.

Wakwa persisted more quietly. "Is the God you worship so different from those to whom I pray? Or do you please to make him different that you may keep unto yourselves? There is one sun over us. The meager fire in your grate springs from the same friction as the one that leaps to the roof of my lodge. Your daughter is ahead of you in understanding these simple things."

Quieted, Charles said, "Would you also convert me to your ways? I want to see her. Could you not have brought Beth here?"

"Very soon. She suffers also to see you. Can we then arrange to solemnize our union with all honor at my town among the Massachuseuck? The Sachim proffers any service to help you be at ease."

Charles would not be pushed so fast. "Where did you learn your English?"

141

"My father taught it me from the Bible by John Eliot. I read that book in both tongues as well."

"Ah! Then thy father is as remarkable as you. Eliot! Friend of the Indians, eh?"

"I know there are differences among you that call yourselves Christians. Will our differences make it repugnant to you to someday say, 'Nosenemuck, he is my son-in-law'?"

The early autumn light receded from the wood-lined room. Dowland sat folded weakly against the high-backed chair. "You are young and comely and in your glory, Silent Fox. You see me crushed beneath your dreams, a wreck of what I was. Beth is the first daughter born to the sons and grandsons of that man." Charles pointed with his hideous hand to the portrait of Peter and his warm-eyed wife. "All those one hundred years of toil went for naught with the death of my son. Beth was all there was left. Seven years has her betrothed awaited their wedding, and in one month's time you have changed all."

Wakwa touched the face of the young woman in the painting and turned back to Dowland with his eyes full of tears. "It is so like Elizabeth!"

Dowland wept, his face and head covered by the knobby hands. The soft center of the man, denied for all his life, opened to these strangers.

The Indians stood together and Wakwa saw the tears as a bitter victory for himself and admired the man for the uncomplaining courage with which he bore his frightful illness.

Someone knocked softly on the door and Worth went to answer it. "It will be her mother."

Wakwa turned his saddened face toward the woman who came quietly in. Thin and small, without appeal, she was dressed in a simple gown of good blackish-blue silk with a lacy collar and a bonnet of fragile stuff.

Mrs. Dowland did not acknowledge her husband's distress but stood directly in front of Wakwa.

"This is the nephew of the Prince of the Massachuseuck and these his kinsmen. . . ." Gil's introductions were interrupted.

"By all means, Mary, greet thy royal son-in-law. His name is Silent Fox!" Dowland was bitter.

Wakwa was appalled at the cruel frankness of the man he had just praised within himself for courage.

Gil said in a low tone, "What happened to the gentle telling, brother Charles?"

The woman did not move nor cry out but stood firm, her bright eyes reading the faces of the men. "I came before I was called and have surprised my husband in some melancholy mood." Then her voice quavered. "I thought no news, no matter how black, could take that long to tell." She looked up to Wakwa's face, afraid of his size and unfamiliar dress. "What is this my husband tells me? You were to bring us news of our child. I want her back with us!"

Wakwa could not bear the mother's outrage and knelt on one knee before her. He tried to frame words that would not hurt her, but the English would not come and he knelt there mute.

Awepu seized the moment and, holding out the velvet bag, began the groomsman's speech to Mrs. Dowland. He coolly deleted some of the old form and substituted new words to fit the circumstances. He finished, saying, "Now, I can only say that Wakwa Manunnappu, Silent Fox, has settled upon and wedded lawfully with your daughter. Never has he done wrong. He is a good man and gentle. He can do everything to make your girl a fitting life. When you are ready, answer if and when they may solemnize their union." With that, he handed her the velvet bag and retreated modestly toward the door.

Mrs. Dowland opened up the sack and pulled out the ancient shells. She felt their weight and saw their beauty.

"Her future, then, is undone?"

Wakwa rose up. "She has chosen to spend it with the Ninnuock!"

"Where do you keep her? Is she imprisoned? No! I see by your face she has realized her girlish fancies. Do you know what she has wrought?" Mrs. Dowland fled from the Indian and stood behind her husband, dropping the shells onto the desk. "How do you simply take their word? You must make them bring her home."

"My wife will not return until you do accept our situation," Wakwa interrupted.

"Your wife! She is my only child. How do I know you even have her unless I see her?"

Wakwa produced the embroidered linen, and the English people gathered around Charles' chair. The coil of Elizabeth's hair unwound by itself as the cloth was spread apart and the mother caught it up.

"It is hers! But what mean these?"

"The upper ribbon shows how I did find her, torn and bleeding. The one binding the lower part shows how she dresses now she is my bride!"

" 'Elizabeth Mary Dowland . . . Bride of . . .' " Gil read the embroidery. "Charles, it is her work. It is even in her hand! See, here, the needle through the word *happiness?* It is one of those I told you we gave her for a wedding gift." Gil turned and spoke directly to Wakwa. "It is fine she uses it with a light heart and brings it to the home of a good man."

Surprised, Wakwa met the eyes of Gilbert Worth.

Gil himself brought chairs for the Indians, who had declined to sit before.

"Brother Gilbert, you are premature in applauding my daughter's state. I have not made a decision."

"With all respect, brother Charles, we are very late in smoothing out this situation."

Mary moved closer to the unarmed Indian sitting easily in his chair. She studied the delicate skins Wakwa wore and admired the noble decoration of his costume and saw him as a man.

"What should I call you? I have never known . . . an Indian. Do I say 'Sagamore'?"

"Call me by my name, Wakwa. It is said 'Fox' in English, Okasu. I have called you mother just now."

Mary moved back a bit.

Wakwa's eyes glittered with tears for the second time that afternoon, but he attempted a smile. "It is not what you think. There is another word, *nokace,* which would mean my true mother, the one who gave me birth. Do you know, I have never had the joy of saying it? Nor will I. My own mother died when I was very young."

"I am surprised to see you weep and smile. I had been taught your race was unaffected by such feelings. So, we share something. You are without a mother and I am bereft of my children."

"Could we not combine our sorrow, then, and make it into joy? I would not withhold Elizabeth from you. We must share

144

our differences back and forth through her. The sachim and my own father are wary too, and I would have them see that English can be tender." Wakwa persisted gently in the face of her hardness.

The Englishmen remarked this exchange, grateful for Wakwa's kindness.

"Why, she has made your shirt! The stitch is unmistakable. I lose hope, more and more, she will come back to us. Gil, come to see it!"

Wakwa suffered their examination as patiently as he could. "It is beautiful, is it not?"

Gil led a humbled Mary to a place near Charles.

But Charles had turned his upper body toward his window, leaving the group to themselves, as his hand smoothed lines from the side of his face.

Gil heard the injunction Hanna had given him to be a help to his brother-in-law and he assumed responsibility. He sat Mary down, stood close to the arm of her chair and said, "Mary, when Beth was home, was she ever grudging in her day's work for you and Charles? Did she not plan with you and work with her hands on those things you required of her?" His questions were met with nods of distracted agreement. "Whether it were fine, pleasurable work or breaking an ill-tempered goat, properly, to be milked when no one else could manage it, did she not give honestly of her time to you?" He wished the Dowlands stocked brandy in the house so he could snap Mary from the shock she felt from this past hour.

"Gil, why do you do this to me?" The mother shook her head back and forth. "You know how I depended on her, missed her even when she went to sew with Hanna." Mary looked up, mildly reproachful.

But Gil turned the moment to advantage and lifted her nervous hand and soothed it. "Can you think, Mary, the girl so cooperative, so unassuming, so sweet, would have changed overnight? Storm or no storm? The nature that made her so lovable to us has caused her to admire the young man you see before you."

Wakwa listened in fascination to Gil's grace of logic and sentiment, and the delicacy of his delivery, and witnessed the Englishman, all unknowing, assume the powerful role of a native bride's uncle.

"But! . . ." Mary's wordlessness expressed her grasp of the awful social complications involved in Beth's choice of a life companion.

"I know, I know, sister. Silent Fox seems strange to us, but not more so than we must seem to him! Let me tell you his treatment of her so that you may see why a girl of Beth's wisdom could lift herself out of one frame of law into another, without wantonness but with courage."

And Gil explained slowly and carefully all that Wakwa had told to him and Charles.

"I cannot believe, Gilbert," Mary dragged words out of herself, "that you are telling me what she has done is right. Charles!" She claimed the man's attention. "Can you both not see that it might be suitable for this man and his people, but Beth has walked in the Light from birth!" Conviction came into her voice. "She is damned without a doubt if she does not come back and repent what she has done."

Wakwa broke into Charles' reflection on this disturbing trend of thought. "Mrs. Dowland, your way is not the only one. Yet Elizabeth came into true marriage with me untouched by me. We both did seek not to compromise Christian law. You feel sure that men and women can as strangers mate and produce families and move through life's troubles, living under sentence that they may never part. I cannot agree. I would venture to say that many vices of you Europeans result from this practice of grimly chaining hearts together like captives in life's war. Or outcasting those brave enough to end a union in which the love has died.

"It is the same to match two people against their will. Or worse. How will hate survive what love cannot? Why else do so many Christians slip away secretly and abuse their partnership? They yet debauch our maidens in the woods to spend their griefs, boundaries or no boundaries! Many of your bickerings even in religion would not occur if you were happier in your hearts.

"Ninnuock are free before they marry that the choice be solid and the bond of love be strong. Our life is hard sometimes, with

146

moving up and down the land, yet when do you see complaint or bitterness between a man and wife? Rare are orphans or poor among us because we are used to opening up our hearts. Even as I told you I had no mother I did not die from want of milk, but was raised by her friend, and my father was welcomed with me that his heart might not stay sore and his spirit heal within this other family. All feed all and comfort all and mourn with all."

Mary Dowland could not respond.

"Young Sagamore," Charles Dowland spoke, "would you philosophize with us? You have told the heart of Christian love in what you've said, but you must know that many of your customs run smack against our laws. I am surprised to find we are a simpler people than yourself. I am only a farmer who spends his life in toil to bring food from the ground. I have sought nothing for myself but to make my child safe and keep her true to the God who is her own. More than that I cannot allow. Now you ask that I forget the natural wish I have to see her wed among her race."

"Old Father, this is not yours to allow, her wishes being different."

Mary Dowland saw the finality of the situation before her husband could admit to it. "Annanias must be told. You must face him, young sir, for he has waited seven years and there is much planning to be undone."

"Yet I ask nothing of you but your blessing on our love! Seven years has the man known of his marriage and can produce nothing but terror in the eyes of her he professes to cherish. Such a look as I have seen pass over my Elizabeth! And from what I am told he has squeezed much land from you as well as gained the hand of your splendid daughter! What would be thy response were I to impose such conditions on your head?"

"I want nothing but the privilege of her society and am come to offer my own back to you, to work, to assuage this difficult transition by my labor."

Awepu kicked away his chair and spoke harshly to Wakwa in their own language.

Wakwa turned away from him. "Further, you may punish or abuse my body as is your right under Indian law and I will not complain. See you that I bend backwards and ask nothing of you but to love? This other man must seek me out and make conciliation for the harm he has done to her. It is I who am her husband."

Wakwa had confuted Mary Dowland's values and dismembered her plans for Beth. The only function left her was the habit of her duty as hostess.

There was complete quiet until she managed to enunciate, "There is a meal prepared, Silent Fox, of the fine birds you sent to us. We should eat it. We shall eat it together. Soon. Mr. Dowland and I will join you."

Gil led the way into the main room, which had caught light from the remote fall sun.

Awepu and Mosq made way for Wakwa, who lowered his head to exit, passing between his men as if through a guard of honor.

* * * *

Remembering Waban's courtesies during the search for Beth, Gil showed the Indians through the house. There were questions to answer about the functions of the simple but beautiful appointments of the place. Wakwa praised the wall hangings, most of them Beth's work.

Gil winked his acceptance of the compliments. "An old blanket would serve to keep out the draught, I suppose, but my wife and niece insist on making a great deal of work about it."

Awepu and Mosq watched from the head of the stairs as Wakwa and Gil went to see the sleeping rooms, spread along the back of the house over the warm kitchen.

Wakwa stepped softly into Elizabeth's chamber. The ceiling of the narrow white room conformed to its beams, slanting from low on the outer wall to the high point opposite. A window was cut between the east rafters, and pale pink muslin stained the light it admitted. Wakwa noted the ingenuity with which the narrow bed was hung from the wall, where she had slept each night of her life before she knew him. He examined the shelves underneath, where her things lay neatly folded. A small bed pillow faced the most arresting feature of the room, a window of tiny leaded panes looking northwest to the line of trees marking the boundary between Indian land and her own.

Wakwa hunched in the small space. "Looking at the forest from on high gives it mystery almost causing fear even in me! How she must have suffered that first night."

"And many the fantastic nightmare her parents have known since then."

Wakwa turned on Worth. "Brother, in whose tracks do you stand?"

"In yours, largely." Gil did not hedge, but chose his words with precision. "I am glad to see my excellent niece rescued in the nick of time from that bull, Hudson. That was certainly beyond me. As you saw, an uncle's opinion is not highly valued among us English. Yet . . ."

"Yet?" Wakwa echoed, keenly interested in this open man's doubts.

"Yet I had plans for her, myself! Away from this sheltered place. There are talents untapped in that child. I had hoped . . . to oversee the blossoming of the rather rare growing thing she is. It doth take time to lay away one's dreams, and then, of course, Silent Fox, there is the living with them folded up, still close by.

"It is a sin, but I am almost glad not to have Charles Dowland's full responsibility today."

The Indian inclined his head out of respect for Gil's honesty as well as the clear images of his speech. "I did not know, new Uncle, English farmers saw into the earth which they furrow. You open new worlds to me. It were these other worlds inside Elizabeth warned me to bring her back to you. But she is rooted to this place like the birch tree. Very deep." Wakwa walked to the window and looked past the treeline. "That is the world she wishes. Day by day, Gilbert Worth, the sap of her is well-run and replenished by the life she leads with me. Her talents will grow. Trust me. You said to save her was beyond you. I have saved her."

"Young man," Gil murmured, "I will try to soften the Dowlands, saying little."

Worth bent to the shelves beneath Elizabeth's bed and found two slim books. He opened one to lines of verse and handed it up to Wakwa. "Those are of John Donne. I gave it her. She may miss it."

The second book was a portfolio of sketches. Wakwa turned

the heavy papers until he came to an ably penciled portrait of a boy, dark hair combed back, the fine features lit by thoughtful eyes.

"This would be Henry. Tell them you gave these to me, Uncle. I would not have them think I stole these, too."

* * * *

The corner of the summer dining room looked like an arsenal, Gil's sword crossed above the discarded weapons of the Indians. The long table was simply set with pewterware and an arrangement of firethorn berries tucked into a bowl of red apples. Mary had put out her finest wax candles.

The strained company was reflected in the bare wood. Charles sat at the head, far opposite Wakwa. Awepu and Mary completed the left side. Gil and Mosq, their backs to the windows, shared the right.

Outside the house, White Cat relaxed after catching Mosq's subtle hand signal from the western window.

Wakwa longed to see Elizabeth. His spirits dragged in the confining atmosphere. He held little hope for them, knowing Charles Dowland had come out of his study without an answer. He endured the prayer and the meal began in silence.

The little maid did all the serving, bringing out platters of food already carved or arranged for eating. Sam cut up Charles' meat, and Mosq, quite helpless with fork and knife, watched the boy at his master's place to catch the knack.

Priscilla carried a frosted pitcher to Wakwa's right side and summoned the courage to ask, "Sir, may I pour you milk?"

The full vessel slipped, splattering milk onto Wakwa's hand. Mary blanched. "Priscilla!"

But Wakwa gave the girl a sympathetic smile. "I will have just this much and some water in my cup, if you will." He blotted his hand with his napkin and the mood around the table lightened for the moment. "Your sohquttahhash is very fine. It was thoughtful of you to make it," Wakwa said to Mary as he savored the bits of tender corn floating in butter.

Privately he regretted seeing the turkeys cut up and served lukewarm, but enjoyed the English squash and cranberry-raisin relish and bowls of pickled cauliflower and watermelon rind.

150

Mary wondered what could be the source of his social ease. Her clouded notion of the red people living so close to her farm was confounded by Wakwa's natural politeness. His persistent conviviality gave her the incentive to bring around, personally, a pumpkin bread she had made. It was when a steaming pie of apples and the mahogany tea table were wheeled in that some ground for conversation was provided.

"This is very beautiful, Mrs. Dowland." Wakwa looked through the hot amber liquid at a white dogwood blossom painted at the bottom of the cup.

"It is our brother, Gilbert, who indulges my whimsy for nice tea things." Softened, she picked up the blue-violet tea pot and topped Wakwa's serving. "I do not like a metal pot." Tears gathered as she sipped her own. "How fares my Beth? She is not as strong as some. I fear the life you lead her far too hard."

Wakwa let a long minute pass. "You see her, I know, selling birch brooms for nine pence in Buzzards Bay. No Massachuseuck has so deep a need. For this do I labor at my traps and in the halls of the mansions in Boston. To keep us free from servitude." Wakwa burned his mouth on the pie. "She is happy as a bird. To speak truth, a little sachim-bird does stay with her all the time and lives up in the rafters of the house. Elizabeth, now she is well, always is singing with it some sweet song."

"She sang as a child, but I have not heard her do it for years now," Charles put in from across the table.

But Mary insisted. "She will ever ignore hardship and make the darkest cellar glow with a touch of her hand. The work your women do is more my concern."

"Do not be so troubled, Okasu. I have been through this with her already. She will never carry nor bear burdens nor work the corn. Her thin shoulders could not bear it. There is no need that she exceed her strength in any task. There are many others who will take on the bundles she cannot lift."

"But how can she go, at last, and live among you, yet be treated specially?" Mary's fork slipped and clattered against her plate, metallic noise amplifying her elemental fears.

"She will never be accepted if she pretends to be what she is not. My people will love her for herself as I have come to do, for she has much to give that is better than a stout back. She already teaches many things to me and I have plans to include her in my work. She does not know—I would not disappoint her, not knowing your decision—but often we will go together to delight her in the cities and she will help me understand precisely what is meant in the councils I attend. Never will she face a day alone but helping hands will be all around.

"Think you women of the Ninnuock are pushed beyond their own endurance? I believe the work you do, Mrs. Dowland, tests your strength and wearies your spirit more than an Indian woman's tasks. More than this, in my lodge on the Twisting River I have servants too, as do you. They are trained to dress us, if we will, and make our meals and care for babes. I would preserve her strength and beauty any way I can."

Awepu glanced their way, opened his mouth to speak, but thought better of it.

Charles asked in careful English, "Awepu, are you a married man?"

"Seven years already, yes, and four fine babes to show." Awepu smiled.

"Four in seven years? Are any of them sons?"

"Three strong boys I have. One at six begins to learn to hunt." Awepu counted on his fingers to get his numbers right.

"I once had a son. I have never ceased to miss him."

Awepu hung his head, then looked into Dowland's eyes. "Good Father, I think that I would drown myself if any of my sons preceded me into the southwest. You are stronger than me."

"Perhaps not so, as your sons live and mine is gone." Charles looked lost in recollection of brighter days.

"Would you like, Father, me to send my middle son to you? He is very special like the night stars he knows so well. Yea, better than I myself. Much you could learn from him and him from you." Awepu chuckled and confessed, "He wishes to be a captain on the sea as he has heard from Wakwa. Shall I bring him when things are settled between you and my dear kinsman?"

"You would do that?" Charles' look was drawn across the table toward the extraordinary man who possessed his daughter as well as the hearts of those he touched in his own sphere. Wakwa's handsome face was relaxed as he followed the thread of another conversation with Mary. Charles pushed himself to grasp onto these visitors not as native curiosities but as real men. "For me you would do that?"

Awepu saw his struggle and gently squeezed Charles' crooked fingers. "It would make smaller your aloneness, and I do not believe you could suffer him in any but short doses. He will have a time handling these cups."

"It is the girls give more trouble, I attest!"

"I should like to have a try at that steam cave someday, Silent Fox." Gil attempted small talk as the meal ended and other topics waned.

"One day I will offer you my pipe, brother Worth, and we will smoke and talk as the bad humors roll off ourselves. I have wondered what you thought of the pesuponk." Wakwa's head tilted slowly back as he recognized his error.

Gil watched the man's embarrassment grow, unsure how the Indian had compromised himself. "Awepu took me in to look."

"It were not Awepu told me you were there." Wakwa gambled on the more difficult course of complete honesty, although he had convenient cover for his slip of the tongue. "Elizabeth was within."

Each diner's attention focused on the speakers.

"I had found her? So nearly found her? I called her name and she spoke not?" The cosmopolitan veneer deserted Gil's face just as the girl had left her family, leaving it dangerously exposed and vulnerable.

"Much hath she wept about it, Gilbert Worth." Wakwa's whisper trailed his destructive revelation.

"If she would not speak to Gil . . ." Mary left her frightening deduction for Charles to complete.

Dowland's attention dipped within himself again, pain filling his head with the mounting evidence of Elizabeth's seriousness of purpose.

On the cleared, empty table only the bright inedible berries, guarded by the candles, remained in their place. Silence fell again with the sun.

Mary spoke when the men would not. "Mr. Hudson comes tonight to pray with us. We told him we would have some news. Sagamore, I do not think you should be here."

"I go nowhere without my answer, mother of my wife. It is

Elizabeth who waits anxiously for your words. Should we care so much what this stranger thinks?"

Agreeing, Gil reproached his sister-in-law with his eyes. "Silent Fox, my wife and I will house you well and be honored by your coming. We will wait together."

"There is no need to wait." Charles Dowland's frail body looked limp against the large chair, but he spoke with sureness. "I have decided." He looked solely at Wakwa. "I acquiesce."

Wakwa's skin took on a deeper tone.

The father reached into his pocket for the embroidered message. "I will not deny that you and she are one, and by your law. You have seen to that, as she attests here." Charles took a moment to phrase his next thoughts, guarding against worsening the rupture in their understanding of each other through carelessness. "She hath excluded herself from her own way of life for good, I would think. If pressed by some authority of either of our peoples, I will hold the marriage real. I will not seek her further, as well you know I could, Silent Fox, nor prosecute you, as I should. You are a man of merit though you break my heart."

Wakwa, his eyes shining, rose up slightly from his chair, only to be reduced to sitting by Charles' next words.

"But never will I solemnize this union with any public approbation. As a man familiar with Boston, you may already know how your marriage with an Englishwoman will be estimated. Rightly or wrongly, some degree of respect is gone from her. I will quietly say to the casual inquirer that she lives somewhere away, in case she change her mind and need a home some day."

"She is as adamant as you! Do you not see by this you close off access between her and yourself? How can she pass between us, thus?"

"I shall do without her, Sagamore."

"Charles, no!" Mary whispered to herself.

Wakwa sat still, astounded.

Charles saw the company falling into the division they had hoped to leave behind in the study and justified himself simply and sadly. "She denies her God, you say, and takes on herself new ways and goes back in time to before our father Abraham. I must teach her by my absence this is most unworthy of a woman civilized. She must learn through bitterness the path of right."

154

Wakwa stared into the man. "How do I bear this news and watch her little face twist with sorrow or, worse, have her heart slowly turn to stone from this abandonment?"

Dowland did not reply, but turned to the lowered blonde head of his brother-in-law. "Gilbert, you will go when Silent Fox arranges to see that she is well and all is as he makes it out to be—though I do believe him—perhaps even tell the sachim of my answer. And do not look so sorrowful, for well you know I am near to death. . . ." Charles raised a hand against Gil's protest. "Hear me, Gilbert! She will fall to your care after I am gone. I trust you will take her in when or if this new life goes wearily with her."

Dowland withdrew the needle from the linen square. "Take this back to her, son-in-law. I have read her message." He tucked the cloth away again.

Wakwa strode to Dowland's side and took the needle from him. He pressed the sharp point into the palm of his hand and watched the blood it drew.

"In your way, Father, you are just and have come far in one day. For that I thank you. I am glad my love is great that I may protect Elizabeth from this new yoke you lay across her back. I trust I may return in safety if I should need some counsel of you."

"Indeed you may. Take care of her!"

Contrary to her husband's demeanor Mary rushed to Wakwa, pleading, "Can I be of help? There is a child coming, is there not?"

"Alas, Mother, the sign of one is lacking." Wakwa held her silk-covered shoulder. "For this I am very sorry. It would do you good to hear the laughter of a child in this quiet house. I do not think you could deny your daughter then, though her son were named after beast or bird."

They stood with glances locked. Wakwa saw in her the determination he had seen in Elizabeth at their first meeting in the forest. But as he continued to search Mary's eyes, he felt had she been the hunted one, she would have turned into the arms of the hunters.

"Then it is farewell." He kissed her and was gone.

Chapter 25

When the house was out of view Wakwa removed his clothing to his apron, embraced his comrades, and ran toward the pines with his neat bundle across his shoulders.

He nearly shouted as he ran free, the rising wind singing against his skin. He darted among the scattered trees at the southwestern rim of his father-in-law's field. He felt he was on the brink of a new world.

His fascination with Elizabeth's people, now that he could approach them from inside their thoughts, might develop into understanding. Even his aversion to their endless piles of books and the array of machines they doted on was subject to change. He had reason to hope that there were depths within white men he had not detected from outside their closed circles.

It may have been the mildness of Dowland's reproach as he pronounced his decision, or the father's crippled hand squeezing Wakwa's strong one as he pleaded "Take care of her!" but Wakwa felt the workings of change after only a few hours of contact. He decided then to take advantage of the safe conduct, if not hospitality, offered him and return soon to persuade the landholder to end Elizabeth's exile.

He would like to have swum the river to crown his feeling of renewal, but he could not squander time, concerned as he was about having left Kayaskwa alone so long. He contented himself with the flow of his loose hair.

While Wakwa shed his tensions, threading his familiar way through the woods, Elizabeth toiled at a surprise for him. She had put on the trousers she had sewn in the wetuomemese and walked up the bank of the river, defensively, with his bow. By night she was just arriving home herself.

The sight of an outside fire worried Wakwa as he stood catching his breath after his straight run. He watched the flames lighting the front of the lodge, puzzled at why she should be outside at night. If she had not lit the fire, he could not imagine who had.

Just then Elizabeth backed through the dark from around the rear corner of the house.

Wakwa saw her as a slender youth with a high fur hat, dragging something with both hands. The figure was merely silhouetted by the fire in the moonless night, and Wakwa struggled with self-remonstrances that he had left his wife unguarded and fears that his carelessness had caused her harm.

He barked from the edge of the trees to make the person turn and reveal his features. The youth stopped. Wakwa imitated the sound of a fox again.

"Fox! Are you there?"

There was no mistaking the delicate movement of the head as the neck arched up, and then he heard the voice as well. Wakwa sighed his relief.

"Here, Kayaskwa!" He came into the open.

She dropped the thing she had been dragging and came close enough to see his face.

"Come to me, young man, what have you done with my wife?" He laughed.

She ran the rest of the way to him and clutched him around his middle. "At last! How long you were gone!"

Wakwa slipped his hand between the furry jacket and her shirt and seized one of her breasts firmly. "Ah! Yet you are a woman!"

"How I wish that I were." She broke away from him. "I should like sometime that you return to a settled house and not find me an hysterical child." She retreated behind the fire, pacing back and forth in long strides. "You do not understand what I have been through whilst you were gone. I have behaved ridiculously as usual, and now you are back you may scold me roundly, for that is all that I deserve."

"Elizabeth. Come here."

She stayed entrenched behind the fire. "Trying to be better I have made the most recent and worst of my messes. I tried, ever so, to be calm and started to work on your great coat, but the time passed and there was no sign of you!

"I took your bow, the big one, the one you love, the best one, and three arrows and went walking along the river. I was frightened when you did not return and felt safer with the bow, in case they should send someone after me.

"Before I knew, I was near the pond where all the fowl stay. And then a goose stuck its black head out of a bush. It seemed to me to be a goose's head! Lord, I have fed enough of them to know! Well, I took aim and shot at the thing and it fell down. I hit it! I aimed into the bush and the bird fell!

"I thought it was wonderful. I would roast it for your dinner and be strong, a heroine, when you arrived! Can you see me responsible for a hot meal . . . the scent of roast goose and berries floating through the trees as you came running home to me?

"But then a great black thing was beating at me and I thought its wing would break my arm off. I dropped everything and ran like an ass!"

Wakwa listened with his hands against his face, trying to make sense of her story.

She stood still, contrite. "It was a swan! A great black swan. I had shot its mate! It went back and moaned over it and cried. Oh! I thought I would die of shame at killing one of your sacred birds and seeing its mate so sad. I nearly vomited with sadness.

"Then some animal came near, a fox I think, and there came a great shrieking, and scores of these birds, like ships, flew down and drove it off. When they flew away I went back to get your bow and thought, 'Why should I leave the bird here to draw wild beasts?' "

"Come here, Elizabeth!"

She paced again. "You will be very angry, I do not blame you whatever you may do, but I made a raft of a loose bough and the bow and pulled this great hulking bird on it. I never could have carried the thing home."

"A raft?"

"A kind of boat . . . I dragged the swan easily through the water until the bough sank with everything on it. Your bow snagged under the water and it lies there still."   .

"My bow is under water?"

"Do you think it truly ruined? I can find it for you. I know just where it is! I marked it with rope and tied the end to a tree."

"My bow, under water?"

"I couldn't help it! And it was getting dark, so I dragged the damnable swan all the way home by the arrow still stuck in it. I left such a trail of blood it is a wonder I am not devoured by this time, except the beasts thought I would make them stupid if they ate me!

"This is the cause of my staying out here. I refuse to be cleaning up blood from the floorboards, nor would I leave the swan unguarded, fresh-killed, like an invitation to the wolves. I made this fire and was bringing her around to start to pluck her when I heard you in the trees. God above, Wakwa! The neck of the thing dragging and bobbing on the ground behind me. I had never seen such a neck nor pulled such a weight!" At last she ran to him and threw herself at his feet, gripped his legs in her arms and cried, "What happened all this long time? What did they say!"

He squatted down to her, held her face against his own, and pressed lightly on the hollow of her throat with his thumb. "I did discover this long day what makes thy fire beat so under here!"

She looked into his eyes for his meaning.

He let his lips wander over her face, explaining, "You never informed me that a warmer sun lit one of your forebears. That is what I have seen shining through your eyes and your laughter."

"They told you of Angelica? The grandmother no one knew?"

"I knew her well when first I saw her picture. In my darkest moments today I did turn to her, and her hot eyes drove me on to make our story straight for them." He smiled. "You did not tell me you were a halfblood!"

"Wakwa, you cannot know how frightened I was for you when you did not return! I saw you drawn and quartered and locked up in the pillory. I saw you shot and tied and tortured. If I had not lost your bow, I would have found my way out of this forest and saved you! I thought surely they would never let you back to me." She cried.

Wakwa pulled her to her feet and covered her face with hard kisses. "Your father lets the marriage stand. He will not part us. He was most just in that."

Her sobs stopped as she gasped cool air. "To have been there! You must be a wondrous speaker! My faith in you was far too small!" She ricocheted from his arms. "I must dance! What a joy to plan a wedding!"

The man caught her close. "That you cannot do, little bird. You are all mine now." Then he began to hurry to ease her shock of realization. "I will go back. Speak with them again. They will grow used to me and relent!"

"All yours?" she puzzled. "They refuse to see me? They accept you and all that we have done and reject me?"

Wakwa grew sick within himself, forced to reply, "Just so." It was the moment her father had sought to bring about.

Elizabeth pranced away from him and kicked the dirt around the fire. Wakwa thought she looked fiercer than the taupowaw, the high priest, at the winter feast.

"So it has been ever!" she shouted, casting rocks and sticks into the fire which grew, leaping with her.

Wakwa closed his eyes, disgusted at the transformation worked upon his wife.

"Ever the dispensable daughter! Always I have known it. Never Henry! Always me! The sacrificial lamb of the family. Here, see before your very eyes the highly marketable Elizabeth Dowland, cow!" She lost sight of where she was.

Wakwa pulled her away from the fire. At his touch she collapsed on his naked breast.

"Kayaskwa! Kayaskwa!" he groaned to her.

"How he must love me, to hang onto my soul this way!" She cried as if she had a wound in her throat.

Wakwa stroked her gently. "If you see that, Kayaskwa, all things will go well between us whether you see him again or no."

"Never, never?"

"I will go back, little wife. Three times, by our tradition, I am permitted to make request. Your father bent far today, deeper into his ground than the poles of the wetuomemese I build for you each month. We have shocked him, but he will change, I am sure. The poor man has your uncle at him, teaching him, always, with his lightning eyes, and your mother softened when the thought of little children came to us all."

The smoothness of his voice and the strength of his caress calmed her, and she accepted the velvet sack of shells to save for

160

their second offering. He dressed in rough skins, made a torch, and led her out to examine her kill.

"What made you think the swan is sacred?" He spread one of its huge wings and measured the length of the feathers against his hand.

"You have said their Indian name means 'shining creature.' "

"True, they are filled with the vapor of Manitto, but they are no more sacred than the deer which we kill when we are hungry."

"But you have never shot one in all our days together."

"I do not go after them. They are such a sight under the moon. Alas, this night there is no moon. I will help you pluck it, though it be hateful work to me. We shall not eat of its meat but bait my traps with it for a hunt tomorrow night." He mussed her hair and smiled. "Perhaps I will draw out the dark fox with the sacred flesh!"

His gentle humor made her smile too, and they walked to the river by torchlight when the swan was bled and hung.

"Wakwa?"

"Kayaskwa?"

"Shall I ever make a proper wife and be a woman? Not just your flitting bird?"

"That I will show you when we return to our house! For now, find the place where you have drowned my bow. There may yet be a little life in it. And do not touch it again without asking. Somehow you will find a way to work it backwards and run yourself through like a cut of venison ready for roasting."

They found the marker and Wakwa disrobed again and dove for the bow while Elizabeth held the torch. After his third try he pried it loose and bobbed to the surface with a yelp of delight.

"Nutahtomp! Dear, my bow! Poor ahtomp, I will take you home and nurse you, and if I cannot hit a deer with you I suppose my young wife and I will starve." He wrapped the bow, himself, and Elizabeth in his blanket. "Didst know, Kayaskwa, my father made this for me to celebrate the eighteenth summer of my birth? Is it not fine?"

"The first day of November marks my eighteenth year, but my papa will not be giving me anything. It is I will give you a gift, Silent Fox." She stopped to kiss his cool hands. Porcupines stared at them through the black.

And the man, grateful for her rededication, delighted her by observing, "Elizabeth, see how our way abounds with creatures? The animals have got wind I am distracted by you and I neglect my traps. They leave the bounds of other hunters and flee to the safe lands of Silent Fox. You will make me rich! I will trap them all while they are in this careless mood. If I do not we will be overrun by beasts and the very deer devour us!"

He laughed out loud at the unsayable repercussions of their relationship upon his life. The laugh reverberated in the stillness and drove the meaner beasts growling away from the scent of man.

Chapter 26

Outside Charles Dowland's house the moonless night was very black, but Annanias Hudson knew the road as well as his own upstairs hallway. He walked his horse through the brisk air, elated by the prospect that Beth had been found alive and that after all his depression his wedding would take place.

He was feeling so amiable with the happy turn of events that he made a conscious effort not to resent his exclusion from the day's conference. The informants, who they were and how they had found Beth when all her family's efforts had proved no good, pricked at him. He was too filled with equanimity to be concerned about his lateness or to rush as he dismounted and led his horse around to the rear door, the front of the house shuttered in somber solidity. The mare shied and whinnied, but Annanias forced her by her bridle and tied her to the post.

Inside, Mary awoke at the sound of the horse. The servants had retired to their rooms after their long day and had not disturbed their master and mistress, dozing before the failing fire.

Mary gathered her shawl around her and was up, lighting the pale yellow candles and tidying her hair under her bonnet. She flew down the few steps into the darkened kitchen to stop Hudson's loud banging on the back door before it awakened her husband.

"Is that you, Annanias?" she called, unbolting the shutter of a kitchen window.

She made a little start when Hudson pressed his face close up to the glass and shouted, "Mother Dowland, halloah! A grand thing has beaten me to the kitchen door and I cannot get over it! Sorry I'm so late that you've closed up! You are looking fine in that cap!"

Mary had the window open. "Come in, Reverend. You are welcome here no matter the hour."

Annanias shook off the portent of her coolness and met her around by the kitchen door as she opened it.

Mary shrieked at the sight on the broad steps.

Charles called from the sitting room in surprise, Sam and the housekeeper rushed into the kitchen in their nightclothes calling questions, and Priscilla, stranded at the top of the steps, alone, wailed in fright.

On the stones lay the carcass of a beautiful young buck. There was not a mark on it, but the broken neck caused the head to turn a little to one side, showing the glassy brown eyes.

Charles, draped over Sam's shoulders, stared at the many pointed antlers encrusted with wild cranberries and laurel leaves.

Annanias hurried to the annex where the laborers slept, surprising them at a forbidden game of dice, and shooed them up to the main house without any reprimand. When the deer had been removed to the smokehouse and the place was settled and orderly, Annanias ambled into the sitting room, having gone back first to his horse for his Bible.

Charles was piqued. "We expected you just after candlelight, Annanias."

"I am sorry to be late, Mr. Dowland, but you know I am so beset by errands, I have a failing in punctuality. I just came away from Hansons'."

"Is there sickness there again?" Mary asked.

"Just the opposite! I am glad to report Prudence is gaining every day and was quite chipper at supper. I think whatever ailed her has left her alone for good. It is very gratifying for us all. She has kept everyone a good bit worried, you know."

Mary sealed her lips shut and stared at the wide buttonholes of the minister's black waistcoat.

Charles searched the younger man's face. "I am happy to hear of Mistress Hanson's recovery. Very happy for all concerned. But I am somewhat amazed at you. Your concerns are more here than there. We have been waiting for hours with the most momentous news, while you sup pleasantly with the neighbors!"

Hudson was brought up short. In his experience, anger had not been one of Mr. Dowland's characteristics. Had it been another man speaking, Hudson would not have let it pass so quietly. He defended himself in his dry, laconic voice.

"I have been impatient for news all day, Father Dowland. I

164

have prayed and kept my mind on other duties since I was not allowed to be present during your consultations. I rather expected to find Beth back among you." Hudson, disgruntled, unwilling to beg for information, forced his glance down from the ceiling, hoping with his heart she lay again, sleeping safely, above them. "I come here, having received some small kindness from friends who are most solicitous of you and myself during this long siege, stumble over dead deer at your door, and meet your ire. You are overwrought but I will apologize. I know how difficult it is to be kept waiting." Hudson settled back into the wing chair and opened his Bible, avoiding the look on Charles' face.

" 'With what shall I come before the Lord, and bow
    myself before the Most High?
Shall I come before Him with burnt offerings, with
    calves a year old?
Will the Lord be pleased with thousands of rams,
    with myriads of streams of oil?
Shall I give my firstborn for my transgression,
The fruit of my body for the sin of my soul?' "

From here Annanias spoke from memory, looking at his intended father-in-law.

" 'You have been told, O man, what is good,
And what the Lord requires of you: Only to do
    justice, and love kindness,
And to walk humbly with your God.' "

Charles looked at Hudson, but returned to the memory of Silent Fox, bowing at the moment of their meeting, his shining black hair spilling forward over his chest.

Charles' voice was thick. "It is an apt reading, Annanias. I might even say, inspired. If you have children someday, Hudson, you will come to know how hard it is to be both just and kind."

Annanias glowed at his swift success. "I do not admonish you, Father Dowland, do not think that! I merely attempt to calm us both."

"I am quite calm within myself, Annanias. . . . Spake you of burnt offerings? The deer you say you 'stumbled' over is a kind of offering."

"From whom?"

"From Indians."

"Why do they bother with offerings to a Christian?"

"You see, Annanias, as of October the eighth they are my relations."

Mary hid her face and looked away.

Still lounging in posture, Annanias grew wary.

Charles bore down on the luckless minister. "Have you a passage in the Testament about forgiveness? The news of our daughter, Elizabeth, is that she is married to a prince of the native people that live hereabouts. Your waiting is negated, I am afraid."

Annanias' weighty body moved forward slowly, his shoulders hunching and his head drooping until he could see the points of brightness from the fire glaring off the buckles of his shoes. "We have an agreement!"

"Mr. Hudson, I have had to nullify it this day. It gives me grief to break a bond we have all favored for so many years. I will never take back any land we had agreed upon. It is yours by right and by default . . . my regrets go with it."

"Your regrets!" Hudson sprang erect in his chair. "I want my bride! Do you mean to tell me that you sat here all night waiting to tell me this? Why did you not seek out the magistrate and follow these lying savages and raid their filthy hideouts and find her!"

Charles looked meaningfully at Mary, then turned to Hudson. "Your advice a month ago, as I remember, sir, was that we should move softly and not raise a great cloud over Beth for what we should find! I took that advice. Had we been more open and persistent right at the beginning, my daughter would sit sewing at the fireside at this moment. But we did not and she does not!"

"You are blaming me!" Hudson boomed.

"I think you must have felt within yourself her reluctance to be your wife and knew she left with purpose, and still you did not tell me this. You persisted and hounded all of us. Well. We shall hound her no further. Now is not the time to be up in arms.

166

The deed is done! She has purposely left us. Never fear she is being held against her will."

"I do not fancy one bit your putting this thing off on me!"

"Sir!" Charles' eyes burned. "I blame myself as well for my willful blindness. She asked me every way in her power to release her from you and I did not listen."

"She did not do that!" Hudson struggled out of his chair.

"Now I reap the havoc I have sown by ignoring her, for she has spoken, finally, through this husband who came here to us today."

"Husband! I am her husband-to-be, there can be no other!"

Mary started up. "I will go to make the tea. Cooke is resting."

"Bother tea, Mary! Sit down."

"I will make tea now." She turned her back on them and left. The men stared after her.

Within the mother mortification and desperation combined, driving her to bury the agreement that had brought her so much contentment a few weeks before. As with a gathering after a funeral, the great frustration of her plans must be laid to rest with some formality. She foresaw others picking up the prize she had groomed for her own daughter and could not control her distaste for Beth's rebellion as well as Charles. She was glad to leave the room.

Charles took advantage of her absence. "Annanias, attend what I say while she is gone! The man is both good and powerful and protected by powerful men. Go raging into the woods and you will be breaking up old treaties and stirring up trouble that may not leave this community the rest of our days. Blood will be wasted if you march in there and start accusing honorable people of acts they do not commit.

"They will not hesitate to cut you down if you so much as look crosswise at this young fellow, for he is greater to his own than you are to your most faithful sheep."

"Do you think I am afraid for my own life? Even were she not my betrothed, I would try to rescue her from the heathen. And you her father and a church member! She is bedeviled, bewitched, to be consorting with such rabble. But a fortnight ago, in Wareham, I saw Judge Dawes pulled in his sedan chair by four of these low savages. They are good for no more than that!

167

You do not know her condition. You have but the word of an Indian!"

"Yet you do not understand me! You will not cause an incident with these people over my daughter. Do you hear? I forbid it! You will not shut off the road back for her! How will she ever return if we blunder in and do injustice to the innocent tribesmen of this man?

"I am not an idiot though I may look like an insect to you, stuck in this accursed chair! I look after her poor soul as well. No one is to blame for this but myself, for what I sought for her with you has driven her away. I turned a deaf ear and she is teaching me, moment by moment, as I long for her presence, the depth to which I made her spirit sink.

"There will be no scouring the woods and ballyhoo, nor hard feelings with the sachim. The old man is probably as upset by this union as I am myself."

"Storm them for proof there is a union! Unholy though it be!" Annanias strained to be rational.

"It is done for you, Annanias! Our bond on this matter is swept aside. Bring me the copies of the marriage contract so that we may cry on them and throw them wet into the fire! This has been a day of unveilings for me and I see my errors. I will not compound them. If you would storm anyone, storm me."

"You are bewitched as well."

"Leave that theme, Hudson, right away!"

"What incantations to one of his thirty-seven gods did the young buck pronounce behind these walls? How did he worm your good will out of you? What secret enemy have I made of him that he uses my own rights and desires thus?"

"Do your thoughts always turn about yourself?" Charles felt he finally knew the man.

Hudson's reply was cut off by Mary's return. She approached Charles with a cup but he waved her away. Annanias accepted his and downed the contents in a gulp. Lowering his head, he whispered into the fire, "It is so like the gall they gave thee to drink, oh Lord!"

At this, Charles explained more quietly the circumstances of his daughter's cure and marriage.

"Mr. Dowland, do you mean to tell me all my hopes for her

168

are lost? The pretty face I watched grow from such a bonnie child into the flower of a young woman? How I have waited to see from it a glance of affection, even the smallest sign of regard!

"You cannot know what I have sacrificed to wait for her. Was I not careful never to offend her? Did I once press my affections on her? I have been like a slave to the image of her as my wife. With all the ability I have to love I have cherished the hope of her!

"Hope. I must hope. I will die, crawl through life, disavow my duties from grief. I need her to come back! She is pure and strong. Together we will walk the twisting flowered paths, pure, one with the other, until death at the gate of Paradise!

"I will still have her as my wife. I will wait until doomsday but she will marry me!" He leaned his forehead against the stones bordering the great mouth of the fireplace and pushed his weight against the spot, holding the empty cup and saucer tenderly, as he would like to have held Beth's face had she been there. He sobbed like a half-grown boy: "Ephesians, chapter five, verses twenty-five to twenty-seven.

> 'You who are husbands must love your wives, just as Christ loved the church and gave himself for her, to consecrate her, after cleansing her with the bath in water through her confession of him, to bring the church to himself in all her beauty, without a flaw or wrinkle or anything of the kind, but to be consecrated and faultless.' "

Surprise and pity at the impotence of the sober minister moved Charles to say, "Mr. Hudson, you are still a young man. Choose another wife. Do you know what I mean when I say she is happily wed to the Indian? Another man has her first. She can never be what she was!"

Hudson squeezed the delicate porcelain and the set of thirteen was broken, the lavender pieces sprinkling to the hearth. He became incensed with the bell-like noise they made as they hit, and he ground his shoe into the frail pieces, grunting his frustration.

Mary stood transfixed, remembering the Indian who had said so cordially that afternoon what a thing of beauty the cup was.

"What is this brute's name who has spoiled her?" Hudson demanded.

"Silent Fox. The nephew of the sachim." The name was bright in her consciousness and Mary pronounced it to him, not really hearing the import of the question.

Charles was beside himself at her lack of caution. His wife caught his look and, realizing what she had done, went into the back hallway and leaned against the stairs.

Hudson did not know where he was and spoke unguardedly. "Silent Fox . . . Silent Fox. I know that name. I have read that name."

"Forget the name, Hudson! Though I be damned for it, I say he is a better man than you or I, and my little girl will find greater peace in his care than she would with us. Happy day that gave her the courage to avoid the snare I laid for her. And the one you laid for me! See henceforth you act a man, not one possessed, *bewitched* is your word, I believe. I would see you docked in public before you besmirch her through this intelligent native." Now Charles was determined to clearly end his association with Hudson. "She is a free spirit now, and I have lost her. I cannot hold her more to this contract with you. Take your land and leave. Find some other woman to support your quavering resolves. She has a man who could have stood without her."

"I will not forget the name! Nor does the all-seeing Lord above forget. Since you will not, I will go to avenge in blood the one true God whom this pagan has offended most grossly, taking the innocence of the lamb and twisting you both into the voices of the Devil!"

"You taste of Salem madness, Hudson!"

"Charles!" Mary stood between them.

Hudson seized the latch, pulling fiercely, shaking the door in his frenzy, unable to work the tight-fitting iron lock. He rattled it with all his strength, helpless to leave the house.

Mary knelt in her dark blue dress and lovingly gathered the tiny pieces of the shattered cup into her hand. "Reverend Hudson, let go the latch. Charles, we will not let all these years of friendship end with such an outburst. We are still members of your church, Mr. Hudson, and need your help this moment, as you need ours.

"I must abide by my husband's wish that you leave Beth in peace. I told you both, long ago, how to get her back, but as usual the word of a woman went unheeded. Beth acted rashly, true, but my husband stands behind her choice and so will I.

"There will be no scandal if you both would act out of charity this moment instead of patterning yourselves after beasts. I think even the meanest savage would be offended at your demeanors, let alone the gentle man who came here today to call me 'mother'!" She went and stood behind her husband's chair and rubbed his shoulders, not saying another word.

All his Boston aplomb broken through, his hysterical outburst cut off, Hudson opened into a more regulated state of mind.

He looked at Charles Dowland. "Did she really ask to be released from me? Does she despise me that much?"

"She begged me. I spoke in your behalf, however."

"I could not have killed him. I suppose you knew that?"

"I knew it."

"Sometimes . . . Mr. Dowland . . . late at night . . . when only darkness lies outside the house, when it is late . . ." Annanias said this again, delaying from shyness the rest of his thought. He folded his arms hard against himself, over his belly, and continued in confession, "I am, naturally, alone. . . . I work at the Septuagint on my own." His arms relaxed and tone came into his skin at sharing this secret.

Dowland, resting from their argument with his cheek against the heel of his hand, tried to register the meaning of this hesitant confidence.

Annanias was embarrassed at the other man's look. "It may seem poor solace to you, sir, used to a family, but," the minister, in his mid-thirties, flushed with adolescent enthusiasm, "I turn to Solomon and Judith for conversation! Oh! It is better exercise for the mind than empty talk with the daringest of college whelps I used to know!"

Annanias Hudson came near to Dowland's chair and seized his hand around its painful lumps of bone. "Have you ever read from Esdras? He says things. . . . You must hear!"

Charles watched the large-girthed man, breathing with unbecoming quickness, hurry to the wing chair to catch up his heavy book of Scriptures. Uneasy, detecting an unstable departure from the overwhelming news about Elizabeth, he looked for his wife, but she had retired to the dining room and was sitting in the semi-darkness, absolved from any part in the men's discussion. Dowland disliked himself for wishing he could move back as Hudson returned, flipping the diaphanous pages to a place past center.

"Never have I shown anyone my Bible! You have seen it in my hand, but you have never really seen it. It contains some books that are better left unseen by most. But tonight you will understand why this second book of Esdras is so appealing. . . ." Hudson chattered until he found his place, but desolation returned as he pored over the verses.

"It is the angel so stern and this miserable Ezra squirming . . . Mr. Dowland, I would not know how to kill the Indian." Annanias looked beyond the book, not needing to read it.

" '. . . I spoke from grief, for my heart pains me every hour,
    while I strive to understand the way of the Most High,
    and to inquire into what His decree apportions. . . .' "

Hudson lowered himself heavily onto a footstool.

" 'Why . . . Why . . .' "

Hudson could not go on. Charles could not leave him lost in his grief and reached for the text to help him. Squinting in the meager light, Dowland found and completed the passage.

" 'Why, sir, then why was I born? And why did not my
    mother's womb become my grave, so that I might not see
    the trouble of Jacob and the exhaustion of the posterity
    of Israel.' "

Charles' hand covered the printed words that called back the remorse he had suffered that afternoon.

But much recovered from this cooperative effort, Annanias dressed their wounded pride in his most gracious clerical manner. "To those who will surely ask, for I mentioned about the town in my happiness that you would have some news, what shall I say? May I hint she has gone among the Indians, perhaps to teach them the gospel? Then if she returns her reputation is still safe."

"That is a lie. It will plague us all if she come back or no. I said to her husband I would own their marriage if asked straight out." Charles waited until Annanias took his hands away from his face. "You would not have her children bastard, would you, Annanias? No. None are on the way as yet. But, I will not see her. Was that right?"

"It is meet. She will learn how serious is her breech with God."

Charles shook his head in the negative. "It seems I have given my firstborn for my transgression—the fruit of my body for the sin of my soul—not to God, but to the Indian. Why do I hold off seeing her, then?"

With Charles' ambivalence, Hudson regained some of his swagger. He fluffed his curls away from his white bands before putting on his hat. "We shall think and pray about it. Something may yet be done to make us all happy once again."

He walked home, forgetting his horse tied to the post. They sent it down to him in the morning.

Chapter 27

On the last day of October, while Gil Worth rode off to order the removal of the notices posted throughout Buzzards Bay and up the coast, Hanna was surprised by a visit from Awepu.

She had horses brought, not knowing what else to do to entertain him, and she showed him the farm with its many buildings.

"Your barn is the size of ten of my own houses!" Awepu marveled, then he teased, "You may find it full of my children someday."

His horsemanship and amiable attitude put Hanna at her ease so that when Gil pushed open the door of the sitting room, unbuttoning his muddy sherry-vallies, he found them chatting over French liqueur, Awepu poised on the silk settee and Hanna bent over her wax board, at work with colored thread making a profile of him.

Awepu spent the night in a curtained bed of down, more and more bemused by Wakwa's choice of a wife. He vaguely saw advantages in familiarity with these foreigners. It seemed clear to him that these New English settlers did not have a uniform character. They possessed no common current of virtues. Living among them was like wandering in a forest sprouting, unnaturally, with thousands of different kinds of trees. Some bore blossoms like the Worths. Some bore thorns.

He was surprised when Hanna would not go to see her niece.

"How can I go to Elizabeth when her mother is not allowed?"

Awepu thought his English too unrefined to understand her reasoning. Wakwa would have to make it clear to him. But he was more than glad to pack the tall gelding Gil lent him with a load of gifts for his new kinswoman and cheerfully lead Gil into the woods.

* * * *

Wakwa had spent the week in assiduous hunting. He provided meat for this important visit, meat for his family in the town, meat for drying for the less prosperous months. He constructed another tanning hut for the furs and skins. He and Elizabeth went there to clean the skins and rub them with the mysterious cakes made of oil, herbs, and animal brains for closing the pores and making them resilient. Together they pulled them back and forth over the poles to soften them.

There was excitement over two bear Wakwa and Awepu brought from the higher country, Awepu refusing the skin of his, giving it to Elizabeth for a wedding present.

One night as they lay down to rest, Wakwa cautioned, "Kayaskwa, you shall wear yourself out with preparations."

She had been cleaning out the lodge and madly sewing the drape which was to hang like an arch, twenty feet from ceiling to floor, making an airy divider between the two great rooms.

He began again when she stubbornly refused to reply. "I should have a maid from my wetu in the town come to assist you. I want your uncle to see you in health, not worked to skin and bones."

"Are you afraid he will think you a slavedriver? My hands are all the help I need. I am too selfish, I suppose, to have anyone share the credit. I could finish the drape if I did not sleep only two nights. Sleep well, Wakwa."

"Sleep well, little Kayaskwa."

"Wakwa?"

"What now."

"I should like to serve him tarts."

"Do."

"Oh, Wakwa! You know I cannot make tarts in an iron kettle."

"Do not serve him tarts then."

"You are most insensitive tonight."

"Kayaskwa! Must I bring my mat outside in the freezing cold to get some sleep?"

"A pudding! That is it! Pumpkins! Lovely pumpkins! Can you get me some butter from someplace?"

Wakwa turned his naked back to the fire.

"If I were not so tired," she kept at him, "I would come to your mat and stay with you tonight. We are at a fine pass if, after all this, I am too weary to love you. Methinks you right again, my Fox."

Wakwa was asleep and had not heard her.

October gave place to November. Wakwa waited for Gilbert Worth outside the lodge in the cold, shadowless sun. Elizabeth joined him, carefully groomed, her hair softly back from her face, wound into a shiny coil at the crown of her head. The hanging, unfinished, lay displayed in folds on the empty quilting frame.

Their guests arrived. Awepu saluted Wakwa and dismounted and stood holding the horses. Gil sat high, looking at his niece.

Wakwa's arm slid from around her shoulders. The Englishman quit his mount with a lithe movement, but stayed distant at the edge of the clearing.

Elizabeth's eyes were very large as she looked at the uncle who meant so much to her. Gil motioned for her to approach, and she walked the twenty feet to him on the uneven ground, almost clumsily.

Wakwa watched Gil's face as Elizabeth stopped in front of him and he tried to read his feelings. But the face was closed against pain, only the green eyes asking the questions Wakwa was anxious to hear voiced and answered.

The girl, for so long so sure of her acts, could not bear his unyielding stare. She lowered her head as her eyes filled with tears, knowing he thought of the day she hid from him in the pesuponk.

"Keep that head up!" the uncle commanded brusquely.

She straightened.

His wrist came behind her neck and he drew her stiffly to his shoulder for a moment. "This has been a time!" He forgave her with the touch.

"Such a risk, it seemed, to speak." Her chin quivered as she fought to be as steely as he. Her head went down again.

"Beth! Beth!" Gil's smooth hand gently forced her head high and he kissed her lips. "Did you purposely choose a man so tall my neck would ache trying to make his friendship?"

The girl cried her shame and relief onto Gil's blue cashmere coat.

"It is a grand and serious thing you have begun." Slowly his arms came around her and they clasped each other.

Hiding his worries, Gil admired everything he saw and made

great to-do about the aromas from the kettle. He loaded their arms with presents. There were thirteen silver cups, an iced bucket filled with eggs, the exotic treat of oranges from the south, and a bundle of gauzy nightgowns.

"Hanna says to tell you these are French. There is also a negligee with a gathered petticoat. She feels the ones you made before are ill-omened and of no use to you." Gil turned a bit pink.

"In my new life neither are these!"

Wakwa, shocked at her frankness, dropped the ruffled dressing gown onto the others in the pile. "Wife, when we are locked in the cold of winter you will learn to sleep in the stiffest buckskin."

Elizabeth served the meal in embarrassed silence. Wakwa began to yield his reticence as Gil guided the conversation gracefully from topic to topic. He showed interest in their everyday routine, becoming involved with the intricacies of each activity as Wakwa described it. He gave Wakwa two books from his own collection, Plato's *Republic* and the tragedies of William Shakespeare.

No one mentioned the name of Charles Dowland.

After the steaming pudding was gone and Elizabeth cleared away the remains of the stew and fish, the men walked out under a pale sky.

Gil pried at Wakwa's reserve, admiring the contentment he sensed in the young couple, striving to extend the security of their happiness with his growing approval. "You know, Silent Fox, I feel foolish here on this errand. It is very necessary to reassure her father, but I would like to have started out as your uncle on a different note. Would you find me a bother if I sneaked over here occasionally?"

"We welcome you when you come out of desire. I do not enjoy being watched like the rabbit by the hawk." Wakwa put his hand on Gil's shoulder as they walked. "Yet it is a small thing to bear, knowing Elizabeth is secure to me. I will go back to Charles Dowland. I will try again, and again, to persuade him to escort her into the otan and settle her among us."

"I like that. I hoped you would. I have even thought you could meet with him at my home. More neutral ground, you know."

"You have been planning for me, Uncle!"

"Indeed. Unlike my brother-in-law, I do not like to leave things up in the air. And this Hudson stays quiet with his bad news but I do not trust him. A worm like that cannot lose without retaliation."

"He is more a snake from what I have heard." Wakwa grinned. "Do you know how we use snakes, Nissese? We bait our traps with their meat and wind their intestines, filled with fresh water, around our middles. This supply lasts a man a week."

"It is a thought. And what a gut he has!"

"Do not brood, Uncle." Wakwa made overtures to Gil's frisky bay. "You will stay the night and I will take you to the sweating room with Waban and so fill you with good times you will return home happier and more vigorous than when you left."

"Let us give Beth a little joy too." Gil reached into his saddle pouch and pulled out a lyre, gilt gold and painted with cherubs of silver leaf.

"Of everything I have missed that sound the most!" Elizabeth settled herself at her uncle's feet when he brought the lyre inside. "Sometimes when I lie awake I hear thy music, Uncle Gil, but it is really the wind singing in the pines. I listen hard and think I read the most complicated tunes up in the air. Serenade for Pine Bough! I come to think all the sounds ever made fly above us in the air, waiting, waiting, somehow to be pulled back down."

Awepu turned to Wakwa. "Your wife is like the sky, cousin. Always seeing everything with a changing light upon her face."

Wakwa came behind her and touched his cheek to her hair. "Ah! Nummittamus, my wife! Awepu, she is more the mist, quietly reaching inside of everything, clouding my own vision so that I see all things through the veil of herself. Sunna matta, is that not so, Gilbert Worth?"

Uncomfortable with metaphor, Gil grunted and struck the instrument. In his surprising basso he sang a poem by Donne he had set to music.

" 'And now good morrow to our waking souls,
    Which watch not one another out of fear;

For love, all love of other sights controls,
And makes one little room an everywhere.' "

From his place in shadow Wakwa combined his voice with the Englishman's in legato harmony. Gil, pleasantly surprised, brought the instrument to him and placed it in his lap.

"Play."

Wakwa ran his fingers across the wires. Hardly a sound was made. He imitated Gil's hand movement and plucked. "I have hurt it!"

"When you play it wrong it hurts you!" Gil laughed. He gave Wakwa a lesson. "Keep it, Silent Fox. I expect you will have taught yourself by the next time I see you."

Wakwa stroked the instrument with interest. "Do not stay away that long, Gilbert Worth. You fit well into this big lodge."

"It is beautiful here. Hanna and I have spent our lives trying to create this effect in our home. I see we should have simply taken a walk in the woods." Gil caught an exchange of smiles between the Indian and Elizabeth. "The handiwork, the peace, the fire, the friendship. You may have two boarders if you are not careful."

Awepu was mellow. "This is nothing to Wakwa's house in our town. The mannotaubana—those are the hangings—the trays, the carvings, make this look very plain. Wussese, you must have seen his lodge when you came at first to seek Elizabeth. You went through every house! You must have met . . ." Awepu strove to right his mistake.

Elizabeth stood in panic, but Gil was unsuspecting.

"I am sorry, Awepu. I looked for only one thing that day and am so glad now I did not find her!"

Wakwa motioned Elizabeth to himself and grasped Gil's hand. "One day, my Uncle, very soon, when this marriage is a settled thing, I will be honored to have you stay with us and come to know all about my other house and how we dwell there. Slowly is the best way to make our bond of friendship strong. You and I will work to open up ourselves."

This was what Gil wanted most from his visit, and he slept a sound, dreamless sleep, sharing the farther fire with Awepu.

The next afternoon, after the delights of the pesuponk and a canoe ride upriver, Wakwa gave Gil two pipes he had carved himself and decorated with turkey feathers.

"Two?"

"This wuttammagon is for you, the longer one for your wife. She too must try. The tobacco I raised with my own hands. You will find it sweet."

"How do you get the time?"

Awepu rode out first and waited at a distance. Elizabeth made her farewell to Gil alone.

"You live in a dream, my girl."

"Uncle Gil, how I would love to parade down the main street with Wakwa and show everyone, at last, what a great man I love."

"Better keep him in the forest for a bit. It is not safe yet on many fronts. Besides, Priscilla has not had a decent night's sleep since she set eyes on you-know-who." They kissed before he rode away. "God help you, child. Happy birthday!"

Chapter 28

A week passed, and Awepu grew more and more regretful about his careless slip during Gilbert Worth's visit. He saw in Elizabeth the effect of her wait for Wakwa's second going to her father. He remembered how much Dowland's hand resembled glass to the touch, and he made bold to cross from the forest directly into Charles Dowland's field.

The ground was frozen and the threat of the first snow was in the air. He held his middle son by his small hand, mollifying him after all the careful washing and dressing his mother had subjected him to. Instead of bringing his little bow the child insisted on the heavy telescope he had received from his great kinsman, Wakwa. Awepu walked slowly, knowing his son hid how badly the band supporting the instrument cut into his shoulder.

The morning was so dim there were candles glowing in the tall white house. Before the man and boy came close enough to be seen from inside, Awepu spotted the grayish mass of the ox on the northern rise and changed his direction.

He held his little son up to Dowland's rough caress.

"This is Tamoccon, my second son. His name means a flood, even as Awepu signifies a calm."

Charles sat the boy in front of himself on the ox. "Netop, it seems I watch that line of trees more these last weeks than in all the time since I was Tamoccon's age. What does Silent Fox want of me now?"

"You are still sad."

"No. I flirt with the idea of driving this ox right into the woods. To visit them. But I warrant none would find or nurse me if I fell off in the wild!"

"You do me injustice, Father." Awepu took the animal's halter, guiding him back down the hill. Tamoccon kicked the beast on the sides, but his little legs made no impression. Charles' arm stole around the stout figure in front of him. Awepu was pleased. "My cousin has no knowledge I am here. He will ask me to come before too many snows to arrange for him to speak to you again. I am here because of you."

Charles closed his eyes and let the Indian lead him toward the wood. He slipped and seized the boy for balance.

Awepu stopped the ox and growled something in his own language. He stood at the Englishman's side. "If you would come to live with us, we would make for you a more fitting pair of legs. I am thick in my head not to bring it to you today." He reached up and took Dowland off the ox, carrying him down the hill in his arms. Tamoccon slid down and ran ahead of them. "If you would take two of your horses and let me tie a certain basket between them, you could rest and swing free, as from a cloud. That strong boy who pushes your chair could ride one horse to guide you. Your cattle are stinking beasts. I would not trust my bones to a devil with eyes that red!"

"Come to live among you? Perhaps I should."

"Nux! Stay the winter with thy daughter."

"You had better get that boy into the house for something warm to drink. He will be cold." Charles came to himself.

Awepu paid no attention to him and entered the trees. They stopped in a small pine glade out of the wind and Awepu swaddled the older man in rabbitskin blankets.

With his head comfortably propped up, Dowland sadly watched Awepu muster a fire and received the little boy who came near him, chattering in his Massachuseuck dialect. The boy made him look through the telescope, but there was nothing to see in the overclouded sky.

"Are you ever confused, Awepu?"

"I know not the word."

"Are you ever filled with doubt about yourself? Are you happy that you are right in your thoughts?"

"I am that."

"Then this fine child should not be next to me. You are a better guide for him. I do not attend the church. I do not know what is right. I can make no sense out of the minister's words. I fall asleep over my own Holy Book."

"The boy is here to guide you, Father."

"Why doth everyone call me father but my own child?"

"Do you eat fish?" Awepu began to whittle some twigs clean.

"You are a magician as well as my friend, Awepu? You intend to roast me a meal on those sprits? My hospitality today is meager."

Awepu did not answer him. He gave his son a stick and the boy opened the top of the carrying basket, pierced a gutted fish, and held it over the flames.

"That basket is a fine thing." Charles noticed the design woven with different-colored fibers.

"My wife made it for you to keep. It will hold wet as well as dry."

"Excellent! You make me independent. Now I shall carry my own noonday meal when I stay out."

"Why do you go around your land when there is nothing growing in the frozen ground?" Awepu brought Charles his portion.

"I plan. I check. I write in my book what must be planted where in the springtime. I look for damage to the fences. Lately, I remember."

"Ah! That is good. What do you remember?"

"Boston . . . as a child. A traveling mime I was not allowed to stop and see." Charles re-explained. "That is a man who is a silent play maker. A man who makes you smile or cry without saying anything."

Awepu only smiled.

Charles rambled on. "I remember the day my son was born and the day my father was buried. I remember striking my daughter, before she was one year, for reaching continually into the hearth."

"And you can hear her weeping, still." Awepu wiped the stray pieces of fish from his son's mouth.

He carried Dowland back to the house where no one was home but Priscilla and Cooke. Charles sent the girl to the attic for something. She came back with a scarlet quilt worked in triangles over a pattern of cabbage roses.

"Tamoccon!" Charles called the boy away from the hall steps, which he had been silently ascending and descending in his moccasins. Dowland wrapped him in the half-folded blanket. "This was the borning quilt used for my Henry." Dowland gave his first smile in weeks to Awepu. "Netop!"

183

"Wetomp is the better word for friend, Father. Henry will be Tamoccon's English name from now!" Awepu patted Charles' hand and opened the door to leave.

A wet snow that would not stick came grayly down.

"Keep him warm, wetomp," Charles said in farewell. "Do come back. Tell your cousin yes, I will talk to him again. But soon."

Charles reached for the thick black book near his chair after the door had closed. It fell open to the New Testament and his eyes rested on the words:

"I have made you a light for the heathen, to be the means
of salvation to the ends of the earth!"

The lines in his face drew firm again and he became impatient for his wife's return.

Chapter 29

Late the same afternoon Wakwa worked his way up the steep river bank, barefoot in the season's first snow.

He was thinking about how to tell Kayaskwa of the new commission he had received from Waban. The errand for his uncle was a nuisance and possibly dangerous. Wakwa was disappointed that he could not take Elizabeth with him. But this was no lofty mission. Waban had asked for the return of his eldest, Wuttah Mauo, and the route lay through shaded portions of the city. Here the diplomatic test involved circling around rum-glutted adventurers, not perfumed politicians. The sachim thought Wuttah Mauo must be very low not to have straggled in for the hard winter season. If he were dead, his bones must be found, and if he lived, perhaps home would look good to him. Years ago the People had named fast-riding Wuttah Mauo their headman for war. But he had grown as useless as his title.

"Kayaskwa!" Wakwa called, but only her sachim-bird fluttered down from a snowy twig and rode inside on his shoulder.

Wakwa walked up to Awepu, who was stirring the meat in the kettle, and teased in their own language, "Don't burn my dinner, cook! Is my wife off at your traps?"

"I did not trap today." Awepu was not humorous.

Wakwa stored the moccasins he had taken such pains to keep dry. "Too bad for us both, with this snow. It will double the effort tomorrow."

He looked into the rear chamber and piled more wood on the fire there. "Awepu, where is Elizabeth?" Then he noticed her cloak missing from the place where she kept it hung. He went to Awepu and took the long wooden spoon away. "I have never heard Meadow-in-the-night exclaim over your talents as a housekeeper. Do you apprentice to the powwaw?"

"Tamoccon and I desired some society today."

"Where is Elizabeth?"

"My son and I shared some time at the edge of the forest with your English father-in-law. He improves."

"Poor wife! She knows!" Wakwa overturned a clothes basket, preparing to follow her, knowing instantly her need to see her father. He jammed his arms into the sleeves of his bear jacket, put on a cap, took his arrows and bow, and ladled some of the stew into a gourd.

"How long has she been gone from me?" he asked, knotting the thongs of his shoes.

"Her footprints will be not quite covered by the snow."

"Why now, Awepu! Could you not have waited? A little bit?"

Awepu blocked his friend's exit. "Her heart is more burdened as his days pass. Through me he is very close to changing. He even asks to speak to you! I met her on her way out for kindling. She divined by my face where I had been. Even such as I would not have told her."

Wakwa tracked her with the concentration of a starving man on the trail of a deer. Before long he spotted the point of her red hood marking her route through the trees.

She moved quickly along the unmarked ways she had begun to learn to read. She progressed through the unnatural stillness, unaffected by the darkness now well-established.

Wakwa saw her pulled toward her house like a wave responding to the moon and forced himself to stay out of view. She surprised him by not going into the open and across the field to her father's home.

She stayed within the trees where the thickening whiteness made a light of its own, struggling toward the northwest corner of the property with her basket and Awepu's club. She had come to see the place where her father had talked and eaten, to catch the sense of his words still lingering in the thicket. She came to touch the land that was her wellspring, wishing only to feel some closeness to the man who had generated her being.

But there was a light in her father's window, and she stopped. Snow fell straight down in the unmoving, almost balmy air. Wakwa saw his wife look from side to side, like a fugitive, then move out of the forest, across the snow, closer and closer to her house.

There was movement behind the light and she dropped the basket to wave. Her father's profile was visible as he turned, distracted from his work.

She stood deciding, wondering if she had been seen. She raised a hand again and kept it high, little flakes of snow collecting between her fingers.

"Papa!" she called into a sudden gust.

Inside the candle went out. For a long minute she did not stir. Then, disheartened when there was no response from the silver-haired man, she lowered her hand and ran back into the trees.

Wakwa's arms encircled her and drew her against his desperate heart. Silent as the snow they went home together.

* * * *

Charles saw little of the snowy landscape from his room. His high-backed chair faced away from the window to preserve him from the draught, and he was absorbed in his diary.

Writing was difficult, but he continued his nightly practice, hoping to keep the muscles in his fingers alive by use. But the struggle was ending and his quill slipped to the floor more times than he would admit to himself. He learned to keep two wells full of pens so Sam would not have to be bothered with frequent picking up.

Charles no longer wrote of pork prices and grain yields, but about the town governments, the Crown, and British incursions into American colonial privacy. Just that past spring Gil had been threatened by customs authorities on account of a shipment of German books stopped at Long Harbor for inspection.

Charles thought of Awepu and his gesture of friendship that morning. His own friends came less often since his illness and troubles had magnified, and the outlet of companionship was rare. He twisted around to see the place where he had lain and eaten with his strange comrade and his son. He tasted the fish again and felt it on his fingers.

Charles saw the trees hazily over the candle stand, falling snow interfering with his vision. His eyes strained toward a small variation in the dark line. A Capuchin figure with no face appeared to move across the snow. He lost sight of it in the shadow cast by the house. A gust of wind blew the top layer of snow and Charles thought he saw the dark robe rising above the swirl of white. He snuffed the candle and turned toward the form, but it was lost in the dark. He kept searching, then spied an upraised hand floating in midair. He turned away in shock. When he forced his sweating body around again the scene was bare.

For a long time he looked at the white emptiness. During the night, while Charles Dowland lay unmoving in his light sleep, the drifts built up, burying Elizabeth's little basket.

Chapter 30

Wakwa brought Pequawus to the hunting lodge to be a companion for Elizabeth while he would be gone. He rebuilt her wetuomemese and started for Boston about the twelfth of November, leaving Awepu with instructions to arrange a meeting with Dowland in precisely twelve days. Wakwa did not plan to spend his winter on the trail of his drunken cousin.

He was displeased that his run of fifty miles took a full day, but thoughts of his father's reaction to Elizabeth and of his errand disturbed his pace.

"She looks too thin and quiet to fill the lodge with grandchildren." Pequawus had commented in disappointment about his English daughter-in-law.

Wakwa made his way straight to Bunker Hill, enjoying the sight of the tall houses with their Grecian colonnades looking down on crowded Long Harbor. Through Dire Locke Wakwa had open invitations at the houses of several merchants and was spared the noise, dirt, and outrageous prices of city inns.

This evening he went to Esau Crosswhite's, a friend of the king's tax collector. An assortment of artists, relatives, and chronic travelers always filled Crosswhite's table with interest, but Wakwa avoided old friends and ate in his room. He had come alone not only to contain the distasteful story of his cousin, but also to lessen the chances of his own identification, which might spoil more legitimate future missions.

In the morning he painted his face somber black, changed into rough skins and a threadbare blanket which concealed a screw-barrel pistol, borrowed from Awepu, and his own obsidian knife. A fur hat drooped over his braided hair, and Wakwa forced back a bitter laugh at his disguise as he examined the effect in the wall of mirrors. He felt the places he was going did not deserve to know it was himself. He left the velvet drapes and spindle-legged chairs behind and moved quietly down the stairs.

"Holy Jesus!" One of the permanent guests, on his way up, backed down again. "Silent Fox?"

"Not today, wetomp!" Wakwa shook the man's hand and hurried on.

He went directly to the wharves, stepping over horse manure and avoiding the pigs and geese which ferreted in piles of rotten vegetables. Markets and public houses on bricked streets gave place to gloomy drinking rooms on narrower lanes. Sailors and women milled about, not noticing the tall Indian, no more exotic than themselves.

Wakwa's dismal search took him from filthy hole to filthy hole.

"Know you a man named King Willie?" Wuttah Mauo's city name began to stick in his throat as Wakwa asked the question and moved on, asked and moved on again.

He was hungry, but the pervasive stink of gin disgusted and depressed him and he held off eating. Finally he succumbed to the sloppy fare put in front of him at a quiet tavern.

It was the first time he had touched this side of English life. He felt he was approaching his task incorrectly. The etiquette of the docks could not be the same as for the governor's mansion.

As he paid, in coin, an idea struck him. Wakwa ordered a drink and spilled the glass of gin when it was brought. He wet his hands and mouth and tongue until he could smell the liquor on himself. Then he asked for a room.

"You're in the wrong street for that, copperskin. Patty's Feather'll take you."

"How much worse than this place can it be?" Bitterly, Wakwa paid again.

Patty's Feather obviously took anybody. The alley leaked its dregs directly into the downstairs drinking room. A long, heavy table separated endless rows of bottles and kegs from the patrons.

Coming in from the morning light, Wakwa was blinded by darkness and deafened by noise. What there was to celebrate this early in the day he could not guess, but women and men seemed transported in marvelous private joking. Sailors of motley origin, molded tough and strong, waited out port schedules, lost in a haze of ale and cheap tobacco.

A plump orange-haired girl came to Wakwa's end of the table to serve him.

Wakwa had never seen a face like hers, covered with little

brown freckles, which he likened to a fawn's. "I wish a bottle of the best you have. Pour for all at the table."

"Well! Welcome to the docks, big fella! Can ye pay for 't?"

Wakwa placed some sterling on the table.

"Here's a fresh one, Sid!" the girl yelled to an older man behind the bar. "Ye can still smell the smoke on 'im!" She poured drinks all down the appreciative line and neared Wakwa with a half-empty bottle and a metal cup. "Ye cum back, Smokey, d'ye hear me?" She blew him a kiss.

Not much older than Elizabeth, the girl's low-cut gown showed her full breasts. The skin of her bosom was transparently white. She placed the coins she owed Wakwa in his hand.

Wakwa chose her for an informant in place of the man she called Sid. "Does an Indian named King Willie stop here?" he asked.

The girl seized his hand with the money still in it and held it against her breasts. "What? Are ye cumin' ta visit? He's entertainin' his nobility just now. Why don't ye get a room?"

Wakwa tried to pull his hand away gently, but the girl pressed it tightly to herself.

"Patty, get goin' down there!" came the innkeeper's voice. "Tell the son of a bitch he's got to pay for it or get the hell out!"

Wakwa looked into her eyes, so green and round, red circling them. He thought she must be an orphan. He opened his hand flat against her chest and the coins stuck to her moist skin.

"Where is he, Patty? What room?" Wakwa said softly, out of pity.

"What's your hurry? I'll show ye." She came back hard.

Wakwa wrenched his hand away and made for the steps at the rear of the room, mounting them four at a time. Patty ran after him, gathering the money as she went.

Sid shouted, "Get that pig outa here, I ain't seen no money from 'im!"

Laughter spread through the large room when the daughter threw the silver at her father from the stairs.

Wakwa was opening doors on both sides of the long hall. Patty squeezed in front of him.

"This one!" She opened the door to a dingy room with an uncovered mattress, stuffed with old straw, on the floor.

Wakwa peered into the half-darkness, keeping his free hand

on the door. Patty took the brandy bottle and put it in a corner.

"Shut the door, Smokey."

"I will not. King Willie is not in this room."

"No. But you are, and I am. Shut it, or I'll scream bloody murder! I want you for a while, Indian."

Wakwa slipped out into the hall and the girl let out a howl. Then another one. Sid came thundering up the stairs with a horsewhip in his hand, but Patty peeked out from the doorway.

"It's all right, Pa."

Wakwa stepped back into the room and Patty locked the door behind him, panting at her little victory.

"Cum 'ere, Smokey, I'll tell you where he is. After a while."

Wakwa came. His painted face was tense as he tried to think of a way to pry the information from her or get himself out of the room without further commotion. The pity he had felt dissipated in disgust. Even his indifference to his cousin was turning into anger.

"I will pay you more. Tell me where he is. I would not have any more noise."

"Would you not?" she mimicked. Then her voice went very deep. "Take some time. I said I'd tell ye."

"I have no need for this," Wakwa refused her.

"Well, I do!" Patty touched his body through his clothes, from thighs to crotch, back to chest. "My, but you're big!"

Wakwa trembled in chagrin and growled, "Nanwunood-squaosue mittamwossis."

Her eyes kindled at his voice and she squirmed against him. "Now there's a wild word! What's it mean?"

He bent to her and put his lips against her fleshy neck and answered, "Whorish woman!" He held the bodice of her dress in both hands and tore it apart.

"Christ almighty! I'd a took it off! Nobody does that!" She was angry and pulled back.

Wakwa did not let her get away. He wrapped her in his arms, seeking to gain control over her, not daring to hurt her. He pressed his mouth against her sweating bosom and wound the torn fabric up short, around his hands.

"Oh! That's better. You're a wild one, after all. All alike except for this." She clamped her hand between his legs.

192

Wakwa gave a final pull and had two long bands of cloth in his hands.

"Now cum fast!" She wriggled down against his legs onto the foul mattress.

Wakwa sprawled across her body and tore the knife from his belt. She gasped and he pressed his right forearm against her open mouth to silence her and took one of her heavy breasts into his left hand.

"Ply your trade less one of these."

"Bastard!" She thrashed her head and spoke.

"Take me to him!" Wakwa released her mouth slightly.

"Couldn't ye have cum first?" she choked.

Wakwa pressed down again, stretching the skin at the corners of her mouth. The girl tore and struggled. Wakwa let her talk.

"An odd one eh?" she had the boldness to say. "Why don't ye just enjoy yourself? I promise . . . no stink about this. Pa'd kill ye." She gave him an agonized look. "Oh! You're handsome . . . cum!"

Her word *handsome* gave birth to a picture in Wakwa's mind of the clean glade where he had talked to Kayaskwa about his dreams for his people. Incredulous at Patty's toughness, he pressed the cold, heavy stone blade against the nipple of her right breast and watched fear spread through her eyes.

"Tell me," Wakwa bluffed.

But the girl ran her hands up and down his straining back, ignoring pain, in pleasure.

"Woman. Say, say," Wakwa begged, releasing her mouth.

But Patty pushed her head up and held his lip between her teeth in passion.

The man pinched the knife against her, seeking to disengage himself, overcome her, and find Wuttah Mauo himself.

Her bite of desire changed to a kiss against a mouth withheld from her intensity. This, not the knife, caused her flush of shame and frustration.

"Two doors down, ye bloody savage! Ye stupid Indian! I'd a told ye. It might 'a been somethin'!" She gave in.

Wakwa stuffed one of the strips into her mouth and tied her wrists behind her. He grabbed the bottle and tried to turn the immovable door handle. In a moment he was back upon her where she lay curled, attempting to rub her sore breast against her knee. He ripped at her clothes for the key but gave up and put his shoulder to the thin panel.

There were footfalls on the steep stairs as Wakwa disappeared behind King Willie's door.

His cousin was lying on a broken bed, dressed in dirty clothes of English cut.

"Rise, Wuttah Mauo. I bring you to your father." Wakwa spoke in their own language.

The man called King Willie sat up painfully, not recognizing his visitor. But when he spied the expensive brandy, so different from the rotgut he was used to, he returned in their dialect, "Come. Share my room, brother!"

Wakwa flipped the bottle, streaming liquor, across the floor. "It is I, Wakwa. I have no time. Will you come decently or shall I overpower you—King Willie!"

Willie crawled back against the wall, confused and afraid, spitting his resentment in abusive language. "I thought you were sachim by now!"

"Thy father loves thee, Weeping Heart. Lift thyself up!" Wakwa saw how aged and grayed by dirt and sickness his cousin had become.

Wuttah Mauo remained inert. Wakwa strode over and pulled him up by a wasted shoulder when angry voices came outside the door.

"Let us go. I am in trouble over you!" Wakwa pushed King Willie in front of himself and opened the door onto Sid's cocked pistol.

"What's goin' on with me girl?" Backed by a dozen sailors, Sid aimed his gun at Wakwa's face.

Very slowly, without moving his eyes from the innkeeper's, Wakwa pulled two pieces of Spanish gold from his pouch. "All goes well with her."

Sid forgot his pistol and studied the money. Wakwa pushed by him through the crowd in the hallway, keeping his cousin in front.

"I didn't say nothin'!" Patty called as he moved past her door toward the steps.

Sid followed, booming, "Say now, Chief, ye cum back! You're always welcome. Pat's a good one for ye."

Wakwa glared at the father and smashed the bottle against the wall at his right. King Willie and the room full of customers below watched helplessly as the costly stuff slid down the wood. The two Indians went out into the open air.

* * * *

Wakwa spent the next days shepherding the sachim's degraded son through the out towns and woods. Ill and unused to exercise, Wuttah Mauo slowed them down, and it was not until the eleventh day that Wakwa deposited the fallen son at Waban's door.

The nephew unwillingly received a wide money belt as an offering of thanks. Waban pronounced a season of rest and plenty over him, vowing his personal assistance in obtaining Charles Dowland's consent to the solemnization of Wakwa's second marriage.

Wakwa took no part in the ceremony of purification for Weeping Heart, but went alone to pesuponk and an icy swim.

The sachim and Pequawus came to his house after several hours to discuss Wakwa's taking more responsibility in the governorship of the tribe. Tame Deer listened and rubbed Wakwa down, cleaned his hair, and brought him a new pair of moccasins, since he had burned the ones with the dirt of the wharf on them.

He dressed in fine leggings and plain arm bands of copper, the costume he liked best. They all ate and considered plans for their meeting with Dowland the following day. And the arrangements for Wakwa's election to the status of sachim by the elder men and women of the otan were pushed through over Wakwa's reluctance. For the second time that year, Wakwa did obeisance to the sachim, stroking his shoulders and saying the words.

Wakwa wished recovery to an unresponsive Wuttah Mauo and started north, along the wet riverbank slippery from melted snow.

The man turned his high collar of gray fox up against a building wind that stung like his skirmish with the girl. He walked across the bridge to his second wife, astounded at the beauty of the sun as it dropped behind him in the west.

Chapter 31

The drifts of the first snow, perpetuated by cold, formed the landscape for several weeks. But the freeze broke, and by the sunny Sunday when Silent Fox returned with Wuttah Mauo, the ground had turned to mud.

Smoothing the way for the next day's meeting between Elizabeth's and Wakwa's families, Awepu, Tamoccon, and Hanna passed the afternoon pleasantly in the Worths' bright sitting room. Dowland's concerned sister enthusiastically cut bands of flannel with the boy as Awepu described the benefits to sore joints that could be gained from wrapping the cloth around applications of the wintergreen oil he had brought along for Charles. Gil was gone again, escorting his brother-in-law to church for the first time in a month. Since early morning Mary had been in their pew, expecting her husband later, since Charles had to negotiate the tortuous walk on the ox in slippery footing.

Knowing Charles' condition had deteriorated in past weeks, Gil contemplated the tragedy of the end of the Dowland line. He wondered what a little of Wakwa's dandelion soup might have done for Henry's and all their troubles. But the sucking sounds his slender boots made as they sank into the mud deceived him into enjoyment of the spring-like day.

Hudson did not hear their silent procession across his cart road nor mark their arrival for the afternoon service, since he remained inside for the break.

Many friends milled around the pair, glad to see Dowland out from under his misfortunes. These neighbors decided their foremost Elder could not withstand a long service sitting in the hard pews. While they devised a more comfortable arrangement, Mary bundled Charles' woolly collar about his ears and threw her own lap rug over him.

When Hudson reappeared at the altar he was confronted by the unorthodox sight of the large west doors wide open, a fire burning in his iron barrow, Charles Dowland on the ox, and

Gilbert Worth beside him, close behind the flames. Cannily, the minister turned his notes back several weeks to a sermon he had been impatiently waiting to deliver. Hudson stepped onto his platform, above Mary in the first pew.

> " 'I was glad when they said to me,
> Let us go to the house of the Lord.
> Our feet are standing within your gates
> Oh Jerusalem!'

"Welcome back, brethren!" He nodded to the two figures outside, wavering in the heated air. "There are several threads we may pull from the sides of this morning's talk, in order to align its fabric for perfect fitting to the needs of this village."

Prue Hanson, sitting between her parents on the mahogany chairs, too new in the parish to use a pew, toyed with the black silk ribbons of Hudson's hat she had coyly asked to hold.

"Recall our discussion of public uprightness." Hudson felt at home with this audience. "What we see in the large cities is no example for us here. It is always greed within men of power that spoils the flower of any good effort.

"All denominations vie for favors with the officers of the king. What a wretched example for our young men and women, just suiting themselves up in moral armor for life. Yea, even Presbyterians bathed in luxuries and seeking more, weakening in their basic resistance to the awful power of earthly thrones. Did we come to this land to resurrect the hideous favoritism of monarchies or Christ?

"Why do we till the fields? To make the land yield booty for the King or bounty for God's people? There is the crux! We must look not to the rich and storied for leadership, but here, among ourselves. It is not to kings but to the Christ, the alpha and omega of creation, that we owe fealty!"

"He's been digging at his Greek." Gil winked at Charles.

But Dowland, remembering Annanias excited over Esdras in the Greek Bible of the early Christians, motioned Gil to hold off judgment. "My own thoughts turn toward rebellion," he whispered.

Hudson warmed to his topic. "What does it matter the sign on the door? Rename our church. Rename the place we live

'Christown'! Let people look from what was Sweetwood and its Presbyters to a new citadel unconfused by vanity, dedicated to purity of purpose, wrestling this sweet earth for the works of the Lord!"

Gil watched a little boy slyly pull a long thread, unraveling the hem of the girl in front of him, and he regretted he had not brought a book along for himself. His attention, however, was immediately reclaimed.

"I stand before you alone." Hudson's voice broke in studied pathos. "Most of you here, leaders of your lives, your farms, this town, and so the life of a good part of this colony, have by your sides women, the salt of the earth, banks on which you lean in moments of doubt.

"I who lead all of you have no such support, left alone by a masterstroke of God or of the Devil. Make no mistake, he is here among us. Here now! Every day you can feel the stench of his work grow heavier. I stand before you with half the armor that other men own, and thus must I pour with the greater fervor all my soul into your service."

Prue began to knot the ribbons. Mary sat staunch as a pillar, every member of the congregation waiting for her to break. Charles and Gil started to chafe.

Hudson blinked, departing from his text, mixing his bid for public responsibility with his need for sympathy. "I have been robbed by a mysterious hand at the threshold of my married life! Was my betrothed, the most careful and graceful daughter of this hamlet, schooled in right by the Elect of this church, dissolved in the rain like sugar, a sham of the rock she was?"

Prue crushed the hat against her stomach.

Hudson pointed toward the open doors with a level finger. "If you wish to see one of the barbs which may have tripped her step from the straight and narrow path, turn 'round!"

The pious people gasped at the slur and the apparition of Gilbert Worth. Red in the face from the fire and anger, he retained the nonchalance of his stance at heavy cost to his true feelings, balancing his riding crop between gloved hands. His rich attire, the yellow moustache above his curling lip, the frightening reach of his green-eyed glare, lent credence to Hudson's condemnation.

"I see no reason to cover the fact! Do you see a former member intruding in our midst?" Hudson was transfigured into prosecutor. "I have dared observe from the safe retreat behind my cloth how he doth play the Sophist! With what carnal joys of decoration, music, games, and company he does surround himself, like an Eastern potentate!

"Ask him what time he doth rise and sleep. Where is his wife today?"

Faint rumbles of objection dotted the church.

"To his house did my beloved repair each day about this time. With earthly splendor all about, why should she lift her burden? Confused she was by his influence, and confounded am I by its effect!"

Still, Worth kept silence behind the crackling fire, waiting Hudson's true thrust. But Annanias goaded this gentility with innuendo.

"Hold onto your daughters and do not let them wander near his land to gather the natural sweets of the forest. For so his own niece did and has not been seen nigh on two months!"

Gil kicked the wheelbarrow in spite and frustration, refusing to defend himself against such lowness. Women screamed as it lurched, threatening to spill the fire into the church, but it righted itself. Charles Dowland's hand was seen to rest on Gil's trembling shoulder.

"There he stands," the minister resumed in an apparently reasonable tone, sure of his listeners, "the personification of the deepest threat to your independence. I do not hesitate to say he imitates the throne in his leanings as well as his living. Mark if it is true, in future years, when the governor grabs you out of your door for this or that, Gilbert Worth will be secure." His voice began to build.

"Refer you to Ephesians, chapter six, verse twelve!

> 'For we have to struggle not with the enemies of flesh
>   and blood,
> But with the hierarchies, the authorities,
> The masterspirits of this dark world,
> The spirit forces of evil on high.'"

"Impudence!" An old man, broad of body and thick of bone, shot out of his seat. His blue eyes burned and he pulled at his white hair, gathering the momentum to match his words to the speed of his reaction. "As long as you're makin' yourself into king, priest, and prophet for today, why stop at judgin'? Why don't ye go an' damn the man? Better yet, let's hang 'im, quick, before he pollutes us all! You know well, you're chewin' on a man with more charity in 'im than all your holy people here you've got all agog.

"For you who dunno' know me, I'm Doctor J. Macmillan Stirling, original of Edinburough, an' I stop here all the way from Sandwich, faithful to the minute every month. . . ."

"Welcome, sir, into our community of saints." Hudson tensed himself like a bulldog ready to squelch a fight. "But this is not a court nor public square. It is a church and you are out of line."

"I am out o' line? What o' yourself? When I came here from Glouchester, to flee the wind and cold after thirty years as a physician, who was it smoothed my way? You? With all your armor and divils? No! It were Gilbert Worth I were told to go and see.

"Never havin' been a farmer, I wasn't used to puttin' out my money to see it comin' in. 'Twas Worth saw my need and holds the deed to my land, so I dunno' stretch meself too far.

"Mind, I am not poor that he be obliged to help, but I need a few solid winters before I'm on my own. Every month I come and pay a bit of what I owe, an' when he reaches out his hand it's never empty, but there's a cup o' ale, a game o' chess, some talk that makes some sense, like ye would to a friend!

"You're chewin' on a man who exposes his anatomy where it hurts the most, in the givin' part, the heart an' the pocket." Looking all around, catching glances that fell before his bright gaze, Stirling said, "It is a fact that half the people here have touched him before they would see their own father for some help, for they knew Mr. Worth would no' hold it o'er 'em but forget it ever was."

"You do but prove my point." Hudson was totally self-assured. "It is the powerful who buy our consciences from us. Undeserved rewards win ungrounded loyalty."

"You are incorrigible!" The doctor's burr magnified his exasperation. "I shall let ye have it!

"While you and all your fancy Hudson folk were wearin' out your Testaments in the fertile fields of Boston, my own father was a minister . . . a better one than you . . . and called himself a Presbyterian without all your reluctance! An' he spoke right out in London with no ocean in between for his protection.

"While all your ilk an' you were fattenin' yourselves on turkeys, he was scroungin' in the furze and hidin' in the heather, dodgin' the wrath of the throne that was protectin' you over here, for the flow of goods ye so disdain.

"Master spirits of this dark world, indeed! I think it's you, not the maids, who're afraid to show your face near Gilbert Worth's place."

The doctor's wife, coughing all the while, pulled at his coat, urging him to sit.

"Thank you . . . physician." Hudson licked his wounds with sarcasm, looking toward the sick woman. "We welcome discontented aliens among us. It is the trademark of the Bay. Since your doctoring, I take it, is to humans and not to cattle, and your religion orthodox, I will give you the benefit of a secret. There are other strangers who surround Worth's farm that a man with your credentials should do his best to avoid. I speak of Indians. Oh! You did not know?

"We harbor on our borders a pack of heathen savages preparing even now for their winter romps! Come on the birthday of the Prince of Light, our Lord, Jesus, and you will smell their fires and their cooking meat if the wind is blowing right! Like the Turkish Christians they march about in delirious celebration of their witching gods. Songs, wild dancing, induced faints, and sweatings form their revelry.

"Ever improvident, they go on for days in a building up of mood that would last any Christian man a life! Still, they renew their accursed rumblings spring, summer, and autumn, too!

"I will not violate this church with the details of what they do and what they fail to do. I will warn you against any softness to them who never stop bleating over land that was bought from them with legal tender and which they enjoy with too much freedom, as it is.

"Speaking of undeserved rewards, Dr. Stirling, I do not approach Indians with the word of God! They are recalcitrant and resentful of past mistakes made by unpeaceful men of a century ago. Thus I can refute, 'Go teach ye all nations,' in Ephesians five, eleven.

" 'Have nothing to do with the profitless doings of the
   darkness.
Expose them instead.
For while it is degrading to even mention their secret
   practices,
Yet when anything is exposed by the light it is made
   visible,
And anything that is made visible is light.' "

Mary Dowland broke down and no one in the church knew
why. Gil bit his own hand in sympathy for her as she wept
miserably, alone in the pew. While the people buzzed about her
expression of sympathy for the spiritual condition of the Indians, when she had been so staunch during the recitation of her
daughter's disappearance and the attack on her brother-in-law,
Charles leaned halfway off the ox, restraining Gil from entering
the church, fearing he would tangle with Annanias. Prue Hanson's mother tapped her and the girl walked swiftly up and sat
beside the mother of her rival.

Hudson skewered Charles with a look and yelled, "As the
Egyptian alliance was denounced by Isaiah, beware these in-
gratiating neighbors. Or,

   'This shall turn to your shame. . . .
   All shall come to shame through a people that cannot
      benefit them,
   That bring no help or benefit,
   But only shame and disgrace. . . .' "

"Annanias, stop!" Mary stood, in tears, and begged for his
pity.

He looked at her, the woman he regarded as his mother defeated by his words, and he regained some composure.

But the slap of leather on flesh caused the congregation to
turn back to the wide open doors onto the picture of the last of
the Dowlands urging his ox away from the church, smoke from
the embers of the dead fire curling to the ground.

✳ ✳ ✳

Gil Worth pulled on the halter, selecting as smooth a course
as he could find, the muddy ground freezing fast into hard ruts.
The men kept silence as they left the lowland, walking against
a bitter wind reinstating winter weather.

They reached the high ground of Charles' farm under an uncertain sun. Charles turned his head to look at the cold Atlantic.

"I will hate to leave this place."

"Will you go away?" Gil asked.

"Of course, and so will you, in time."

"Brother Charles, that does not show your customary fight. You have much ahead of you before you skip out and leave me and your family floundering without your guidance."

"When is the meeting, Gil?"

"Why, Charles, I have repeated that to you several times. It is tomorrow. Awepu stays with us tonight."

"My mind slides. I cannot hold any thoughts except recriminations toward myself. How was I so enthralled with that madman? You do think him mad as well?"

"Imagine his sin if he is only mean!" Gil enjoyed that prospect for a moment. "He would make his mark in politics and be a potentate like me!"

"Poor brother Gil. I shall withhold my share of his stipend for what he said of you. I fear he has made his mark, Gilbert."

"But he is only the minister of Sweetwood!"

Charles raised an eyebrow to his brother-in-law, making his point, but then his face changed and his eyes filled with tears. "I want to touch her before I die. Doth that make sense?"

"Touching her, yes. Dying, no."

"It is my secret hope that Silent Fox spring her on me, in surprise."

Gil made a mental note. "Still so afraid of compromise, even after hearing that gutful of misread chapter and verse?"

Charles withstood his persuasion. "Interesting. You have quite a friend in Stirling."

"That I do! I think he even plays. I could use a violin for some Italian music I have gotten hold of."

"Do you think, as Hudson said, Beth was distracted by frivolity?"

"The life she lives is hardly frivolous!" Gil could not hide his annoyance at the implications of Charles' clinging to Hudson's view.

Gusts of cold brought a haze to the sky, and the ox, so sure and wide of stance, lost its footing on the frozen mud. Charles hung on and refused to turn off toward the barn.

"Take me to the trees, Gilbert. Since my lunch with Awepu, I often go there to help me think."

The ox's breath stretched out in front of its muzzle in a bolt of hot vapor, and the temperature dropped more.

"What do you think of the Indians, Charles, now you have had some time?"

Dowland lowered his head. "I have been wondering of late how we must seem to them. I would certainly rather roast fish with Awepu than have my stomach turned in the church."

"Then rejoice! Announce it from the common! See Beth! They are a handsome pair."

Charles turned toward the thicket which gave him such consolation. "What is that thing?"

Gil left the ox's head to investigate a dark shape resting in the mud where several days ago there had been snow.

"Just a basket!" Gil called from fifty yards away.

The ox responded viciously to the sudden thrashing Charles administered to its quarters. It lurched forward in a lumbering run, bearing down on Gil. Charles sank his fingers into the ox's fleshy neck, vainly trying to deflect its course. The man moaned with the effort of staying on.

Gil felt stupid to have left his brother-in-law and came running toward the face of the animal. "Merde! Merde!" He cursed his inadequacy as he slipped on the marshy earth, now hard in spots.

Charles screamed in pain and gave up his hold, slipping off the ox onto the hardening ground with a cracking thud.

Gil jumped out of the animal's path and half ran, half crawled to Charles' side, unconsciously dragging the basket with him. "Christ almighty! Sacre bleu!"

Charles smiled at the odd coupling of these expressions as he lay stifled for breath.

The ox was grazing off pine cones in the thicket by the time Gil came up to Charles.

Dowland tried to move his upper body toward his brother-in-law's reaching hands, but he snapped back with the pain of a broken rib.

Gil's voice thundered for Sam. He knelt, unbuttoning clothes in the chill wind, trying to examine Charles. When he found the blue mark where the rib had broken inward, he was sickened. They looked at each other, wondering why Charles' breathing came so hard.

Gil's beautiful kersey coat made Charles' pillow. Crouched on the frozen mud, Gilbert Worth framed his first prayer in years.

Sam galloped to the church and a farm hand rode away to tell Hanna.

The breaths came slowly to Charles Dowland, looking at the basket and thinking. Close to the earth he heard an approaching horse. He breathed.

Awepu slid from Gil's unsaddled bay in stride and hovered over Charles.

"Nosh! My Father!"

Charles exhaled, answering with an unrestrained smile.

But Awepu's lips were taut with regret. "This is my fault for being not careful with you."

Tamoccon lay down in the crook of Charles' arm and Charles breathed.

Mary was helped from the horse she and Sam had shared and was surprised to find Awepu at her husband's side. She stood apart where her husband could see her.

Stirling and the Sweetwood doctor clattered up in a cart and Tamoccon ran to Hanna as she came. Awepu backed away.

The doctors slowly felt the bruise and listened to the man's faulty breathing under the rising wind.

Suddenly the ground shook with the impact of a ton of falling weight as Charles' ox succumbed to the iron-tipped arrow of Awepu.

Astounded by this swift judgment, the doctors stepped back to whisper to the family.

"His condition is poor," the village doctor spoke.

"Be plain, sir!" The visiting Stirling dominated him explaining with merciful candor. "A rib has broken inward. One lung is punctured, sure. He can breathe on the other one . . . a while."

"An hour, I would say!" The affronted physician wiped dirt from his hands.

"A while yet he's got, dear." Stirling held Mary around her

shoulders. "But he canno' go on one lung forever, do ye see?"

"Can I take him home?" Mary saw.

"Somethin' happens, dear, inside, if we move him. The air," Stirling held Mary's hand in both his own and brought it to his throat, "stops here." Stirling looked at Gil.

Awepu knelt near Charles again, on the forest side.

"The men of medicine are with you! Take heart, friend! I will build a little hut around you to keep you warm, and we will wait for your sure breath together, like two snow rabbits, nux?"

Charles managed to wobble his head in the negative.

"Gather all your courage! You are to meet the father of Wakwa tomorrow. It will be a day of beauty."

His face marbled with purple, Charles choked out, "My own father I will see."

"Matta! No! You will not die!"

The doctors and Mary tried to force Awepu out of the way, but Charles' bony fingers closed on Awepu's long braids.

"Last but one hour under the shelter I will build!" Awepu shielded Dowland's head with his hands. "You cannot go to your fathers in the southwest before you see Elizabeth!"

Charles' eyes roamed to the basket, ice forming like silver berries on the thin branches stuck inside.

Awepu pushed its handle into Charles' grip, taking away the braids. "Then you are ready, for indeed she came to you."

Almost easily, Charles breathed in. "Lost. Lost . . . to God . . . am I." The words escaped with his air.

"Never be lonely, wetomp! There is your direction." Awepu pointed over the corner of the house toward a pale yellow sun on its way to setting.

"Kautantowwit, to whose house all good souls go, opens his arms!" With big tears dripping onto his thin cheeks Awepu lifted the man and pointed his face toward the sun.

"Go then southwest, to your Henry. I will join you there with my own."

The basket fell away with Charles Dowland's cares.

Chapter 32

Elizabeth heard Wakwa call from the bridge, and she came clean and straight to the precipice, awed by the ball of the sun blanching into a lavender sky.

She waved him up to her. "I had given you up for tonight. I was tempted to trundle along tomorrow with your father in your stead."

"Neesintuh! Lie thou with me!" Wakwa translated his yearning.

Elizabeth drew his fur-framed face down to hers. "Neesintuh," she whispered, responding to the hurt she saw.

He followed her into the lodge, closing its new door behind them. The floor was littered with her cutting board, embroidery hoop, and all the makings of his new coat.

"You will blind yourself doing this work!"

"Let me show you what it will be. Lay that out flat. This is the inside." She walked around, flattening the cut pieces of the lining. It was on an ample scale to fit Wakwa's dimensions. "Of course when you wear it, no one will be able to see the embroidery."

"Of course." Wakwa came close and kissed her neck.

"But it will keep you warmer, knowing each little thread is so privately beautiful against your back."

She knelt in the middle of the heavy fabric. "I am starting from the middle, and all these little laurel leaves I have drawn with chalk to guide my stitching will be an overlay, and, alas, must hide some of the embroidery underneath."

Wakwa was taking the pins from her hair.

"Starting at the shoulders are the ears, and further down the head, and at the center the curious nose. Across the hem all the claws of a . . . wakwa, the black fox!"

Wakwa fought against captivation in the mystic game she was playing with her needles.

"It will be done so that close up it is only pretty stitches. Even under close examination, should some stranger be taking a look at the inside of your coat, I cannot imagine why, they would see only little leaves and undecided lines.

"Please do step back! Stand there. Imagine from a distance the huge face of the secret fox, glowering from behind the laurel, as big as the coat itself! Naturally some of it will be lost when the coat is stitched together, but the total effect . . ."

Elizabeth sensed Wakwa's introspection, even though his eyes traced the pattern she was describing with her hands. She lay down in the center of her work and extended her arms. He came, removed only her doeskin trousers, and admitted himself immediately into her person.

Wakwa covered his young wife with a bearskin robe, but he could not sleep. He had left his degradation with Patty behind, but looked ahead to his second interview with his father-in-law. With his small pipe between his teeth he laid out his things for the morning. He added a second string of wampum to the velvet bag of shells.

This long loop, bought from a Passamaquoddy, contained five sections of beads separated from one another by red, pink, and blue ribbons. Even though his common-law marriage was fact, Wakwa saw some value in impressing Elizabeth's relatives with the marriage ritual among Ninnuock.

Awepu would re-offer the Williamsburg shells to Mrs. Dowland. Then he would give the formal speech with the loop from the northern tribe. As he spoke the words, Awepu would touch each section of the beads; the first for the proposal, the second for Wakwa's wish to have Elizabeth until death, the third for the willingness of all the relatives to approve the marriage, the fourth for the dreaded refusal, and the fifth for the celebration if all were agreed.

Wakwa fingered the pink ribbon, color of happiness, passed over the dark blue, meant for gloom, reminding him of Mary Dowland's dress at their first meeting, kissed the red, color of good, matching Kayaskwa's warm cloak.

He put out his pipe and forced himself to lie down on his bare mat. Cold, he crept in beside Elizabeth. He touched her delicate contours as she slept and, finally, dozed and dreamt.

In his dream he saw himself seated on a red horse, bringing Elizabeth to her father to show him the serenity she had achieved. Dowland was waiting, standing freely at his back door. The horse did not stop its circling of the field and cantered just out of Dowland's reach, dipping away into the arc of each new circle. The horse called "Wakwa Manunnappu!" repeatedly, but Wakwa's mouth was filled with its blowing mane and Wakwa could not shout the order to make the beast obey.

Silent Fox awoke to chill and silence, brushing Elizabeth's hair from his face. In his state between sleep and full awareness he formed the idea of bringing her with him to the next day's meeting. It was not traditional, but neither was their marriage.

Then he heard the hooves of a horse and his name shouted in the night. The dream came back to him with force. The terrible significance of the red horse in the Bible swept over him and he sustained the sensation of falling. But he reached for his blanket and went out to meet Awepu under the stars.

Awepu told his news in a few sad sentences. Wakwa stepped quietly back into the house and lifted Elizabeth, awakening her.

"Kayaskwa . . . Kayaskwa . . . mauo . . . mauo . . . Kayaskwa!"

Sleepily she wrapped her arms about his neck. "Why should I weep, my love?"

The husband carried her into the cold and lifted her onto the bay stallion's back. She sat, wrapped head to foot in the huge robe, in front of Awepu, listening to the story of her father's death, Wakwa's face against her knees.

Chapter 33

At the sachim's direction, the news traveled fast. Awepu reached the Cape Cod Indians, who lived near Dowland's seaside property. Others walked north and south along the River to tell different bands and tribes about the death of the man who had always dealt with them fairly.

On the third day after Hudson's vicious sermon against them, beautifully robed delegations, from the Cape to the Great Ponds, crowded into Sweetwood, waiting in silence on the lawns outside the church.

When Gilbert Worth seated Waban, his wife, their second son, Awepu and his family, and Wakwa's father with the Dowlands in Charles' long polished pew, Annanias Hudson did not disguise his displeasure.

"This is my church, not your notorious parlor. How can I speak with this rabble before me? Dispatch them to a more becoming place, in the gallery with the blacks!"

Gil was glossy with self-assurance. "I have never observed you at a loss for words, Reverend. If you insist on removing the Massachuseuck delegation from the front, I shall remove Charles Dowland's body from your pale and bury him with my own hands in his own meadow. Think you, another lost soul!"

The oration went forward, but the established farmers who had assembled from all over the Bay pondered other things. The story of Dowland's last day, Gil's and Awepu's role in his death, the sight of Mosq heading Waban's armed guards at the edges of the room, would yield them conversation to fill the rest of their long winter.

While Annanias navigated through his classical ode about the Dowlands' predetermined election to the beatific vision, the Indian representatives seated throughout the church considered the conspicuous absence of their spokesman, Wakwa.

Charles' coffin was lowered deep into the dirt between the graves of his father and his son. The Christian families began to leave the site for refreshment at the Dowland house or their own kitchens.

210

Only then did Tamoccon, dressed gorgeously in furs, brave their scandalized looks to walk to the edge of the grave with a burning torch. Awepu, his face delicately etched with black symbols of mourning, spread the mannotaubana his wife had painted for their wedding on the freshly dug earth. He held Elizabeth's gathering basket to Tamoccon's torch and tossed it onto the pyre.

Not one English person dared move away from the last rite of their most exalted member until Awepu's offerings were smoke and ashes.

Chapter 34

For two days after her father's death, Elizabeth Dowland went slowly about her tasks. Wakwa stayed near, protectively, preparing his equipment for the winter hunt. He watched her withstand the pressure of her exile, when for a walk of a few miles she could have offered solace to her family. Knowing she suffered this loneliness for his sake, he overlooked her indifference toward himself. He had begun to sense her shifts of mood, recognizing the alternation of warmth and coolness from his dealings with her uncle and her father.

Elizabeth discontinued work on the third day, the burial day, and left the house, alone, in the gray unpleasantness of coming snow. She walked aimlessly for a long time, conscious that Wakwa followed at a distance.

He was already sitting at the fire when she returned, cold. She lay down, not cooking as she usually did in the early afternoon, and faced away from him.

"You are unwilling to share your sorrow, my wife?"

"I apologize for being withdrawn."

"I understand your trouble."

"I have not been able to think of you these past days, nor receive you to me, if you have wanted."

"Do you think that I expect it?" Wakwa was annoyed. "Who can think of such things while in mourning!" More patient, he came to her and attempted to remove her cloak. "I am also sorrowful. For as long as your heart is heavy you should remain unto yourself. It may take much time to heal the wound. You know that I will wait. The time will come."

But his wife gathered her cloak back around herself and said, "I know not when that time may come again."

He set his face. "You have not wept."

"You are unfortunate in your wives! How can I go on? I will only bring calamity to whomever I love."

"Why do you not unburden yourself of the tears that weigh down your heart?"

"I am past tears!" she snapped.

Wakwa touched the strings of his gold and silver lyre, trying to remember Gilbert Worth's instructions. He saw her stiffen, resenting the distraction of his many mistakes.

"Kayaskwa, my father will hold thy mother's hand today in thy stead. Through him, she will know thy heart."

"That will be small comfort, considering the little he has ever said to me!" Elizabeth covered her ears.

Wakwa kept on with his practice. Finally playing a simple melody without error, he sat near her.

"Can you sing to this, my gull?"

"We do never sing in the house. Only in church, and that holy songs."

"Will you sing with me? I will teach you words." Wakwa continued to pluck.

"I do not wish it."

"I wish it."

"What difference can it make if I sing or do not sing!"

"You live by my fire now! When a man dies, we sing! Therefore, thou shalt sing!" He struck discordant notes.

Stung by his uncustomary dominance, tears gathered under her eyes like sweat. Distressed by her own predicament, tears mounted for herself, not for her father. She struggled against letting Wakwa see, but when he put the lyre aside and began the loud wail of his people for her father's soul, her reserve was broken.

She cried, unabashed, her voice climbing in agony to the spaces under the beamed roof, hitting against the sweet stream of his own. Expanding in the emptiness above, the sounds of their lament touched across the distance she had let come between them.

Chapter 35

In early December Wakwa prevailed on Elizabeth to make use of the furs he had given her for her eighteenth birthday.

She had not touched her needles since the funeral, even refusing to work on Wakwa's coat, wishing to deny herself any pleasure.

Wakwa fought against this attitude with gentle persistence, finally appealing to her need for warmer clothes. He wanted to see the gold needle moving rhythmically with her hand, absorption and energy glowing on her face.

He had begun to leave her for small spans during the day, dividing his time between his house in his town and the hunting lodge. One day he brought back a pair of snowshoes his father had made for her, and she was delighted at their novelty in spite of herself.

They continued on separate mats, using layers of bearskins to keep the cold away. Elizabeth extended herself, surrounding his bed with balsam-filled pillows to sweeten his sleep in the close atmosphere of the long winter nights.

Elizabeth knew Wakwa did not have intercourse with Tame Deer, but had two wives and lived without comfort from either of them.

One morning when she awoke he was gone. She followed the marks of his snowshoes to the riverbank but could not find his canoe. She trudged over to the tanning hut, leaving her own set of elliptical shoe prints. The place was almost bare of skins they had cured the month before.

Transforming into energy her regret that she had not seen Wakwa off on his trading day, Elizabeth went home and scrubbed the lodge, aired the mats, counted their supplies of stored foods, and planned which baskets to re-bury and which to keep in the lodge for immediate use.

She cut a doeskin coat for herself with a close-fitting hood, basting gray fox throughout for the lining. She worked a fringe of fur from inside the hood outward to frame her face. Not having Wakwa's company, she worked continuously and made good progress in one day. Making clothing was the most elementary skill to her. She preferred to lavish time on less practical projects she called "artifices." By the following evening there were only the finer seaming and the ties to do.

It was time for her to live in the female hut again, and she was glad Wakwa was not there to build it for her. She suspected that in the otan it would not be so lonely an ordeal. There would be activity all around, and voices and laughter and other women. For now there was only the little bird and the knowledge that Silent Fox came and went alone.

She finished the coat after two and one half days of concentrated sewing and visited the pond in order to see herself in the still water. The effect of the gray and red fox across the shoulders, cascading front and back in strips to her knees, was not less than regal and brought a new vibrancy to her eyes dulled by sadness.

She walked on thin layers of melting snow to the back of the lodge. She stopped to listen to the low rumble of Indianne unnontoowaonk, as Wakwa called his language.

"Wakwa!" She rushed to the front and called his name, as was the etiquette, happy he had come and brought people with him.

Before she could step into her own door men came pouring out, crowding behind Awepu. She stayed stranded on a circle of snow, certain Wakwa had been hurt when she did not see him with his men.

"Saunks!" One of the strangers gasped, reacting to her bearing as she faced them in the stately richness of her new coat, the hood thrown back revealing her coronet of glossy braids.

Elizabeth turned to the man, recognizing the word for queen. Among the score of respectful men Elizabeth was enveloped by the same feeling of safety she had known when she encountered Wakwa.

"Awepu?" She sought reassurance against more bad news.

"Elizabeth! Bride of my kinsman, we greet you." He saluted formally, pleased with the impression she had made on his fellows.

She paled under windblown cheeks. "I greet you all, Awepu!" She refrained from the question that burdened her.

"When we last met, under the sky, I told you of Charles Dowland's journey to his fathers, southwest. Now these, the bravest of our young men, are sent from the sachim to seek your counsel."

"Your kindness to my father, Awepu, has lightened my sorrow." She returned his answering smile. "Wherefore does the sachim turn to me, a woman, for counsel?"

"It is the matter of the winter feast. Nickommo will not be celebrated unless you raise your hand, so much is your departed father mourned. Only the return of Weeping Heart to his father's arms moves us to come across the bridge to ask for your advice, disturbing your mourning. If you say nay, the feast will not be held and Waban rest content, so highly does he regard the wife of the man who brought Wuttah Mauo back to him."

Warmth toward the people who had adopted her and were willing to recognize her marriage made her answer flow easily. She knelt on the snow and crossed her breast with her arms.

"I am honored by the sachim's gentle care of me and so happy Wuttah Mauo is reunited with his father. I did not have that sweetness with my own." She sought control of her voice. "Say to Waban nux! Celebrate with all haste."

It was the right thing to do. Happy faces surrounded her, anxious to greet her when her answer had been translated. She met the man who had called her "queen." He was Nuppohwunau, the sachim's second son. At ease since her foods were in good order, Elizabeth asked them in and served them a spread of dried fruit, maple sugar, and Asian tea laced with honey.

Wakwa came through the wide-open door in the midst of the impromptu party, laden with parcels from the city. He placed his things in a corner and walked up behind Elizabeth, deep in conversation with Nuppohwunau.

"I see you are not lonely, Elizabeth! Am I come in time for high tea?"

She whirled to him and took his hands, lowering her forehead against his knuckles.

Quiet fell as the group caught a glimpse of their intimacy.

"As you see, my lord, I am surrounded by my family. Yet I was lonely 'til just now!"

Wakwa answered her skillful repartee with a nod.

216

"And if you have brought tea with you from the city," she continued tauntingly, "I will gladly make you more, for that from the kettle is all gone."

For just a moment Wakwa's arm slid around her back, down the silky fur of her coat in irresistible caress. Supporting her arm English-fashion, he led her into the center of the company.

"Make the town ready, brothers," he warned pleasantly in his dialect. "You see what shall soon be coming among us. Clean it and fix it so she will feel at home."

Elizabeth repeated, "Hawunshech, farewell!" to each man when the gathering broke up. She cleaned the cups and swept the floor while Wakwa put his purchases in place.

She pirouetted for him before she untied the closings of her coat. He stopped her with a hand on her breast and one on her back.

"Then you will stay? You will live again?"

"I am ashamed I ever gave thee cause to doubt it. Remove thy hand from my breast or I will trap thee as a spider would a juicy fly!"

Wakwa took his hand away and replaced it with his lips.

"You will be upset when you find I must refuse." And Elizabeth gathered his loose hair into a periwig tail.

He drew back, disappointed, never having misread her mood before. "Do you play with me?"

"Never that!" She flushed. "I flow. I will break your rule."

Wakwa thought, then burst into a hearty laugh. "Dost mean you entertained in state this afternoon twenty brave men of my tribe, in this condition?"

"What should I have done? Build a hut myself? Burrowed underground like a frightened rabbit to await your return from who knows where? When civilized company doth come, I serve tea!"

He grinned, remembering the appreciative group of captains chatting under the blue and green drape while she served them. "See they do not wear out their welcome." He came and held her tenderly against his tall body. "Do you judge me civilized as well? Will you be hospitable to me? It is no time to break off, now I have thee back again. Tomorrow is time enough for wetuomemese. I will play the Englishman tonight."

217

Chapter 36

When she returned from the wetuomemese Elizabeth spent the night in a sweating fear. The winter feast was in progress and Wakwa was in the otan. Work overhung her after ten days of idleness. Excluded from Sweetwood and the Indian town, she kept company with soured memories and frustrations. The shadows in the hall finally reached out for her. She drove back the haunting projections with work, baking, cleaning, and bathing. But when faraway screams of human voices slipped past the smoke hole on a frigid wind, she crawled under her fur robe and watched, almost unblinking, the dark corners. At last she lapsed into nightmare.

At dawn she came into the cold to find new snow. The undisturbed forest was innocent in streaks of green and gray and bright white. She remembered the winter's first snow and her walk to her father's house. The image of a new hanging came into her mind. Cloth, cut into shadows of tree branches on snow, should be sewn onto the backing, handmade of stuff that would make the sheen of frost. With other tasks to finish, she left the decision of what this fabric should be to future inspiration.

Returning from the spot where they made their toilet, she found White Cat waiting. He seemed startled by her blood-red cloak against the forest of gleaming snow. In practiced English he said that Wakwa would meet her on the bridge at sunset. Then he ran off toward the south.

Thinking of her mother, and how she was bearing her own total loneliness, Elizabeth wandered outside, wearing both coat and cloak in thin winter sunlight. She was drawn to the bridge, hours early, and hesitated. Then, for the first time, she crossed.

The beauty of the river, almost placid in the cold, made no impression on her preoccupied senses. She marched, unseeing, across the gradual upward slope to the top of the western bank. A plain stretched away from the crest of the hill for a long distance, dropping into a valley toward the southwest.

She caught her first glimpse of Wakwa's town, nestled in this drop-off. From her high place she saw it as a collection of ant hills.

She turned toward a gathering of men, involved in some kind of game, across the plain. She trembled at the loudness of one man's invocation and his scream as he ran with a polished pole aloft, then released it, snapping and whirring down a corridor of ice dug from a drift. Thrust after thrust was made in turn, each time with a measuring by rope and loud cheering for whomever threw the farthest. She grew disgusted at the sight of their almost-naked bodies lost in aimless occupation.

One of the players saw her and trotted over. His limbs were painted in thin lines of yellow and red and his facial expression was lost in geometric design.

"Mistress Elizabeth!" His small white teeth showed.

Her throat went dry and she could not answer.

Laughter bubbled over from his smile and Elizabeth knew him. She curtsied to the sachim's second son. He laughed again and waved her on. She left him, uncomfortable, unable to tell if he was being pleasant or insolent.

Occasional sentries did not interrupt her progress as she walked across the snow toward the valley. She wondered who had prepared them for her presence or if they had noticed her exchange with Nuppohwunau. She never went close enough to be seen from the valley. Appalled by the noise, she stopped, watching ant people milling about the smoking houses. There were many more than the two hundred fifty people Wakwa said were permanent in his village. Smoke settled in a haze over everything, and it was impossible for Elizabeth to pick Wakwa out from among the men. The air smelled of roasted flesh and she could make no rhyme or reason out of the movements of the throngs.

After so many months of quiet, Elizabeth looked down, seeing a pit of garish devils. Here she would pass her days, here share a husband with another woman. Here her children would grow up, live, grow old, and die, knowing paint and ritual. They would pass out of life unremembered among whites for their achievements, unpossessed of property, and unmarked in the circles that had given their mother life.

She retreated into her English self, knowing the horror her

parents must have felt as Wakwa stood before them, saying she was his wife.

Unreasoning, she scrambled over the hill back toward the bridge.

It was night when Wakwa found her, hidden, enduring falling snow.

"Wife!"

She moved back when she saw him. Covered in fur wrappings, his face highlighted by strong tracings of white paint, he was angry.

"I told you when the sun did set! You were late! You did not come at all as I asked! I grow tired of not finding you where you should be."

"Methought my body would be discovered with the flowers in the spring. How did you find me?"

"Even an Englishman could have found the marks of your feet in the snow!" He spat on the ground. "Do you think I have been looking all this while? I have waited the evening meal, I have read until my eyes hurt, I have given you time to come home and explain yourself. Yet you drag me out and make me vie with yourself for your company. I had planned to let you come and watch if you would. Now all is ruined. Wuttah Mauo was to pray with his father. I was not there because of you!"

"I saw."

"Explain thyself!"

"All of you. The town. Where I am to live. How I am to worship."

"Uninvited you came?" He pushed his face close to hers, kneeling on the snow.

She snorted at him.

"I see. Bright colors frighten my little gray sea gull. She would rather hover in a church filled with grim-faced coatmen wearing black than light upon the plain amidst some paint and merriment!"

"You can be cruel. You must see what a struggle this is for me!"

"You struggle over everything. Can you not live?"

"Withdraw your face." Her voice was ice. "I know it not, disfigured as it is."

The man did not move back.

"You could be great!" She raised her voice to him. "Why do you squander your days throwing pieces of wood, as I saw, dressing up like a child in a garret, making such to-do about your trapping. What will our children be?"

"We have none."

"That is unfair!"

"Perhaps it is."

"Perhaps!"

"It would not be good enough, Englishwoman, if they were like me?"

"It is no matter. As you say, we have none. Think only of yourself and how you will improve your people, playing every day with the sameness of rabbits in a warren! Every year the same and never an advancement!"

He pushed himself away from her, gulping back his hurt. "When will you change? When will your untutored English mind cease to value your days like a squirrel, measuring out your work and pleasures? When will you cease to honor only glory, gold, and property?" He turned to her, his face ugly with outrage. "Until quite recently you were up for trade yourself, or did you forget that and also me!"

He had hurt her in his turn and, regretting it, stood apart. He said very quietly, under the rustle of building snowflakes, "Someday . . . someday . . . you and other English will honor the soul of a man. This is the hope that pushes me out of the forest for the talking that I do. I cannot believe that never, never, will you understand the splendor of a man or woman. Me, Awepu, even wasted Weeping Heart, your father, or yourself. Understand! I thought you did. . . . I am this place! I will not move from here, no matter how you would distort my talents or my prowess into gain." He leaned against a tree on the side where the snow would not reach.

Elizabeth moaned her turmoil, at last whispering, "I try. I try."

He came close to her and offered her his hands and pulled her up. "This anger must not be. Charles Dowland is not buried yet?"

"I would not have it so."

"Kayaskwa, let him live, but as he was becoming!"

She drew her hand along the pure line from his temple down along his cheek and forward on his jaw, smearing the white paint. She daubed her own face with the residue.

"I will never run in fear again. I may be afraid, but I will not run." Timorously she clung to him. "My beautiful man, why is it I am not fruitful?"

"Look at all the years and rivers of different blood the seed must cross. It will find thee, I know. In time you will make a man who will bind us close together."

She held his head between her freezing hands and slowly kissed each part of his face, drinking in the form of it with each touch of her lips.

He sought her body underneath her coverings but was unsuccessful. "We are clumsy in the snow. Come home."

She followed, almost running to keep pace with his long strides. It took hours to become warm. But in the middle of the night Elizabeth threw off the fur robe and exposed her sleeping husband to the light.

She studied him, his face still streaked with white. She looked down the length of his strong body and touched the soft, relaxed penis, remembering her surprise when she discovered that he was circumcised. An odd sameness, she thought, between their peoples. Wakwa's eyes fluttered open.

She said, "I would love you if you were stout or aged or plain, but have I told you I am mightily glad you are made the way you are?"

He rose up on his elbow and blinked in the firelight. "Cowammaunsh!"

"Thy word for love is beautiful. Can forgive, I am a fool?"

He yawned. "You are not that. But young. Your son will share our souls. I am depending on your brilliance."

She kissed the penis, grown long and sleek and firm, and tasted its silky smoothness with her tongue. The husband folded her in his arms and she listened to the beating of his heart.

"Kayaskwa, how did I live before?" He entered into her and strove gently and slowly to bring them together. She felt nothing but his weight against her legs, but raised up to kiss him at the end. She did not sleep well.

222

It was Wakwa who woke her from restless dreams with slow and loving kisses down her back. When they joined she was all alive inside, but was not conscious of the man alone. As she moved beneath him, a silver picture grew before her eyes. Streaked with shining slippery gray, it formed into branches, after snow.

She felt with joy the throb of his release and the picture turned deep blue. Her eyes still open, she saw nothing but dark spreading color overhead, the branch-like shapes glowing where they intertwined.

When Wakwa returned that night from the end of the feast, the house was running smoothly.

"I grow lonelier and lonelier off by myself during my monthly sickness. While we live so alone, may we make some new arrangement?" she questioned carefully, working over her hoop.

"Little bird," he smiled, "that is not a problem anymore. Know you not you have conceived?"

"Can you tell that, too, with your sensitive self? I was blinded by a vision of it when you came to me this morning."

Wakwa spread his hand across her belly. "I am grateful for a son who is made of white rock and red earth. Please, Kayaskwa, do never go away from him or me."

Chapter 37

"I begin to tell the stories of the People in the otan, in place of my old father, but the story I carry from Gilbert Worth even I cannot believe," Awepu said at supper with Wakwa and Elizabeth.

Awepu had been in Sweetwood to arrange a meeting with Mrs. Dowland for Wakwa's final proposal to legitimatize his marriage. It was the deepness of his attachment to Elizabeth that Wakwa wanted to impress on his people with public sacrament.

"Your hopes, cousin, to reconcile mother and daughter seem black as the ashes from your fire. Mary Dowland winters in Salem with her own people. In the company of Annanias did she travel. He makes council with his fellow holy men. A big mia-wene. Gilbert calls it 'synod.'"

Wakwa changed his plans and prepared to bring his case to Gilbert Worth. About fifty days after the winter nickommo Wakwa made his solitary way to the Worth farm through a light February rain, his lyre strung over his shoulder as an afterthought.

He was intrigued with the shape of the house, blending into the northern slope, not obstructing the land with height or solidity. Acres of dormant fruit trees clacked their branches audibly in the wet night.

Wakwa's knock interrupted a flow of music from inside. The matron who answered left him standing where he was on the uncovered stone steps.

Gil, in his shirt sleeves and velvet slippers, and Dr. Stirling, stuffed into a well-loved, well-worn waistcoat, appeared in a wide doorway.

"Great God! Winke has left you in the rain! Come in, come in, Silent Fox!" Gil quickly drew him into the vestibule. "I have never seen you carry a weapon. Are you looking for a fight?" Gil laughed and they embraced, arrows and all.

Stirling recorded their affection.

"Mac, meet my nephew, Silent Fox, from Twisting River.

Fox, this is Dr. Stirling, our friend and physician. Doctors get bigheaded when one uses titles overmuch. We call him, simply, Mac."

Stirling fumbled with his violin, changing it to his left hand, to shake the hand Wakwa offered him. "You're a sudden man, Gil Worth!"

The white swan feathers knotted into Wakwa's long black hair, the fur collar turned up to his cheekbones, his moccasins heavy with black shell money, stimulated questions, but the old man said only, "Honored, sir, eh . . . Fox, I am sure!"

"I regret coming to you unannounced, Uncle, but . . ." Wakwa turned his eyes to Stirling for a moment, "my lyre needed tuning."

"Haw! The spokesman for his tribe, with reason, as you witness, Mac!"

"I am more than that now, Uncle. I serve, since the winter nickommo, as one of two young sachimmauog. But do not call me sachim. I would retain my head in its present size!"

This time Stirling laughed with Gil. But the uncle turned serious.

"This is news! The best news!" Gil bowed elegantly from the waist.

"I hope, Nissese, this will not change things between us."

"Only if it makes us better friends."

The sharp Scot pieced his scanty information into a cohesive story. "I'm beginnin' to see, I'm beginnin' to see. This is somethin' to do with what that brayin' minister was yellin' about in the church! Your missin' niece isno' missin', is she, Gil? And this no nephew, but thy nephew-in-law!"

"He speaks of this in his church?" Wakwa looked sullenly over Stirling's head. "What doth he say of my wife?"

"Well now, lad, I've a cousin in the Pennsylvania hills, won't go out his door without a rifle cocked, he's so put out by yer folk. An' I can hardly believe I just saw ye huggin' a Briton. Why no' lay them arrows an' pistol down, an' I'll tell ye!"

Stirling's humor was not reciprocated.

The Scotsman continued with a challenge in his voice. "He said naught but good about your wife, who, I take it, is poor Dowland's daughter, one an' the same. Hudson was not over-kind in his opinion of the local Indians nor, for tha' matter, of your precious Uncle Gilbert here."

Wakwa looked sternly at Gil as he put his weapons and jacket in a corner. "Why was I not told! This must be corrected."

"All this talk in the front hall!" Hanna had come. "Let us please to get out of the draught!"

She was presented to Silent Fox. Unable to hide her admiration, the light full upon his face, she curtsied deeply.

"How doth our Elizabeth?"

"For Elizabeth, most well, wife of my uncle! She will not rest until she have a thing she calls her treadle wheel. Truly, she was recovering until the news of Mrs. Dowland reached her. That Hudson continues the favorite disturbs us both. I have made her calmer now."

"Believe me, Silent Fox," Hanna's big eyes were full of sympathy, "this latest action mortifies us all."

Wakwa registered the hurt in her voice and although his curiosity about Hudson's statements grew sharper he said, "You bear the mark of Angelica's portrait, as doth Elizabeth. Your face, Hanna Worth, has much the same sweetness and is a comfort to me, parted from her as I am this night."

Hanna slipped an arm through Wakwa's and led him into the sparkle of her dining room. An after-dinner spread of coffee, cakes, and liqueurs was set out in silver servers.

"This is finer than any room in the mansion of the governor or even Crosswhite's on Beacon Hill! Nothing here is less than perfection."

"Do you then know Mr. Crosswhite?" Hanna asked, showing him around the room.

"I stay with him and other kind families like his when I am in Boston."

"Always first class, eh, Silent Fox?" Gil cut in.

"The forest has more splendor, Uncle, in the place where I daily wash than even your abundance of dainty glass." Wakwa was standing in front of shelves set across a window, stocked with imported crystal. "Crosswhite's is the best that I can do when in the city, for what is offered my people for lodging makes your barn a palace."

Gil was muted with the implications of this statement.

226

"If ye don't mind, Hanna, I'll do without the coffee and be practicin' this unnervin' stuff across the hall. I dunno' think this young man came out on such a night for idle chatter with the likes o' me." He eyed the cake.

"Oh, Mac! Gil will let you off for at least one cup. Stay a minute." Hanna was a pretty and gracious woman. Not polite, but genuine, she combined the best of what she had known, Dowland's competence and Worth's flair, into her own personality. At home with herself, everyone was at home with her.

"Yes, Dr. Mac!" Wakwa opened up to him. "Stay. You must be my white taupowaw. It is as if Squauanit, the women's god, has moved the earth to make you present here just this rainy night. I am much in need of counsel from an English doctor."

"Scotch, if ye please!"

"Why do you need a doctor?" Hanna's interruption was passed over by the men.

"Are you then from Scotland? I have a dear friend who spends much time there seeking out wool from the best of your sheep."

"They are not mine anymore, my friend, I have not been on those sweet shores for thirty years. I have taken root in your soil."

"You try."

"Humph!"

"May I know who your friend is, Fox?" Gil asked.

"The finest agent of Kirke's trading house, Dire Locke."

"Jove! I know him slightly. Who do you think has located half the stuff I have about my house? Why, those violet cups and pot of Mary's that you liked so much were his doing."

Hanna brought the men's conversation back to course. "Why do you need a doctor, Silent Fox?"

But Stirling began to glow, more trustful of Wakwa. "All the years I spent up the coast, doctorin', I was wishin' for a few Indian remedies. I hear you've got a thing takes infection from gunpowder wounds. Never found a soul who'd tell it me."

"You have found your man, as I have mine." Wakwa's smile, revealing so many of his hidden hopes, made him look like a boy. "Elizabeth newly carries my son."

Hanna flushed as red as the ribbons on her frail cap and turned from the men, her shoulders shaking.

Gil took her into his arms while she cried softly, and Wakwa and the doctor stood, each wondering what clumsy thing he had said to bring on this reaction.

"Storms from that Corsican island sweep over Elizabeth as well, and I am at a loss what to do about them," Wakwa apologized.

"You see the effect of mixing blood, Silent Fox." Gil soothed Hanna with his hand. "The storms pass. They pass of themselves. You will learn."

"Do not think me selfish!" Hanna defended herself quickly. "It is only I am so happy Beth is not cursed as I am myself."

"Come, Hanna." Gil lifted her chin with his thumbs. "You have me to take care of. That's child enough for anyone."

Stirling left the couple to themselves. "You are mighty sure you have a boy comin', laddie. Have you people found a way to divine that, too?"

"This must be a son. It means much, now I am sachim."

"Beth will have a beautiful child." Hanna came to Wakwa and led him to a place next to Dr. Stirling's. She and Gil sat opposite to them.

"You too have a child now," Wakwa said, "for I perceive the natural mother hath deserted Elizabeth. My wife will turn to you in her travail, which will come at nunnowa, our harvest time, the middle of your September."

"But Mary has not deserted Beth! She is coming back! Her return is any day!"

"Deserted." Wakwa reached across the table for her hand. "This is why I came to your house tonight. She forfeits her power over her daughter by denying her husband's word which was given as law. Elizabeth's father foresaw this and gave his daughter into Gilbert Worth's care. I remember his words, spoken at another table."

Buoyed, Hanna served the steaming coffee and the little cakes herself. Sweet aromas spread through the warm room.

"Then do these Roman-Frenchmen make many tears and nothing more?" Wakwa spoke mildly to Gil, referring to Hanna's outburst, but Stirling answered.

"They also make hellish hard music to play, friend."

"But they are fine companions," Gil paid Hanna tribute, "and

228

do such marvels with a simple chicken's breast a man would swear he dined in Paradise!"

"This is true! You should see how my Elizabeth boils a shoulder of moose."

Hanna was all laughter. "I would love that. May I come for some?"

"If you still wish to after I tell you what is in my heart tonight."

Gil saw nothing in the remark. "On the contrary, your news is very cheering. Why ever would we hesitate to visit her?"

Wakwa said nothing.

Stirling filled the gap, licking sugar from his forefinger, preparing to leave. "I told you it was time for me to quit the room! Imagine, Silent Fox, an old mutton like me awake at such an hour, workin' over a music stand! Worth kidnapped me when I stopped by from the Cape—every four weeks I ride in—an' he will no' let me go. He regales me with stories about some gatherin', but won't say if he'll hold it here or there or when or why. He locks me in his sittin' room, bids me saw away at allegro, andante, allegro 'til I'm blue from standin' and have to send a rider to my family so they know I'm not . . . swallowed up alive!"

"Or attacked by wild Indians?" Wakwa's mouth lifted slyly at the corner. "I am glad to see music in the house relieving the family's sadness after Mr. Dowland's death. But his wife is unremitting in her grief, as would have been Elizabeth without my help. I cannot understand the mother allied again with her daughter's tormentor. From what Dr. Mac has said he has offended you all. I must know what the snake has said. I act for many people now."

Gil had lost his bravado. "Give us time, Fox. Some others and myself are tired of footing this man's bills. We are casting about for another minister. If Hudson were foisted on a less vulnerable township, poor souls, he could not do any more harm here. If I had not resigned my status as Elder when Hudson came, it would be a great deal easier to open the eyes of the other members."

"I shall remember this in my own work. I am reluctant to hold power myself. It seems always the evil run after it." Wakwa saw the picture of scornful Wuttah Mauo asking him if he were sachim. "Still must the damage this Hudson does with his tongue be contradicted! Askug! Snake!" Wakwa would not yield the point.

"Done," Stirling piped up. "Let Silent Fox come, Gil, to the Session Sunday next. We'll make Hudson debate your nephew Fox over the insults we sat through on Dowland's last day. If the Elders see this civil man next to that shouting ape, it might save us a bale o' time." Stirling chose another cake. "Back to more important things. Young governor, know you what party your uncle-in-law has in mind? It would no' be a weddin' we're to celebrate with this Venetian rot I've been ruinin' my fiddle on, would it?"

Until Gil agreed to the meeting with a thoughtful affirmative nod, Wakwa held off introducing a topic even closer to his heart. Then he said, "I would like to hear this music that raises up your passion so, Dr. Mac. But it is not for me to say when I may celebrate my new life. I came here without strings of wampum, or delegates, so wary am I of spoiling my chances with premature requests."

"Why, Fox, you know my mind!" Gil was surprised.

"Uncle, my first suit was only half-successful, my second refused by virtue of your brother's death. I have but one chance remaining to make Elizabeth happy among her own folk. Thus I came to clear my path of all resistance and not to talk about Elizabeth tonight."

Not understanding, Gil insisted, "Who better to talk about? With your firstborn on its way, you should settle this posthaste!"

"It is not my firstborn."

"Not!"

There was no reply. Wakwa felt they had slipped into the most vital subject unprepared. He studied Gil's surprised face, searching for the least offensive way to make the Christian man accept the fact of his two wives.

Stirling turned longingly toward the door, wishing he had taken his previous opportunity to leave.

"You were married before Beth?" Gil was incredulous.

"Yes!"

"Never did I suspect. You are so wholehearted in your affection for her."

"I am that."

"So, you are a father like Awepu. You have a son?"

"I welcomed a daughter two years ago."

"A daughter!" Hanna grew soft.

"And are widowed and afraid I shall not approve this tiny child?" Gil pressed, sympathetically.

"There is no person who would not love the glowing flower that is my daughter Sequan. But her mother lives."

"I see." Gil stopped in thought.

"I think it true that Indians may divorce?" Hanna supplied her husband's unspoken question.

"It is true."

Gil relaxed. "You should not quake at our feelings toward your divorcement. There must have been some good reason, knowing you, as I do."

Wakwa's skin went very cold. "My first wife dwells in my sachimmaacommock. There has been no divorcement."

Dr. Stirling stayed his chewing. Hanna, bewildered, turned to her husband, who was on his feet, his face suddenly red.

"Sachim! Have you played us all for fools? I have heard of that kind of rudeness from your meaner sort, but I thought I had measured your character better than this!"

"Uncle, I have sought to make none of us fools. I thought only to withhold pain when it were not necessary to give it."

"This turn of events gives me pain! What do you mean by this, Fox?" Gil stamped his foot and his voice broke at the breach in their understanding.

Wakwa looked at Gil, but his concentration was within himself.

"I recall!" Gil barked at him. "There was an inkling of this when I visited you and Beth months ago. How deftly you glided over Awepu's slip! Strong bonds of friendship, indeed!"

Wakwa unbuttoned and removed his shirt as Gil gave vent to insult. He stood across the table from the Englishman, his body, in its largeness and beauty, shocking in the room filled with delicate, inanimate objects.

"I come to bare my soul to you, to let you see through me, as from our word, *michachunk*, a notion of soul to us." He held his long hands to his breast. "That looking at my naked self you may

231

discern my view, as in a looking glass. The bridge between us, Uncle, was very nearly finished building. You cannot walk to me nor I to thee unless you know what love a man of the Ninnuock beams on those close to him."

"He is more subtle with our tongue, Mac, than you or I who were born with it in our mouths. Stay by, lest he trip me up and I plunge into the river from his damnable bridge!"

"As your doctor, Gil, I bid ye to sit, both o' ye, and allow your blood to cool."

They both sat, meek before Stirling's words.

"Mr. Worth," Wakwa retreated into formality, "it was my first wife, Tame Deer, who urged me to have you present during that first meeting at Dowland Farm. With Ninnuock, the uncle is much respected and has more sway in such matters than a father. My wife saw you in your search, so long ago, and judged you a feeling man."

"A foolish man! She is clever as her husband. You won me over, it is true."

"Enatch keen anawayean. Thy word shall be law. I will put my first wife aside if you say it, Nissese. I lay the fate of this good woman at your feet, for I saw I could not trust her to your brother-in-law."

"Do not flatter me! What have I to do with the fate of this woman I do not know? It is the fate of my niece that concerns me. How swift I was to condemn Charles! Now I am lost without his wisdom. But I shall do my best not to be duped again."

Wakwa controlled his face as best he could, realizing the damage extending from Gil's disillusionment. His voice was strained as he asked the doctor, "Will you answer me a question?"

"I will try, young man, but I would rather ask you a few!"

Reflected in the gleaming surface of the table, Wakwa's presence doubled. "When an Englishwoman conceives and bears and gives suck to a child, does she embrace her husband during that time?"

Hanna was wide-eyed at his frankness.

Stirling took his time. "The answer is yes. She does her husband's will."

"Her husband's will." Wakwa spoke to Stirling as if they were

232

in private consultation. "Then women of the Ninnuock are more powerful than are Christian ones. Indian women decide whether to receive their husbands.

"It is not the custom from many months before the birth even to a year after for a husband to know his wife."

"Holy God!" The doctor studied the crumbs on his plate.

Gil seethed. "This is your excuse for taking my niece? If you all observe these customs, why is Silent Fox exempt? I suppose this is when she unwarily met you in the rain?"

"I met her in the sun! And yes, amongst us this long separation can be a reason for taking a second wife.

"In my case, it was not. Almost another year yet passed. That makes two and nine months!" Wakwa held up his fingers for emphasis. "Still, the excellent woman whom I love refused me."

"What could be her reason?" Hanna mused to herself.

Wakwa made use of the Scot's impartiality. "Dr. Mac, if an Englishwoman did this, what would her husband do?"

Dr. Stirling thought again. "A harsh man might whip her. A kind one, send her to physicians, who would, most certainly, do her not a bit o' good. I suppose, in the end, he would put her aside. Very few, except a popish man, would live a martyr to this behavior. Of course, to avoid a whole lot o' mess, he could seek companionship outside his house, illicitly, mind ye."

"Yet I was patient." Wakwa made his appeal to all of them. "Did I harm her who had been at my side since I was a boy? Did I whip the mother of my baby? Did I expose her to the public scorn and drag her to the taupowaw? Did I agree when she asked to leave me so I might remarry or permit her to live apart, never again to have her sweet presence in my house or to hear the laughter of the child we had made? I did not do these things!"

Hanna spoke, unable to resist the mention of the child. "But was not Tame Deer wise to annul your union if she could not love you?"

Wakwa fretted on the slender chair not made to his size. "Twenty-nine, thirty moons had flown, yet I had been silent about our trouble. Then, unlooked for, came Elizabeth and the love I felt for her, separate from all else in my life. Tame Deer's request had come too late to be coldly fit to my convenience.

"Who would believe I had need of another wife? Should I put

aside my faithful partner for a white girl I had found like a crystal under a tree? Such conduct would be considered lewd by the town. The sachim would not grant Tame Deer the separation she sought, nor me my new wife. I would be justly punished for violating the bond that tied me to Tame Deer.

"Leaving one to love another for caprice is a fearsome sin among my people. This is no reason for separating or having to oneself two wives."

"Two wives!" Gil was thunderstruck.

Wakwa turned his attention on only him. "A man takes a second wife to extend his family, to love more widely, even to grow more corn! If his first marriage be unhappy, he makes an amicable settlement with his wife, divides the children between them, and departs gracefully from the union. After half a year or so he may seek to wed again.

"But could I hide Elizabeth in the forest for half a year while dragging Tame Deer through the mire that we might divorce, the delicate and sole cause of our unhappiness being so shameful to her?

"Could I visit Charles Dowland and beg him wait until I, an Indian, disposed of one wife to gain his only daughter away from her betrothed of seven years, and her wedding nigh?"

The group around the table stared at the shortened candles.

Wakwa watched Hanna turning a piece of ribbon from her bonnet around and around her finger. "It was like the twisted knot of a certain trap we make which kills the hapless animal below by dropping rocks as he seeks the bait. I was the hungry beast with the stones menacing my head.

"Thus I told Tame Deer to stay! And she obeyed. And keeps unto herself."

The English people sat staring at him.

Wakwa gathered himself to clarify the rush of new concepts he had unveiled. "From my people's view, it were more proper that I love two wives. Rejecting not one person to favor another. If, after all I have described as my necessary course, Tame Deer chose to break away while Elizabeth dwelt with us, it would not stain the second wife nor me.

"Had Dowland agreed to solemnize the marriage, taken upon us by Elizabeth and me, the People and Waban would have been more satisfied with my seriousness. I would have allowed Tame

Deer to melt from my house like ice, not obliged to reveal to you English she had once been my wife.

"Sweet Elizabeth chose not to break Tame Deer's heart, even as I would have. My acts now are directed by your hand." Wakwa heaved a sigh, exhausted.

"It is damnable. What you say always makes so much sense to me," Gil complained, very unhappy.

"Then, no matter what you do to my Tame Deer, our bridge is mended."

Stirling lumbered toward the door. "I'm off to slave at my Vivaldi. I'll take a look at the condition of your little wife when you would have it, Fox. I'm growin' cowardly in my old age and will let Gil settle this labyrinth." The old man closed the door with remarkable softness for a man of his brusqueness.

Gil was ashen under his responsibility. "So then I hold power over a woman who thinks me a feeling man, yet I do not know her at all. Will you put her aside if I say you must?"

"Nux. If by doing this Elizabeth will bask again in your light and be not a prisoner more for love of me. They both are captive souls for my sake. We two must seek to make them free."

Hanna had not listened. "Fox, how doth Tame Deer have such a clear idea of my husband, if Gilbert cannot remember her?"

"She noted him by his hair!"

"I should like to meet her!" Hanna said with spice.

Gil spoke from his concentration. "If Tame Deer change her mind, Silent Fox, and would be a wife again, what would happen to Beth?"

Wakwa could not keep back a grin at Gil's inability to visualize this point and said happily as he put his shirt on, "She will also be my wife! It is not so rare among the People. And it was Elizabeth who suggested this! The house will be filled with babes and I . . . I be supremely content, where but five months ago I was lonelier than the wolf."

"Content indeed!" Gil wandered over to the window.

"I cannot imagine it." Hanna rested her forehead on her hand.

Gently Wakwa said, "There is a reason that a man with two wives builds another room, having its own fire, for his second bride."

Hanna looked at him sadly.

"We behave," Wakwa dropped his voice, "not as netasuog, as we call your cattle."

Still Gil heard him, and the devastating bigotry of Hudson's sermon sounded in his memory. "Hanna, show Silent Fox in to Dr. Stirling. I am going out to walk."

"Not in this rain!"

"I vow Beth dares not fuss over her husband this way." Gil's eyes were moist. "I shall stand near Charles' grave and listen for some guidance. I have not his deepness of perception but I have the sense to wear a coat!"

* * * *

Stirling mopped his face with his sleeve, relieved at having his practice interrupted by the Indian. He listened with a young man's alertness as Wakwa answered his questions about the details of childbearing among Ninnuock.

"This fearless ease you talk about is nice to hear. I should like to come an' see it sometime, if your . . . what d'ye call him would permit."

"Taupowaw. If you could get a woman to allow you near her, what should the powwaw say!" Wakwa's smile faded. "What Gilbert Worth decides tonight will not change the progress the child makes within Elizabeth. She argues with me that she will do as did Tame Deer and quit the house when comes the hour of travail and bear the babe in peace."

"You do not trust she can do it, young friend?"

Wakwa meshed his fingers together, squeezing them until the knuckles showed white. "What hath been her knowledge of these things up until this time? Who among her kinswomen has borne a child? I do not expect her mother shared with her the birth of Henry. It is not the same as seeing a lamb brought forth in the spring!"

Stirling emitted a jingle of laughter. "Has she been feedin' ye this to get her way?" the doctor continued over Wakwa's baleful look. "There's a great difference between bornin' lambs and people, yet your little wife is in the right somehow. I think we doctors and midwives only bustle about to keep our own nerves at rest. There's terrible little I can do save hold her hand, if everythin's pushin' along all right. It's when there's somethin' goin' wrong I can perhaps reach in with a bit o' help."

"Is there more pain for sweet Elizabeth than for my wife Qunneke?"

"Poor soul, I shall have to come at least to comfort thee!" The doctor leaned toward Wakwa confidentially. "In thirty years of standin' by while babies deliver themselves, I can tell ye I've found two kinds of women. Them who's scared by other women's tall tales, makin' all kinds of trouble for themselves, and them who's calm an' happy an' look somehow as if there were nary one pain at all. Then, of course, there's the few with somethin' wrong."

"Come to see her, please. See for her sake there is not this 'something wrong.' I cannot speak to her of the weight of my worry."

"An' don't ye dare once mention it, laddie! That girl is on the right path without any help from you. Englishwomen are tough of fiber. Or don't ye know that yet?"

When Gilbert Worth opened the door to his sitting room, he found Silent Fox seated crosslegged on the floor, his back to the fire, rapt in Dr. Stirling's memories of his native Scotland. Gil was not struck by the differences between the man with the feathers in his hair and the one whose stubby pink hand gestured from his black coat cuff, but by their lively unity.

"Loitering again!" Gil boomed. "You both have a deal of practice yet to make you ready for this great event of solemnizing. Will you bring me your lyre, Silent Fox, while forgiving my abruptness in our previous conversation?"

Gil sat and removed his dripping boots, Hanna beside him with his slippers.

Wakwa pressed the instrument against his breast.

Gil came to him, relaxed and happy. "How should I play God with Tame Deer if you are all agreed?"

"Nissese, my Uncle! You are then what I thought you!"

"You are even more than I thought you. Nephew! Now, to make a musician out of a sachim." Gil extended his hand for the lyre. "God help me!"

"He does!" Wakwa could not see Gil's gesture through his tear-filled eyes. "He does!"

Chapter 38

"You are another person when this Elizabeth of yours is involved!" Pequawus admonished his son in private.

Wakwa stalked around the room of his sachimmaacommock, waiting to meet with Waban and his counselors in preparation for the confrontation with the Sweetwood churchmen. Waban was to deliver an explication of the religious life of the Ninnuock at the next day's Sabbath meeting. Wakwa would interpret and answer any questions which followed.

"My father, I am weary of bargaining for her. Think you they will ask about the fine points of prayer under the trees? They will, at last, have at me for what I must reveal has happened to the daughter of Charles Dowland."

"Son, it is all of us on trial here. With her uncle's sanction and the torn marriage bond, they cannot single you out an offender. They care not so much about this girl as you do! They must simply be convinced we do not desire to mingle with any other of their fair-skinned daughters."

"Why did you agree to make me sachim? You are wiser than am I."

Pequawus' lips twitched with a smile. "Think thou anyone would listen to the wisdom of Pequawus? There is no one who becomes not enraptured listening to you. Learn, Sachim, my son, to think with breadth, regarding your subject as from a height above the sea, and be not so distracted by every grain of sand along the way."

Wakwa paced again. "But will these dour Elders, so fickle with this snake of a priest that they would turn him out, when but two months ago he stupefied them in his church, accept with grace this sanction of my English uncle?"

"Wakwa Manunnappu, you have gained victory after victory since you met this new woman that you love.

"You will soothe their feathers. You will quote for them the story of Sarah, who suffered the slave girl to make sons by Abraham to lead the Jews. You will liken Elizabeth to the fearless men who came to our shores from across the sea in their ships to join their souls with a new land. You will stress her freedom from their principles that they may see she outcasts herself, choosing the way of the Ninnuock. They will want nothing to do with her then.

"You will say how she leads you into understanding and thereby helps you preserve the peace by the mixture of your blood. You will have her ready to receive and reassure them here among all of us if they wish it. Do not try to convert them to us, but disengage them from us!

"More, you will remember you have one man to blame for this unrest. The minister. And this man soon to be cast from leadership. He it is who frightened Elizabeth and it is he who fills Sweetwood with venom, arising from her love for you.

"You will go, not as a man weak over a woman, but as sachim, to protect the whole of the River Indians from the slight we have suffered. They will see our wound and our numbers more troublesome than parting ways with this snake of a priest. And you will stop fretting and twisting your hair!"

A call, relayed from the forest to the camp, interrupted their conference. Over his father's protestations, Wakwa raced out to meet the visitors, described as three white horsemen, crossing the river.

He returned to Waban's house with two Presbyterian Elders and Gilbert Worth. The two strangers sat uncomfortably on the floor of the great council room. Gil Worth, much at home, sat in the place of honor opposite the door, totally dejected.

Observing all the forms of politeness, Gil addressed by name all those men he recognized. "I come, forced to disappoint the People of their chance to tell their story clearly to the Sweetwood townspeople. These two Elders of the church where false thoughts were spread will relay your words accurately in your defense. Tomorrow is not a propitious day to welcome you among the congregation."

Waban drew on his pipe. "Gilbert Worth does not lightly break a promise. What builds this new wall between us and our rights?"

"Mary, Charles Dowland's wife, is dead at Salem of pneumonia." Gil watched this disaster fall like a stone on the assembly.

But in their remarks the Indians gave no sign to the church leaders that the event affected them personally.

Gil went on. "Added to that, Reverend Hudson lies on his deathbed in the northern town. None on the council of Elders thinks this a proper time to be undermining his position. They hold aside, temporarily, negotiations with a new minister, one Mayhew Low, of Sandwich.

"The Session feels that since the words which offend you, me, and all the knowledgeable Christian members were from Hudson's lips, he must be whole before you speak in the church. Annanias Hudson cannot travel until the warmer weather, if he lives." Gil and Wakwa were ashamed to see the hope in one another's eyes that he would not.

"Delay will allow the damage he has done to live as fact in many minds." Waban was exasperated. "We will come among you to clear the vision of your people. Do not ask us to wait forever."

Gil could not stay on to visit and risk raising the suspicions of the Elders after they had been given their basic outline of the Indian feasts and sacramental life. He took his leave, sadly, with the others.

Wuttah Mauo caught the long handclasp between Gil and Wakwa. When the horses had disappeared behind a veil of snow, he turned and said in the hearing of the rest, "Cousin, I see you are in trouble over more than only me!"

＊＊＊＊

Wakwa's guard of five carried the crates of dried fish and boxes of fine paper Worth had blatantly brought for "Wakwa's forest lodge."

Elizabeth came to him when the men were gone and, just reaching the crown of his head with her fingertips, brushed the snow from his hair.

Wakwa surprised her with a kiss at the hollow of her throat, which she liked best, and played with the ruffle of her new bonnet, which covered her neck from nape to shoulders to keep ash and draughts away. He buried his fingers in the pretty folds of her gown, styled high under her bosom to leave room for the expansion of her middle. He could not tell her yet.

They each tasted an anchovy encrusted with crystals of yel-

240

low salt, but Wakwa threw his into the fire and broke open the paper, faithful to his nightly writing lesson. The constricting lines and points of the printing they had started with weeks before frustrated Wakwa's natural hand movements and they proceeded directly to the circular, connected letters of script.

It was not long before Wakwa could write all the inane sentences with which Elizabeth teased him. "Is not the fire hot? How glad am I, I'm not a pot." He often hid little notes of his own in the baskets, which she read with a blush and burned. Now that he was started Wakwa wanted more than a legible hand. He was seeking a uniformity between the words he wrote and his thoughts. When he looked at the paper he wanted the satisfaction of seeing himself reflected there, in the same way he stepped back to regard the finesse of the tied rope in his traps. He gave up searching for a signature when his wife began undressing for bed.

He came behind her and ran his hand across her abdomen. "How tight and hard you have become. The little sachim rests soundly under here! You are well and strong. You do feel strong?"

"See how I came to this pass, lovely!" She brought his hand to her lips. "Yes, I am stronger every day. Do you know how far I can walk? Don't you see how my legs improve? I am not such a confection as I was when first you touched me there! Is this why you never have a horse to carry you all the distances that you roam?"

Wakwa fastened the door and fed the fire. "Nux, Kayaskwa. Come and feel how strong my legs. They have become like iron with all the running I do between two homes and into cities for all your English cloth. As well, I would be foolish to meet the price for a horse that would suit me. Come. Come and feel."

"You are a subtle Lucifer tempting me tonight. You know how well I resist the touch of you!"

He lay down with her and held her close against himself. "Perhaps you should resist. Should you still receive me?"

"As long as it is comfortable why should I not?"

Wakwa hid her face against his neck and spoke close to her ear, looking into the far shadows for a hint of how to lead into his news.

"I wish instead of closing yourselves in houses and crumpling

241

your bodies over books and weaving linen sheets indoors, and eating trash like salt and cakes, when the sun and air await outside, you English had more healthful habits. You were frailer when I met you. Now you are so sleek."

"When you start to hold a council and weave lengthy sentences with me naked in your arms, I am afraid."

"Kayaskwa, your mother never learned to be strong the way you have."

"She is very strong in ways you know by now."

Wakwa held her tighter. "It has proved not enough. She fell ill in Salem with your brother's sickness."

"No!" Elizabeth struggled to be free, as if she would rush out to her mother.

"It is too late, and too far to see her." He kissed her eyelids closed. "Keen kah neen! You and I! Keen kah neen. You and I are both without our mothers now."

In the silence that ensued, Wakwa felt her skin grow hot, then cold, and hot again. He left her with her thoughts, but did not release her body under the fur robe.

At last she spoke in a painful whisper. "I am glad our child shall have two mothers. How wretched he should be if I were taken from him and there were no other breast to comfort him."

It was a long night of low, regretful talk. But, after she had slept awhile, Elizabeth reached out for him and Wakwa responded to her need.

He was strong and unyielding in his approach, making her ache from her connection with him, now that the ancient tie with her mother was broken forever in her earthly life.

242

Chapter 39

Wakwa and Elizabeth stayed together even on the hunt while she recovered from this second great blow. When other hunters considered the stream exhausted for the season, Wakwa showed her the smoke of beaver's breath coming from one of their enclosures. He split the house open and came away with two fat black ones.

They stayed outside on a February night, too far away to return home after a successful moose hunt. It was so cold the moose froze as Wakwa skinned it. Fighting time, he cut up some parts and bundled them into the skin and hauled this burden to the foot of a hollow pine. He sent a fire screaming up the inside of this tower of bark and they made their bed close to it, as if it were a hot chimney.

"Colonial woman," Wakwa laughed as they walked home in the morning, none the worse for exposure, "you have witnessed a costly crime. Your Sweetwood tyther would have five pounds out of me in court if he knew I had burned a tree."

"They are, perchance, afraid that live trees will catch." Elizabeth was unsure about this new method of keeping warm.

"That is because the Selectmen do not know how to burn it right. In addition to a hearth, I have made me charcoal for mending my canoe."

＊＊＊＊

Wakwa went to Kirke's that week to trade his heavy winter catch and hear the news about Dire Locke. He left Elizabeth to fish with Nuppohwunau and Wuttah Mauo, promising to return by nightfall.

Wuttah Mauo, now unproductive as a hunter, his wind ruined for the river and running, sat next to Elizabeth with his line of twisted willow branches, using a hook she had made him of a partridge breastbone.

"English squaws, a dozen men will sit around your fire, hungry, by dark. Are you quick at gutting fish?" He had brought up scores of bass and filled a huge container to the brim, while his brother quietly added his share.

Always afraid of the lean man with his dark, creased skin, Elizabeth raised her chin. "I will ready ample food for my husband's friends. Will you be among them, Sachim?"

Wuttah Mauo spun away from her toward the trees, his calf catching the side of the basket, upsetting it. Fish rolled everywhere, still writhing for breath, and the more congenial man scurried after the ones that flopped farthest away. Neither Nuppohwunau nor Elizabeth could tell if it had been done on purpose.

Wuttah Mauo mocked his brother with his eyes as Nuppohwunau lifted the heavy basket onto his own back.

"Do you resent I have the courtesy to help the little wife, if she needs it?" Nuppohwunau reprimanded the sachim in their own language.

There was silence all the way back to the lodge.

* * * *

In morning darkness, the sky indistinguishable from the sea, Wakwa left his second wife on the rocky oceanside to gather seaweed and dig for clams. He went in a larger canoe with fifteen others and made for open water.

Elizabeth made stacks of the vegetation and put clams in her basket. Wakwa was going to teach her to make a brine of them and combine it with corn cakes for the salt she craved.

As the whitecaps leaped ever larger on the gray water, the men came, their nets loaded with fish for the Indian town.

They filled their stomachs from the abundance of the land, working and resting with the cycle which moved all life.

244

Chapter 40

Just at dawn one March day, Elizabeth shivered down the path to the stream to wash. The trees were far from showing buds, but in cheerful promise of things to come early violets popped up in protected places, looking more like little spots of paint than living things.

Delighted, Elizabeth picked the slender strands until she had a handful. She caressed the tiny petals with her cheek and breathed the sparkling morning air, blending her awe at the beauty of the day with her thanks to its creator.

She ran the rest of the way and discovered Wakwa standing dripping wet in the stream. He was facing away from her, toward the sun, his arms crossed on his breast. His face was happy when he stepped onto dry ground and reached for his small apron.

"Good morrow, Kayaskwa!"

She poured the flowers into his hands and he lifted them to his face.

"That is just what I did with them." She tied the leather band about him and picked up his blanket. "Dearest, is not the whole forest like a church with a round blue roof this morning?"

"You are learning how to pray, Elizabeth."

"My dear, I believe I always knew."

He held her red cloak while she immersed herself in the shallow water. As she raced for her blanket, he could see the change in her breasts, their shape more prominent, the nipples darker, her stomach no longer flat.

"Elizabeth," Wakwa dug around the pink crocus near his toes, "the earth, during her long winter sleep, yielded to the embraces of the sun and blushes now with these early flowers. She will ripen until she nearly bursts with greenness, then, working no longer from within, will present us with a rich harvest."

Color came into Elizabeth's face. He touched her gently.

"This is so with you as well. After you give up the fruit of our making at nunnowa, should you not come to live in the town?"

245

"Surely, Wakwa, he will be born by Taquonk. And I would love to see that. Uncle Gil, as well. But now I am used to this life, I dread the change."

They each filled a bucket and the morning issued from the frost of early spring.

****

Later they walked north in the direction of the ponds, stringing birch buckets around the trunks of the maples, boring holes to release the silver sap.

They ate at the pond and watched the swans at their matings.

"Elizabeth, look at that pair!"

"I am looking, Wakwa. The cob is greedy of his pleasure, think you not? He climbs so many times upon his mate!"

"Never greedy, Kayaskwa. He speaks his affection better than most men. They have made a nest together every spring for fourteen springs."

"Why, she is an elderly lady!"

"They have grown old together."

"I hope you will love me like that when I am as old as she."

"I hope I have not changed climate when you are as old as she."

"Wakwa! You can be morose. When I am seventy you will be only eighty-four. Ninnuock traipse about the woods at over one hundred, I have heard."

Wakwa laughed, showing his even teeth. "Those were better times. Eighty-four! What do you expect of me?"

"That."

"The bird does not feed on fancy stuff I grow used to at your uncle's, nor does the cob have two wives!"

Elizabeth shot him a panicked look. Wakwa lifted her single braid and wrapped it around her throat, continuing pleasantly, "Elizabeth, Tame Deer may take you at your word, permitting me near her."

She gripped his hands, still under her chin. "Has it happened then?"

"Should you ask?" He kissed the back of her neck. "It has not."

The second wife threw a stone into the water, ending the

246

swans' rendezvous. "I will keep my promise to her, but I would rather think about the sugaring!"

They went off to collect the syrup.

Wakwa covered the buckets and lined them up against an outside wall of the lodge. In the morning he would remove the ice, pour off the syrup into a storage container, and repeat the process day after day until a year's supply of sweets was laid in. But Elizabeth's desire that day was maple sugar candy, and she borrowed an Indian method, heated scores of smooth stones, and dropped them into a wooden bucket full of sap to boil it.

Wakwa drizzled a cup of the seething liquid onto an unmelted strip of snow and they lunched on the sweet strings it formed.

While the rest of the boiled syrup cooled outside, Elizabeth bent over her embroidery hoop. Wakwa persevered with one of the books Gil had given him on his only visit to their lodge.

Wakwa's progress had not been quick. He was straining within the compass of his natural experience to understand the thoughts of Plato. The book was translated into academic English from the Greek and he felt many times removed from even its surface meanings. Elizabeth was of some help with word definitions, but she felt inadequate to touch its deeper implications.

She went for the bucket as Wakwa placed the book on his mat and rubbed his eyes. "I understand more by touching the cover of this book and seeing its edges of gold than by reading it. This man Plato must be a fool or a conjurer. Such terrors he puts himself through to arrive at being an Indian!"

"To you everyone boils down to that sooner or later." Elizabeth beat the cooled syrup with a wooden spoon.

"Not so, little bird. Most foreigners will never grow into this kind of understanding. I wonder even about the Greek.

"He describes the rulers of his perfect place as people courageous, just, untinged by lust for property and goods. I perceive he means them to live in common as Ninnuock. They are temperate he saith, possessing their power by virtue of excellence. They do not wound but live in harmony with the land."

She sweated over the stiffening confection. "Continue, chanticleer!"

"I speak fact and you fill with mirth!" Wakwa scolded. "He

talks of ordeals and tests to separate the best from the unworthy, and would lower those born not so perfect to be growers of food and makers of pots!" Wakwa paced in front of his mat. "Like a horde of starving animals they would cut off their own offspring if they do not measure in perfection as high as themselves. Cruel. Without honor!"

"Silent Fox, Plato is correct. Your cousin, Wuttah Mauo, is not worthy to be at your side, to govern."

Wakwa studied the woman beating the maple syrup, the bucket between her legs. He threw off her train of thought. "They understand nothing about living and working in this world, as we must, to raise ourselves even to the level of the trees, which stand in one spot yet know more, and speak more clearly, than this man made with a head and no body! What does your uncle want me to learn from such a book?"

"Is this creamy enough?" Elizabeth asked.

Wakwa came and tasted from the spoon. "If you grow not too weary, beat it more. But only a little.

"Do you see! How do I know this? Because my senses are molded, as Plato would have, by poetry and music? He cannot see there is more poetry tasting your sugar than memorizing rhymes about it!"

"Dearest," Elizabeth panted between swipes with her spoon, "perhaps that is what Uncle Gil wants to convince you of. Think you not white men are increasing and taking hold on this shore? You call me foreigner, yet I know no other place than America! It is mine as much as yours!"

"What has this to do with Plato? And I do not push you out . . . it is you who are always pushing us!"

"There you have it, my Sachim! If Master Plato stirs your thoughts enough, you will devise a way to deal more handily with all this pushing and those who do it. Waiting in the woods is no defense, and you will never kill us! Them, I meant to say." She spooned the tan-colored sugar into walnut shells Wakwa had saved from the fall. "You tried that once, under Massasoit's son, and were defeated."

"Only because bayonets and men and food came from the English king. Your towns were fortunate, Elizabeth. On and on would Philip have fought. It took an Indian to kill him yet short of his victory. He was shot through his broken heart after his own wife was used by those red-coated savages as a whore and sold with her son into slavery thousands of miles from her shores!"

"Nevertheless, you were defeated. England is a place you ought to go to see, to convince you they have more weapons and ways to do you in even than they did one hundred years ago."

Wakwa lay half-curled on his mat and concluded with painful reality, "In Massachusetts we have given up war against you. We could be killed in an afternoon fighting with our puny numbers against the guns of the new England as well as the old. True, we could begin picking off Englishmen one at a time or burn, without direct cause, whole towns and be reduced to murderers. We could hide and survive on roots and such trash as poor Philip did, but to what avail? Massachusetts Bay, the pirates of Rhode Island, Williamsburg, and the bloody robbers along the Miami to the west will try to make this, my earth, secure to themselves alone. You will see. Then Ninnuock will judge if it be worth a fight, a helping hand from us to win security once more for our way of living."

Elizabeth tasted the warm candy. "Mayhap this New England you seem convinced will run away from her mother will grant you some land, a fertile part, and you need never be bothered by white men again."

Wakwa looked at her, amazed she did not see herself in her words. "You have fashioned me a reservation, Kayaskwa."

"Oh!" She stared at the empty shell.

"How would you fare on a reserve, Elizabeth? I have stayed one night with the poor people of the Hills tribe in Quinicticut. Even before the war they were herded there like cattle. A century they have lived like sheep and know no difference, except the stories of their old men and their terrible dreams at night. Compared to me, my wife, each one was weak and sick."

"Compared to you, anyone is weak and sick."

"Hear me, woman! I never ran so fast as out of there! No. It must be two sachimauonk, two governed places, two kingdoms. One New English. One Ninnuock. Or, as becomes my new hope, a place for Ninnuock within this coming English-American country. Both with a voice and listeners, taking part in the guardianship of the land, as this Plato would call it.

"Next winter, when you are safe in the town, I will go north and talk to the Chippewa and Penobscot and Abenaki and venture onto the private shores of the Passamaquoddy, to see if they will join in a league to demand such a place when the time is right. For so long we of the south have kept innocent, like children, of such possibilities."

"Now you talk like a sachim, truly. There is fighting brewing there. I want you safe with me."

"Sweet Saunks, I thought it was thee who said staying in the woods is no defense. So it is not. We are agreed."

"But you are a speaker, gifted with persuasion, not a red-coated ruffian, nor warrior!"

"Think you I can fight only with my mouth? Alone, I have killed Mohicans! Head eaters, we call them.

"Five, by myself, so careless were they to attack Silent Fox, seeing he was alone, and they out of their heads with rum! These bloodthirsty men encircled me on my path in the Dutch colony.

"Five sets of their big ears have I, strung onto a necklace I wear when in those parts. Would you see them? No? And this knife you have used upon your body fetched off as many heads, which I bundled together and, finding their sachim ere those heads were yet green, threw them at his feet! Dogs that they were to attack me whilst I looked for food, my party separated from me!"

Horrified, Elizabeth cut herself as she shaved some maple sugar over a bowl of dried currants for him.

He came and sucked the blood from her wound. "They being in the wrong, their sagamore gave me slaves as bearers for our burdens home, slaves of his own from other tribes. One and her mother I kept. The rest were never any good. I thought to send them home in disgrace, but Waban said it would cause insult. Thus I packed them off to Black Earth as a gift." Wakwa slapped his leggings. "How would this Grecian man live in the woods!"

He went laughing out into a north wind building toward the last vicious snow, and his English wife was not sure she should believe the tale he told.

250

Chapter 41

It was the spring of Wakwa's ascendancy. His plan for forging a link between the River Indians of Massachusetts and the northern tribes won approval after several weeks of consideration by Waban and his Council.

Even Wuttah Mauo found no fault with the idea. He proposed to accompany Wakwa to the surrounding Indian bands who must agree to a delicate alliance between themselves, the French allies, and English-Americans.

Because of his fallen status, Wuttah Mauo was asked to stay home and win the trust of his own village before adding his name to Wakwa's revolutionary pact.

The tribute the common people brought to the lodge of Silent Fox when the old sachim overruled his own son in favor of the youngest sachim further increased his prestige. Tame Deer made sure the gifts of meat and skins, wampum and service, were carefully redistributed among less fortunate families.

Wakwa began to exercise his privilege with quiet visits to the scattered Indian settlements, gathering a base for his next winter's journey north.

In April the women of the Massachuseuck could be seen on the heights, laden with their household belongings. Hours later the town was buzzing in its new location south of the winter quarters to catch the warming sun.

Planting began in the fields they worked in common, and the huts were set up where women could sit, protected from wind, ready to chase the crows away from the seeds.

This year Tame Deer was not to plant, but supervised her servants and lent advice to other young women. She spent more time working on the mannotaubana and found the preparations for Elizabeth not work but recreation, enjoying with it a new celebrity among her kinswomen and friends.

Wakwa began work on small surprises for the second wife as well, and as he sat carving or curing a skin would speak to Sequan in English and treasure the sight of the child turning to teach Tame Deer.

Elizabeth wished to bring something of herself into the otan and, resorting to her golden needles, embarked on the delight of designing presents for her new family. Her need for her old spinning wheel and loom and stuffs for making the silvery cloth for Pequawus' hanging gave Dr. Stirling his excuse to meet and examine her.

All gentleness with a patient, Stirling resumed his banter as his concentration lifted from the physical. He motioned Hanna into Elizabeth's chamber and turned to the pregnant girl to tease.

"Bonnie, you're as pretty as a Scottish lass and as headstrong, too! You an' your brown eyes will keep your wild king from roamin' any more."

Elizabeth blushed as she tied the little ribbons of her shift. "You do, then, like him?"

"What matters it if I like him? It's you must do that!"

Her face fell.

"All right." The doctor saw her tenderness about their racial blend. "I think him grand. More? And mighty. More!" His terseness opened to her dissatisfaction. "And mighty good, an' good to ye, and much surprised am I at all his kindnesses in your behalf. I should 'a thought a redman rough an' growlin'. *Grrrr!*" Stirling looked at the group around the fire. "An' there he stands, King Arthur himself. His great fault is he grew too big!"

"I can see where a man might object," Hanna quipped as she came in.

"Salty! Salty woman." The doctor moved away.

Alone with her niece for the first time in over half a year, Hanna shyly sought her hand. "Child Beth! As much as you will suffer me, I will be here to help. He makes you glad, even thus?" Hanna glanced around the high room of rough wood.

"Glad! There is no word for companionship such as his. But it is not only him. It is his life I love. How clear and deep and sweet run the thoughts of the Indians. Even were there no Silent Fox I would live close to them as they would allow. I hate Sweetwood now and long to lose myself among my child's people."

"I have never heard such a word as hate from thee!" Hanna was distraught.

252

"Aunt! You know my tongue. But does it not irk you to walk among such people as you meet at the tanner, and in the cottages and church, who look askance on the great possessions I have learned to see in the very dirt!"

"Yea, dear Beth, I am saddened every day."

"Then why do you bear it? Aunt, are you unhappy for me or thee?"

"I would not, nor wish that you, look askance on others," Hanna pleaded in a soft voice.

"Dear Ana. How sweetly you mother me!" Elizabeth accepted her appeal for moderation.

"Never can I presume to be a mother to you, Beth." Hanna was helping with the buttons of Beth's spring gown of the last of the rosebud cotton. "But I will be your friend. Remember, you have more experience than I. I have never felt the mystery you have growing inside you."

Elizabeth looked at her father's sister. "Let me share this mystery with you as he grows. This babe is more than only a grandnephew to you."

Hanna could not return her look. "Indeed, you must learn to share!"

"Mean you Tame Deer? Doth my decision shame you?"

"Oh!" Hanna cried. "My Beth! How? How?" The aunt searched the girl's face for some reassurance.

But Elizabeth retreated to a corner out of the fire's light and leaned weakly against the wall. "How, indeed! I do not know. Dear Aunt, I do not know!" She reached up for a basket of sassafras bark for tea.

* * * *

"Dunno' worry, lad, no more. Thy missus has enough room between those bones for a litter!"

Wakwa's look pierced the doctor as he tried to interpret his exact meaning.

"Rephrased," Gil mediated, "are you saying my niece is in fine condition and should expect a safe delivery?"

"Did I no' say that? As far as the date . . . I canno' be completely accurate, not knowin' by a calendar a few necessary things. Your little wife's lost track o' time."

"There is no trouble over that." Wakwa translated dates on his fingers. "He was conceived on the fourth day of nickommo. That would make it . . . December, the twenty-eighth day."

Dr. Stirling and Gil crossed glances.

"Fantastical!" Gil left with his guitar and sat on the hill above the river.

The doctor took the Indian aside. "I think, Silent Fox, I had better do my best to be in ridin' distance about the end of September."

"I thought he would come sooner."

"All this spinnin' of silver threads, an' livin' in the woods, an' the ghostly knowledge you profess, make me think I must come to witness this nativity."

"But you said yourself not to turn her from her purpose. I had much trouble with her even about your visit this day!"

"Never mind. I can sit under a tree and ne'er approach her side unless she calls for help. She never need know I will come."

Wakwa smiled. "Now it is you who have lost faith in her."

"Not so! I simply have the desire to play this pipe by the runnin' water yonder, an' may as well be nigh keepin' you out o' her way an' busy at your lyre." Dr. Mac drew a flute from an inner pocket. "Let us go an' find our elitest, Gilbert Worth. Him with all his violins an' harps an' Moors guitars!"

"Here, m'friend, is the instrument that has kept up me courage through many a dark night on an empty road or in a lonely cottage. A flute is all the music man needed a thousand years before the Greeks. Ye can pluck as many fancy strings as ye like, but it's this ye should be learnin', Silent Fox, for the singin' of your heart comes out on your breath, like a bird's!" The old man danced out the door, blowing his flute. "Strike up some L'Oiellet on your box o' strings, Gil."

All Wakwa could think was Gil's new word, *fantastical!*

* * * *

Left largely to himself by the special wish of Waban, Wakwa ran through the ever warmer spring nights to visit the Worths, always with the golden lyre.

Stirling came down from Sandwich twice each month and learned the path from the Worths' to the forest lodge, becoming more friend than physician to Elizabeth.

She blossomed with the child with this sudden acceptance and lost herself in the loveliness of her work.

Still in progress on the great coat for Wakwa, she finished the silver cloth, four feet in length and three in width, for his father. On this, in shades of gray, she sewed a complexity of satin strips, linking her visit to her father's house, the conception of her child, and her introduction to the father who was new.

She decorated a capelet of beaver skin for Tame Deer with a covering of feathers from small bright birds, rendering English flowers encircling the moon. It was how she saw herself and the first wife. She lined it with swan's down extended over the collar, which could be turned up and tied under the wearer's chin.

She stretched a quilt of fine wool for Waban's house and struggled at the effort of making Wuttah Mauo a wide-sleeved shirt of silk with a random embroidery of broken half hearts.

As she worked on these things she mulled over various gifts for Wakwa's daughter, not having arrived at anything suited to the child she was anxious to please.

The young wife's person was absorbed, but with the work time expanded, increasing her knowledge of the Indian who had revitalized her life.

Chapter 42

"Prithee, Fox, must I endure the surveillance of a group of strange men while you are gone? I will do nothing foolish."

June was well-advanced when Wakwa was called into service for Waban.

"Hardly can I leave you to the mercies of the forest, even in summer." He silenced her objections. "Kayaskwa, you must submit your will sometime to better sense than yours. The men will be no trouble and come to see that you and your baby are happy. You will be glad of them since you cannot go to your uncle's yet."

"I will end up entertaining and get nothing done! You Indians are great talkers."

"They will not ask a cup of water, as you well know. They will be here to do my will. What kind of sachim would keep his town protected but leave unguarded such as thee? Live alone, if you would, they will sleep under a tree or in a shelter of their own making. They must, at the least, tend my traps. Remember, thou art no longer a farmer's daughter, but Saunks."

Elizabeth lay down with him for the last time before his journey. While he held her in the fragrance of the evening, their fire bright, she asked, "What squabble between a common squaws and her mate is so important that it drags the great sachim of the Massachuseuck all the way to Rhode Island?"

The man placed his hands on her rounded belly. "They call me not so much as sachim, but as a man who can speak the woman's dialect. She is of our tribe, living with her husband's people. I used to know her."

"I did not know your peoples mixed."

"She mixes!" Wakwa brightened. "That is her trouble. She has played false for the last time with her husband's bed."

"How are you so sure?"

"She has been found lying with a youth. She was seen. There is proof this time."

"Then what can you say for her that will be of any use?"

"The punishment for such a crime . . . and she is beautiful . . . is mutilation."

"Mutilation!"

"You see then why she needs someone next to her to talk in circles around the town's anger. And the youth no less, for he will be blamed and punished in public at the whim of her husband."

"In an English town the girl would be blamed as a devil. Beautiful, you say? How well did you know her?"

Wakwa disregarded her possessiveness. "I would not step into this swamp were not the town under partial rule by an English overseer. He does not care too much for such sweeping judgments over a matter that seems trivial to him." Wakwa put his ear to Elizabeth's middle.

"What will be your position?" she puzzled. "Take the white man's view or support the old custom?"

"Custom! It is more our survival! We must keep each wetu straight. Living so closely without fidelity would make terrible confusion."

"How will it be done then?"

"Elizabeth!" He was horrified by her curiosity. "In your condition!"

He did not dwell on the grisly topic, for he was busy stroking her belly and looking at the golden light in her eyes.

Chapter 43

While Wakwa was crossing Fall River with twenty men from his tribe, Gil Worth was bathing. He dressed in plain, clean clothes of blue, an open-necked shirt, a short leather vest, and his incongruous straw hat.

Its broad brim, high crown, and long black sash were made to order for overseeing his orchards, stables, and fields in the high sun. He had bought it in France directly off the head of a farmer. When Gil Worth's straw hat began protecting his head from aches, Sweetwood was sure summer had arrived.

He was taking the afternoon off from farming and music to visit his neighbor, Annanias Hudson. Going to test his mood, perhaps by now one of repentance, he would try to smooth things out before the public solemnities of Elizabeth's marriage were undertaken.

He could not resist a slow trot over to his greenhouse after Matthew brought him his horse. Other New England men raised cattle, grain, and vegetables. Gilbert Worth excelled in fruit.

He had his smattering of milk cows and a kitchen garden which sustained his household. He had a large flock of sheep crowded into the northern pasture. But his corn was notoriously bad and he bought what he needed from others, not wasting ground on grain.

Apples, peaches, cherries, walnuts, chestnuts, acres of cranberries, strawberries, blueberries, gooseberries, and flax were his pets and had no peer in the region.

Without intending it, he showed increased earnings every year, shipping fruit out of Wareham to the burgeoning cities. He was scientific in his approach to his favorite crops and lay awake nights planning for the wormless apple, the sweeter cherry.

This year Hanna was almost jealous of the new tenants of the greenhouse. They were a family of citrus trees. Since Italy Gil had pined for lemons and oranges and decided to find a way to raise them in New England. Dr. Stirling considered this design akin to latent madness, but patiently he accompanied Gil to the glass house, week after week, to watch the progress of the cuttings as the spring passed and the summer wafted in.

****

Annanias, too, watched the farms and forest burst into flower and turn green as he convalesced in his upstairs chamber.

The Elders saw to the seeding of his land in April, because he was still unable to work the ground himself, weakness necessitating his use of a cane. But it was to Worth they made appeal for financial help in hiring farm labor for Hudson.

Gil had agreed and now supported a small group of Irish immigrant laborers out of respect to his sister-in-law's memory. But he used this powerful wedge to force an agreement that a permanent assistant minister should be brought in at the public expense immediately. His plan was to make painful the strain of financing two preachers, causing the sensible farmers to compare between an upright man and Annanias, forcing them to let Hudson go.

Yet the farmers' wives surrounded Hudson with sympathy, and his kitchen was so swamped with puddings and confections that the housekeeper begged the goodwives to stop.

Without fail each day Prudence Hanson baked and brought him an apple cobbler, securing most afternoons a few minutes of conversation with Hudson himself. He ate, and mended, and heard the urgings of his friends to quit his waiting for Beth's return and begin anew with a different woman.

The element which escaped his townsmen was the hot sting in his hide that he had been bested by an Indian.

****

This day Hudson woke from a nap determined to walk to the barn without his cane. Slowly strength was returning and with it his yearning for some connection with the life he saw waving in every stalk of corn. His manhood depended on leaving the cane behind.

He shuffled into the kitchen to check for his cobbler, his black summer coat buttoned wrong. The pie was there but Prue was not, and without waiting until supper he downed the whole thing then and there.

He sweated more from weakness than from the sun as his

shoes pressed into the soft earth. The barn seemed far away and he stopped to rest against a crabapple tree decked in new red leaves. When he saw the high doors open he pushed himself away from the tree and walked purposefully toward the barn. He blamed the Irish workers and walked faster as he fantasized the scolding he would give them when they came in at sunset. All the animals were out except an old mare in need of shoeing, yet this carelessness was against his specific wishes.

Annanias stopped in front of the stack of wood inside the door. Neatly arranged were the boards to finish the dressing room for Beth. The oval tub plated in lead remained unpacked in its crate. He had engineered an underground drainage pipe of copper-lined wood from tub to meadow as a joint experiment in bathing luxury for her and an irrigation channel for himself.

"Spoiled girl," he muttered, caressing the wood. A splinter caught his skin. He went toward the harness room for an implement to remove it.

His heels scraped the cool earthen floor. Light glowed in a single shaft from the open shutter in the loft, and Annanias experienced pleasure as he passed through it, sensing he had been seen by some angel of the day.

There was a surprised sound from the mare's stall that could not have come from the horse, and Hudson peeked through the open top of the door.

In the shadows stood Prudence Hanson, her form curving abruptly away from the rough boards of the sidewall. Her arms came up to hide her bosom. The minister made no move, but only looked, trying to interpret the picture before him. Her full calves arrested his attention. Their strength and whiteness, so unmoving, supporting the rest of her body, made Annanias think of his white sow, standing after suckling her new litter.

The mare flicked her tail at a black fly and Hudson pulled open the door. The girl clasped her hands at the small of her back, revealing her short, conical breasts. Annanias searched the stall and saw her clothing bunched in a corner. He gestured feebly toward it. But Prudence stepped across the floor and stood just within the minister's reach.

Annanias tore the horse's blanket off a hook and clumsily pushed it against her front, but Prudence did not accept it. The blanket slipped to the floor.

260

"Prue!" Hudson hid his eyes.

The girl's slight flush made her pinched face pretty for a moment. "Never did I expect you to come to see me!"

"Put on your things. What do you do?" Annanias could not resist looking at her body again. "I came not to see you!"

She stepped one step closer to him.

He began again. "Dress thyself. Please. I came only to test my strength. To walk alone without my cane."

Prudence Hanson came closer still. "I have never been seen unclothed. How strange, I am not afraid! Some girls run away in fear. I am here. I will be your crutch."

Annanias stepped out and back into the glittering dust motes behind the door. "Why came you to my barn today? Dress and leave me to myself!"

She took up the hay-smattered blanket and draped it over one shoulder, hiding most of her body.

"Each day I come to your barn. It is warm and smells of life. I have no life, I dream of you. How massive you are, lit by that halo of gold!"

Deeply flattered by this new view of his self-conscious bulk, Hudson softened. "Each day you come, child? To do what?"

Prue smiled and drew the blanket totally to one side. Her arms came over the door and she pressed against it, only the wood separating her from the man.

"Stand back! You will damage your body!"

"Care you, Mr. Hudson? Annanias I may call you now, granted you have seen me. I will press and press until I'm blue so your care for me will grow."

He disliked her then in her selfish assault on his senses. He disliked himself for his arousal, judging her unworthy even to be tempting him.

She grew petulant. "What must I do to show you that I love you?"

"Love? What know you of love?"

"Nothing! Teach me about love! I stand here of an afternoon stroking this horse, enjoying its warmth against my skin. At night I wake my mother with my screams of pain over you. Come and wed me! My dowry is not so great as a Dowland's but I will bring happiness to you. Must I teach you to love?"

Prudence Hanson moved from the door and approached the

rump of the horse, talking to it as she moved. She leaned against its dappled coat and caressed the flank with her hand.

"Stop!" Hudson could not bear the degradation she caused him. He rushed in, angrily grabbing her away from the animal.

The glow of her skin in the diffused light, the little creases where her breasts curved away from her armpits, the closeness of his face to her light brown, waving hair, overrode his opposition to the idea of her, and before he knew, the skin of his own stomach was pressed against her yielding body, and he searched for the place where he could pour his bitterness and release the pressure of his frustration.

* * * *

As Prudence Hanson leaned against the stall door, persuading Hudson toward her satisfaction, Gil Worth laid his horse's rein loosely over the post and knocked at the front door of the manse.

"Best of afternoons, Millie!" He tipped his outlandish hat and loaded the middle-aged woman's arms with Hanna's pink roses.

"Why, Mr. Worth, sir!" She was flustered. "The minister's not in. Not yet."

"Still out, is he? Makes he rounds on such a day?"

"You did come to see him? You came to talk to the Reverend."

"Oh, yes. But we'll not tell the town about you and me!"

"Master Worth! It has been ever so long since you have come down to us."

"Too long, Millie. How are the Irish coming on?"

"Well enough. Great workers, but they never seem to eat, you know."

"Give them some of your bread and jam, Mother, I miss it myself."

"Ah . . . sir! If you want to know where Mr. Hudson's gone, I . . ."

"Very much."

"Well, he left this for the first time." She held up Hudson's cane.

"He has ridden out somewhere?"

"He walked up to the barn without it! He's been all of half an hour now. He may need some help. Shall I come with you?" She reached for her bonnet.

Gil snapped off one of the buds she still held and laced it into his hat. "No need. You'll only get mussed in this warm sun. You could ready me some jam, though."

He strolled toward the big gray barn, enjoying the balmy breeze. He held Wakwa's pipe unlit between his teeth, thinking it best not to bait the minister with smoking. Gil saw the doors slightly open and boyishly tried to slip in between them without moving them, but the hat brim was too wide. He became conscious of a scraping noise from within and thought he heard a moan. Anxious that Hudson was ill and would be embarrassed or startled, Gil was now in earnest to enter unseen. He tossed his hat onto the grass and stepped lightly through the tight opening.

He peered into the dimness and caught sight of Annanias' feet in the beam of sunlight, protruding from a stall, one stocking still clinging. A girl's tense grunts grated on Gil's ears, and the sounds he heard from Annanias made him move with a jerk back through the doors. He grabbed his hat and fled out of sight, midway between the barn and the house.

Gil swabbed his face with the hat's black sash and found himself cursing in a whisper to the chickens in the coop.

"Bastard! Hypocrite! Filthy swine! I would say he needs help! Blundering, oafish pig!

"Lord, I begin to believe in thy Providence! Thank thee for Beth's safety!

"Bungling, incompetant, two-faced bastard! I should have stopped him! Poor little bitch." Gil lit his pipe with a shaking hand. "I'd have had him if I'd brought Millie along, goddammit!"

Prudence came limping down the gravel path, her bonnet strings dangling, her wicker pie basket empty.

Gil wanted to approach to be kind, and while he decided if he should, she went past without seeing him.

He leaned against the crabapple, puffing quick little rings in the hot air. "That one will be back for what's owing to her. Better I did not stop them. They will meet again, and I will be the avenging angel."

Hudson appeared in his shirt sleeves in front of the barn. He flung his jacket over his shoulder and marched toward his house on the now-empty lane. He passed Gil up, then sniffed the fragrant smoke, turned, and riveted his frightened eyes on Gilbert Worth. He had no choice but to step onto the lawn.

Gil wagged his hat in Hudson's direction as the minister lumbered nearer.

"How be you, neighbor?" Hudson was sweating.

"O tempora, O mores!" Gil rolled his eyes.

"Have you just come?" Annanias licked his lips.

"You have just come, Reverend! I feel so Ciceronian today! Is this not a day from southern Italy?"

"I have never been, so cannot compare. You lament the times and customs, brother?"

Gil let his eyes roam over to the barn. "Not lament! I am more encouraged with each passing day. How does it feel . . . to be well again? I see you are willing to own me brother. Behold, even that improves."

Annanias looked down at his dirty shoes. "I have been meaning to thank you for your help and support. God knows, I would have been ruined without you."

"God knows everything, as the papists say!"

Hudson blinked his dilated eyes.

Gil was moved by the minister's embarrassment under this relentless innuendo. Hudson was a man after all. Would it not be easier to reason with a fellow who copulated in a barn than one who screamed the Old Testament to a church full of worshippers?

Gil knocked out his pipe. "You look tired, Annanias. Won't you sit on your grass with me?"

"I have never been so tired."

"That will improve as well." Gil could not resist a quip, his seriousness reversed by Hudson's self-pity.

And Hudson grew infuriated with himself for seeing things through guilty eyes. He shook his big head, trying to clear it of recent visions. He looked at his graceful companion, sitting in glacial coolness while he sweated with fear and fatigue, and his candor was covered by a cloud of self-forgiveness.

Gil, not sensing the moment of rapprochement had passed, continued, "Look, my man, we are never going to be friends. You've said some things and done some things, and I have offended you, I am sure. Perhaps I brought it on."

"Yes?"

"But though we are different men," Gil pulled the rose from his hat, "can't you believe that I and everyone in the town would see you happy? Break away from here. You are wasted in this place. There's much needs doing in Pennsylvania, and all along the Miami River the first settlers are crying for a man to lead them and tame that frontier mob into a unified settlement."

"The Indians are hostile there."

"And here?"

"Here they are just Indians."

Annanias' hardness brought up Gil's defenses. "Your assistant is due in August. With your slow recovery, Mayhew Low will keep the sheep in the pen for you, I vow."

"There is but one stray lamb I seek."

"Hudson! Give Beth up! It was her father's last word to you. He lies sleeping not a thousand feet from us! I am her guardian and I have given her her head. Don't get caught on the common with your shirttails hanging out for her." Gil waved his shapely fingers at Hudson's disarray. "Summon your dignity and realize she will come into society soon, and travel."

"Society!"

"Better to marry some willing girl, fast, and know happiness."

"Worth, the things of this world mean much to you, do they not?"

"Leave the Dowlands and the Indians and the Eastern potentates alone, Annanias. You will never understand them. Take a post in a good college and teach your otherworldliness! I'll buy you a new damned church anywhere. Let go here, preacher."

"You would help me resettle?"

"As I say, we are not close, but I have no need to see you miserable. You could have a family! Think of it! To make your own flesh and blood walk after you. Life would mean something again. Remove!"

"A stone church? My own mill?"

"What do you need with a mill? All right. A mill."

"A stipend, 'til a town be formed and support forthcoming?"

"Within reason."

"Total silence to the Elders about the whole arrangement?"

"Annanias, they would take me to a madhouse if I told them all I will do for you."

"And never a word to dearest Beth why this sudden change of place?"

"That would be unseemly. In the end, I suppose you were a well-intentioned fellow. I am silent as a trap."

"Get thou behind me, Satan!" Annanias stood, drawing this cliché around himself like a mantle of righteousness.

Gil was incensed at having been made into a monkey when his offer had been so sincere. "I would not trust the old boy at my back, Annani-ass!"

Gil whistled for his horse and sprayed Hudson's shoes with dust as he rode on past.

Chapter 44

Elizabeth received her uncle only once during the three weeks Wakwa was away. Gil came, abstracted by the crisis of his orchards.

His peach trees had developed a powdery stigma on their barks, and the young leaves had yellowed.

"Uncle Gil," Elizabeth felt inventive when alone, "could you not simply clean the trees? Cause a rain-like shower of something uncongenial to this powder?"

"Aside from the detail of what this uncongenial substance might be, you are not a bad farmer, Beth! But I fear the fruit would dislike your nasty shower as much as the powder.

"For you to fully understand I must paint the picture of your Aunt Hanna's kitchen in these past few days. Between the bark and the wood of the trees I found small worms."

"Yes?"

"I isolated them in glass jars, Winke bemoaning the expense the while."

"How is your housekeeper niggardly with her jam pots when your farm is at stake!"

"I understand Winke. Winke is all right. Well, here we are, your aunt and myself, Winke and Matthew, disgusted over these jars because the worms hatched a form of winged insect."

"I do not think I would raise peaches, Uncle."

"I say to myself, Gilbert Theodore Worth, winged insects cannot fly betwixt bark and wood. They must fly free! Like a knight, I ride to the orchard. Simple observation shows these mothers of mischief laying eggs on my peach leaves! The eggs hatch into maggots. The maggots feed on the leaves that were their cradles and, devouring these, eat up the bark. My peach trees strangle right at the ground."

"Then you must kill the maggots!"

"Think you so? *The Sussex New Jersey Register* warns of a peach wasp scourge. It tells me that the wasps leave a powder on the trees which cause their death.

"I ride out to find the wasps. Thank Providence for my straw hat which allows me the leisure to sit long hours under the sun without stroke, though my Hanna disputes it!

"Contrary to the opinion of *The Sussex New Jersey Register*, the wasps are depositing not powder but baby worms of their own. The wasp worms burrow into the holes left by the maggots, the grandchildren of our worms in Mrs. Winke's glass jars!"

"Let me think, Uncle Gil . . . the worms in Mrs. Winke's jars . . ."

"It is simple, child! There is a war between wasp worms and worm maggots, and the sickly powder is but evidence that Nature herself, through agency of the wasps, is providing antidote.

"But I cannot wait for the outcome of the battle between two sets of worms to decide the fate of my farm!"

Elizabeth laughed so hard that her child kicked her in retaliation. She held her plump belly happily, thinking of the joy the uncle would undoubtedly bring the baby when they could finally be companions.

"I skulk home, seeking a way to murder the lot. Like you, I devise complicated potions, wondering how to poison the bugs and not the trees.

"And now I have a method. And I have written to *The Sussex New Jersey Register*, claiming a discovery!"

"Uncle Gil, you are wonderful!"

"Winke is wonderful. Hanna and I sat at tea, watching these creatures writhe on the table, Matthew swatting at our escaped, experimental wasp. Winke walked over with the kettle and an 'I'll not bide these things in my kitchen, more!' She scalded them to death with water from the kettle. Splash!"

"Oh. Good." Elizabeth was doubtful.

"I've refined it a bit." Gil had descended from joviality. "I must stay in Sweetwood until all the trees on all the farms are scalded. I hope to God the farmers will accept this method. These things travel. They spread. They cause a blight which may last generations."

* * * *

And so Gilbert Worth worked, sweating at the side of his laborers, mixing boiling water with cool, digging shallow moats

268

around the trunks, filling them with scalding water to heat the bark, executing the insects almost one by one.

They wrapped the few healthy trees with sheep's wool to protect them, and his orchard became a parade of mummies in the moonlight. They carted their equipment to the other farmers, lending their backs and advice.

Matthew traveled with his master, the value of his presence far greater than his ample muscle. His entree into the servant quarters made him invaluable in dealing with farmers not so willing to use "wild Worth's" experimental cure. Matthew walked into back doors and front ones opened up to Gil. The former slave had an extra usefulness—gathering the gossip. He appeared suddenly from anyone's barn, loaded with lengths of wool, his ears tuned to the whispers about the secrets of the more illustrious class.

Annanias Hudson grew uncomfortable with this new invasion of strangers on his land. The Irish, the black, the farmers, all helping him, all beholden to Gilbert Worth. He made rounds again and found himself searching the neighborhood for some quiet haven where he could lie with Prue, to steal some respite from surrounding eyes that seemed to condemn his stubbornness or coddle his loneliness, as if he were a jackass in a ditch.

* * * *

Elizabeth's guards were pleasant men, anxious to supply her needs of sustenance and security. Her unusual status in the tribe, due to her personal merit and her position as Wakwa's wife, afforded power to her wishes in their eyes. But demands from the white saunks were nonexistent. She was self-sufficient.

The young woman carried her own water, collected her own kindling, made a tasty samp of corn and berries for them in the mornings. She was solitary as a man on her long walks by the river. She was never indolent, but worked over her sewing during her free sunlight hours. The captains respected her merits as a woman and a wife and attributed her acquisition by Wakwa as a sign of his special blessing by Manit. They spoke softly of her unique beauty and grew tender over her care, bringing in delicacies for her to eat. A week passed in this way, the hunters considering their assignment a holiday.

Summer rain came and the rhythm of their lives changed. Wakwa's second wife grew even quieter with them, resting at peculiar times, leaving their tasty morsels untouched or spoiled before she could prepare them. The men breakfasted on jerky soup of their making and murmured suspiciously about the woman's one-sided conversations which she seemed to be holding with her unborn child. The hair they so admired was left in a neglected braid, and she grew so heavy and sickly they made her a staff to assist her to her private spot in the woods where she saw to her physical needs. They discussed calling in the taupowaw or at least a woman to advise them, but were relieved of the responsibility of decision when, at last, the English-woman made a request. Almost gladly, they left in a canoe for the ponds to fill large baskets with swan feathers.

Humid heat returned, and Elizabeth was relieved to have the men away from her private corner of activity. The embroidery of Wakwa's coat, more than half-finished when he went away, was the outlet for her affection. As the weather closed her in, her gage of time became hazy. The vacancy within her from Wakwa's absence transfigured itself into the norm. She fed on work, not meat. She resented the time invested in the very process of cooking and eating. She subsisted on dried fish, loving its tantalizing availability.

She was tempted to actually finish the great wolf-sleeved coat. And in the touch of the brilliantly red wool, and the glossy intricacy of black thread, she was seduced into abandonment of herself for her art. Other objectives misted into the animal taking life before her under the flash of her needles in the firelight.

The design became more ambitious, growing weed-like. She dared the aching of her back, and fell off to sleep while she sewed, and dreamt of the sewing while she slept.

The frenzy of her absorption led her to ignore the tingling, then prickling, then pain, of her swelling limbs and body. She became a servant to the beauty of the concept becoming reality through her hands and neglected her outer person. She saw her inner self culminated in her work.

It was only when the doeskin shell was sewn to the finished lining, and the black fur sleeves were in place in the arm holes, and the piping of wolf hair bordered the coat from hood to hem, that the smells and sights of the real world pressed her.

270

Elizabeth awakened to her needs too late. She needed help and care and sleep. She needed proper food and air and exercise.

Her predicament dawned in almost pleasurable discomfort, and she tumbled from the glory of her work to fright of necessities she could not meet.

It took almost an hour for her to drag a pail from the stream and set the water to boil. It was a great effort to lift her arms over her unnaturally distended breasts and belly to untangle her hair for washing. She rested and was conscious of an obscene change in her shape, her body enlarged by an abnormal retention of fluids.

The baby floated very still within, and she grew afraid for it as she hobbled to a basket for some toweling. To be clean would be a beginning. She must improve her condition before her husband came home. He might not even recognize her.

It was as she slowly drew her basket of toiletries toward herself that she realized Wakwa was standing in the doorway.

"Wakwa! Not you!"

"This is my greeting, Kayaskwa?" Wakwa lounged outside against the door frame, one naked foot braced against the opposite side, the broiling July foliage as his backdrop.

"You are come as I was about to bathe. And is it not more usual to call out your presence? How did you fare?"

"You are sly!" Sun-blinded, he blinked into the dark interior, unable to see her clearly. "Dost pretend to be the fox in her lair, luring the hunter inside only to devour him?"

She tried to push back her annoyance at his flippancy and easy grace as he leaned strong and supple at the entryway. "I have good news."

"As have I! What passions we have unraveled, like the mad spider's web, in these few days." He wiped his face, grimy with council grease and dust.

"It seemed longer to me, alone."

"Oh! My mistress. I do detect a scolding there. Spare me. It is too hot here in the sun."

"Do not strain yourself to enter, lest we argue further." Elizabeth secured soap, despairing that she could hide herself from him, yet pushing him away with words. "How long does it take to cut up mischievous women in Rhode Island?"

"Ah! Thou art curious, my love, yet will not nod thy head that I may enter my own lodge."

"Heaven, come in! I do not bar the door! You seem content loitering there like a wayward schoolboy."

"That is what I am, truly. I have learned so much about people's hearts in all this time."

"I have finished your coat."

"Have you?" He smiled up and away, lost in his own remembrances.

"Methought it would be pleasing to you."

He laughed at the sky.

Elizabeth snapped, "I take it this evil woman is not divided up?"

"You 'take it' rightly." Comfortable, Wakwa crossed his arms over his chest.

"Wherefore did his highness Silent Fox change his august mind?"

"I told you she was charming!" His eyes gleamed through the dimness.

Elizabeth struggled up, incensed. "If that is an example of the native wit, you may as well put on the stiff countenance your people enjoy credit for. Rude man! How could you distress me with her when I am in this condition?"

"Elizabeth! You are serious!"

She began to weep hot, bitter tears.

"Is it the child makes you so tender? Little bird, come to me. Thou knowst I would never make thee weep! It were unseemly to say. My spirits are high from all the noise and entertainment we suffered them to give us."

"I hope, husband, it is not rum drives you home so insolent!"

"Wife! Come. A little air will do you good. We will walk and begin again. I cannot believe your anger at such a small jest."

She moved toward him, her bare feet tingling as her swollen soles padded across the floorboards. She rocked her body like an old woman's to keep balance.

The man was horrified at her struggle to obey and went to her and put his arms around her. He was surprised at her girth. He turned her face up to himself and felt its fullness, worry coursing through his eyes.

"What is it!"

"It is nothing. It happens."

He looked in her eyes. "You cannot walk?"

Elizabeth sighed. "I will walk."

She moved to take a step and Wakwa screamed. He saw her foot swollen far beyond normal size, the bloated toes splaying apart. He knelt, passing his hand up underneath her skirt, against the hair of her unshaved leg. He grabbed up the gown and stared.

"Your legs are like trees! Your feet . . . your shape is gone! What is it?"

"Wakwa. There is water in me. It will go away. I suppose."

"You are unkempt! You are weary! Have you been ill all this time? Where are my men? I must bring Dr. Mac!"

"Fine. Race off again. I must go to my spot in the trees." She passed him by, taking her staff for support. "This is an event I have waited for all day."

Wakwa stood transfixed, repulsed by the ruin of his beautiful wife. He caught up to her and blocked her path.

"Where is my guard, Elizabeth?"

"Let me pass!"

"Why is it you have waited the whole day to make water? And where are the men? I shall thrash them with my own hands for this!"

"I will soil the earth like a dog if I am not allowed by!" As he let her go, she lashed out, "And try to control your mighty power over us common souls. It was I sent the men away. They bear no fault in this. They are off in the canoe gathering down for Waban's quilt. They have been most cooperative."

Wakwa was deeply angry with her attitude and stormed off to the stream.

When she returned he was standing in front of the door with an expression on his face that would have driven her into Annanias' arms had Wakwa looked that way the first time they met.

She made an attempt to reconcile their argument. "I would go to bathe, husband. I must sit before I fall."

"You will stand until you make this clear!"

She threw down the stick and met his anger. "Are you not done torturing women?"

"Say no more words like those! You, who have spoiled your-self with some foolishness! Tell me what you have done."

"What do you mean? What do I ever do!"

"Evade me not. It is the cause of this I wish. But tell me, what occupied thy time whilst I was at Council?"

"I sewed."

"This is all?"

"All! Night and day, alone, I strove to finish the presents for your family. Time is growing short!"

"Did you, perchance, eat?"

She hated him that minute for hitting at the center of her problem. "I ate . . . when I was hungry."

"Then explain to me why the weir in the stream is next to breaking with the fish that strain against it. You had only to reach in for one!"

"I ate not of them."

"Of what did you eat?"

She squirmed away from truth. "If I were hungry when the men brought meat, I ate it. If not, sent it back to the otan."

"How does a woman grow to such a size and not eat?"

"I ate! Oh, let me sit!"

Wakwa hid his eyes. "No!"

"Nights I have stayed up with my back splitting from bottom to top for you, and you use me thus?"

"This is your gift to me? This thing you have become that I behold! Wherefore did you without sleep for my sake?"

Tears glittered at the crudeness of his observation. "I say I have finished the great work of my life, and you remark it not! You laugh rudely about your comely adulteress, when your wife has pricked the skin off her fingers to make a gift worthy of a prince. Fool that I was!"

"We are agreed in that. Your great work is the child in your womb. Can you not see you are killing him? What bloats you like a drowned thing?"

"Do not tell me our excellent Tame Deer never held some water in her when she carried your daughter!"

"Never! Never do I remember such as this."

"Perchance you have forgot. It hath been so long since she conceived." Elizabeth purposely plunged him into pain.

274

He was silenced, grief-stricken at the wound she had torn open. But then his voice rose in a screech like a bird's. "What poison passed into you while I was gone? Where is Kayaskwa?"

She could not speak although she saw his lovely nature transformed into rage.

He left her to look in the house for a clue.

She was kneeling on all fours, relieving the stress on her back, when he reappeared.

"Elizabeth, there is nothing there! You have not readied a cake. The new basket of corn is untouched."

He dug by the side of the house where they kept the dried foods cool. "Even the fish is gone!" he moaned. He came and sat in front of her, pitying her condition. "Must you stay there dumb and crouching like a forlorn animal? I am home. I will help you. Are you poisoned? Are you starved?" He was gentled by concern and parted her dangling hair from her eyes.

"If only I could sit . . ." she whimpered, tears skidding into her nostrils, her head pitched forward between her shoulders. The heels of her hands were hot on the dust and she despised herself for excluding him from her confidence. She gambled with his anger. "I craved the salt."

"You ate salt?"

"It was so convenient. It kept my eyes open and my hands moving and my spirits up. I do not know when I slept, or if I slept. I sewed and sewed and my mind got tangled in the work that breathed and talked to me like a being come alive!" She fell to the ground and gave in. "I ate salted fish until it was gone and burned the box since I could no longer walk out for firewood." She turned her eyes to his unbelieving face. "The salt ran out two days ago and I am growing weak. I cannot stomach the food the men bring to me, but only drink and drink in all this heat."

The man seized her shoulders, using all his strength to bring her to her feet. "Mad! Ignorant! Filling yourself with trash! Know you not you have poisoned not only yourself? Must I be father and mother too? Go in the house! I see what I must do to cure you."

If he had been angry before, it was nothing to his outrage now. She lay trembling on her mat in the heat and covered her head with her fat arms, cheated of his forgiveness.

The bathwater in the kettle had dried up, and the scalded iron let off a foul smell.

Wakwa fixed it, ranting, "A man comes from a journey, he is tired, he expects a smile and some food from his wife, and is met by snarls. How you are paid by Manit for your monstrous selfishness! I am weary! Weary after all these days of sitting in the sun, sorting out the disgusting life of that woman. And I come back to find my own wife destroyed by her own hand!"

He took something from his carrying basket. "Here! I bought you wheat flour for you to make your precious English bread!" The sack split open where he tossed it on the floor.

He began to braid his hair and ready his bow. "Now, when my bones are ready to fall away, instead of resting I will go to hunt. Will that make you happy? Since you have sent my men off on some old woman's errand, I must go to shoot a hapless deer that I may cure you."

She was in a turmoil over his disrespect for her work. It was the inside of herself, more important to her than comfort. Yet the child she had longed for was suffering.

He bent near her, his face showing his hurt. "You will learn, tonight, to act better than a child and behave not as a sucking infant, but a mother at last." His voice broke and he petted her swollen cheek. "Do not move. Not a finger! Let not the poison course through thee."

She gripped his wrist. "Why say you I am poisoned?"

"The water must go somewhere if it does not pass out of you! Unlettered Indian that I am, I know some little things. Stay still. Pray!"

"To whose god shall I pray?"

It was dark when Wakwa came back. The fire was only a red glow and mosquitoes flitted in and out the open door.

Elizabeth was asleep, her position unchanged. She woke at the thud of a carcass on the floor.

"Wakwa? Forgive?" She had resigned the luxury of acting with single purpose.

"I forgive. . . . I only wonder why you do not love yourself."

"I love you too much!"

This brought no reaction but cursing, as Wakwa's knife slipped and slashed through the skin of the doe.

"Why did you bring the deer in here? There will be a mess."

276

"There will be more mess than this, ere long!" He disposed of the skin and feet and head for later use.

The sights and smells sickened her. "All this effort! I only wish some cool water."

"Cool water you will not get, but hot broth of dandelions to draw the water out of you."

Then Wakwa stood, straddled the skinned flesh, lifted his breech cloth, and urinated on the meat.

"Jehovah! What do you do!" The English girl recoiled, disgusted.

"I prepare your dinner."

The wife lurched off her mat and crawled against the wall. "What is this revenge! Savagery!" She screamed short, helpless screams. "I am alone!"

Disregarding her hysteria, Wakwa tied the deer up above the ashes and made a high fire underneath. He went out for water to wash down the floor and returned to find her sobbing, her face pressed against the wall. He sat near her and felt her first fear of him as she drew away. He stayed with her, downcast, the acrid smell of the scorching meat circling them.

She summoned what was left of her reason. "Wakwa Manunnappu, I am your match. I shall not eat that. Your anger is out of bounds. Punish me some other way. I have said that I am sorry."

"Elizabeth Dowland, I do not punish you. I am not trained in London. This is the only way I know to make you well. My urine will make your salt. Many times, in the north, I myself have eaten thus to keep alive."

At this irrefutable claim she lost control and squealed, "I will not eat that!"

Wakwa stepped away and snuffed the fire. He looked at her terrorized face and said, evenly, "You will eat it. All that I give you. You will be greatly ill for three days. Not from this food, but from what you will lose out of yourself. Weak, dizzy, and . . . other things. Then you will rise, stronger than ever you imagined you could be and you will run like a cat. You will never require your kind of salt again."

The husband tore off a joint of meat and divided it with a powerful twist of his hands to make it easier for her to hold.

She sank heavily onto her large belly and spilled out more tears. "Papa! Papa!" she groaned in helpless litany.

"Dear wife, crying will not melt the poison out of you. Calm thyself to eat." He stood ready, the pink meat on the bone oozing its juices.

"It is yet raw!" She gagged and turned away.

Relentless, Wakwa sat her up and pushed the lukewarm flesh into her hands. "Now, eat."

Still she fought him. "You do take advantage of my promise never more to run away!"

"You are not my slave, Elizabeth. You may go. Go. Go and die of this insanity and take with you all my heart!"

She was ghastly white as she bit down and felt terrible shame as her teeth tore away meat permeated with the waste liquid from his body. She made her first swallow, choking down her degradation.

"Won't you join my evening repast, Sachim?" Warm blood smeared her cheeks.

"Do not be hard, Elizabeth." He took the bone from her and held his other hand behind her neck, and slowly, very slowly, drew her changed face toward his own weary one. He pressed his lips against hers, but there was no response. He pressed harder, licking her mouth inside with his tongue. "Now I have tasted of your remedy."

It was then that her arms came around his bare, sweaty back, and she answered his kiss, lifted back into herself by his acknowledgment of her suffering. They clung together in their sordid state in the hot black room until flies began to bother the meat.

She ate steadily then while Wakwa rubbed her back.

She chewed, distracted by this miserable end to her ecstasy of creation, seeing no graceful way to admit her fault.

He had called her a child, unwifely, and she articulated her failure internally. Her concentration gave rise to the memory of Proverbs, and she repeated phrases to him so he could know her aspirations.

" 'If one can find a good wife,
    She is worth far more than corals.' "

278

Wakwa rose and mended the fire.

> " 'Her husband puts his trust in her,
>   And finds no lack of gain.' "

Wakwa reached for a clean cloth and fresh water and cleaned her face as she chewed and prayed.

> " 'She sorts out wool and flax,
>   And works it up as she wills.' "

Elizabeth gave in to tears, then bit down again.

> " 'She perceives that her work is profitable,
>   So her lamp goes not out at night.' "

Wakwa found the coat and spread it to the light of the fire. The meat was cold and bitter, soft to the teeth, but too tough to chew well enough for swallowing.

> " 'She lays her hand on the distaff,
>   Her fingers grasp the spindle.' "

The old words about the good wife filled her with their irony.

> " 'She is not afraid of the snow for her household;
>   For her household are all clothed in scarlet.'
>
> 'She makes coverlets for herself,
>   Her clothing is linen and purple.' "

Wakwa was touching the black figures on the red wool with admiring hands.

In a thick voice she kept on.

> " 'Her husband is known at the gates,
>   And he sits among the elders of the land.' "

Wakwa came to her in awe of her work. She chewed and talked.

> " 'She is clothed in strength and dignity,
>   And she laughs at the days to come.' "

Wakwa wiped away her tears as she broke again.

> " 'She opens her mouth in wisdom,
>   And kindly counsel is on her tongue.' "

279

Elizabeth hid her face in the crook of her arm.

" 'She looks well after her household,
And eats not the bread of idleness.' "

She was finished with the meat and held the bone out to him,
ashamed to look at him. Repeatedly she attempted to speak, but
could not go on. Wakwa threw the remains into the fire, continuing for her, surprising her with his knowledge.

" 'Her children rise up and bless her,
Her husband also, and praises her:

Many women have done well,
But you have excelled them all.

Charms are deceptive, and beauty is a breath; . . .
Let her deeds bring her praise at the gates.' "

* * * *

Elizabeth suffered through her purge on an outdoor bed and
measured the days by the changing sky. By the first evening
her toes rested normally, one against the other. Vacillating between shame and sensibility, Elizabeth talked and slept under
stars.

"Poor boy! Was he very damaged?" she asked as she gingerly
bit into a tomato Wakwa had given her to slake her constant
thirst. She had been taught from childhood they were poison-
ous.

"He will have a different nose when the swelling disappears.
The husband showed much control with him."

"But you say Panther Eye seduced the youth. They did not
beat her, I vow!"

"Her husband did, Kayaskwa." Wakwa grew very quiet. "Until the blood ran. She stood very still for him. He would have
killed her but for me and the overseer."

"You sided with the English!"

"It may seem so. My purpose was to do them out of another
Indian to hang. Were the husband to kill his wife, the English
would have taken him and strung him from a high tree for
murder. His protector would then seek to avenge him. Revolt!
I strongly urged the Nipmuc to forbear."

"She lives with him again?"

"Never. No one wanted her."

"Alas, lonely woman."

"It makes me glad, Elizabeth, you see her view. I thought to send her north, but never mentioned that. How should I make friends with those people, sending such a siren into their midst? Her husband sent her back to her own people."

"Her own? Your own! Are her own, then, my own? What is becoming of innocence? Is there innocence in this world, Wakwa?" She crawled behind the bushes.

"I brought her to our town and she will live ever so chastely or change her climate prematurely."

"Panther Eye, the monk!" Elizabeth moaned as she made her way back to the blanket and lay down.

Wakwa stroked her damp hair away from her face. "You are thinner, Kayaskwa."

"She traveled with you?"

"Does your head spin?" He fanned her with a broad leaf.

"It makes me sick to move."

"I am her protector now."

Elizabeth vomited then, and with the weight of the child pulling against the heaving of her stomach, she felt as if she would suffocate. She washed herself with shaking hands and lay down in a new spot which Wakwa chose.

He conversed to distract her. "Panther Eye dwells now with two useless servants I cast from my house months ago. You need never see these unfortunate women. So few are troubled families, they will receive care, perhaps improve."

"I wish to run. The wind in my clean hair. Run to the pond where we used to sit."

"Soon, Elizabeth."

"May I visit with my family?" Her gaze was glassy.

"Soon."

"Such a miser you are with favors." Without warning she was cool. "Can we not leave the cows to themselves and run up the hill to dine with mother and father? Leave your prayerbook behind, Annanias. None of us prays anymore."

Wakwa was unsettled by the steepness of her slip into fantasy. He had expected her to talk in her fever and to require his comfort. He did not know how to respond to her grotesque mental lapse.

"Why have you no coat on, husband? You surprise me." She looked into Wakwa's eyes, seeing a phantom of the man she despised. "You sit without your shirt in the open!

"Did I tell thee of a mad dream I had? I believe I was married to an Indian." She cried hard. "A man, a man he was. Nothing like you. Unworthy of him, I have fallen to your hands." She brightened up and touched Wakwa's leg. "My, but you are become handsome and tawny in the sun!"

The sweat rolled off her. As the hours passed her ankles appeared and the thickness of her legs decreased, while Wakwa sat with his face to the sun, terribly afraid.

On the fourth day Wakwa awoke to find her gone. He went to the ridge above the river and saw her below, running, slender again but for the pretty swell in front which was his child.

He sat in the pesuponk, considering the lesson of her delirium. He had been harsh. She had begun to escape again, to reverse direction, bedding with hate rather than imperfect love.

Their difference of reaction astonished him and he returned from his swim dedicated to finding and touching their cords of similarity.

She was clean and lovely, kneeling near the fire with her hands in the flour, starting a batch of bread.

"Cowammaunsh, nummittamus," he greeted her.

"And I love thee, nasuck, my husband." It was hard to speak in the aftermath of their bitterness.

She had changed more than physically from his treatment. Although her pride in her art was reinstated with strength, submission to the cure displayed her desire to live in grace with him, even in the face of tempering the delights of solitary life.

She nodded shyly when he asked if he might sit and watch her work. In the heat she wore the negligee Hanna had sent long ago, its fragile skirt met by a loose sacque, crossed over her bosom, showing the fall of her ever heavier breasts.

As she worked she found it necessary to soothe herself of sharp pains that stabbed her. Since her hands were covered with flour, she rubbed her breasts gently with her wrist while she relaxed with Wakwa in silent harmony. Finally a soft groan

282

escaped her and she forgot the inconvenience of the flour and held her breasts through her robe.

"My beauty, have you pain?"

"Wakwa, I wish not to make complaint, but yea, from time to time I hurt." Still shy of him, her voice was husky. "It is a thing happens to all women, I think. Now must I rinse my hands and clean my gown." She smiled to herself. "My, my. Then I will ache and rub and rinse again." Her smile broadened into a grin, and merriment lit her tired eyes. "Wakwa, do not try to cure me, please. I will never hurt badly enough for that!"

"I am no nurse, it is true, Elizabeth, but a thought comes to me which will help to put you at your ease."

"Goodness, no!" She crossed her arms softly against her bosom and rocked back and forth, looking at him sitting cross-legged, shining clean and rested.

He made no verbal contradiction, but dipped his fingers into the flour, spread her gown apart, and massaged her nipples and breasts with a touch like silk.

She closed her eyes, relief from waves of pain causing a trill to sound in her throat. Pain overcome, pleasure rose within her.

Wakwa redusted his hands with the white flour, but before he could touch her, she kissed his own breast and shoulders reverently, gladly submitting to his patient desire.

The touch of his hard body against the round rise of her abdomen warmed her. She knew pleasure in his company and he in hers.

So through the long summer days they mended their affection into new soundness.

Chapter 45

On a blue and blowy August day Gil Worth set out for the Dowland property on foot. He split his time between the two farms, planting, nurturing, managing his and Charles' laborers and accounts. He sought to keep the old place productive until Elizabeth could assume her right to the land.

Gil had held the household together, only quiet Sam returning to his father's carpentry shop in Acushnet. Cooke and Priscilla cared for the house and the farm hands.

Dowland relatives stopped in town now and then as they received news of Charles' and Mary's deaths and their daughter's disappearance. They slept in the silent house, visited the graves near the white church, and wrangled details of the will out of Gil and Hanna.

Winter weather, the shock of two sudden deaths, the emergency of the fruit trees, and the nearing birth of Elizabeth's child had detained Gil in his search for legal counsel. There were several men in Sandwich and in Boston who supervised the deeds to his lands in America and his holdings abroad. But the advice he needed required a specialist, well-known but discreet, versed in the complications of large inheritances and unsavory concepts like written codes against racial mixing.

This was the day of the month Gil brought the workers' pay. Even this unremarkable duty etched more deeply the void Charles' lost friendship left. But Gil's depression lightened with the beauty of the land as he made his way along the rills abounding with their summer yields.

As the house became visible over a hill, Gil spotted an array of little dishes spread near a basket in the alfalfa field. He smiled at the thought that someone on the farm had caught the spirit of summer and enjoyed a meal in the open air. He came up to the picnic in progress, the dainty spread of duckling and jelly, buttermilk and cocoa cake, left open to the pleasure of the ants. Seeing no one, even the workers hiding from the noon sun, Gil thought of Priscilla.

He always tapped at the kitchen glass rather than assuming

ownership by walking in unannounced. When she was there Cooke chuckled at him for this, assuring him the house was his.

Priscilla scurried to answer today, coming nimbly down the stairs from the dining room, her pale hair rolled modestly at the nape of her neck, her child-like face smiling at the benefactor who maintained her position even though her master and mistress were dead.

"Cooke's washing up, sir, just finished with a custard." She curtsied and Gil entered the coolness of the kitchen.

"I understand. But what are you doing here, young lady? I just passed the basket of goodies you left on the meadow."

"I?"

"Admit it! There must be someone you like to share lunch with on such a fine day."

"Master Worth, I do never entertain no one, save on a Saturday eve, and poor Cooke peeking through the door the while." She blushed.

Gil sat down at the long table. "Sit, dear child. Sit. I have no wish to embarrass you. The basket belongs to someone else. In any case, I have been thinking about you for a while and your situation here. Is this not wearing on you? All this quiet and not any young friends to talk to? Tell me if there is somewhat more I can do to better your position. After all, in a year and a half the decision what to do with the old place is made."

"Sir? You do not like my work?"

"Little maid! I'd gladly have you part of my own house but for the fact I am overstaffed already.

"I refer to your settling in some better situation, to launch your future. Someday you will be fond of someone and will marry. I wish you would help me help you. This will not go on forever."

The girl looked at him squarely. "You are kind. I, being so alone, never expect it. You and Master and Mistress Dowland have been good as family to me. Yet . . ."

"Yet summer has come to Priscilla Marley too?"

"Since I have no father is it too bold to tell you, sir?"

"I have no daughter. It is my privilege to listen."

The girl hurried through her hopes. "I am fond of the carpenter's son. . . ."

"Our own Samuel? How natural. How did I miss that?"

"Sir," she flushed, "little do you miss. It is only that sad things have you preoccupied."

Gil stuck his chin in his hand, charmed by her womanly wisdom and her girlish presence.

"It is since Sam's been gone we have thought of each other. We've been used to working together, you see. Do you know, he wants to break away from the farms and have a shop in Boston? Sam thinks there be a great need for furniture and wants to make cabinets, and wardrobes, and tables, all solid things—from American wood—that a man could hand down to his children.

"I would help him keep his shop shining. Oh, sir, can't you see Sam with all his hardwood around him made into polished pieces? And him staving off customers who want to avoid the wait and duty on all the English wares?"

Gil opened his mouth but her excitement swept his comments aside.

"He has apprenticed to his father now and soon can set off on his own! How carefully he has planned! He don't want a bit of waste and will use the very sawdust for something!"

Gil drummed his fingers on the table, lost in active concentration about all she had said. "The most fortunate of his careful plans is to include you in them. A great thought, that! Domestic furniture for the gentry. Why, you and Sam shall buy me out ere long! But I am afraid he will need more than his back and good intentions if he wants to set up in Boston. Even more than you."

"It may be he does not have me, Master. I plan to wait."

"For what?"

"For Mistress Beth."

"Eh?"

"I speak this to no one. Not even Sam. My mistress is with the savage, isn't she?"

"Priscilla, what good will it do your Mistress Beth if I tell things she must reveal herself? And the savage is not so."

"Ah! I guessed that too. Is he not frighteningly handsome?"

"Priscilla Marley! You have changed since the day you opened the door to him."

"Excuse me. I did not wish to pry. I am bolder with my happiness over Sam. But I am resolved to wait for her 'til she

286

come back to her home. How terrible to find it empty." The girl's voice went husky, sharing their orphan's sorrow.

"She comes not back. She is part with his people now. I cannot have you wait when she is settled somewhere else. Let us walk out in the sun. Come, child," he said to the crying girl, "you'll mess your bib."

Gil offered Priscilla his arm. She was shy at first, always careful of the lines of class, but, needing support, held onto his blue-shirted forearm.

She listened to Gil's description of his niece's situation as the wind from the Bay blew her starched apron stiffly out in front of her.

"But who does her washing? And who will help her when the child is born? And who will talk to her in her own language when she lives among the Indians and is lonely?"

"She manages all these things herself somehow. She has never been so radiant. She relishes her tasks and stays alone for weeks sometimes. I do not see how myself."

"I could leave the house and join her in the forest. Let me go to her! She needs me, I am sure."

"I will ask her, Priscilla, but you should know, women of the Indians will wait upon her soon, or wait upon things with her, as they do. It may be wrong for her to bring you too. And what of Samuel?"

"Sam will keep."

"You are a true Englishwoman, Mistress Marley."

"Sir!" Priscilla was honored by the title.

"Yes, you are born with service for others in your heart and let your private comforts wait their turn. I say you should come to their wedding. How would it be if I wangle an invitation for you? Since you are discreet we can smuggle you in to her as Hanna's maid. What say you?"

There was no need to ask. Priscilla had danced away, clapping her hands at his cleverness.

"Matthew will be along keeping me buttoned straight and doing some fancy things with some beef I intend to send into them. It will be just fine." He tempered her thankfulness. "And send Sam to me with his plans. I have been thinking of investing in a native manufactory."

The maid ran to him and kissed his hand in hearty gratitude.

Gil patted her shoulder as they progressed toward the abandoned picnic basket. "Take thyself to Mrs. Worth, quick and quiet for some new things to wear. It is to be a marvelous gala."

"This is not our crockery." Priscilla crouched down near the assortment of plates.

"Priscilla," Gil cleared away the wasps with his walking stick, "as a test of his skills, have Sam make a chair. A rocking chair . . . low and wide, inlaid with cherry . . . oh . . . some maple leaf or other or . . . yes . . . wound around a stalk of corn."

"This basket is not ours. Ours is a dark color. That is new."

"Yes?"

"Cooke and I have not roasted ducklings, nor baked black cake."

They stood, puzzled, Gil idly turning over each dish with his stick, maneuvering them into a line. He followed their direction with his eyes and noted the roof of the smokehouse at the foot of the hill. He nibbled at the handle of his stick in thought, then cut at a serving of duckling meanly with its tip.

"Priscilla, how deep runs your loyalty to your Mistress Beth?"

"I would go to the ends of the earth for her."

"Have you ever seen a horrible sight?"

"Once. My mama and papa, after our house burned."

"Child, do you know what marriage is?"

"Sir?"

Gil had gone white. "Do you know what is the function of a married pair?"

"I do not understand why this question, sir!"

"Answer it. For thy mistress."

The girl looked at his eyes, hard, shining like metal. "Cooke has talked to me. And Mistress Dowland, long ago, of this connection. I know that much."

Gil covered his hair with his hat. "If I am forced to show you some evil connected with this basket, could you be a witness before a court?"

"What must I see?"

"You must walk with me toward the smokehouse and not say one word. But look, and think only of serving Mistress Beth,

. . . knowing you must declare what you see before the assembled town."

The girl started ahead of Gil across the slope.

The breezy northern hollow held Charles Dowland's smokehouse. In line with Charles' habits, it was the most modern of its type of structure. It was very large, built two feet off the ground for dryness, and the smoke for curing the bacon and other meat was funneled in through a pipe as needed. Any time of the year a man could enter and choose what he wanted to eat and find it cool and fresh. The meat for both households was still cured there. A purist's source of pride for Charles during his life, the smokehouse continued in flawless function after his death.

The building was tightly made, but the smoke pipe formed an excellent conduit for sound. Gil led the way around the back, and they stood listening. His instinct had been true. They tensed when they heard a murmur of voices. It cost Gil all his strength of soul not to build a fire and smoke Annanias Hudson and Prue Hanson out.

Priscilla left him with his struggle and inched along the ground on her belly underneath the house to be closer to the speakers. Gil crawled after her.

They stopped at center and silently camouflaged their hiding place with stray branches.

"I have no more excuses to offer to Mama. You must speak to her at last." The voice of Prudence Hanson came clearly through the floor.

Gil pressed his face into the dirt. Priscilla reached for his hand and squeezed it, urging him to listen.

The female voice wheedled, growing angry. "You shake your head, but you do take advantage of my good nature. That timid bit of vanity you suffer over is off enjoying herself somewhere else, I'd swear, while Papa and Mama wait for you to call!"

"It is so common in you to say, 'swear,'" Annanias spoke.

Priscilla Marley jerked her head up from the ground in surprise.

Then came Prue's bitter laugh, followed by tears. "Still you disdain me, though I have given all and she nary a thing."

"I shall bloody your lip if you ever speak her name again in my presence! Let us not twist up our give and our take, Prudence Hanson.

"There is at the core of that angel the breath of all that is beautiful. No one, not any man, nor thing, nor demon, nothing, can change her mystery.

"You think you suffered over me? Ha! Your most violent screechings to your mama, your meanest deprivation here," his partner squawked as he touched her, "your most heartfelt prayer for my attentions, were but the chirp of a cricket to the death song of the swan.

"My heart, my soul, my very bowel approach a decade of exquisite longing for her love. She is more than beauty or goodness or desire. She is the wholeness that the classics broach to us as art! A soaring combination of all the elements of life, a sparkling, brilliant, turning, dazzling, eternal orb, of which I, unlike you, have an inkling, and, through her, the possibility to hold in my grasp! You are fodder. She, elixir."

"You do live on pretty speeches!" There was the muffled sound of bodies readjusting their positions. "Did she ever plant a kiss like that upon your mouth?"

"Prue! It is too soon again for me!"

Many minutes passed before voices again reached outside. But Gil's pallor converted slowly to blood darkness as the couple's heavy shuffle on the smokehouse floor opened the imagination to their activity.

"Prudence Hanson, you confound me! Why did I not know you long before?"

Gil uttered a stifled little bark at Annanias' satisfied rumble.

"Annanias, you know me now!"

"Wife of the flesh, it is too late, and it is wrong. How can I marry you, before the people, when you are so impure?"

Gil's hands writhed in the dirt, impatient to deal directly with this brutishness. Priscilla shook so she could not keep her head up. They heard Prue crying again.

The couple walked about inside, and when they wore shoes again the sound of their feet on the wooden floor was deafening to the pair who lay concealed.

The minister put his arm around Prue when they emerged. "Let us not quarrel but go enjoy the meal you have gotten up.

You may laugh at eating it on this land I might have owned. Now, now. Do not be sad all over again. Give me but a few months. Mayhap I will change my mind." The wide man rubbed the girl's posterior and she curled her arms around him as they disappeared up the hill.

Gilbert Worth and Priscilla did not move for a long time. They missed seeing the shocked look on Annanias' face when he discovered the overturned dishes. They missed his wild-eyed search of the alfalfa. They missed seeing him tip his hat to his consort and hurry swiftly away, leaving Prudence alone to carry the basket home by herself.

Finally the master and the maid stood.

"Now. How may I assist my dear mistress?" Priscilla asked in her light, steady voice.

"Keep this day fresh in your mind. Store it up. Relish every word that you heard that you may give it back to the tyther, the Selectmen, and the judge when you are called before them."

"When will that be, sir?"

"Never, I hope. The minister may yet give himself away to others in less jeopardy than you or I. Elizabeth's marriage must be solid before I venture into accusations of this charlatan. But we have seen and heard, and if Elizabeth needs defending at some future time we shall be there to do it.

"Hudson has wrung the town's heart with his plight, while they are told to distrust me for prospering." Gil twisted his hat.

And the girl amazed him with a skillful attempt at comfort.

" 'For seven times will the righteous man
   Fall and rise again,
   While the wicked will stumble to ruin.' "

Gil hid his distraught face with his hat. "Only two regrets have I in my life. That this man uses unreproached my brother-in-law's clean and saintly ground for his fornication and that I have smudged forever the whiteness of your apron."

Gil was in a quandary about his next step in regard to Hudson when he arrived home and found two church Elders and the Selectmen waiting in his sitting room. They presented him with an overdue letter from Mayhew Low posted July the sixth, 1747.

Still standing in the doorway, Gil read the letter and looked past the worried men to his wife. "Gentlemen, if the new minister is to be waylaid and go to England before coming to us here, I charge you with a duty.

"Think you I enter my house with dust from head to foot on any ordinary day?" His green eyes lit them like two lamps face by face. "I have passed my afternoon underneath Charles Dowland's smokehouse! There is a trespasser comes there with a woman, which blasphemy I shall not abide! Notwithstanding sides of meat hanging all about, he houses his lust in my brother-in-law's outbuilding. I will not name the name with haste, but charge you to catch him. But I stand ready, and another witness will support my word. I hope, when I must reveal this information, if I must, you will usher the party out of town, like the German man last year whose accent so displeased you! Meanwhile, I am getting me some Scotch-Irish with guns to patrol on these joint lands. Such men are conscientious about efficient use of powder."

"Why, Mr. Worth, we will not fail you!" the officials assured him.

"I trust not. Hanna, serve them something. I am gone to bathe." And Worth retired, his new course set by the pressure of circumstance rather than craft or care.

Chapter 46

Awepu's soft, slow laugh circled from the front to the back room of the hunting lodge. Elizabeth had enjoyed the night of listening to the men's quiet voices as they ate and played at reeds. She spent the time readying baskets of infant clothes and rearranging the stores of wood dust, crushed corn, and other supplies she had prepared for the child's arrival.

During the last part of the summer the hunters relaxed, saving themselves and the deer for the harvest drive which was to come as soon as the first freeze threatened. But this year had been moderate and summer was dying a leisurely death. It was more comfortable than the September which had driven Elizabeth into the woods, and she remembered and reverenced the unbearable heat of the year before and the violence of the storm that had swept away her dependence on her old life.

While the men lost uncaught pheasants and furs to one another, reclining about the outer room like Romans at a feast, Elizabeth worked late at her preparations. She did not seem able to stop her hands from arranging and rearranging the baskets. She had in the last week scrubbed and made rope, set the herbs to dry, and hung them in great bunches, making the most of their beauty and usefulness. She was intent on bearing the child in the native way to make Wakwa proud of her strength and had collected wood dust, which felt as soft as down, for the baby's bed. The child would lie on the fluffy substance which absorbed moisture and could be changed as needed. She had also hemmed some cloths for him in the English way, but would try to do without them.

Wakwa had provided a coverlet of mink and a lining of fine skins for the stiff-bottomed basket that Tame Deer had made. Wakwa, determined that Elizabeth should not carry the baby on her back, devised a narrow straw cradle with a rounded shade against the sun, fitted with the footboard and ties that would keep the child's wrappings close and his body steady. The first wife wove it, adding a handle and a sling so that Elizabeth could choose the most comfortable way to balance the weight, and made a great effort over the painting of yellow, black, and white flowers and animals on the outside.

Elizabeth had not yet met the shy woman who delicately remained aside so that her shadow would not fall across the peacefulness of Elizabeth's pregnancy. But she began to admire Tame Deer through her work. Elizabeth detected her patient presence in the exactness of the pattern the plaits made as they fitted together and in the precise points of light that appeared when the sun shone through the tiny spaces between the fibers. She prodded Wakwa constantly for information about Tame Deer. He was also asked for details about Elizabeth by Qunneke and was oddly unresponsive to either of them, embarrassed to be caught between his wives' mutual curiosity.

"How can a man with your ability for words not know how to tell what his wife of four years looks like?" Elizabeth demanded one day, provoked by his reticence.

Wakwa thought, then laughed in sudden relief. "She hath not yellow hair!" He gladly left her to her frustration and the second wife bothered him no more.

Now, in the mid-September night, Elizabeth came to the arch of drapery and watched the playing men. She was massive, her abdomen a low, immense bulge, emphasizing the fragility of the rest of her body. She waved to Awepu, who threw down his reeds and pleasantly came to her side.

"Your Silent Fox is losing to me, dear sister! Have him retire. The tooth, it is big with soreness."

Elizabeth smiled and nodded to the guard of five who played with their sachim. Waban's second son was there with them. She spoke in their language, still simple words, but her effort was always appreciated.

"I go to rest. Take care of the sachim!" She came up to her husband, her hair loosened and brushed, her high-waisted robe revealing the sunburned skin of her neck and bosom. She felt the yellowish lump on the left side of his face. "You look a perfect monster! I am afraid the jimson does nothing to take down the swelling."

Wakwa rose with effort, holding his aching head, and walked her back to the smaller room. "A few leaves of dragon's claw is

294

all I will chew. With my son so close to birth I shall not let jimson weed turn me into a fool just for a pain in my tooth." He could hardly make himself understood.

Awepu teased, "Lo! The spokesman for the People, who can move only one side of his face. Sister, I tell him to find Dr. Mac. We have not much cure for the teeth."

Wakwa made a disrespectful noise and rubbed his temple.

Worried, Elizabeth prodded, "I am glad of one thing, my warrior, that there are no Mohawk lurking near the lodge tonight!"

"Wife! You both make too much of a toothache! It will go away."

"Help him, Awepu. Finally when he needs me I can hardly move myself. Bring the doctor. I am redder than Wakwa is tonight. I fear he has infection."

"Matta, Elizabeth!" Wakwa struggled to be understood. "Dr. Mac is not in these parts for twelve days yet at the least. When he comes to see you he may judge, although tonight I would not mind so much if one of those Mohawk dogs ate my head."

"Dearest, come to rest."

"Soon, Kayaskwa. I enjoy too much losing ermine to thy good friend."

Elizabeth looked at Awepu, telling him with her eyes to watch over Wakwa. As she turned to go into her chamber Wakwa stroked her hair, then walked slowly back to the game.

She lay on the raised bed he had made to ease the constant pain in her lower back. She closed her eyes and heard the men counting their scores in the long words of Indianne unnontoowaonk.

"Neesneechick, neesneechick nab naquit . . ."

She saw her uncle's farm through the haze of her comfortable fatigue and wondered how the late summer scalding progressed. A wrenching passed along her belly for an instant. She had sometimes seen her abdomen rise as the child pushed against her from within, but she did not remember having a sensation like the one that jarred her from her thoughts about Sweetwood. It did not return and soon she was asleep.

Daylight came, shooting a beam of light into the high window Wakwa had cut in the rear chamber. Elizabeth rolled over onto her hands and pushed herself up. She could not tell if she had dreamt it, but it seemed she experienced a repetition of the pulling on the side of her belly. She waited. Nothing stirred except the breaths of the men in the outer room. Wakwa had not come in to her the night before. They must have played very late.

Elizabeth stood without the motivation to get the morning meal. She took a light, loose summer dress, her blanket, and two buckets and made her way toward the door, trying not to awaken the men. The floor was strewn with their big bodies, lying in the mild morning light which sifted in under the matting at the open door.

She stopped near Silent Fox, who lay like a child with his hands curled near his face, and almost cried out loud when she saw how the swelling from the sore tooth had progressed. He was almost unrecognizable, the left side of his face distorted and discolored. She went quickly for water.

Awepu did not move when he awoke at the footsteps of the white saunks. He dozed again, guiltily, after she went out. He stayed more and more at the lodge as the time grew near for the child's birth, feeling a strong responsibility for Elizabeth since her father's death. He used to bring her strawberries, which she loved, but now she refused, saying they should spot the child. The English, Awepu thought, had more superstitions than the Mohawk head eaters.

He watched her return and place the full buckets on the floor, straighten herself up, and wait with her eyes closed. From his secluded corner he saw her bring one bucket near the fire for the men and one to Wakwa's side. She went for clean cloths and soaked them in the cool water, wringing them as hard as she could. He saw the effort she had to make to bend to kiss her husband's forehead, and he saw Wakwa's arm circle up around her, his hand familiarly pushing against her glossy hair, gently putting her mouth against his own. Awepu saw Wakwa awake fully, surprised at the pain the kiss caused him, and heard Elizabeth's sympathetic whisper.

"My poor, dear lamb!"

"When will you part with that child?" Awepu's kinsman gurgled sleepily, his hand on her bosom.

Awepu watched Elizabeth tenderly wrap the once handsome

face in the cold cloths and heard Wakwa sigh his relief. Wakwa closed his eyes again and seemed to sleep, while the wife combed his hair away from his face until it lay smoothly out from his head like a black cloth against the mat. She soaked the rags and wrung them out again, then stopped and waited quietly.

"Wakwa, I cannot find the knife." She ran her fingers across her husband's dry lips.

The man rose halfway on his arms but snapped back to his mat in pain. He pointed to the place where the knife was hanging.

"I must rest my eyes, Kayaskwa."

Awepu saw her tie the cool white bands around Wakwa's head and leave him like a wounded warrior while she went to get the knife. Again she stopped and waited, backing against the wall for support. He saw her wipe away tears and slowly walk into the back room.

When she reappeared with blankets and a mat and a large round basket, Awepu was already up and out. Elizabeth noticed his place empty as she went through the room and out the doorway, stopping again and waiting with her head bowed for fully half a minute before continuing on past the clearing and into the trees.

Awepu followed his cousin's wife and watched with interest as she searched the groves with her burden balanced in each arm. She stopped several times and stood still, once falling to her knees, but regained strength and continued toward her objective. At last she found a thicket, walked around it smiling at some memory, and put her bundles down. "Nonantum," Elizabeth said aloud, blessing the spot. She ran her hand up and down the gray bark of a maple, set out her mat, making a pillow of one of the blankets, and lay facing east.

About an hour later Awepu arrived back at the lodge with a string of bass for the men who were beginning to stir around the low fire. Only Wakwa had not moved. Awepu turned the preparation of the fish over to the guard, White Cat, and sat by Wakwa's side. He ate next to his friend, thinking, wishing Pequawus were there to settle his doubts. He felt Wakwa's forehead with his wrist. Finally, leaving Mosq to watch the young sachim, he motioned the other men out of the house.

"Nuppohwunau," he addressed Waban's carefree son, "will

297

you perform a service for your sachim who lies too sick to ask it?"

After listening attentively, Nuppohwunau raced off with three of the guards toward the east and the sun which rose steadily higher above the trees.

Awepu went with White Cat to the grove where he had left Elizabeth. They saw her black and gold book open, propped on her full belly, her thin arms and hands resting on the blanket. Her eyes were open but she was not reading. Her glance was cast far up into the spreading green leaves, and wisps of her hair and the translucent pages of the book caught the movement of the breeze that brought them fresh ocean coolness.

Worried, Awepu circled through the trees, coming into the clearing where she could see him. She remained silent, occupied with the sensations that passed along her side, then exclaimed, "Awepu! You came here?"

Disregarding her flush of embarrassment, Awepu calmly stepped close to her. "Elizabeth Dowland, it is good, is it not, I am here? Was it not I who lifted thy father's dying face to the southwest? Shall I not be favored to be at your side, to help him be reborn through the tomb of your body?"

Elizabeth held her hands up to her friend and he took them both, kneeling on one knee at her side.

"Saunks, thou hast hands of snow, so cold and white. Fear thou?"

"A fool am I, Awepu," she complained, but the man shook his head in the negative. "Was it pride made me refuse Dr. Mac's offer to attend me? What do I know of such a business as this? I am all very well for the moment, but have I the strength to do all that I must to place a healthy babe in its father's arms? For this he will love me, not caring if I bear it alone or with a court of physicians and old wives dancing round me. Awepu! Shall I break it ere it see the light of its first day?"

Seeing her change of heart had come much too late, Awepu reassured her with more hope than he felt.

"You think too much of things you cannot know. Your heart is filled with courage. Your back rests against the earth. The glade is filled with the spirit of the man who caused thine own birth. Four little ones Micuckaskeete-nokannawi washed in the

298

stream and brought to my wetu after doing what you do now. Today you too are Ninnuock. Fear not."

Elizabeth gently pulled her hands from him and let them rest on her blanket, turning her face away. She felt in unison with the growing intensity of the contractions of her muscles only when she avoided tenseness and withdrew from the activity around her. Her countenance was lax as death, enlivened only by the glow of her sun-streaked skin. Some minutes passed, then, perfectly relaxed, she turned back to him, looking to Awepu as fresh as she had been a year before.

"I am happy then. If you have such faith in me I will rise to it. Tell Wakwa I have the company of the sun and birds and that at last, having to lie still, I eavesdrop on the weighty talk of the trees."

Awepu patted her cheek. "You have also White Cat thirty paces off, who sits with his back to you, winding rope, ready to answer your call or protect you from beasts. Thy husband sleeps, little Saunks, yet tired from the ache in his tooth. But he will be better soon and wait with me for news of your papoos."

"Awepu, he needs care. Stay with him. Send for someone to help. Poor Wakwa! It is no normal toothache that could keep my husband asleep so far past sunrise."

Her control had slipped in her concern for Wakwa and she yelped in surprise as the pulling began again, now on both sides of her belly. She lay flat, watching the sway of the leaves, resting as the tautness increased, allowing herself to sense the working of her body. The tightening maintained its strength, and slowly she began to realize the enjoyment of the unrelenting pressure that signaled the long-awaited birth of her child.

Awepu broke into her thoughts. "For the first time I feel smaller than the least of women. The happiness that fills your eyes when you lie so still like that shows me secrets I may never know, being but a man." He was glad White Cat was out of hearing. "What little help I may be, I will be, most courageous sister." Awepu lifted her fingers to his forehead in farewell and slipped quietly behind her, through the trees, and back to Wakwa.

* * * *

Gil Worth had just sat down to his harp after his early morning inspection of his orchards. With the new schedule forced on him by the late summer scalding, keeping accounts for two farms, and preparing for his niece's wedding, he had formed the habit of stringent practice before his breakfast. This calmed him and clarified his day's horizon, as the sun served to open his eyes.

For ten days he had lived alone, Hanna and Priscilla driving up to Boston with dependable Matthew. The women had gone for fittings of their gowns, which Gil desired to be extraordinary, suspecting this nuptial would be a once-in-a-lifetime celebration even for the Massachuseuck. Gil's own clothes were being tailored in Boston to his never changing measurements, he having neither time nor patience this season for personal fittings. Elizabeth's things were being made in the city as well, to fit her figure of just before her pregnancy. Hanna was praying for the fabric's sake that her niece would soon be small again, but sagely designated that the bodice be cut away in a deep square to take advantage of the fullness she expected from her niece's nursing of the infant.

Gil began this day's practice with Bach, working back to the Italians who so bothered Dr. Stirling. The doctor was due in ten days for a stay in Sweetwood, to wait for the signs of Elizabeth's labor and to practice for the fete in the woods. With all this happening in the midst of harvest, Stirling had arranged for his son to split his time between Harvard and the new farm. Israel, an able trumpeter and an uninspired but competent string player, would make the thin duo into a trio at the Taquonk feast. The theology student had allowed himself to be drawn into the coming nuptial with a mixture of repugnance and academic curiosity.

Gil sat squarely in the light of his bright window overlooking the yellowed leaves of the cherry, plucking in abstracted perfection at the strings of his harp, lost in the contrasts of this day to the events of exactly a year ago.

The Dowlands, except for Henry, had been living as a family, enduring the limitless, moist heat of mid-September. Now the Dowland house stood empty and the day was a true Cape Cod affair, soft, airy, unbothersome, late summer. Last year he had sat dripping perspiration, his collar open, working hard to pacify the two women he loved most in the world. This morning, as he made music alone, he was fitted out like a gentleman in linen coat and silk vest, his throat wound with a stock of crisp gauze resting in even furrows on his shirt front. Then the threat of Annanias Hudson loomed over the family. Now that same man tottered on the brink of being discovered in his guilty dalliance with Prudence Hanson.

As Worth contemplated, his fingers unconsciously melded tune into tune, until both his body and mind were caught up in the solo expansiveness of Wagenseil's G Major Concerto, giving him freedom to produce almost continuous melody without accompaniment.

It was at the most tender intonation of the graceful allegro that Gil became conscious he was being observed. The hair at the back of his neck raised a little as he moved his eyes from the shadows of his playing fingers to the sweat-glistened, winded figures of four strange Indians. Their wildness was magnified by their closeness to the thin panes of glass, where they stood listening in awed silence.

One man's smile smoothed the dissonant moment and Gil recognized Nuppohwunau in the nearly naked man surrounded by three others. He met the Indians at the door himself in his enthusiasm, but the sound of deep voices in the hall brought the housekeeper from the back of the house. She tucked in her chin and drew up her chest in disgust, scolding her master with her voice for yet another welcoming of such "divils," as she termed the native people.

"Will it be tea then, sir?"

"Yes, Winke!" Gil was quick to catch her tone. "Tea. And herring. And eggs. And currant bread. And baked apple, and porridge, and potatoes. In a quarter hour! In the summer dining room." Worth turned away from the stout woman, hoping the Indians had missed her vindictive disapproval.

He ushered the men into his sitting room, moving the harp into his customary corner as he spoke.

"Came you, brothers, to share my lonely table? My wife is away in the city. I appreciate your company. Aspaumpmauntam sachim?"

Introductions were made all around by Nuppohwunau, the only English-speaking visitor.

"Wetomp! Wakwa teaches well!"

"Nux, Nuppohwunau, as he does everything. But I have far to go before I master two thoughts together."

The guards observed the room, silently appraising the many foreign appointments, the collection of clocks, the hung instruments, Hanna's sewing frame, the books, the silk-cushioned chairs. But the graceful son of the headman broached the topic that he could see caused his host distress.

"You dress enough food for twenty men. I had rather hear the voice of your gold strings than fill my stomach."

Gil, full of appreciation for this flattery and understanding, increased his effort to use Indianne unnontoowaonk.

"Taubot mequaun namean. Mattapsh!" He turned a bit red. "I am at a loss. I meant to thank you for your kind remark and ask you all to sit."

The guards looked with misgivings at the dainty furniture and began to seat themselves on the carpet.

Nuppohwunau waved them up. "Gilbert Worth, we have not such freedom. The sachim rose not from his mat this morning."

"He did not?"

"Matta. No! I come on the wish of Awepu, to bring help. Wakwa Manunnappu has a grievous pain."

"Great God! What is it?"

"His tooth."

"His tooth? You jest. Ha! I cannot believe that mighty man felled by a simple toothache."

"The white powwaw must come to Silent Fox." Nuppohwunau was very serious.

"But will it not keep? This is harvest! Do sit and take some cool water. You are all overheated." Gil went to a small table to pour out goblets of cold water from a crystal pitcher. "You see, my friend, the doctor is here within ten days to wait in attendance on the Mistress Elizabeth."

Nuppohwunau smiled broadly and Gil took this as a sign of friendly interest. But Waban's son would not be refused.

"I am sent to bring the man of medicine to my cousin. Silent Fox is the color of birchwood and his face is swollen like the belly of the osacontuck fish."

"Aye?"

"Nux." Nuppohwunau was proud that he had won Gil's sympathies. "Your powwaw will come if you ask him."

"By all means! But let us ride out after breakfast, I am famished."

Nuppohwunau nodded his contentment with this as Winke poked her head into the room announcing breakfast. Gil led the way toward the door with a gesture to the guards.

"Peeyaush, netompauog!" Gil was looking forward to some company at his meal.

"Ten sleeps, my friend, is far too long for your powwaw to wait," Nuppohwunau said casually as he passed in front of Gil into the hall. "Mistress Elizabeth wants not to delay."

"I fear, Nuppohwunau, she has no say in it. She must wait her time."

The young man stopped and pondered this expression.

"Her time? Ah! Then her time is waited! She quit the lodge at sunrise, friend."

"Quit the lodge?" Now Gil stood mystified.

"Neechau!" Nuppohwunau patted his stomach.

"You cannot mean . . ."

"Nux! She brings forth the little one."

"But you cannot mean . . . she . . . now? Now! While we stand about talking of Wakwa's tooth! She quit the lodge? My niece? Alone? The daughter of Charles Dowland, in travail, without the house, unattended?"

Winke, anxious about her master's reprimand, entered the dining room to check the maid in the serving of Worth and the Indians. But the maid was fluffing the ruffles of her apron near the laden sideboard, the men not yet at the table. Angry, the housekeeper marched across the sun-swept floor into the main hallway to the sitting room. It was empty. The front door stood open. Only the rising dust on the road east revealed that the diners were gone on horseback. Winke closed the door, worried about her master riding alongside the savages.

* * * *

Awepu waited in the quiet lodge while Mosq patrolled the path to Gil Worth's house. Wakwa had stirred only once and that was to open his red eyes and complain of thirst and ask for Elizabeth. But he sank back onto his mat and did not move again. Awepu felt caught between Wakwa who did not move and Elizabeth who did not return with the child. The sun had reached its high point. They had arrived at midday and his efforts to alleviate their discomforts were at a standstill. He could only assume that Nuppohwunau was riding in Worth's company for the doctor.

Awepu went out for water. When he returned he untied the bandages from Wakwa's head and dipped them in the pail. He called Wakwa's name repeatedly, afraid to touch his face, observing before how sensitive it was. He shook his friend's shoulders but Wakwa only grumbled and curled up on his other side, away from the bothersome Awepu. Having little choice, Awepu made a ball of the dripping rags and wrung them out over Wakwa's forehead.

Wakwa cried out and sat up, blinking back his headache.

"What are you doing?" he muttered.

"It is time you awoke, my friend. I have tried every means."

"Have you nothing else to do, Awepu, than play at games with me? You have many mouths to feed. Why do you not follow a deer?"

"Should I have kissed your forehead, kinsman, to awaken you?" Awepu paid no attention to Wakwa's bad humor. "I am but your cousin, not your wife."

"And where is my wife? She helped me greatly this morning. Was that morning?"

"She has left for the woods."

"A child she is, my friend. A lovely child, newly in love with her mother earth," Wakwa rose uncomfortably and made his way to the doorway of her part of the house, "whom she seeks always at times inconvenient for her unfortunate husband."

"You have no complaint with her, old friend!" Awepu stood in front of Wakwa. "You must know the earth is within her, she need not walk the forest paths to find it."

"Awepu! Do not defend her. I but act like an old woman over my tooth." Wakwa was forced to talk out of the side of his mouth.

Awepu grasped his friend's arms tightly. "She is no child after today. Since the dawn she has rested on the breast of the land that forms the bond between you, seeking not only comfort from her mother but to become such a one."

Wakwa's limbs went sore and he bent to lean on Awepu,

304

looking beyond him into the empty, airy chamber. He saw that the baby's basket, prepared with the wood dust and covers, and Elizabeth's mat and blanket and basket were gone. His burning face rested against Awepu's cool, thin one. Tears sprang into his eyes and his swollen cheek widened as his mouth stretched into a smile.

Awepu told the story. "Six hours by her uncle's clock your English wife has labored to produce him. She cries out not, but glows each time the child moves nearer to his birth. Manittoo! Such a bride you have!"

Wakwa reeled away from the door, holding his head with both hands, and loped clumsily toward the stream.

"She cannot stay alone!"

Awepu followed close behind. "White Cat guards from a little distance. Think you I would leave her unprotected?"

Wakwa sank into the stream on his stomach and held his painful head under the rushing water. He clambered out with a sigh, gripping Awepu's waiting hands.

"Six hours, you say? She must be dying! What should take so long if all were well? I must be with her!"

"Disturb her not! She is strong and happy."

"Then why has White Cat not returned with joyful news?"

"Would you go and bother her? She has work to do! Do I visit with my wife while she brings forth our babes? Where were you when Tame Deer retired to bear your Sequan?"

Wakwa hung his head.

"Yes! Like a man you went fishing and brought back the finest eel I ever saw, and my Meadow-in-the-night cooked it and we all ate together with your daughter sleeping at her mother's side."

"This is not the same! This is Elizabeth Dowland, no Ninnuock! She will want me near her." Wakwa saw her in his memory, lying with her face averted before he first had knowledge of her, wishing only to be a perfect wife to him. "Why did you not wake me before!"

"First it is too soon. Now it is too late. You must settle your sleeping yourself hereafter."

"Come, Awepu," Wakwa grew persuasive, "see you not her father's spirit filling every glade, charging me to keep her safe while she lies alone and I grunt in my sleep like a pigsuck over a little pain in my tooth?"

They rushed back to the lodge, Wakwa tying on a pair of leggings.

Awepu chided gently. "Since when does the mighty slayer of Mohawks moan over a little pain?" He worked around his message, afraid Wakwa would be angry that he had sent for the doctor. "You are sicker than you think. For days your jaw has been increasing, and now your skin is gray. You have fever and you only chew jimson weed which throws you in a stupor!"

"Why does everyone insist that I chew jimson?" Wakwa snapped.

Awepu cursed his own timidity and Wakwa turned to the mild man in surprise.

Awepu blurted out, embarrassed, "Nuppohwunau has been sent to your English uncle to fetch back Dr. Mac to serve you."

"When was this?" Wakwa burst into full consciousness.

"I did this at sunrise."

"This is fine!" Wakwa clung to his friend happily, as tightly as he could without hurting the nerves in his head. "There is hope, then, he will help my Elizabeth! Awepu, there is no better friend than you."

Awepu growled. "I sent for him to fix your mouth. How should I know thy wife would lie so many hours in the birth?"

Wakwa limped along the pathless way, stopping several times, nauseous at the sudden activity after the past sluggish days. He draped himself across the branch of a tree and rested, growing gloomy.

"Could it be there is something wrong with her? Dr. Mac said this is when he would be needed." He saw Elizabeth as she looked on his return from the court in Rhode Island, puffy, sick, and exhausted, and he pitied her for the harshness he had shown that evening, feeling sick in his stomach now himself. "What can be done even if he should find her in time?"

They walked. Wakwa whirled around to Awepu. The friend hurried to support him as Wakwa reeled and spoke in sudden dizziness.

"It is something wrong! This child wounds his mother. Dr. Mac said it was not to be until almost frost! I have been lying across a tree that is still green and hot in the sun!"

306

Silent Fox pressed on, tangling his legs in vines and tripping on hidden stones, while Awepu trotted at his side, amazed to see his cousin in this condition.

Following the direction which Awepu pointed out, Wakwa broke through some crossed branches, reaching up to steady himself on the bough of a maple. He was certain Elizabeth knew of his presence, although the slackness of her face remained unchanged. Her eyes were fixed on the edge of the clearing and seemed to light when they saw his hand grip the branch.

"Cowaunkamish nummittamus!" the husband said and came softly, holding her with both his arms behind her head.

"Ah!" She leaned her head back against the blanket and translated his words, enraptured. " 'My service to thee, my wife!' Then you remember what day this is?"

Wakwa dared to kiss her exposed throat, then placed her gently down. He wished to tell her of his exquisite memories of the past year, but saliva pooled under his tongue and brimmed near his lower lip. He sucked it back and hid the swollen side of his face.

She continued for him, her voice softly monotone. "This very day, a twelvemonth ago, I saw thee and loved thee."

"Even then?"

"Remember thou this place, dear one?"

"The purple sky," Wakwa sucked again, annoyed at himself, "the glory of the leaves, and the softness of thee." He sputtered and stopped speaking while he settled the straying hairs around her face. "The feelings I knew within thee when I returned . . . after thy first flowing!"

He touched her tenderly, but she moved his hand away and turned her face and waited. He sat on his heels and watched how pearly her skin became, how distant and independent she grew, like a verdant mountain in the distance.

She turned back to him. "Without knowledge, I pray, dear, do I well? If I bear our child smoothly, will he love me? Oh, pray, will he love me?"

"I love you! I see only you! He does not hurt you?" Wakwa leaned on his elbow with the effort of speaking.

"And if it be not a son? Another daughter? Oh! Could you love her and me?" Knowledge of the disappointment she had caused by not being born male made her turn her head away again, the gigantic tautness coming more frequently and lasting longer each time.

Wakwa planted his hands on the blanket on each side of her, holding his own body above hers. "Elizabeth! Do I not love thee now? Care I for the wife who brought me a daughter before?" He was forced to stop to prevent his dribbling. "Does not Sequan fill my thoughts and dreams with her grace and sweetness? Should I not adore another creature such as thee, who will turn with the years to bring happiness to a man as you do to me, that from herself, as from the moist earth, shall spring another in the circle we have begun?" Exhausted, Wakwa sat holding his head in his hands. "We shall name her for the forest which gave you to me. Touohkomuk, or, in English, Sylvan, Sylvia, or would you like . . . Sylvana? Elizabeth, Sylvana, Qunneke, Sequan, my beloved women." He covered his face with his arms, hoping to hide his tears of anxiety.

She sought his hands but could not reach them and found it was more comfortable to touch the inside of his thigh as he sat crosslegged. She stroked it up and down, reassuring him. "I try to remember all the doctor told me to do, yet I only breathe and wait out each feeling as it comes." She squirmed over to touch his naked side and felt it hot with fever.

"Wakwa. Leave now! I would help you, but I cannot do both."

"Matta. I must help you."

"What can you do? Now go. Before it starts again. Find Tame Deer. Please! She will know how to help you. Tell her I am sorry to fail you yet again." With a sigh, Elizabeth turned away, immersed in another muscular tightening as the opening for the child grew ever wider.

"Never could you fail me!" The husband put his hand on her belly but she squawked and batted it away. He saw he had caused her her first discomfort and drew back.

After a time she said, "Sweet, my Fox, will you go? As a favor to me, let your wife help you. I grow frightened to see your poor face."

"Matta!"

"Why no?"

He forced himself to keep back his worries.

"So. You are afraid for me. Never be! Oh . . . perhaps you are right. Perhaps I cannot do this task. Were you afraid for Tame Deer?"

"No, Kayaskwa." Wakwa could not look at her. "But she is Ninnuock. She knew much by talk with others, by staying with others. You have been so alone."

"How sweetly it doth go! Alone though I have been, or because of this. Travail is a poor word for a mother's first work. You must make me a new word, Wakwa."

"Yea, little gull. We will find one."

She looked at the sky through the leaves and tried to talk through the gripping pressure that she could feel gather and heighten, then diminish, depleted. "In waves he comes to us. As on the blue swells of the ocean, riding into shore."

"Always it is the sea with you. Pull away from it and stay with me. In a short time you will truly be of this land. Thy grandmother salutes you from her shore."

She lay, loose and abstracted again, and Wakwa thought she looked pale and still as the sleeping swan on her nest.

"I ride the waves of this pulling, pulling, I am powerless to stop." She laughed a little. "Am I not like a manufactory filled with working members until the product is finished at day's end?"

He ran his fingers admiringly down the line of her nose and lips and chin.

She rambled on. "Nor sorrow, nor pain, touches this bringing forth! The curse of Eve is another falsehood."

"And what is the curse of Eve, Elizabeth?"

She blinked, turning her concentration to remembering the words. "How could you have passed it by in the first book of the Bible? Every little child I knew had it all by heart. 'The Lord God said to Eve. . . . I will greatly multiply thy sorrow in thy conception. . . . In sorrow . . . thou . . . shalt bring forth children.'"

Wakwa's mouth curled in disgust. "The claws of this Genesis grip at your root still!"

Defiant tears threatened. "We must part. I grow so very tired." She waited to summon energy before she could continue. "I beg you, seek Tame Deer. Tell her I was brave."

Her eyes were again fixed on the bright blue sky of midafternoon. After the sensation subsided she would only pet his hand and not look at him. And so she wore down his resistance until he could no longer reason with her. "Matta" became "perhaps," "perhaps" changed to "soon," then finally, reduced to the guttural affirmative, "oo," Wakwa stumbled off to find White Cat and Awepu.

When he saw them he was grim. "Awepu. I go to Qunneke. Stay and tell Charles Dowland to open his arms. The daughter has no more strength to work longer over this child. White Cat! Give me your shoulder."

* * * *

Elizabeth reacted to his parting with secret regret, feeling truly alone, picturing herself poised on the outer edge of the ball of the earth, all fullness in the void.

Seven and one half hours she had lain and felt her insensible body performing its singular function, while she with all her powers of thought could do nothing to bring closer the outcome of her union with Silent Fox. Nor could she escape the advancing moment of complete openness and the entrance of a new person into time and space. The anonymity of the small lump inside her, which had quickened and grown powerful enough to cause her to cry from the strength of its kicks, was giving way to sudden intimacy.

"Keep yer buttocks raised up a mite, stay as pleasant as ye are right now, let your body do its work. But push down slow an' easy at the end for as long as ye must. Rest yerself between the stretchin' of the openin' an' give some breaths short an' quick when the head is born. That is all there is to it, Bonnie." These were her instructions from Dr. Mac.

A breeze struck up along the river, blowing in the watery noises, snuffing out the songs of the birds. Her muscles seemed to twist with the severity of their contractions. Without warning, pain spread through her lower back and for a moment she wondered if the child would burst out of her body, so extreme was her discomfort. The pain mocked her inability to relieve it with counter pressure, and while she lay confused she began to shake. A trembling started in her feet and worked its way up her calves, seizing her thighs and hips, shaking her ribcage until the next shiver began to climb her body once again. A mighty pressure followed in her abdomen, but, familiar with that sensation, Elizabeth mastered the force which seemed strong enough to wrench her insides loose.

Flames from a fire caught her eye as she lay rapt in the powerful, untouchable movements. Awepu clutched her hands which lay loosely under her breasts.

"Thou art cold? I beheld thee shaking."

"Something happens! I cannot tell what it is. Awepu, I am not cold!"

Awepu strained to judge her mood. Desperate to comfort her, he said, "Dr. Mac is coming to care for you. Soon he will be here."

Another huge shaking took hold of her. "Lord, God! My back! Awepu, it will be too late, I am at a loss. I do not do what I should do."

Awepu's mention of the doctor brought back Stirling's instructions, and she squeezed her eyes shut to concentrate, but saw only a greasy blackness like a wall of dripping coal. She trembled again.

"My wife saith she leans against a bank or hill when she brings forth. Shall I take thee?"

Elizabeth grunted as she gave a push against the new feeling and the shaking stopped. "Ha! I have found it!"

"Can you be carried?"

"Oh! Please, no!" Elizabeth bore down inefficiently, out of rhythm with the swift, strong contractions.

"Then Awepu will be your hill." And the strong man with knotted black hair deftly lifted her from behind her shoulders, slipping his feet against the small of her back, resting her upper body against his legs, her head cradled against his knees.

Her sigh of relief at the firm support against the searching pain became a trill of happiness as, in the next moment, the fluid sac split and the waters gushed from her in sudden release. The woman sighed deeply again and again at the rewarding advance of the all-present event that had begun to yield her satisfaction unimaginable.

Now Elizabeth threw off the light quilt, openly accepting the intimacy and assistance of the gentle man. She grappled with the loose dress, soaked underneath her.

Undauntable Awepu tried to help her pull the gown up to a

more convenient level but could not reach from his position. He pushed against her back with his hands, shifting them both into a more mobile arrangement, while she responded to the inner demand with a slow, steady push. Her face grew wide and red with effort as Awepu moved himself to her left side. He bent his knees, putting his weight on the balls of his feet, making a rest for her shoulders against his right thigh. With his hands free he was able to slash the skirt away with his steel knife, bundling the dry part for her to slip between her buttocks and the wet mat.

Again she bore down, seeking a place to brace her feet. Finding nothing, she made ready for the next contraction by bending her legs out from her body so that she could hold her knees with her hands. Awepu surrounded her head with his arms and bent his spirit toward the hope that her strength would hold, that Dr. Mac would come, that someone would think to bring Meadow-in-the-night, and, especially, that Elizabeth would not die in his arms as her father had but be the way to a second life for the man he had understood. So they remained locked in patient labor, while the eighth hour expanded into the ninth.

* * * *

When Wakwa careened into camp leaning on White Cat, he had no intention of letting Qunneke nurse his abominable tooth. His young captain had set up a call in the forest before crossing the river, but Tame Deer and her daughter, Sequan, had not been located by the time Wakwa entered his uncle's house.

The sachim's lodge went into action at the news that Elizabeth Dowland's child, by Mac's calculation, was making an early entrance into the world.

Meadow-in-the-night found the saunks bathing in a pool of water at the foot of a small fall in the western arm of the river. Qunneke and a group of women were relaxing after several days of work in the field, bringing in the first of the harvest. Tame Deer was caught by the news as she was washing her hair. She tossed back its wealth with one movement of her arms and ran wet and naked toward her house, winding her skirt around her on her way.

Halfway there she was met by suffering, explaining Wakwa,

in his haste ignoring Sequan, who was racing at his heels. Once inside, Tame Deer took command, giving brief, quiet orders to the young maid she had been training as a servant for her husband's second wife.

Wakwa shook in his anxiety. "Qunneke! Will you take time to dress yourself in finery while Elizabeth lies there needing you? Sequan! Be quiet! Do not shout to make me look at you when I am speaking to your mother!" Despite his disabling headache, Wakwa picked her up when he saw the little girl's dejection.

Tame Deer looked at him with calm eyes as she slipped into a sleeveless, beaded bodice and sprinkled her wet hair with fragrant water.

"Gilbert Worth will come there! What matters it what I put on, as long as I must put on!"

The husband stared blankly at the wall opposite, his agonized mind unable to accept what he had heard. The maid raced for a large basket of cloths and other supplies which she strapped around her forehead. Qunneke slipped a small painted gourd filled with her perfumed water into a pouch at her hip. She caressed her husband's sore face and went past him on the way to her mother's house with Sequan.

As she took their daughter from his arms he asked wonderingly, "Have you everything? You are ready?"

She called back as she hastened away. "I knew you would come to me!"

Wakwa counted the hours that had passed each time the guards' paddles cut the water. Absorbed, he gave no consideration to Tame Deer's feelings as she approached her first meeting with his other wife. Qunneke's efficiency pleased him and her hand upon his knee calmed him. His own aches and pains were forgotten in the rush. He could not know the woman was regarding the lengthwise cleft in his forehead, above the bridge of his nose, that always appeared when he was frightened.

The husband and wife were left down on the bank while the maid and the guards went on to the big lodge to ready the fires and seek news that may have come from the Englishmen.

In the tenth hour of Elizabeth's labor, Wakwa and Qunneke made a run for the far place she had chosen in the forest.

Afternoon was waning and the sun was not warm anymore.

Elizabeth had done prodigious work but was unaware of how fatigued her body was, growing more exuberant as her exertions increased. She fought excitement and attempted to rest in between the rhythmical demands her body made to urge the baby downward with her pushing.

Awepu remained unmoving in his position of support, sometimes saying small words of encouragement to her, sometimes singing in a whisper to himself, sometimes lost in the beauty of their closeness, sharing unspoken memories of her father and longings for her child. He looked over his shoulder to check the position of the sun and was startled to see how the haze rising from the river had bleached the blue of the sky and the yellowness of the sun to nearly white. There was a long time until dusk, but the memory of another white sunset and the wizened old man he had coaxed into happiness at death was strongly in front of him.

"I burn!" Elizabeth completed another strong, slow push, expelling her pent-up breath in a throaty rush.

"No. The sun has gone cold now." Awepu put his head down near her ear so she could hear through the stress of her effort.

"The sun? No, no! My son! He is here! He is coming! Tell me it will be soon!" she shouted. "I burn! Now it is gone. . . ." Her voice trailed off, disappointed.

In her eagerness she bore down too soon, and her body rumbled against the unwarranted force. Anxious about failing after coming so far, so successfully, her breath came short. Then she remembered Dr. Mac.

"Give some breaths short an' quick. . . ." She heard his words again, trying to comply, teaching herself to space her panting, gliding over the force of the expulsive contractions.

"Short an' quick when the head is born," she remembered further. Afraid of that strange expression, "when the head is born," she attempted to touch the opening of her body in hesitant fascination. Her legs wobbled without the support of her hands on her knees.

Awepu reached his arms around her and grasped her firmly just behind each knee, his right arm crossing above her face like a beam.

Panting again, her hands free, she felt with gentle fingers a tender, hairy bulge which grew larger and larger.

314

"Oh! Oh!" she sang out. "It is come, Awepu!" She screamed in happiness. And then into the cradle of her waiting hands came the forehead and face of the baby. "Can I? Can I?" she called out in worry, directing the infant, as it emerged, upward toward her abdomen as she had been told to do.

Awepu moved his stiffened leg, raising her up more so that she could see what he was seeing. With a slippery sound the tiny neck and shoulders emerged, then the torso and legs shot out, pushed by pulsating force.

Emptied and filled in the same moment, Elizabeth's breath was suspended while the infant sucked in its first air, and a sound of suffering, anger, and want tore from the baby's open mouth. While Elizabeth did not breathe, in the flood of acceptance of the tiny body that weighed down her hands, the gasping, reaching child opened his eyes.

"Neetu!" Awepu cried. "He is born!"

"She?" Busy Elizabeth, trying to clean the choking matter from the baby's mouth, misheard.

"It is a man!"

"A son? Yes! Dear God! I cannot hold him!" Elizabeth's eyes were wide.

Awepu reached his left arm over and opened his hand, and Elizabeth released her child, still connected to her by the cord, into his confident grasp.

The infant was momentarily face down, Awepu's forefinger supporting its forehead. Pulling his cramped leg from under Elizabeth's back, Awepu knelt with the young boy in his hand, then with great respect turned from the waist and showed the reclining woman the fruit of her love. He laid the baby on her stilled breast, and while the mother encircled him with her arms and hands to keep him warm, Awepu took a piece of white flannel from the top of the basket and spread it on the mat near her shoulder. Together they placed the tiny boy on the soft blanket. Suddenly calm, his color reverted to its original fairness from the purple tone that lit his skin when he had been crying. His mother laughed lightly, turned back to him, and saw the little hand reaching out aimlessly. She gave him her finger. His hand closed on it, and she loved him from then, connected to him at last by touch. She lay back, all smiles, her work not yet done, waiting with impatience and interest the afterbirth, the mysterious shelter, transmitter of security and food, the mother of the inside.

It took all her habits of mental discipline to bear down again to squeeze herself free of the wonder that had become an encumbrance. Finally it slid from her, a small, pulsating, blood-streaked heap of softness. Though afraid of this moment before the birth, Elizabeth was surer what to do with the strange sac than she was about the child. Gathering the flaccid matter in her hands, she bundled it, still warm, into the cloth with the baby, who was crying again, marvelously loud and unrelenting.

With the machinations of the birth quieted, Elizabeth looked at her little son and saw his father, although the baby was so new and very pale. His head, already covered wildly with long strands of black hair, showed the same long shape as Wakwa's, the skull a pleasure to view in its balanced perfection, the aspect of the tiny features, now round and even, betokening the same equilibrium that lifted Wakwa's countenance into the extraordinary. At that moment his large wandering eyes were a surprising deep blue-green.

Elizabeth rested, soothing him with her hand, enjoying the squall he made. Awepu sat against a tree, his face mirroring Elizabeth's beatitude. He leaned over and rubbed his stiff legs, smiled broadly, and repeated over and over in his own language, "Nutonkqs, neetu!"

Elizabeth understood the words from the language that was her own son's birthright and was thrilled by their import. Through them, Awepu gave her belonging in the tribe and a renewed sense of worth, by saying to her, "Kinswoman, he is born!"

She saw she must put the baby to her breast to comfort him. Her hands and arms shook as she loosened the buttons of her ruined gown. She had no experience even watching a baby suckle, Mary Dowland's milk having been insufficient to support Henry from his early days. The little brother had been fed watered goat's milk from a silver pitcher-like container.

Awepu's presence did not embarrass her, but she was awkward. After a day of cooperation with the new experience of bringing forth a child, her calmness was sliding from her as she realized how unprepared she was to care for the babe. There was

316

the desire from within to simply hold her son close and hope that somehow he would naturally know what to do to take nourishment from her. There was the directive from the old doctor, "An' when it's born, Bonnie, ye've got to cut the cord!"

"Awepu! I can wait no longer. Bring me the knife."

The friend put his hand down to his own, but Elizabeth persuaded him with her eyes to bring Wakwa's great stone blade.

He cleansed the weapon in the fire and doubtfully held it out to the exhausted girl. She rose on one elbow, afraid, holding the wet cord in the fingers of one hand. She sliced through it with a strong upward cut, Awepu taking the knife immediately. Clumsily, she fingered the cord, deciding where to begin the tieing.

"May I not try?" Awepu suggested. "Hunting with your husband has made me an expert tier of knots!"

Gladly she abdicated this duty, trying to sit up to watch, but a hot wave passed from her chest to the crown of her head and she felt only the support of a pair of wonderfully smooth, strong arms and the touch of damp, fragrant hair to her face.

＊＊＊＊

When Tame Deer and Wakwa came into the vicinity of the second wife, they slowed and caught their breath, hoping not to frighten her with their approach. Their sudden stillness allowed them to hear the sound of the forest. They were drawn together in the beauty of the misted afternoon, little birds caroling busily as they set about finding their evening meal. It was as Wakwa slid his arm around Qunneke's shoulders and proceeded forward more slowly that the infant's cry fought its way to them against the easterly river breeze. They waited, as still as the tree trunks, then bolted ahead as the unmistakable sound of the newborn grew and continued.

Qunneke followed her husband as he made his way through the foliage, past the place where White Cat had kept guard earlier in the day, to the western perimeter of the thicket, behind Elizabeth.

Wakwa moved a sapling aside and they saw Awepu holding Elizabeth's son for her to see.

317

"Lo!" An exclamation escaped Wakwa.

"Kusseh!" Tame Deer echoed his sentiment.

"I have a son!" Wakwa would have entered the green space but Tame Deer's hand detained him.

Together they watched Awepu and Elizabeth care for the infant boy, holding back until their presence would not be an intrusion. Wakwa raised his eyes and crossed his arms over his chest. But Tame Deer watched the disheveled girl staunchly going about her business, openly sharing her son's birth with Awepu. The Indian woman could not see Elizabeth's face. Only the matted hair, her fragile shoulders and arms, and one bare leg were in view. She thought Elizabeth was as white as the growing mist which diffused the half light of the sun into unearthly brilliance. She pushed forward when she saw Elizabeth struggle to place the wailing baby into a position to nurse. Now Wakwa held her back, and, feeling he was right, Qunneke obeyed him. But she noticed Elizabeth's strength failing about the matter of the cord and saw Awepu gamely offer his assistance. She watched the other wife sit up and she felt dizziness pass through her own body as the younger woman reeled backward. Qunneke was there to catch Elizabeth Dowland as she slipped insensible onto the mat.

It was only for a moment that Elizabeth lost consciousness. When her vision cleared she was looking full into the stately countenance of Tame Deer. One of Qunneke's hands held her shoulder, the other wiped away the gloss of sweat from under her eyes.

Uncontainable joy freed Elizabeth's reaction to the impact of this introduction, and her arms came around Tame Deer's neck and were lost in her loose, abundant hair which covered her body like a cloak. Knowing without having to be told that this woman was Wakwa's wife, Elizabeth whispered, "So glad am I, Qunneke!" Her arms locked around Qunneke's neck in perfect happiness, and she closed her eyes, enjoying the summit of her achievement and the floral aura surrounding the tall and lovely woman.

Shyer, Tame Deer looked up from Elizabeth's face for help from Silent Fox who was coming quietly toward them. He knelt and passed one arm underneath Elizabeth's back and one over

Qunneke's shoulders, catching and caressing Elizabeth's clasped hands. The three of them remained in triple embrace, Awepu standing in awe of the sweetness of this rare encounter, the child nestled close to his face. Finally Elizabeth opened her eyes and released Tame Deer.

Awepu said huskily, "Kusseh kenaumon. Behold thy son."

Tame Deer rose to see the baby, but Wakwa lingered to kiss Elizabeth's eyelids and whisper, "Thee I love."

The Indian woman watched them together, then took the baby from Awepu. The child was crying again, and Qunneke held him to her heart, comforting him with its beat. Wakwa rose to greet his son.

Awepu joined Elizabeth and sat next to her proudly. She saw his hands bloody from holding her baby and tieing the cord at his middle. She took Awepu's hands and kissed them and refused to release him. They stayed contentedly together, watching the product of their common effort being adored by Tame Deer and Silent Fox. The murmur of Tame Deer's voice reached Elizabeth, who was marveling at the woman's hair, which fell to her heels.

"Nunnaumon, nunnaumon, my son!" Wakwa spoke to the baby as if he would understand. He touched the infant's silky cheek with a long finger and tears filled his eyes. "Ah! Qunneke! At last we have a son." Wakwa pressed her head against his shoulder and kissed her black hair.

Elevated by her victory, Elizabeth was happily at ease watching their affection. She felt she could die at that moment and have lived the purpose of her existence. She had provided Silent Fox with his continuation.

"Nunnaumon!" she called out in her ecstasy.

"Yea, Kayaskwa!" Wakwa turned to her and smiled as the baby continued to cry. "Wakwa Manunnappu has an English son. Alas! The hope of our peoples desires to suckle."

Tame Deer passed in front of her husband, drew one half of Elizabeth's unbuttoned bodice aside, and adroitly placed the baby near the nipple of her left breast. Elizabeth trembled as Qunneke's fingers softly slid against her skin and the nipple formed into a bright bud. The baby frantically twisted around until he caught the prize in his warm, little mouth. Qunneke stayed closely bent over the pair, anxious for the white girl who was making little high noises of discomfort.

While the wives were occupied, Awepu and Wakwa removed from the thicket and sat next to one another, exhausted.

"Walk in sunlight all your days, dearest cousin. Such a service you have rendered to my wife and to me!"

"Wakwa, I but watched and made easy her poor back. It is I would thank her for such a happy day as this has been."

"Poor Dr. Mac had a wish to see the loveliness of a brave woman bringing forth a child in the forest. You have worked his magic for him. My faith in Kayaskwa, I see, is not enough. She is indeed a woman!"

"Think of it!" Awepu sprawled against the earth on his back. "Because of Elizabeth, I now know all that Meadow-in-the-night has passed through to bring my children to me. My friend, I shall have to father yet another, so that I may be at my own wife's side to see such a wonder yet again."

"Is this the man who would have sent me off to fish! Does it not seem Manit smiles again on my path?"

"Nux! And feel you not Charles Dowland is also pleased? This mist is his spirit touching the son of his daughter. Oh!" Awepu groaned. "How do women bear such trials? I am sleepy as a bear in Taquonk!"

The men almost dozed, content to speak quietly, freed from the English tongue, worry drifting from them, leaving them devoid of energy. But at a scream from Tame Deer they shot to their feet and burst into the thicket.

Again and again Qunneke had gently helped Elizabeth put the tender nipple and its surrounding circle of darkened skin comfortably into the child's mouth. Repeatedly she had to place her finger under the infant's nostrils to force him to release his hold and lessen the pain the English girl was experiencing. In frustration, Tame Deer bared her own breast to show the second wife how simply all could go, given some experience and calm.

Coming on the women, Wakwa and Awepu stared in vicarious agony at the sight of Elizabeth writhing on her blanket, holding her breast in one hand and her stomach with the other, and Tame Deer biting her lip, attempting to remove the baby from her own breast.

320

"Yeu peisses sunna touohkomukque puppinashim!"

"Qunneke!"

"Tame Deer saith the papoos is like a beast of the wilderness."
Awepu replaced the quilt which had slipped off Elizabeth.

"I would try again." Elizabeth opened her arms and called to
Tame Deer, "Nunnaumon!"

Resignedly the woman placed Wakwa's son at Elizabeth's
other breast. He turned his little face with a snap and latched
onto the nipple of the smaller breast, grinding it between his
toothless gums. Tears slid from the corners of Elizabeth's eyes,
and her legs sliced across the mat like a shears as she fought the
temptation to scream.

"Yeu muckquashim!" Tame Deer spoke sympathetically as
the men stood aghast at the discomfort they could only try to
imagine.

Again Wakwa scolded his first wife, this time with more authority. The words flowed too fluently for Elizabeth to catch
any meaning. And she did not object when Tame Deer removed
the boy. She fell back against the dank blanket, her elation
turning to misery. Awepu brought her water as she all but hid
under the quilt. Elizabeth received it gratefully and watched
how Qunneke listened to their husband, not arguing her own
point with him, but shaking her head and letting the baby nibble
at her finger. Qunneke gave Wakwa a little smile, saying when
he was finished, "Muckquashim."

Although tired, Awepu found some humor in the situation
and sat down with a twinkle in his eye, like a man prepared to
watch a wrestling match.

"Elizabeth, my sister, Qunneke calls thy son a wolf."

"Poor little thing." Her hands massaged her breasts under the
covering. "But she is right."

"But the father complains she curses him with such a name.
Thy son must not be seen as a lonely, hungry creature wishing
but to take."

"Tame Deer means it not! Or doth she?"

Wakwa took his son from Tame Deer and held the voracious
little mouth against his neck. The infant gnawed his father for
a moment, then dropped off to sleep.

Wakwa crooned, "Oh. Oh. Nunnaumon. . . . He wishes not

to devour, but only is filled with hopes. He will be difficult to satisfy, but is this not the image of hope itself?"

"I thought to name him after Papa, but I see his name will never fit." Elizabeth's voice was small but she was relaxing now that the child was resting too. "What is the word for hope, Wakwa?"

"Ah! I perceive thy thought. Annoosu. Hope." Wakwa soothed his infected jaw against a raised shoulder. "Matta, Elizabeth. Hope is nothing of itself. If it pleases you for a name, little wife, he shall be Noh-annoosu, He-hopes."

"Yea, my sweet, Noh-annoosu! I can say that!" Elizabeth was growing sleepy. "Bring him near that I may see him. See the light as it forms around his face in the mist!"

"Noh-annoosu." Wakwa sounded sure.

"Muckquashim," Tame Deer mumbled as she cleaned up the articles strewn on the ground.

"Matta Muckquashim, Qunneke." Awepu fingered the air and turned toward Elizabeth. "My sister, it is true he is too beautiful in this mist for 'wolf' alone." He paced in front of Qunneke. "Ouwan! Elizabeth, is it not beautiful? He emerged with the mist! Muckquashim-ouwan!" Wolf-of-the-mist! A name for a man! Not Noh-annoosu."

"Muckquashim-ouwan-Noh-annoosu." Tame Deer settled it.

Wakwa translated to Elizabeth. "Wolf-of-the-mist-He-hopes."

Poor Elizabeth, caught among the metaphors, began practicing the mouthful of syllables. Wakwa gave the baby to Tame Deer and stood looking lovingly down at the English girl.

"This name will serve until we find a better, nux?"

"Nux!"

Awepu had disappeared in the direction of the lodge. Tame Deer began to walk toward the stream to wash the infant. The baby woke and wailed again. Qunneke turned and saw Elizabeth's head raised in anxiety for the baby as she struggled to stand. But instead of walking toward her crying child, the second wife hobbled toward Silent Fox. He held his hand out to her and she kissed his palm and said, "He is as beautiful as thee! Cowammaunsh, Sachim!"

Tame Deer understood the pledge of love in the last two words and faced away, continuing toward the stream.

322

Wakwa began to see the details of the thicket for the first time, now that the joy of his augmented parenthood was accepted as fact. He saw the ruined mat, the disordered basket, Elizabeth's little book half-buried under some early fallen leaves, the stained flannel holding the mass of the afterbirth. He saw the cut-up skirt dangling around Elizabeth's thighs and the line of blood trickling down the inside of one leg. Where she had been full and in blossom hours before, she was shrunken and thin.

He remembered her as she had been, glorious among his tribesmen in the bright afternoon when she had surmounted the tragedy of her father's death and had accepted him again and all his ways.

And he swept her up, carrying her after Tame Deer, bringing her to wash. Then he withdrew to find Awepu and go home.

Chapter 47

The sound of horses' hooves on the forest floor was hushed by the floating damp that had replaced the mist. Their rustling against the close foliage, and the plodding of their iron shoes, stopped a little way from the lodge. Gil and Dr. Stirling made the last few yards quickly on foot.

They panted into the clearing and found Silent Fox propped against a listing maple tree. He had not heard them or was not conscious, for he did not turn his head as the white men approached.

Gil bent close to his niece's husband, hardly recognizing him, pale, puffy, glazed in expression. "Great God! What is it?"

"I think the lad needs a tooth pulled." The practical doctor, coat sleeves rolled up, felt Wakwa's face and rummaged in a fat leather satchel he had dropped on the ground.

When Dr. Mac took his wrist, Wakwa responded to the touch with a dreamy smile. "A man child it is."

Gil rose up, remembering the purpose of all his haste. "Beth has done it? She has borne it alone?"

Wakwa began an explanation but the doctor pulled him back to the ground.

"It is no surprise to me," Stirling said gruffly, "an' I'm sure she an' the babe are in better health than ye, laddie!" He began his examination, addressing himself to the more pressing need.

The doctor's response confused Gil, and he turned toward the lodge door alone. Still suited as in the morning, his neckcloth had long ago been torn back from his throat, and it hung against his coat like a rag. His pale hair was white with dust.

The painted mat moved, and the doorway was filled with the figure of Tame Deer. Gil blinked back the image, irrationally expecting to see his niece come running and smiling, as she always did when she heard the sound of his horse in the trees.

The woman and the man stood in the chilly quiet of gray dusk with the woodland smells all about them. Gil saw the strength and grace of her body underneath the black veil of her hair.

There was no question in his mind who this woman was, so fitting did her presence seem in the muted brownness of the entrance to the place that should have harbored Beth.

Gil looked back toward Wakwa. But the husband was making no introductions, his head pinned against the ground, Dr. Mac daubing his gums with whiskey.

"Qunneke!" The woman spoke for herself, holding her hands over the fullness of her bosom, waiting with her head down.

Gil squared his shoulders and walked to her. Only his shoes tipped their equality of height in his favor.

Qunneke looked into his face, suffering with her inability to tell him of her gratitude for his benevolence.

"I am Gilbert Worth, Qunneke." A smile pushed at the corner of his mouth and was touched by his fair moustache.

Qunneke's full lips parted in fascination. She tore her dark eyes from the gleam of his green ones and forced out her word for uncle, her fingers shielding her mouth. "Nissese!"

Worth was jarred with regret at her reminder of their familial relationship. He had seen Qunneke as a creature apart, a mine of amicable experience, and fully appreciated her statuesque allure.

He purposefully took her hand away from her lips and rested it between his hands, seeing he must modestly seal the approval he had given Wakwa's plural marriage before touching the tantalizing psychical cord that drew him toward her.

Gil pressed her straight, strong fingers warmly. "Keen kah neen . . . you and I are . . . wetompauog . . . good friends?"

A sound of pleasure escaped Tame Deer, and she reached for him with her free hand and led him to Elizabeth with his arm tucked high against her side.

Wakwa half rose as Gil spoke and watched Qunneke and the Englishman disappear inside. He turned to Stirling, mystified by his first wife's rare responsiveness.

"I'd look out for tha' fancy feller, laddie!" Stirling cackled and sneaked a long metal implement from the bag.

Nuppohwunau and the men from Wakwa's guard rode up, late, slowed by crates of lobsters and clams strapped to their horses.

Wakwa had no choice but to submit to the fearsome-looking

tool, comporting himself like a man going to certain death with his fellow warriors looking on.

* * * *

Earlier, when Qunneke reached the lodge with Elizabeth, she was displeased to find that the maid had not lit the fire in the rear chamber. But this mistake allowed the woman to see the room as the younger wife had left it. She saw the cleanliness and felt the freshness of the air, appreciated the organization of the numerous baskets and the charm of the hung herbs and wild flowers. She stood under the blue and green drapery and appraised its artful appliqué of birds that seemed to fly in the breeze filtering through the open door. She was roused from her silent acquaintance with the habits of the second wife by Elizabeth's great sigh as she stretched out in front of the dead fire. The child had been settled in his basket. Qunneke went to the English girl quickly.

"Elizabeth?" Tame Deer had practiced the name. "Neen-kuttannum-ous!"

"I will be better, Qunneke." The girl looked up helplessly and apologized, terribly tired and sore after the birth.

Qunneke soothed her sister-wife and mended the fire. She bathed her again, this time with heated water and the soap which lay ready near the buckets. As the fire warmed the room, she persuaded Elizabeth to spread her legs to its heat, while she quickly poured cool water onto the tear in the skin where the child had emerged. Qunneke talked all the while in her cordial voice, sorry she could not be understood. The girl lay more abashed before the first wife than she had in front of Awepu.

Relying on her hands to convey her meaning, Qunneke asked for and found the clothes basket and devised a breechcloth of soft doeskin and linen for the bleeding.

By the time the little maid could be heard moving about the outer room, Elizabeth was resting on her raised bed against the softness of fur, robed in a nightgown of white lawn, covered with the borning quilt she had made for this occasion.

Qunneke left softly, smiling back at her charge, her thoughts turning to Wakwa's needs. But she came across the maid stemming strawberries.

326

"The son of thy sachim entered a cold house!" The uncustomary sharpness of her voice woke Awepu. "Are you idle or ill-taught? The fire comes before pleasant gathering with White Cat! In my place, what would you do?"

Ashamed of herself, the girl went to the woodpile, chose the greenest branch, and presented it to Qunneke for a whip.

"If that is how you would be treated, guard you do not make the same mistake again in my house!" Qunneke was surprised at such harsh thinking. She broke the stick across her knee, added it to the fire, and motioned the girl to come close.

"Now! Go and clean thy mistress' hair and call me in to comb it." Qunneke shook her head at the frightened maid. "Be gentle with the new saunks."

Before she heard the sound of the horses in the woods, Qunneke had finished cleaning the strawberries.

****

Gilbert Worth found his niece looking tired, peaceful, and pretty. Awepu was by her side, spoon-feeding her crushed berries. As Tame Deer urged him forward, Elizabeth saw them, exaltation replacing fatigue.

"What a smile!" The uncle was relieved. "What has happened?"

"He has happened, Uncle Gil." Elizabeth wrapped her arm about the hood of the baby's basket.

"My God!" Gil knelt and looked in awe at the baby. "How did you? . . . Was it? . . . I tried so to hurry to you, dear!"

Qunneke pulled back the fur coverlet and displayed the child's perfect little form to the uncle of Elizabeth Dowland. Gil studied Wakwa's son in silent affection. The baby opened his eyes, then sneezed, and the Englishman put the cover back into place.

"Mink! He is a prince! And big! A nice big boy. Ha! A great-uncle am I! Where doth a baby Massachuseuck get green eyes, eh? And what will you call him?" Gil turned from the baby to Elizabeth and Awepu. "You understand I could not bring the Sweetwood doctor in. The property deed aside, I could not chance that bunch getting close to Silent Fox at such a time."

"Awepu was my nurse, Uncle Gil."

"Awepu? I do not follow."

"Did you see the sunset, Gilbert Worth?" Awepu attempted Wakwa-like diplomacy.

"I rode into it, Awepu."

"She brought him forth the same as her father let fly his spirit. With the mist. I was there to offer the old man and the new man my hand."

Gil looked haggard.

Qunneke took up the comb and contented herself playing with Elizabeth's hair.

"Poor, sweet Uncle," Elizabeth said lovingly. "See how well I am? They spoil me. Were I alone I should be up and get your supper."

"Well! There are some lobsters crawling about the other room. Shall I have you chase them into a pot of boiling water?"

Elizabeth laughed happily and reached her hand back to squeeze the first wife's arm. Gil watched them touch. But laughter was short because it hurt the new mother's insides, and she became rapt in reciting the adventure of the birth.

She grew careless in her enthusiasm. "Such power I have and never knew it! Oh, Uncle Gil, that someday, somehow, you and Aunt Hanna . . ." She saw Gil's face change and whispered, "Forgive me."

Gil came and kissed her then. "Dearest, your aunt and I will never know your joy, but it does me good to see you well, and strong, and jolly."

Elizabeth started to cry and the baby woke. There were sounds of men walking in the outer room, fish crates being opened, and Dr. Mac making his way through the crowd toward the sound of the baby.

Qunneke withdrew from the English people, not following their swift change of mood.

Wakwa and the doctor appeared in the doorway and saw Awepu explaining to Qunneke in a far corner, the maid preparing the screaming infant to nurse, and Gil pulling Elizabeth's hands away from her eyes.

"Would I could have named him after you, Uncle Gil, but you see how it would fit!"

"No, no, I do not expect that, dear!" He forced her to look at him.

"You will come often and be with him?" she cried to him and clutched him. "So he knows you and I do not lose you, too!" The new mother groaned her depression.

"Tell me! Tell me! Have you pain?" Gil put his smooth hands on her cheeks, afraid to hurt her by holding her.

Disregarding the turmoil, the determined maid brought the baby to Elizabeth.

She accepted her squirming child. "Thy nephew, Noh-annoosu! Muckquashim-ouwan-Noh-annoosu." Then Elizabeth was lost looking at the baby.

"Jehovah! Muckquash what?" Gil asked above the boy's yowling.

Wakwa came, removing a wad of cotton from his bleeding mouth. "Wolf-of-the-mist-He-hopes."

Gil looked hard at Tame Deer. "I remember the time you said Beth was like the mist, that you saw everything through her!"

But Wakwa was not listening. He regarded only his wife, Elizabeth, his fingers worriedly working the pretty ruffles at her shoulders.

"Shoo! Shoo! Scat! Every last one o' ye! Yea, you too, Silent Fox. Out! Yes! Now, ye go an' rest yourself somewhere's else! Bonnie an' I, an' the bairn, have got some visitin' to do. Lady in a hurry, not willin' to wait for an old man!" J. Macmillan Stirling cleared the room.

Chapter 48

Nuppohwunau left for the Indian town to give the sachim the news of Wakwa's son, leaving Wakwa and Gil to rest against the thick maple.

"A relaxing way to wash, Sachim!" Gil held his face up to an intermittent drizzle.

Wakwa smiled. "So, Uncle, now we are one."

Gil could only look at the man he wished to have for a friend.

Wakwa took up his thought again. "I would like my son to grow to be like you, Gilbert Worth."

"Why, whatever for?" Gil was too surprised to be flattered.

Wakwa dodged away from his strong sentiment in their first brotherly talk together. "You are tired in my service, Uncle. It is good to see you with dusty boots."

"I am not a wise man that your son should be like me!" Gil did not wish to let the subject drop. "I am a seeker, an incomplete, who wonders about everything and can answer nothing. Even the simplest deed for the most common laborer on my land I cannot perform."

"What is it a man like you cannot do, Gilbert Worth?"

"I cannot beget children. It seems."

There was a lengthy silence.

"What is it, Silent Fox, makes for this lack between a man and a woman? Such a beautiful thing is a newborn babe."

"This is not the only lack, and do you see now why I would have Noh-annoosu follow after you among the heights of your thoughts? Gilbert, have you thought of the comfort of another wife? Come, Englishman, and live among us. You will be a lord and live in a house with many fires and give us strength with your blood, as does Elizabeth."

"I cannot take up your jest now. The day has been too long. Beth has been through too much. I am afraid for us all."

"Why afraid?"

Gil snorted. "You certainly would not want young Wolf in there to follow after a man who grows afraid because he hears a baby cry!"

Wakwa threw his blanket around them both. "See how the rain gently builds, as last year it poured down upon us, flooding all our lives with change."

"You deceive yourself, Silent Fox. It were not the rain but a woman changed our lives."

"Now you see that I did not jest when I asked you to leave the life you live now. You could yet father a son, mayhap a different woman would place one in your arms, and your dear wife Hanna share him with you?"

Tame Deer came out of the house then, looking for Wakwa. Gil watched her move toward them, the drizzle coursing down the bare skin of her breast.

"There is a woman could induce me to break the habit of monogamy, but I am afraid she is out of reach for the likes of Uncle Gil!" Gilbert Worth did not take his eyes from Wakwa's wife.

Wakwa, still recovering from his bout with Dr. Mac, gripped his forehead and narrowed his eyes. "Now it is I cannot tell if you jest with me."

Tame Deer's attention drifted away from Wakwa, answering her questions about his infection, for she was watching the Englishman drink the cup of steaming tea she had brought him. When he was finished she took the cup, less anxious about Wakwa's sickness, and returned to the lodge with a message for Awepu to escort Dr. Mac to pesuponk.

Wakwa rose with Gil and they turned down the path to begin their own cleansing in the steam.

"Perhaps I should free her to thee," Wakwa said without humor. "Son or no, I perceive you could do what is impossible for me! To make that woman happy."

"I have spoken too freely. And you must be sore discouraged to think of parting with the woman you worked so hard to keep."

Wakwa stopped moving for a moment. "Gilbert, would you not be discouraged?"

"Yes. But not defeated! There is some other need to be filled in her than the one so apparent to you and me."

Wakwa struggled with fluency through the wads of cloth that packed down lye where his tooth had been. "I see her full of fear.

Of me? And why? I cannot tell! I fear myself when I am with her."

"Not at all, nephew!" Gil saw Wakwa's mood as a result of days of sickness and hastened to calm him.

"Should woman not be with man? There is more to gain than children through a union, nux?" Wakwa grew excited.

"You are right! You are right! And how well I know it. The Creator was, at least, a little kind to me in his plans."

"Very kind, knowing Hanna. You have a wife and no child. I, the child, but no wife."

Gil was distracted by a small bird that flew onto a nearby branch, making a spray of droplets in Wakwa's face as it shook loose the twig's coat of water.

Wakwa flicked at the branch with his fingers and the frightened bird flew on. Gil had never seen Wakwa's resentment.

"What is there in me that so repulses her?"

"Nothing! You love her and cannot see her without seeing yourself. Just now she is alone, a chrysaline being, her mystery wrapped within. How can I tell her difficulty? All I see is a rare woman."

"You secret your meaning from me, Uncle. I see I have more English words to learn."

"Just farmer's talk, Fox. Is not the butterfly encased in a golden sheath before it comes into its own, its perfect, state?"

"Nissese, you begin to think like Ninnuock and although you do deny it, your eyes see far. But the woman has lived thirty-six winters! Wherefore remains she incomplete? And should not a husband be loved for piercing this shield to bring to blossom her life within?"

"I wonder." Gil attempted to cool him. "Suppose some women would rather never admit a man into their secrets, even their persons."

"Tame Deer married me not from force." Wakwa was bitter. "And we have camps for such women as you describe, where they are left in peace to do their will with each other and not disturb happier families."

"I did not describe a woman wanting women, but a woman wanting herself. And you do force her now, Fox, to stay with you out of loyalty to your past love. She wants not to be a wife. Simply a woman!"

332

Color came to Wakwa's sallowed skin. "After Taquonk, she is free to go."

"But you do not wish it, Silent Fox?"

"I do not," the tall man whispered painfully. "Yet I will keep her no more against her will, nor tell her more of the hole she will tear in my days if she go."

"Tell her! Beg her!" Gil was irate, logic lost.

Wakwa looked coolly at his confidant. "No more."

Gil slapped at his rain-soaked suit, exasperated.

"If she wish, I will hold her warm and safe and solitary. But I suffer to bleeding at her unhappiness. Elizabeth, my child wife, is alive with life."

"I envy you your dilemma."

The two men walked the last mile to the sweat hut in silence.

* * * *

The roof of the big lodge resounded with steady rain. The delicate aroma of boiled lobster and steamed clams clung in the smoke of the sweet wood.

All the men were relaxing together after the experience of the sweat hut. The five guards were off in a corner, passing the time at reeds. Awepu and Wakwa had taken on a special vibrance after their sweating, smoking, and swimming. Gil, sitting opposite them, was merely very pink. Dr. Stirling was dozing near his sleeping patient and the baby. Tame Deer sat next to Silent Fox, disturbing Gil again with the fitting presence she supplied his niece's husband.

". . . thus, my Uncle, I have been deciding between you and Awepu as Noh-annoosu's special protector."

Gil was barely listening to the new father, his mind occupied instead with the practicalities of a man living with two wives.

"It is necessary, I have come to think," Wakwa re-explained his tradition and its adaptation to the child's circumstances, since there was no response, "that Noh-annoosu, being both bloods, requires two men to turn to in time of need. Two men with power enough to allay the hurts or sorrows that will come his way, as they do even the strongest forest creature."

It seemed strange to Gil that he should be upset to see the first wife sitting comfortably, her forearm casually resting across Wakwa's leg. He thought with annoyance that he had known countless men, entertained them, or mingled with them in the cities, who without a qualm entered in and out of romances with this or that pretty woman when their home lives were troubled or routine. He had heard their glib exchanges about their new amours and never felt them reprehensible. Adults snatching happiness in the face of life's pressures.

But now, in the presence of a friend honorably linked with both Elizabeth and this native woman, Gil was fighting back distrust of the arrangement.

Wakwa resorted to directness to elicit interest from Gil. "May I ask you, then, to watch over him when he travels in the world of his mother? Awepu can affect little good for him there."

Awepu, occupied making a little doeskin sack to hold the pieces of Wakwa's tooth for a memento, grunted.

"Wakwa Manunnappu," Gil stammered, his doubts, as usual, diminishing when he looked at the Indian's face, "it is the first time I feel I can call you that. . . ."

"Uncle, I am glad!"

". . . even without your asking I have taken the boy to my heart. And, if you will, my purse. He will have any benefit I can offer that you approve. I must possess a little of him, like a grandson, for I think you know how close his mother is to me."

Wakwa beamed through his fatigue. He had attempted nothing more strenuous after pesuponk than to sit, talk, and crack lobster claws with his hands, passing the slippery pink meat around unbroken.

"Wakwa, I wish to see Waban now you have a boy and, I think, a successor." Gil's attention had been reclaimed.

"I will take thee, Gilbert."

"I would tell him what will happen to my land when Nohannoosu reaches his majority under English law."

"Uncle?"

"The land shall freely revert back among your people."

Wakwa clutched an empty claw, his eyes changing with the potentials of such an action. A coup indeed to regain that rich earth as a result of a life of delight with Elizabeth.

Gil was all business. "I realize it is a mere seventeen hundred acres, but it was a long walk across it when I bought it as a young man from Dowland. Of course, if we play things right, Elizabeth will inherit all of her father's land, which will bring it up another two thousand. That is, I suspect, the best I can do. The rest of my British neighbors are not so fortunate as myself to have learned we are foreigners but forcing peas and turnips out of land that truly belongs to someone else."

"Terrible battles have been fought over less land than this! You would give my son his first victory before he can turn from his back to his stomach! You sacrifice all this earth to us?"

"First, friend Wakwa, it is your victory, which fact I intend to make well known to your uncle, Waban. It is you who have conquered my ambitions. I return the land to you, not sacrifice. My soul is in the place. If you annex the soil, you annex me. By this trickery I will extend my life after my bones are carted away. You have the farm, for what it is worth, and I hope only I have not spoiled the face of the land too much for you."

"Land cannot be bought or sold or owned! It is the mother feeding and yielding to us all. Why do you do this with the land that is your life?" Wakwa said, genuinely confused at the notion of inheritance. "How do you keep the earth like pearls in a chest?"

Gil cleared his throat to hide a thickness of tone that had grown from his good will.

"This land is always ours, always yours!" Wakwa said. "So anxious was Charles Dowland to keep his farm, he lost the person for whom he kept it. Do not give away thy life and Hanna's!"

Gil thought back to the day he had given Beth the case of needles. The transfer of wealth had now become his burden. "What would Waban or your charming cousin, Weeping Heart, say to your rebuffing this inheritance?" Gil could smile again. "You know I am right, I see. Little Wolf, if he is anything like his mother, will have definite plans what to do with the place the moment he is old enough to get it legally."

"Legally! Legally this ground is guarded still by the spirit of Will Connet, the sachim who from the first would not sell it, but only permit its use. What is legal is different between you and me.

"Legally Elizabeth may have forfeited her rights because of

335

loving me! Dire Locke is not hopeful about our union. I think I should hide her, forever, that you may take the land for yourself according to Charles Dowland's will, disposing of it as you wish. I must not lose her heart over this."

"You do have a mind for it!" Gil enthused privately, then spoke to Wakwa again. "It may come to that. But there must be a way to do justice to both you and Beth. I am in agony when I think how Hudson encroached on Dowland's estate, and encroaches even now, by his never-tiring, impossible aspirations." Gil grew hard. "I have decided, your son gets the lot."

"But the snake will not like this gift!"

"Hudson? Do you really think Wolf-of-the-mist will be put to a fight for this land by that jackass?" Gil lounged back and laughed, unable to sustain his vehemence. "If my fine nephew has no room for his old uncle, I'll slip away and lose my soul to the cities once again."

Wakwa's smile brightened his face. "To prevent that I will defend this gift of land as that on which we sit! Less and less do I know what to expect of you, Uncle. Where are your limits?"

Awepu expelled breath in satisfaction as he tied the thong of the pendant around Wakwa's neck. His day's chores were completed with the sight of the vanquished tooth. "Never have I seen such a root on a tooth!" he exclaimed as Wakwa looked inside the bag.

Gil talked around the interruption. "My niece has taught you to write?"

"She has!"

"You read, I remember. You talk more tongues than I can name. I am told . . . you have memorized passages from the Bible? . . ."

Wakwa was uncomfortable, suspecting Elizabeth had confided to Worth their argument over the coat.

"Listen now, Fox, to what I say! There was an offer two years ago to the Six Nations from the scholars at William and Mary College, to the south of us, where they teach the sciences, religion, philosophy, the law. But a few moments ago I said you had a mind for it."

The lengthwise crease returned to Wakwa's forehead.

"The Iroquois put them off, but I know people there. They

336

would have you! The discipline you know least is the one you need most. You should learn the law. All the gyrations of English law. Who but you is better suited for such study? Then you will be the man of the moment with all the scattered tribes. I feel, from things I hear and see, we will tangle with the king before long to keep our sweet little farms, and you your rivers and trees. What a help in keeping the lands I will turn over to you if you can fight the Crown with its own code!"

"And go from here and live in the city?" Wakwa's vision turned inward.

"For a time. Of course, I will help you house your . . . families."

"Live where there are streets, and never run, and forget the way to hunt, and become a stranger to my very self? Perhaps these gentlemen should send their sons to me, and I will make men of them and teach them how to live!"

"All that in time, Silent Fox." Gil's disappointment showed. "Think about it nevertheless."

Wakwa was so intent he missed Elizabeth's appearance in the doorway. Gil stopped speaking and looked past Wakwa to her in surprise, remembering her mother bedridden for a week after Henry.

Elizabeth was beautiful, her hair wreathed around her temples in a braid, tumbling loose at back in arm-thick coils. She came, a bit hunched over, but steadily, alone.

Gil wanted to rise to greet her and spell the shock he read on her face, more lucid after rest, as she gazed with wide eyes at Tame Deer's closeness to Silent Fox. Her skin glowed red in the firelight. But in the time she stood isolated behind her husband, Gilbert Worth never moved.

Nor did Wakwa, rapt as he was in the radical design Gil was drawing for his future.

Elizabeth hesitated, then chose a place next to Tame Deer.

Wakwa seemed unaware of her presence as Beth moved softly behind him to sit. But the Indian recognized the sudden tenderness in Gil's green eyes.

His voice made them all tremble with its depth. "Come, Elizabeth! There is room on my other side for thee!"

* * * *

Wolf-of-the-mist-He-hopes was hungry. A long, strong child with an insatiable need for comfort, he had no talent for settling peacefully into the loving arms around him.

He chewed Elizabeth's breasts, rather than sucked, and by the middle of the night the circles of delicate skin around her nipples were grazed, the nipples twisted and bleeding. The mother and the child had found no enjoyment in their first intimacies.

Again Doctor Stirling was out of reach. He was spending the night with Waban, Wakwa, Gil, and the Massachuseuck men at the Indian town. The doctor could not have come if he had been called. The elderly man was worn out from riding and from tending five other troubled mouths as a gesture of good will and an exhibition of skill to the taupowaw.

It was Qunneke who helped Elizabeth as she lay distracted, the baby howling in Sparrow's patient arms.

"I am nothing. Can do nothing." Elizabeth sought Tame Deer's eyes.

"Toh kittinnoowam, Elizabeth?" Tame Deer gingerly daubed a salve of honey and walnut oil onto the broken skin.

"I am nothing. Can do nothing," came the rhythmic response through tears.

Tame Deer rehearsed the sounds, determined to ask Wakwa for their meaning in the morning.

Rain continued and increased during the night. Sun did not light the little window at daybreak. The doctor puffed in from the storm, covered by a newly acquired bearskin, and found Elizabeth lying on her bed, a heated sack of fine gravel placed on each breast.

The Scotsman wrote in his notebook, recording this new lesson, then slammed it shut and shouted to Tame Deer, "I've an idea meself, Mrs. Fox!"

Stirling and Qunneke cooperated on the construction of two shields of soft skin to cushion Elizabeth from the pressure of the baby's mouth.

The doctor watched the child cry, then suck and cry again. There was something inefficient about the action of the baby's jaw and the old man soothed Elizabeth as he took Noh-annoosu away once more.

338

"Bonnie, me bonnie, you'll be doin' fine! The bairn's tongue-tied is all."

"All!" Elizabeth was frightened.

"Imagine! The son of a talker like Silent Fox, tongue-tied!" The doctor clucked over the irony.

Then, with a deft flick of his scalpel, Stirling cut the extraneous membrane that had spoiled the coordination between the boy's tongue and the roof of his mouth. "Drink up now, lad, poor pet." His blunt, hairy hands handled He-hopes with a woman's tenderness. Dr. Mac began Elizabeth's son's first normal feeding at Tame Deer's breast.

By afternoon, Elizabeth regained a degree of self-confidence as the filmy liquid preceding milk began to satisfy her son.

* * * *

Gilbert Worth spent that morning in negotiation with Waban about the solemnity to come. The formal exchange of Waban's pipe among the men, marking the progression of their dialogue, guided the blonde man, the three sachimmauog, the taupowaw, the sagamores, and the young lords into understanding in clear, smooth conversation.

The grant of land, the invited guests, the transporting of the beef and the small cargo of gifts were arranged.

It was when Waban reached across the circle to lay a belt of wampum at Gil Worth's feet, as a record of their relationship, that Wuttah Mauo took the pipe and put in sourly, "Why, fair brother, all these favors to a tribe of dirty Indians?"

"If that is how you see yourself, I pity your children!" Gil snapped in feline reaction.

"I have none. I see farther than does my illustrious cousin."

Wakwa sat mute, the etiquette denying interruption.

One light eyebrow raised and Gil's voice sliced defensively. "Intemperance breeds dreary vision, friend."

Wuttah Mauo smoldered. "What do you want of us for all the valuables you laden our camp with!"

Waban, dismayed by his son's hostility, studied its effect on Worth.

Gil lost sight of protocol and chose the moment to open his deepest self to Wuttah Mauo. "What is worthwhile having from

339

any man can ne'er be bought. That should be so clear to a man of your worldly experience, Wuttah Mauo!

"The extent of my gift shows how highly the daughter of Charles Dowland is regarded among her own, and how highly she should be prized among the Massachuseuck! The depth to which I draw from my resources shows with what trust I give her over to the care of Silent Fox. Never forget, this gift shows but a small measure of my sorrow at losing Elizabeth from my own home and ways.

"I want nothing! It is I who am vulnerable and open from all sides! If you see so far, Weeping Heart, you should know that my own kinsmen will not hesitate to find ways to cut up the ground that I have labored to keep in one piece. Where would that leave your people, Sachim, snuggled so close to my now unbroken boundary?

"Your blood and mine pulses through the body of Wolf-of-the-mist-He-hopes. He is our heir. Yours and mine. Ah! You had not considered that! Do not forget to love him."

"I am the first and last of my race," Wuttah Mauo sneered the traditional sentiment, outmaneuvered.

Gil forced back a smart retort and digested the philosophy spat at him. No Machiavellian, Wuttah Mauo! "I am the first and last of my race." Responsibility to the whole People lay in the responsibility of a man to himself. With such belief, self-compromise was more than distasteful, it was treasonable. Gil's memory traveled back over the reports he had read of Philip's War. The pictures drawn there of savages subjecting their own children to hunger and death rather than forego a raid were blotted with misunderstanding. It was a richly poetic principle that tied the self-determination of one man's rights with the future of his whole people. Gilbert Worth appreciated for the first time the deep division between red and white that Beth's baby must meld into a heritage.

Gil would not give Noh-annoosu the example of dissension on his English side and agreed with Weeping Heart:

"As you have no son to follow you, I am also childless. Like sterile trees we blossom but do never make fruit. The world ends with you and me, Sachim. What have you made of yours?"

The pipe lay where Wuttah Mauo dropped it.

340

Wakwa could not speak. Waban took control of the breakfast meeting.

"Think not, brother Gilbert, the life Charles Dowland's daughter brings among us will ever be denied.

"If Noh-annoosu follows Pequawus, the man who engendered Wakwa, he will be wise. If he is part with the flesh of his father, Wakwa, Noh-annoosu will be eloquent and powerful. If he bears the mark of his English mother he will be courageous and loving. If he is all these he will be a leader of his people. And if he places his feet in your footsteps, Gilbert Worth, he will be a warrior!

"Elizabeth, the mother, will walk as in the midday sun, guarded always by my people in life and glowing in the warmth of Kautantowwit after death, though thy gifts perish before they reach our hands. Only, share, Gilbert, the pipe with my first son. He is the lonely one of my children."

* * * *

"So, Uncle, you have found your voice and are a spokesman, too?" Wakwa, preparing for business in Boston, shouldered a tremendous basket of pelts and started across the bridge with Gil in the rain.

"By God, Fox, the man makes me foam at the mouth! I like Wuttah Mauo about as well as I do Hudson."

"Come, Nissese, at least Wuattah Mauo has the advantage of being an Indian!"

"I would not be so fast to claim him, Silent Fox. I do not want him near Beth while you go up to Hanna. I am too busy with harvest to remain here longer. I know this Weeping Heart will worry her."

Wakwa withdrew. "You are decided not to tell Hanna yourself? You will not come to Boston?"

"No. I think I must stay. I should also tend some things in Sweetwood. Take the horses and anything else you need. Give Hanna my love and this note, although I am sure you will explain things better."

"Thy wife will prefer it in thy words, dear Uncle. And when you are in Sweetwood, can you do something in my behalf? Look around you. I believe poor Weeping Heart hath found a running stream of liquor here in the forest." Sorry he had burdened Gil even further on Wuttah Mauo's account, Wakwa stopped in the middle of the bridge, water shooting by underneath, and dropped his basket to his feet. "Look at these! They will make Kayaskwa a mate to the coat she has sewn for me."

Gil hovered over the open basket, protecting the pelts from the rain. "Never have I seen such a store of gorgeous mink!"

"Yea. One year's time it took to catch and trade for them. My good friend, Meadow-in-the-night, has kept them in her small house all this while, warding off all the little fingers of her children. Think you Elizabeth will like the dark color?"

"She will!"

"Dire Locke will try to buy them from me." Wakwa grinned. "But they are not for sale. I want them made into an English coat with a shining red lining. Dire doth not know yet, but he will bring it himself to the feast."

"It is always interesting to see him, but all this trouble. . . . Why not use our tailor?" Gil led him.

"This is a thing between Dire and myself. He will keep any excess for his payment and give the clothesmaker silver money. Dire may then also ask for different pelts of a certain kind, or color, and I will please him and surpass his request if I can, or send Awepu and others with their catch."

"So! Now I am privy to Locke's dealings in the wilds. I cannot tell sometimes if he is to be trusted. A man like that must know every buccaneer on the Atlantic Ocean."

Again Wakwa rejected Gil's exclusiveness. "Dire Locke is a white man who never offers rum before the trade."

Gil pushed through the branches and wet leaves on the incline, weighed, as he had been months before in his own dining room, by this second indication of the sad experiences Wakwa had suffered at the hands of whites. When they reached the lodge, he stopped outside.

"See now, Fox. I am using Kirke's to import a few surprises for your wedding. I have written instructions directly to Locke, as usual. Yet he does not know for whom the merchandise is meant. I thought it prudent to let more time pass before being public about you and Beth. Do forgive me, and wish him hello if his ship is in."

342

They found Dr. Mac putting samples of herbs into little vessels Tame Deer had supplied him.

"Mornin', Gil! Laddie, your little son's settlin' in."

Worth stepped over to the Scot. "You will have to get over calling yonder prince 'laddie.' His relatives are somewhat touchy on the subject of Silent Fox."

"Aieam-nuthing, kandoo-nuthing?" Tame Deer sought her translation from Wakwa.

But when he sorted her phonetics he bolted from his first wife and sought the second, who lay, lightly asleep, in the rear chamber. He could not resist kissing Elizabeth's lips. He moved quietly to the door, sorry he could not comfort her before he left for Boston.

"Did Tame Deer paint your suit?" Elizabeth's voice was thick and slow.

Wakwa came back and gently conformed his hand to the shape of her breast for greeting. A trill of pain escaped her and Wakwa took back the thin quilt.

He fought to keep his face from changing when he saw her mangled, bloodied nipples and whispered near her ear so she would not see his expression, "How beautiful you will grow as you fill with milk! I will turn strange as the loon waiting for thee."

She covered herself. "I sense it. You are going away!"

"Someone must tell Hanna, and I must bring some few things to Locke."

"Dire Locke? Such an odd name, Dire." Sound spilled from her like cream. "With all this care about Noh-annoosu, how did his parents light on Dire?"

"I think, sweet wife, they were none too happy with his entrance into this world. The story is he is half a Jew and half a Walesman."

"A Jew? And Welsh? My, he shares Noh-annoosu's burdens with such mixing." She smiled sleepily through her insight.

"Can you not see him taking to the sea to bury such a name? Dost like my coat? Tame Deer made this last mark to record my success for Panther Eye, the woman from Rhode Island."

"Will you wear this at Taquonk?" Elizabeth sharpened her awareness.

"Nay, Kayaskwa, nay. Qunneke has bleached a skin as white as snow and wishes to know from thee what decoration you would like to see on it."

"Fringe, my love, fringe and more fringe!"

Chapter 49

Rain separated Gil and Wakwa like a translucent sheet as they parted at Worth's barn, each man bound on a different mission, each man in a hurry.

Gil galloped past the Indian and his three borrowed horses with a call of "Godspeed!"

He was heading, first, to Isaac Bearing's Tavern for the mail, but energized by the baby's coming he hoped to catch up with the tyther there for news of his progress in the hunt for the August trespassers, Hudson and his mistress. Next he planned to collect his year's supply of boot leather at the tanner's, put in the vats just before Beth's disappearance. His last errand would be to the cobbler, to order clogs and boots out of the leather for himself, Hanna, and the household.

He passed the church, bright in the downpour, and caught a glimpse of the sweeper driving a goat who had taken shelter there back out through the door.

"Must ask Mayhew Low about a viol for the worship, Grandee." Gil conversed pleasantly with his horse. "When the man decides to drop in to town!"

Someone crossed the road where it narrowed far ahead, and in the grayness of this noon Gil had no way of identifying the person. But he could tell from the posture of the figure the traveler suffered discomfort. Gil released the tightly buttoned collar of his canvas cloak as he neared and called out, wishing to be of help.

"Good morrow, neighbor!" He mastered his rebellious mount and looked down, surprised, into the face of Prudence Hanson. His instinct was to ride on and splash her gown with mud, but he felt it unworthy of himself and asked, instead, "Mistress Prue, are you unwell?"

The young woman blinked back through the rain drops, deciding what attitude to take.

Gil supplied one for her. "Go you to the cobbler with those shoes? Shall I drop them for you on my way back from Bearing's?"

"That is very kind." Prue showed her pink gums with her smile. "They are heavy up this hill." Her smile faded as she handed the boots up to him. "I will only be arriving there when you are through with the village."

Gil flipped his hood up, shrugging off the rudeness of her indirect request for a ride. "True, Miss. Many things to catch up on." He watched the daughter of prosperous Nathan Hanson resettle her wrap and noticed she was dressed in an ill-fitting gown. "Remember me to your parents!" Gil trotted down the road, not daring to look back, ashamed to be leaving her alone and sick in the rain. "Well, we know what kind of talk that would cause next Sabbath morn, don't we boy?" he confided in Grandee and picked up his pace.

There was a letter at the tavern from Hanna, written from the Poores' Boston house, detailing a problem about a pair of shoes along with other news.

> ". . . miss you, dear! No fun alone. Steph. Poore on holiday from school. Asked to see Beth if not bound still to A.H. I did it. Had to tell him. Poor Poore! Booked passage back to England right away, mumbling about the wonders of philology. Gillie, how easy all might have been!
>
> Cannot stay with Gwynne P. again. Will explain. Can you believe, Poore the senior is a snob? . . . And since, m'dearie, I have not got Gwynne to cajole her shoemaker into producing an overnight miracle, I cannot think what you will put on your feet. Moccasins? Your loving etc., H."

"Damnation!" Gil railed out loud, putting his ale down with a snap.

Heads turned and the busy room was hushed. In New England public swearing was an untolerated offense. Men had spent nights in the courthouse cellar for statements such as Gil Worth's. Fines were frequently added as punishments and proved a greater deterrent than a night in a dark basement. Added to this, the tything man was present.

Will Cooper, Sweetwood's tyther, walked toward Gilbert Worth. The tavern served as Cooper's base for gathering news

346

and keeping an eye on the public morality he was paid ten pounds per year to survey.

The official cleared his throat.

The yeomen and masters who filled the tables set themselves, with pleasure, for a fiery display at Gil's expense. The patrons squinted at Cooper's red plush coat and silver-striped hose. The deference with which he approached their volatile neighbor Worth caused resentment in some. But old friends smiled and shook their heads at Gil's bravado, amused by the man of quality and the tyther who dressed the part.

Gil went lightheaded with the mixture of the morning ale and Cooper's serious face. His exertions of the past twenty-four hours had drained him of propriety to suit the picayune code recorded in the village ledger. He slid a fresh, full tankard across the table to the tyther.

"How goes the Town's Eye?"

"What's so bothersome, Mr. Gilbert Worth, thee should swear among good Christians on a pure day like this?" Cooper's voice carried through the room. "More bad news from important folk abroad?" Cooper tried to skirt trouble.

"Good Christ, Cooper! Have you nothing better to do than fork up gossip and spread it in my face?"

The customers froze at the repetition of the offense. Cooper folded his arms across his chest.

Gil's annoyance gave way to a giggle, the obligations he felt since yesterday's events evaporating in playfulness. "I am sorry. I am only making noise about a letter from my loving et cetera in that temple of morality, Boston. The bad news is about a godblessed pair of shoes! Were to be blue, you know. But they've danced off the boat white as angels. Now wouldn't I look an ass in those!" Gil laughed at his private vision. "How would you like me to give you the damned things?"

Poor Cooper bristled, growing red as his clothes, his position growing more difficult.

"Lost your tongue? Will! You've got 'em free! Aw, shit, Coop. If a macaroni like you won't take them, who will? There's"—Gil referred to the letter—"'Brussels lace about the vamp.' Think of it, white pumps with the lace, gold hose, and that stunning fire-red suit you're wearing!"

Cooper polished his tankard with a nervous hand.

"Hell! If you don't want 'em I'll send 'em down to the Devil!" Gil roared with laughter.

There were grumblings and delighted, scandalized laughs over Gil's immunity from Cooper's authority.

Cooper hurried a sip of ale, quenching the heat of his quandary. "They'd be too small for my feet."

Gil burst into laughter again and the place broke into guffaws.

"I've made a joke?" the tyther blurted.

All tension eased, and in the uproar the men forgave Cooper's leniency and Worth's profligacy. The rumble of general talk started again, leaving Worth and Cooper to themselves.

Gil pressed the official for his report. "I'm telling you, I've a witness and I'm not to be kept waiting forever. After a while, approval of Elders or no, I am going to dredge this thing up. Sweetwood's tidy image will be ripped as by a cannonball. It is far more important than the looseness of Sweetwood virgins."

Cooper set his face. "Worth, we're knowin' on several points now. One. Since you placed your gunmen there's been no repeat of said offense. To my mind, you should have held off. We could have trapped them unawares. . . ."

"Oh, Jesus!" Gil buried his face in his hands, seeing his action, for the first time, as a mistake.

Cooper did not have the heart to object, feel·ng the man's sincerity.

Gil drank his beer to the bottom. "What else?"

"Two. A man's been seen with a certain Mistress P.H., who I am not about to name outside a hearing."

"Aye?"

"But no one's seen the man's face."

"Goddammit! I don't believe that!"

"Now, Worth, you'll have to stop. You'll have to stop that behavior. I can't show favoritism just because you are . . . you!"

"Let it pass, Cooper. Where were they seen?"

"Well, now, you'll laugh at this, 'cause it may take away guilt. There was strange voices heard 'round the church very early of a Sunday. Then this certain Miss came from the rear of the altar past Millie, just entered, puttin' in some flowers, last of the day lilies and some ivy vines, I think. . . ."

348

"Mr. Cooper, spare me the decor. What was said?"

"Much askin' for forgiveness is all, more like prayin', Millie told me."

"And the man? His voice?" Gil's eyes startled the tyther.

"Already gone. Just a dark coat disappearing into Reverend Hudson's gate in the south pasture."

"Well, this is nothing."

"What I told you, sir."

"But have you asked yourself why Millie would come running to the authorities about the penitents of a Sunday morn?"

Cooper balked.

"Come, man!" Gil pressured. "I've got to go have a pair of shoes made! I can't spend this 'pure day' choking down ale with your tall tales."

"I shouldn't say this outside an official hearing, but all right. Was a thing found right back of the steps going to the dais."

"What thing?"

Cooper whispered. "A woman's thin yellow sock!"

"Well!" Gil's hand slapped the tabletop and he saw Prue again, pathetic in the rain, slightly swollen in her summer frock. "Complications," he clucked. "I saw a goat coming from the church today. The place is becoming a regular barn since I left the Session. Do you suppose some female has taken to doing her washing on the altar?"

"Mr. Worth, how do you joke? This is damned serious!"

"Now you're doing it, Cooper! There is no joke here, but a frightening thing unfolding. Catch him before the winter is out, or I'll do your work for you and snatch your salary from you for incompetence." Gil slapped the man's shoulder and yelled back, as he wrapped up at the door, "Watch your language, governor!"

* * * *

Gil moved through his transaction with the tanner, distracted from the beneficence of spirit he had known since the afternoon before when he found Beth well and had met Qunneke. His spontaneous plan to have Hudson depose himself through his own blunders was successfully fermenting like the tanner's vat. But Gil was disgusted not only by his involvement in Hudson's affairs, but also by his old friend's bias, which Hanna had hinted about in her letter. He hurried his horse up the hill toward his last errand, as if speed could break his connection with both Hudson and Poore.

* * * *

Gil winced at the clatter of cheap bells as he pushed the door open. "Miss Hanson!" Gil nearly tripped over the girl seated just inside the shop. "Have I kept you?" The men's boots dropped at her feet, and while Gil went through the machinations of picking them up, still holding the broad, sturdy pieces of tanned leather, he missed the soft closing of the door to the bedroom at the back of the shop. "Good day!" Sorry to have involved himself, Gil turned his back on Prue and looked around for Tim Bottle, the master shoemaker.

Only Jack, Bottle's assistant, the town Indian who had found the Massachuseuck encampment for Dowland, sat scraping a leather heel into shape. Gil spotted a news sheet and searched through the list of merchant ship arrivals while waiting for service. There was a wet ring on the corner of the paper and three half-finished mugs of cider were huddled out of the way on a sideboard.

Suspicious, Gil continued to run his finger down the columns of print. "Was it the sound of bells, Jack, or did I hear men's voices as I came in? Perhaps the rain has frightened away our usual coven of political experts?"

"No can tell," Jack mumbled.

Gil had always despised Jack's lazy use of English, knowing he understood all the intricacies of the country people's quaint dialect. "Looks like you've had a batch in here this morning!" Gil pointed to the mugs with his free elbow.

"Jack know nothing." The Indian made no move to serve Worth. "Jack not good for much no more. No. Get old." He grinned. "Jack work all time. Have saddle I earn, no horse."

"Have you sudden need of a horse, Jack?" Gil pried, angry that the man would be indiscreet about his part in the search for Beth, bringing Charles Dowland's faithfully kept bargain into the open.

"No. Horse no good to old Jack. Jack no blacksmith. No good,

350

give horse leather shoe!" Pleased with his humor, Jack slowly rose to help Gil.

"Take the young lady first, Jack. She's got a long walk home." Gil watched Prue watching him.

"Thank you ever so, Mr. Worth," Prudence refused, "I twisted an ankle on the way here and must needs give it a rest."

"Why, then, I shall ride you home!"

"Oh!" Prudence squirmed. "It is rest will fix me! And it is awfully out of your way!"

"Well-spent time." Excitement played in Gil Worth's eyes. "I can see your father about some corn."

"You first, kind sir. I am all right."

"As you wish." Gil searched the room for an explanation of the third cider mug. "I suppose you and Jack here will want to finish your discussion of the weighty events reported out of Boston."

Gil put in his order for clogs and workshoes, marveling that Jack, who never wrote an order, never confused one. Gil sensed he was not privy to some secret Prue and Jack guarded. The town Indian's memory was good. A horse to go with his idle saddle might one day nudge it to reveal something that would help Beth.

"Ever do any satin work, Jack? Or soft leather? Suede work?" Gil bought time, anxious to see the other side of the deceit he felt heavy in the air.

"What you need?"

"Oh, a pair of opera slippers came off the boat too small. Season's upon us and it's too late to send away again. Thought perhaps you or Bottle could measure me up something."

"Bottle make shoes good. Suede, kid, satin, anything. He not here."

Although his back was to them, Gil saw the three cider mugs in his mind's eye. "Just left, eh?"

"No. Bottle sick today." Jack's eyes were pulled toward the drinks as he realized his mistake.

Gil, sure now that Hudson was behind the door to Jack's quarters, marched over, his most engaging smile cast back toward Prue. "Tim resting in here? I'll pop on in and wish him a speedy recovery!"

351

Gil swung the door open fast and revealed Weeping Heart, Waban's eldest, sprawled across a chair, balancing a silver flask against his palm.

Both men were immobilized by shock. Wuttah Mauo's eyes were hot with overindulgence, but he was alert enough to choose a stance of brash indifference.

"Come you in, Englishman?"

"Sorry, friend!" Gil saluted jauntily. "It was Tim Bottle I meant to barge in upon."

Gil slammed the door shut and turned on Prue. But the girl was gone and had not left the boots for mending. Jack was already straddling his bench in front of the low window, digging at the boot heel.

"Prudence Hanson!" Gil shouted her name and burst out of the shop looking for her, not knowing what he would say if he found her. He stamped down toward the road and called again, but he was frustrated there too. He turned back toward the building too late to see the back door of Jack's quarters open to the farmer's daughter as she entered the company of Weeping Heart.

* * * *

"Wily bitch! Wily!" Gil searched from the high perspective of Grandee's back for Prue as he galloped down the cart road toward the minister's manse.

All restraint dropped from his movements as he ran from the post through the flagging rain to Hudson's front door. He pounded on it but Millie did not answer. He splashed to the back and discovered the kitchen door open, admitting dampness and wind into the house.

"Millie! Millie!" No answer came. "For Christ's sake, where is everybody? This whole town is empty!"

Gilbert Worth tracked wet leaves all through the house as he searched it room by room, seeking contact with the people who threatened Elizabeth. Mud marked his route.

"Disappeared like a dream they have. Every last one of them! Yes. I am dreaming," he muttered. "Oh, Charles, when will I wake to find you running Henry through his prayers?"

Unsuccessful, the man strode to the church, tossed by the powerful wind which was clearing away the rain.

He threw open the big rear doors. "Millie! Go home! You have a week's work waiting!" Gil's sonorous voice struck the thin window glass high above the altar.

The housekeeper, hovering near the overwrought minister weeping in prayer, obeyed.

"Lose something, brother?" Gil walked to the front and bent over Reverend Hudson who continued in tearful supplication. "Looking for some jonquil-colored hose?" All Gil's patience was gone and he kicked back at the cause of all the confusion in his life. "Washday is past, you bale of blubber, and your dirty linen is in plain view!"

Hudson cried out.

Satisfied, Gil hissed, "So, you managed it, you fucking bastard! Got her pregnant, didn't you? Congratulations, Papa Hudson!"

"Irked?" Hudson faced his tormentor.

"For God's sake, don't make me ruin you! With what I know I could have you up before the Presbytery on the morrow. And you know how long it would be before this nightmare would burst open in the faces of the General Assembly! I was not ordained Elder for life for nothing! I could get back into the Session with a nod of my head! I left it only out of despite for you."

Hudson was ready to dissolve in tears again. "Before I came, did you believe? Not for a day!"

"Fly out of Sweetwood on the Devil's coattails! Slip away, you faggot! It would give me the greatest joy to slit your throat and hang you in my brother-in-law's smokehouse like the flitch of bacon that you are! When? Tell me, when are you going?"

Hudson gathered his coat from beneath his knees and struggled to his feet. He looked his best, aside from his distress, his white bands pressed and lying neatly across his front.

"You did not come here this afternoon." His voice wavered, uncontrolled. "I do not see you. I did not hear you."

"You have only to look at your dowdy carpets, you ass! I have left a trail that cannot be denied. And more have you! By God, I know your innermost diary and you will not trample over me or mine again!"

"Worth, you can prove nothing against me, therefore you know nothing."

"Jesus!" Gil reacted. "I have seen you before, during, and after your ineffectual romps. There be another witness!"

"You! . . ." Annanias was stricken. "What other witness?"

"That is my little secret, Hudson. My first. Willingly I will lose everything . . . my farm, my name, my life, my soul, but I will bring you down, you . . ."

"No more invective, please. Though I may deserve it." Hudson appealed to his adversary. "I am a converted man this day, though I am sure the state of my soul holds little interest for you." He sucked air, gaining equilibrium. "I never go back on my word. You know that well. Yet I am a desperate man, Worth, and shall defend me any way I can." Hudson limped toward the water pitcher Millie had brought for tending the cut flowers. Without regard for place, he watered his sweating head.

"Use the trough outside, pig!"

Hudson turned his dripping face up. "Let us face the hard fact, sir." The shock of cold had revived his faculties. "You do not want my hide badly enough to lose Beth the land you hold for her. Dear, dear Beth! How good I could have been with her."

"Not good to her," Gil said, disgusted at this lingering and hopeless love.

Hudson blotted his face with a rumpled handkerchief and grew composed. "It is I would expose that savage who has taken her, only now I am strapped with this other thing. But say one word and I will also speak, having nothing more to lose, and out of the dust the townspeople kick up will come not one winner but the two of us losers."

Gil saw himself trapped in this vindictive rationality.

"Mr. Worth, you will be an inspiration to the bereaved of this locale, bearing your in-laws' misfortunes with resignation and humility. I shall live, continent—more, a model minister—and the people will weep when I leave this musty village."

"You would leave? Leave now!"

"There is this matter of Prudence Hanson must be squared away. I must see her through some trying times, lest she spill her knowledge and turn herself and me, even you and the Indians, into fools. And then there is this promise of a new church. You were sincere in that? I must last here through May. Nathan Hanson is the kind of man, by his own admission, would sell his daughter out for labor if she produce a bastard child. My blood will not suffer that!"

"Annanias, simplify! Marry Prue. Be a father to thy child and still have the new place."

"Impossible."

"Why, dammit!"

"I have always disliked her."

Gil's skin began to crawl and he lurched away from the cunning man, feeling inept in the face of his calculation.

"You have despoiled her and say this?"

"*Au contraire*, that is the phrase, my fine gentleman? It is she who hath ruined me.

"Mayhew Low must come by summer or the congregation will select someone else. Whoever arrives will wave me farewell with sorrow, so great will be my competence between now and then. We have struck a bargain?"

"A pact with the Devil!" Worth backed down the center aisle of the church between the high pews that hid the sitting worshippers from one another on Sunday mornings.

"Put it any way. June, then, you will be rid of me. Great respect will be shown mutually. At least politeness, no hostility. I swear . . . pardon, another habit acquired from Prue. I promise to tread softly, copper skins and everything, and you have only to donate for a building. Fertile land west of here, near the Ohio. It is the coming place, Uncle."

Sweat broke out on Gil's body when Hudson mouthed his title. "Yes. All right. Dear God, help us!"

"I am so glad to hear you pray, Mr. Worth. Only yesterday I petitioned the Elders to receive you back into the Session. It will make it so much more direct deciding Low's salary, fitting the place out with little luxuries, admitting and prohibiting from membership, as you will be wont to do. You see, I do not forget charity. You saved me with the Irishers."

"I know!" Gil was enraged.

Hudson gave a wild laugh, detecting how ingenuous was his major foe. "You and Low will get on marvelously well. Good day, brother Worth!" He dismissed him.

The rain had been swept away and Gil could barely see in the sunny glare. He made for Grandee, a dark shape roaming near the manse. He had no strength to hold the reins, but slumped across his horse's neck, longing to be home.

Without warning, Grandee's giant body reared, and Gil forced his knees against the horse's withers and clutched the hair of his mane to keep his seat. In the bright and dripping unreality of the afternoon, Gil watched a long brown water-snake wriggle away from his horse's hooves toward the pleasant brook that crossed behind the church.

Chapter 50

Gil knocked at his own front door and left Grandee fretting for his rubdown and oats. The housekeeper answered, crisp and plump.

"Winke." Gil stood like a child on his own threshold.

The woman appraised her master. He was not shot. She circled her arm around his waist and led him to the sitting room. She sat him down, undid his soiled neckstock, lifted his mud-encrusted boots onto a silk-covered stool, and gave him water.

"Last I saw thee, Master, you were raising dust, riding in the company of Indian divils. Look at you a day later!" She pulled at his filthy boots. "Mistress Worth'll have at me if she comes home to see the state I have let you get into."

"Winke."

"Yes, Master?"

The man did not respond.

The housekeeper covered him with a shawl Hanna had left out. "Now don't refuse the whittle, sir," she crooned. "It is good for you. There! Tea is coming and a hot bath. I know how you'll like that. What did they do? Why did they come? Poor Master. It is old me, old Winke. Come tell."

Gil eased his head back against the settee and covered his face with his arms. Could it have been only yesterday that Nuppoh-wunau had admired the sound of the harp in the sunrise and galloped off at his side to bring back Doctor Mac? Was Wolf-of-the-mist-He-hopes only twenty-four hours old? Gil yearned to tell his troubles to a friend. With Hanna away, Tame Deer's hair and shoulders shaped themselves in his mind. He felt surrounded by the depth of feeling with which she pierced the barriers of speech.

"There is a woman can comfort others so deep is her own pain!" Gil's words came out in a garbled jumble, even though his thoughts were crystal sharp.

"Spake you to me, Master?" Winke lifted his elbow and stuffed a pillow underneath.

He would not go to Qunneke. She was helping settle new life into comfortable surroundings. He must not transport Hudson's malevolence where the atmosphere was pure and hopeful.

Now he knew the desperation that had driven his niece away from Annanias into the solace of the forest. Yet Hudson was not threatening him with his continued presence, as he had Beth. The minister was merely extorting time to reshape his twisted existence.

There was hope in that Hudson's steps were directed out of the village. Slow steps that would require a delicate patience of those who wanted him gone.

The tired man summoned a sigh to cover his inclination to cry. "Charles!" he choked.

The housekeeper rang the silver bell for help. "Do those red Indians bully you, Master, about poor Mistress Beth? Do they tease you about finding her whereabouts? Divils they look and divils they be. She's not to be found more. Don't give them another penny, nor ride with them. See how they wear thee down!"

"Winke?" Gil managed a whisper.

"What is it, sir?"

"Believe you this? Answer straight." He forced himself to sit erect, prying beneath her cooing with hard green eyes.

The woman washed Gil's face as she would a muddy puppy's. "I know it, sir! They are dirt and sloth and cruelty in one fearsome package. I hate 'em so, sometimes at night, remembering my mother's tales of what they did in Braintree in the war, I pray a plague shall take them off to where such beings go when they die and leave the country safe for good working people."

"Winke," Gil exhaled, expelling the bad air of the day with her name.

"Aye, Master Worth."

"You are an excellent housekeeper."

"Why! Thank you, sir. I am that sorry I made you angry yesterday in the morning."

"Take yourself to Dowland Farm at your earliest convenience. Your things will be sent after you. Tell Cooke to come up here in your place. If you run that house properly, you may remain in my employ, at least for a time. If you wish to return to the auction block at the tavern where I hired you, you may.

Priscilla will fill the maid's place, whom you will let go now with three months' advance wages. To give her a start. Good afternoon."

Gil leaned back and closed his eyes against the orange light signaling the end of the day. He felt the woman's eyes on him, and, without moving, met her outraged look. The fine wrinkles in her cheeks converged into the pucker of her lips. Tears had sprung in her blue eyes, but she refused to let him see and sailed toward the door in her dark widow's gown.

When the lock clicked, Gil said to the white ceiling, "I shall not have it in my own house."

All that night Gil sat propped up in the chair. Neither Winke nor the maid brought him supper. He was grateful to be spared talking to them again. He walked to the washhouse before dawn, checked the stable, and found that at least the horses were being cared for.

The stable boy showed surprise at his master's appearance, but he tipped his cap and obligingly turned away as Gil examined and caressed Grandee by the light of a whale oil lantern.

Gil bypassed hunger with anxiety and annoyance and lay on the floor, face down, behind the settee, waiting for the sun to wind its way from the dining room to his large window to warm his back. He heard the cart pull slowly away from the house, but did not lift his head to watch it go. Wuttah Mauo filled his vision.

Gil pondered the question of how the man had gone so quickly from the morning council between himself and the sagamores to the cobbler's back room. Jack must be his source of supply. But what other link between them had forced their secrecy? Certainly Gil had seen a man drink before. This was a problem he could unload onto Wakwa's big back. Yet why had Prudence Hanson lingered at Bottle's when Hudson was wearing his kneeler smooth in the church? He would have to carry this worry with Hudson's plans on his own shoulders.

Later, soft footsteps came across the Persian carpet. A linsey-woolsey petticoat brushed against his elbow, but nothing was said. Gilbert Worth continued to soothe himself, passing his hand gently across his hair. The footsteps retreated, then stopped again.

"When Master Dowland went like this, I baked him a raisin pudding. Shall I bring you the same at midday? Master?"

"Many thanks, Mrs. Cooke!" Gil rasped. Then he fell off to sleep.

For the rest of that day, and through Sunday, Gil caged himself in the sitting room. He took no time with his toilette but allowed his growth of beard to speckle his chin and cheeks with gold.

Carefully he made a book as a record of the related events of the past year. He recorded in detail his new agreement with Hudson. And on the Sabbath, while that minister preached a revolutionary sermon relating the doctrine of the fore-ordained damned to forgiveness, Gil paced his favorite room, shirtless, absorbed in finding an alternative to Hudson's blackmail.

He diagrammed the advantages and disadvantages of an aggressive stance against Hudson. In order to protect Wakwa, he must not push the plodding Cooper in his investigation. If Hudson desisted from his relationship with Prue, Cooper's investigation would lead nowhere. Perhaps discovery would dovetail with Prue's delivery of her illegitimate child.

The net around Gil allowed little hope of detachment from the minister's activities. To shield his niece and her native family, must Gil mollify the Hanson girl with money or security?

If he found the right lawyer, would it not be better to sue Hudson openly for the unnatural threat he was holding over Gil's head? But it became clear that not one in a thousand white men would uphold the claim of an Indian over that of an Englishman. No matter how diffuse Hudson's taint, the minister did not pose a threat to colonial persons or lands. Love stories would wield no weight on the American judicial scale, overburdened by vested interests.

"Good Lord!" Gil sighed as the small hopes he had had of battling Hudson in court slipped from him. Tame Deer was also Wakwa's wife. By his acceptance of her, Gil had forfeited his niece's chance for a Christian marriage and an open and legal settlement of Dowland's will. What a mammoth comedy it would be to secret Tame Deer away in the forest until the inevitable cruelties of investigation finally dissipated.

360

The more he and Beth tried to pull away from convention, the more tightly they chained themselves to it.

To lie low, to wait for May, to believe Hudson's self-seeking veracity, to pick up the deed to Hudson's acres if he were graceful enough to sell out to Low, to be patient, became Gilbert Worth's course.

Tidy in his habits, Gil locked his statements into a peachwood box made from one of his own trees. Naked except for the ruin of his gray linen trousers, he abandoned both mind and body to his fears.

Cooke left him attractive tidbits and a flow of good tea, coming and going silently to change the used tray for the fresh. He rarely saw her enter and did not acknowledge her presence when he knew she was there. His thought was that Charles and Mary had done an excellent job finding and training her. His pride in his own competence sank lower until at last, late Sunday night, he retreated like a dog under the settee.

Sleep descended potent as an apothecary's dose, blotting out the frustration of the past days. But anxious dreams tore at Gil's veneer of youth, weighing his hopeful spirit, robbing some of the brilliance of his glance when he awoke.

Chapter 51

Monday, midday, Worth lay there still under Cooke's watchful eye. She was satisfied that his sleep had become healthy and took the liberty of airing the house, opening the top portion of the front door, admitting the warm afternoon and the smells of mowing into the hall.

The high halloah of Matthew circled in the still air, reaching Cooke before the sound of the coach wheels. The woman stood in the kitchen, undecided whether she should greet her new mistress or wait to be called.

Three men of the Ninnuock, the sachim and the guards, rode fanned out at the sides of the carriage, racing to the mounting block. They slid from their horses in front of Worth's amazed stable boy.

Wakwa dispatched the guards to the hunting lodge and waited for Matthew to aid Hanna and Priscilla out of the coach.

Exhilarated with the delights of spending money on gifts for others, and largely removed from the deeper cares surrounding this particular feast, Hanna welcomed Silent Fox into her home with the lightness of a girl.

"Winke never has the door open this time of day!" she remarked as she passed in front of Silent Fox to the inside.

Matthew heard this as he followed them, his arms loaded with baggage.

"Please wait in here, Silent Fox, I will find Gil. Priscilla, dear, are you too tired to go ask Winke for tea? Where is everyone? Gil! Dear! Naughty man is gone! We are here!" She called out at the foot of the east staircase.

Matthew stayed close behind her with his burdens.

Wakwa entered the sitting room alone. Where the Dowland house had been silent and efficient at its core, the Worths', in all his visits, had been filled with cheerful clatter from the kitchen, the company, or the music. Today the air was stale and the harp covered. The room suffered from a layer of dust on its shiny objects. Wakwa grew uneasy. He sat on the soft blue carpet and

362

thoughtfully ran his fingers over the intricacies of its gray-green designs. It was then that he saw the graceful white ankle and foot camouflaged in the hot light of noon.

"Wetomp!" Wakwa's voice was falsetto as he lifted the whole settee away from Gilbert Worth.

Priscilla ran back with Mrs. Cooke, but Hanna was left behind, blocked by the baggage Matthew dropped as he rushed toward the sound. Matthew pushed his way to his loved employer.

"Leave him to me!" the black man growled jealously, glaring at the Indian who was trying, gently, to wake Worth.

"Matthew! Let Master be!" Priscilla stamped her foot.

Looking from Priscilla to Gil, Wakwa backed away. Hanna screamed when she appeared and found Matthew shaking her husband without result.

"Gilbert!" She fled to the side of the former slave.

Matthew pulled Gil to a sitting position with a thick arm wrapped around his shoulders. He twisted Gil's bearded chin, his muscles straining against his tight jacket, hurting the man into semi-awareness.

As his lids opened, Gil's eyes rolled back. He gripped Matthew's dark face and enunciated clearly, "That bastard! He knows I cannot select the pastor if I sit with the Elders again. Congregation only chooses!"

"Darling!" Hanna soothed him, but the husband squeezed Matthew's cheeks tighter and hid his face against the burly shoulder.

"Are you here, Matthew? Truly?"

Matthew lifted Gilbert Worth easily in his arms, circling toward the door, his look defying interference with his care. Hanna alone was allowed to walk next to him, her fingers softly touching the fine skin of Gil's shoulder, almost feminine in its allure.

"Hanna, dear, you are here? What is happening?" Gil squirmed in Matthew's arms, yawned, and took her hand, waking more fully as they passed through the doorway.

Wakwa sat very still in a hard chair across from the window and looked at the yellowed cherry leaves. Priscilla and Cooke were busy straightening the room, unfamiliar with the arrangement of things. They restored it as best they could, cleaning and ordering its specialized riches.

Wakwa looked at Priscilla as the servants excused themselves. "It would be well for you to stay."

She hesitated. Cooke nodded and left her standing alone.

"Be comfortable," Wakwa invited her to sit as he addressed himself to removing the harp cover.

The young maid came and helped him fold it and found its place in the music cabinet.

"This bastard . . . that is the word?"

"Yes, sir!" Priscilla looked up in awe of him.

"Would be Annanias Hudson?"

"I surmise, sir."

Wakwa sat crosslegged in front of the instrument and removed his sweaty headband. He thought for a long minute. "I perceive, young maid, a connection between thyself and Gilbert Worth. Are free to speak to me of what you know?"

There was no avoiding his eyes. "Why should I break this confidence, good sir?"

Wakwa's even teeth showed as he smiled. "I would protect thy master from snakes. Woman. You are brave and faithful."

Briefly, without passion, Priscilla described Worth's agony under the smokehouse. "What this present trouble is I do not know, but I suspect Master Worth has lost another round with Satan."

Cooke knocked and entered with the tea. "Thy new mistress comes!"

Priscilla curtsied to the Indian and stood close to her superior.

But it was Gil who came instead, transformed in a shirt of green India muslin, the afternoon breeze fluttering its sheer folds. He kept Wakwa sitting with an affectionate pressure on his shoulders.

He turned to the women, hands casually stuffed into the pockets of his corded silk breeches. "Welcome, dear ladies, to your new home. I believe we are a family now. Mrs. Worth awaits across the hall. Your first duty in my service, Priscilla, will be to tell Samuel to please hurry with that chair!"

Wakwa studied the man from his position on the floor. "There is a great change in you, Nissese."

364

"I am a good deal cleaner than when first you saw me this afternoon." Gil relaxed on the long seat that had shielded him when he was alone.

Wakwa scrutinized him. "I know! Oo. The line of hair above your lip is gone."

"Think you I can pass for an Indian now?"

"Never!" Wakwa embraced his uncle by marriage. "I like what you are."

In the flattering gold of the September sun, Gil unfolded the story from the village. "To watch and wait and believe Hudson's rule of terror will soon end is the only course I can see. I will be the buffer between you and him, for, excuse me, Fox, I must say, none but his own kind would know how far to mistrust him. And God forbid he find out Beth has delivered you a son."

"Gilbert, shall I learn to fear?"

"Rather, remain discreet. That is your fortress, not my own. I suffer in the attempt, as you saw when you came in."

"I am not ashamed I was afraid for you when I found you. You have suffered. Your weapons buried out of wisdom. We will await battle together. Let Askug be alone, fearing us. Because of Snake, who has become more like a pigsuck, you have no news of my Elizabeth?"

Hanna was there, the brightness of her eyes belieing her new worries. "Dear Fox, go tell her to make ready. We are coming down to see if all this Palestine gauze has been put to waste. There is a party in thirty-five days and the gown must fit!"

"Then it is time, Okummes?" Wakwa took a heavy roll of papers from his shoulder pouch.

"Aye, Sachim, go ahead."

"What are you two about?" Gil was sparked by their support-ive presences.

"A gift to you, dear Uncle, from Thomas Kirke."

"A gift from Kirke? For me? What were you two doing con-sorting with Kirke? I have never met him!"

"Gil, he is a lovely man." Hanna turned from inspecting her geraniums.

"I like him not already."

"But he came from New York to greet the shipment of our goods expressly."

"He what?"

Hanna rolled her eyes, delighted at her revelation.

Wakwa intervened. "Dire Locke could not please you with goods to fill your order, thus . . ."

"Thus, my dear farmer," Hanna took up her story, "this marvel Kirke sent to Ireland for the pick of his own . . . you know whats!" Hanna whirled once around, entranced by this commercial coup.

"Oh, God. What have I done?" Gil sat looking tired again, but his good humor extended to this extravagance. "Silent Fox, after this solemnity, Hanna and I may reconsider your kind offer to live on your hospitality."

"Will you also change your mind about the number of your wives?" Wakwa's eyes were wicked.

"What is this?" Hanna withheld Gil's teacup.

Gil began breaking wax from the opening in confusion. "I see I should have let Matthew run errands to the tanner and have gone frolicking up in Boston myself."

"This were no frolic, my husband. What is this about the number of your wives?"

Wakwa attempted to balance their discussion. "Uncle, Dire and I passed Kirke upon the stair at Crosswhite's. So it was arranged he should meet your Hanna. A wondrous evening of dancing it was!"

"An evening of dancing?" Gil was grateful for the chance to divert his wife's question.

"Now, Gil, I had been stuck with pins for nearly two weeks, scurrying to the docks, frightful work you refused to do. Checking every day for the arrivals, poor Priscilla faint from the sight of all those rude people in one spot."

"It sounds terrible hard work, my dear. Dancing with moneybags Kirke, while I wrangle with the cobbler."

"Nissese. She is a very skillful trader. Dire Locke sails for England soon and cannot assist me with the coat for Elizabeth. Hanna, by herself, persuaded Kirke to have Elizabeth's coat made. . . ."

"Pleasant persuasion for a doughty old bachelor." Gil did not use a light hand in his retaliation.

". . . and to avoid the eyes of Wareham, he will send it on the river with these other goods you have ordered."

366

"I do not understand all this. Do Locke and Kirke know whom these things are intended for? Do you know, Fox, what I have been at pains to keep a secret?"

"Gilbert Worth, break the seal of this gift. Locke knows fully but Kirke does not. Dire introduced me as the hunter who had brought in his two matched beaver. He told Kirke I was to be married and these gifts you had ordered were to come among my tribe."

"What did old man Kirke say to that?"

"Nothing. But his eyes grew small in thought. After hearing Hanna praise you Kirke rode off, returning the same night with these papers, saying this would surpass in value all you had bought of him."

"This had better be quite a gift!"

Gil unrolled the papers and discovered the libretto and musical notation of a year-old opera. "Jove! Do you see what this is? Look at this!" Gil opened the corners of the handkerchief table, handed Hanna the heavy tea tray, and spread the composition to full view. "Ha! It is what we will be in a few weeks!"

"We?"

"Hanna, how fashionable of us to hold Beth's wedding in the woods. See here? Shepherdesses and gods, satyrs and monsters, playing in the forest! The French court is evidently staging such dreams for amusement. How I should like to hear this performed!"

"Uncle, we shall perform it."

"Wakwa! Could we? Would you try? You humor me. How nice that is. Why, then we shall live their fancies. Look at the date! First produced October fourth, seventeen hundred forty-six. Why, that is almost to the day when . . ."

"Yes, Uncle." Wakwa's eyes were bright.

Gil hid the sudden pink of his face by turning toward the tapping on the sitting room glass.

Dr. Stirling grimaced at the group, then made his own way in through the open front door.

"Now ain't this pretty? The whole bunch o' ye derelicts together, while Bonnie an' I are prayin' for your safety and coddlin' that hungry boy! An' the lot o' ye dandlin' teacups an' makin' merry. Why, laddie, I'm surprised!"

Wakwa nodded and smiled at the scolding.

"Mac! Your manners! Hush, and come here and see!" Gil pushed away the teacup Hanna offered the doctor. "Now we add Leclair to our repertoire."

"More Italians?"

"French, good fellow."

"The same."

"And wonderful! See the violin. Look at the bowing that shall demand! You will shine at the feast, good doctor. I do not know why I did not think of Leclair myself. This Kirke is a singular man." Gil deciphered the notes, singing from the script.

"Scylla et Glaucus? Air des Sylvains? Satyrs and that lot?" Stirling wrinkled his nose.

" 'Part-man, part-goat, and extremely wanton!' " Gil worked over the tuning of his harp. "Get a fiddle, man, never mind the cake!"

"Nothin' else to keep the lad's mind occupied." The doctor took an instrument from the wall.

Silent Fox and Hanna were glad to rest and watch the temporary cure.

* * * *

They descended upon Elizabeth the morning of the fifth day of Wolf's life. The lodge was quiet when Wakwa and Hanna and Gilbert Worth entered. Only a steady squashing noise added a rhythmic beat of life to the house.

Wakwa touched familiar objects as he passed toward the rear of the structure. "Tame Deer has left for the otan. I am sorry, Hanna."

"How can you tell, Fox?" she whispered as they passed the first fire.

Wakwa let his glance roam over the space between them and the limits of the walls, as if Tame Deer's absence had left a vacuum. He went ahead of his in-laws through the drape.

"Tawhitch!"

Hanna and Gil crowded the doorway at his dismayed exclamation.

Elizabeth sat opposite the door, smiling. "Greetings, my love." She held a mortar against her stomach and had been pounding boiled corn steadily with the pestle.

"Elizabeth! Tawhitch?" Wakwa refused to advance toward her.

"Why ask why, sweet?"

"We are here, Beth." Hanna peeked around the disturbed man.

Wakwa glared at the sleeping Sparrow. "Who is the maid and who the mother here? Why does the servant lie abed soft pillows while you labor at the corn?"

Elizabeth stood and shook the grains from her long apron. "Hello, dear Aunt. Come. Come and see!" Very proud, all sly smiles, Elizabeth held her aunt close.

"Sparrow certainly is asleep," Gil ventured from Wakwa's other side.

"Oo." Wakwa looked into the front area to control his distress.

"You need not be embarrassed, Wakwa. I am not," Elizabeth said.

"You shame me in front of your family, Kayaskwa. What brings thee to grind the corn?"

"Go to see my babe, Auntie. Wakwa, you forget I used to milk cows."

"I do not forget. But there is always something new with you, Elizabeth!"

"There now, you've made him wake. Well and good. You can all see how the green of his eyes has darkened into brown. Shhh. Shhh. Muckquashim!"

Wakwa, too fascinated with his child to scold from afar, came near and put his arm around Elizabeth's waist. "Shhh, my son. You should not wake the maid!"

"May I?" Hanna's skin looked dewy as she reached for the blinking child.

Elizabeth helped her hold him, more self-assured in her movements than she had been a few days before.

Wakwa said more gently as he took her waist again, "Tell me, Elizabeth, why is this?"

"You touch the reason."

The husband let go quickly, not understanding.

"Wakwa, it is Tame Deer shows me what to do to firm myself."

369

"Tame Deer has put low work into thy hands?" Wakwa was angry again.

"But I can walk so far I almost joined thee up in Boston!"

Hanna walked away from the squabbling parents, always fearful of relations between her niece and the Indian wife. She sang in a soft voice to the round-faced baby.

" 'Rock a bye baby, thy cradle is green,
Father's a nobleman, mother's a queen . . .' "

"That point is moot at this moment, dear wife." Gil filched dried currants from an open jar.

Hanna ignored everyone as she walked at the outskirts of the room.

" 'And Betty's a lady, and wears a gold ring,
And Johnny's a drummer and drums for the king.' "

Hanna kissed her great-nephew.

"Royalist!" Gil whispered to his wife, elevated at the sight of her with the newborn relaxed and dozing in her arms.

Elizabeth continued to clarify her activity to Wakwa. "First, Wakwa Manunnappu, you do not think it low. The work is necessary."

"But not fit for thee!" Wakwa spat into the fire. "I made my promise to your father. You must not wear yourself down!"

"Second," she kept on, "there is corn a' plenty done by Sparrow. It is still there in sacks waiting to be eaten."

"What then doth Qunneke mean by this?"

"Feel here!" Elizabeth forced his hand against her belly, unmindful of her aunt and uncle's presence. "Feel thou! Am I not thinner, and firmer? Think what I will be five days from now, and ten, and twenty! My stomacher will hang away from me and I shall be able to stand and curtsy to our Uncle Waban like a saunks instead of a sow. I follow Tame Deer in this! Today I finished corn for Awepu's house, and tomorrow Nuppohwunau's, and who knows who else's the day after that. Tame Deer sends up the sacks and I grind when I am not holding our son. I feel well again!"

"Yes. You are well." Wakwa rubbed her flushed cheek. "I am pleased you are stronger. Yet is there not some other way?"

370

Elizabeth opened her mouth to argue, but Wakwa kissed her hard, in company, and left her speechless.

"Do as you wish. Only grind the corn for my house. I will not have it said Wakwa Manunnappu has made a slave of his white wife! And why doth Sparrow sleep?"

"Through the night she walked and rocked our babe. Thy Muckquashim-ouwan-Noh-annoosu knows not night from day. Master!" Naughtily, Elizabeth abased herself at Wakwa's feet, holding tightly to the fringes of his moccasins.

Too angry to speak to her, Wakwa extricated himself, removing his moccasins, and left the room. Gil slipped out behind him.

Hanna passed in and out in front of the men as they sat deciding how much to tell Elizabeth of the village news. She dropped several small boxes near the entry to the rear chamber.

"May I help you, Ana?"

"Gil, you call me Ana when you have done something wrong. I shall be back to pick them up myself, if only to eavesdrop on the plots you hatch."

"Why so spicy, Mrs. Worth?" Gil was enjoying the sight of her pretty face after her long absence.

"I have not forgot the color of your cheek when Fox mentioned a multiplicity of marriage partners to you!"

Gil smoothed the skin where his moustache had been. "Only his oblique sense of humor, Goody Worth!"

Hanna looked to Wakwa, but his discomfiture at the results of his careless joke was obvious.

"Oblique. Oblique." Wakwa reaffirmed Gil's excuse without understanding of the word.

"Oblique, indeed!" Hanna stepped close to them and whispered, "I advise you both not to drop any such pin pricks in Beth's way about this pudding of Hudson's. Let the child enjoy her peace of mind a little while at least." She bustled away, then turned again as she reached the drapery. "Why don't you two overlords fix us up something lovely for luncheon? We shall be occupied."

Gil threatened her with the addition Wakwa had suggested, wagging two fingers for two wives, but she hissed and disappeared with a show of confidence into the far room.

In privacy, Hanna had Elizabeth remove her clothes. She

circled around, assessing the damage the birth had done to her niece's body.

"I am delighted, really! Relieved. You will be prettier than before with the loss of a very few pounds."

"Aunt, is this necessary?"

"It is."

Hanna untied boxes and arranged them on the matted floor. "Tame Deer uses you with kindness?" Delicately she urged Elizabeth's confidence.

"I love her, Aunt, already. One cannot help it."

Hanna looked away, thinking of the change she felt in Gil. "Put something on, Beth!"

Elizabeth decided to be patient. She lifted her arms as Hanna wrapped her in a stiff undergarment.

"See, Beth, new, longer stays. They are invented by a woman."

"Aunt, I have not worn any all these months. How free one is without! You should try the feeling."

Jittery, Hanna began the fastening. "These are really more comfortable for a slender person like yourself. And rather pretty."

"Such tenderness Qunneke shows our child, as if he were her own."

Hanna winced both at the reintroduction of Tame Deer into the conversation and at the sight of her niece's healing breasts. She strained to hook the stays past Elizabeth's waist. "I hope you like the color of the hose. They are awfully fine for wearing out of doors, but I assume this is a onetime affair."

Elizabeth fingered the embroidery on the garters her aunt held up for her inspection. "Qunneke teaches so lovingly, Auntie. How Noh-annoosu would have survived without her guidance I do not know."

Hanna made a noise, her mouth too stuffed with pins to speak.

"She will come back in a few days to see how I fare. By then I hope to work up my walk to five miles, carrying Noh-annoosu. I could be almost what I was."

"You are a marvel right now. Do not let Tame Deer push you."

"Aunt! She wants me to be the way Wakwa first loved me. Without words I know that."

"Is there no escape from ash!" Hanna barked, dismayed over Elizabeth's train of thought. "I will ruin the petticoat if I try it on you in here!"

The women maneuvered themselves into a corner, as far from the fire as possible, and tied up the heavy skirt of Chinese silk sewn onto a four-foot hoop.

"Aunt!"

"This is nothing, my dear. Kincob is not rare, but so pretty with the sheer stuff going over, I had no choice. Simplicity was your uncle's dictum for you, to let your little face show."

As they built up the costume with the bodice, the stomacher, and the overskirt, Beth thought back to the unhooped gown she had been sewing for her marriage to Annanias Hudson the year before.

"Aunt Hanna! I am shocked."

"Oh, come. You?"

"I am not covered!" Elizabeth touched the pinked edges of the squared neckline, made without the usual ruffle of modesty lace.

"There is some Dowland left in you yet, Beth." Hanna adjusted the gauzy overdress and the sheer puffed sleeves, tapering Quaker-fashion, close-fitting at the wrists.

"Voilà! Your hair I shall ponder. What think you?" Hanna stepped back.

Elizabeth could not speak. Her hands saw for her as they coursed over the rich fabrics, her eyes closed. "Never have I worn such, nor shall I again, dear Aunt." She looked at Hanna. "The work is superb, but I have left my pretensions behind and am so comfortable in my straight, soft deerskins. My own needles will likely stand idle the rest of my life."

"Nonsense!" Hanna was harsh. "Get out of those fripperies. Your husband saith he will travel far and wide with you. You are to help him in his work. If he consents to study in Virginia, you will have to be properly clothed to do him honor.

"You are English and shall never match this woman Tame Deer. Can you imagine the velvets, the taffetas, the Flanders lace, the figured silks, he will provide and you will sew, that will stun all manner of snobbish folk into respect for your choice?

"Get not so lost in this forest that you exist like Eve, with but a few leaves for a skirt! Be clean and practical when you are at your fire. Never forget you are an English colonial married to a native American man. Be wise! Bring him glory when you go abroad.

"Speaking of which, something must be done about your skin. Wear the bonnet and mask if you must. Cover up and stay in the shade."

"But I feel so healthy all brown!" Elizabeth regained some buoyancy.

"My dear, you are all in patches! The dress will not do if it is to cover a human quilt! You think me a ridiculous person as you stand there lost in love, but humor your poor uncle and me. He has poured his lifesblood into creating some security and joy for you. He envisions you an angel on this great day to come."

Elizabeth carefully removed and folded all the parts of the ensemble, replacing them in their containers with precision. As her hands made knife-sharp pleats in the delicate sleeves of the gown, she thought how generously this aunt and uncle had yielded to each startling demand she and Wakwa had made on them.

"Aunt Hanna, I am grateful. Truly. You are more than a mother to me."

The older woman reached over with a kiss for her niece.

"Auntie, if you can get some watered silk I shall unearth my golden needles and make some ribbons for my hair."

Hanna nodded happily, picked up the band boxes, then stooped to whisper, "Gil set me to buy cloth of bodkin and padasoy for Tame Deer. What is she like?"

"Come. I will show you."

Elizabeth let her plain dress touch Wakwa's back as she passed him, her face blocked by boxes. Both women avoided their husbands, Elizabeth intent on her revelation and Hanna frightened of the coming moment.

"Hanna, will you talk to me?" Gil took her parcels. "Where go you, ladies? We have roasted you fish."

"I am sorry, Gil. I was lost in thought. The list of things I must bring Beth grows. Foremost on it are a pair of chicken-skin gloves."

"Chicken-skin gloves!" Wakwa said, disgusted.

"Whiten the hands, nephew!" Gil went out to pack the horses, leaving the Indian by the fire examining his own hands.

Elizabeth led her aunt to a shaded area thickly grown with tall, green, flowering plants. She broke off one of the hollow stems and gave it to Hanna.

"From this plant Tame Deer makes perfume which she showers on me when I wash, or feed my baby, or feel lonely. She seethes the leaves into broth for me to bring back my color when I am fatigued. She knows without a word when my thoughts have turned to Wakwa, when he is far away."

"She gives you such attentions?"

"Yea, Aunt."

Hanna ripped the spreading leaflets into their three parts and tasted the moist, slit edges. "I believe this to be angelica."

"I am sure of it. Our Grandmama's name again." Elizabeth pulled some of the plants out by the roots to have them ready for the first wife in the lodge. "I think about Angelica much of late, Hanna, and what made her cling to her soil with a death grip and not cross to a new world with the man she loved and her only son."

"Child Beth, you have too much time to think."

* * * *

When the Worths had gone, Wakwa led Elizabeth to her raised bed. Words would not come as they stayed close in a gathering chill. The glitter and turbulence of the last week and the strain of the involved wedding preparations left Wakwa voiceless.

He undid the ties of Elizabeth's nightdress and pulled each side gently back, studying her body where the child had left her raw and broken on the day of his birth. He was pleased with the progress of her healing and gave each sensitive nipple a single kiss, carefully covering her again.

"It seems everyone is examining me today." She reached for him and he encircled her upper body with his arms as he sat on the floor at her side.

Wakwa let his face move against her bared arm by way of comfort and came to rest with her tiny wrist between his teeth.

"Lovely man, you are distracted and cannot speak. What happened to you so far from me?"

Wakwa hid his face against her palm, struggling against openness, Hanna's dictum fresh in his mind. When he lifted his face his eyes had achieved a sparkle.

"I met Kirke whilst in Boston."

"That you did not!"

"Vaughn Thomas Kirke."

"You wish me to believe that? The actual Kirke? The House of Kirke, Kirke?"

"Your aunt danced as his partner."

"I would give anything to have been there! Danced as his partner! They say he lives like a king and holds more money and influence than royalty. Tell your bumpkin wife, what is such a man like?"

Wakwa shrugged his shoulders, unimpressed by her description of mercantile power. "He is like an ermine."

"Why an ermine!"

"He is very white, very thin, very sharp in the teeth, beautiful in movement, but difficult to touch."

Wakwa kissed her eyes closed and said with a catch in his voice as he slipped a thin package into her hand, "I have brought you silver hairpins. Hanna did say you have always wanted some. You, Kayaskwa, so brave in bearing my son, should wear them like tokens of honor. Sleep well, Elizabeth Dowland."

He left the house and made his bed under a tree.

Chapter 52

While Elizabeth spent the long days walking, working, and caring for her son, restoring her vigor and faith in her future, the farms gave up their heavy yields to be transformed into food, candles, soap, cloth, and all the necessities of life.

Matters in Sweetwood tempered with the cooler weather. Gil watched Hudson's keeping of the terms between them and calmed as a gentle autumn hesitantly felled the leaves, leaving much of the forest still a collection of bright torches, in all the warm tones of earth, late in October.

Strangely, Annanias became a frequent visitor at Nathan Hanson's table, openly friendly since regaining control of his aims and, to some extent, their daughter. His presence was balm to the Hansons, troubled about Prue's returning melancholy. But Annanias remained unpersuaded by the familial warmth they showed him and held his plan before his eyes like an amulet, while the neglected girl hoped to win his affections through discretion about his part in her pregnancy.

It was clear to Prue that if she were to marry Hudson the wedding must take place publicly before her state became obvious. She wielded Hudson's guilty parenthood like a club in their snatches of hushed conversation to break down his reluctance. Another plan, to leave the town, forcing him to join her with threat of disclosure, began to emerge as days passed.

Yet Prudence could not keep herself from walking the long, uphill path to the cobbler's back room for the excitement of talk with Jack's worldly friend, the red man Wuttah Mauo. It was not long before her harmless pleasure extended from the shop to the shed and Prue began an intrigue of innocence before the father of her illegitimate child and of experience to the disenchanted Indian with the smell of the city about him.

She relished the thrill of this secret, seeing herself soon married to Annanias, the social life of Sweetwood in her command, knowing as she progressed through days of fishbowl propriety that she had been touched intimately by a savage. Fundamental questions burst silently within her insulated ignorance before the first time Wuttah Mauo took her. Prudence Hanson dreaded his Indian body, his yet unrevealed mode of lovemaking. But as he coaxed in sweet cynicism, making use of her availability, suspicion fermented into hope that relations with Weeping Heart would be less painful than with Annanias.

That season she learned to endure the disdain of the man she revered and to drink gin and enjoy the casual warmth of the eldest son of the sachim.

In the otan, the settlement of the Massachuseuck, Waban felt Wuttah Mauo's lapse with self-reproaching pain, but was carried above his disappointment by the imminent welcoming of Wakwa's son, the hope of his tribe, aptly named, he thought, Noh-annoosu.

Waban marked it as a favorable sign that Wuttah Mauo refrained from entering the camp drunk, a decency he had not shown in his Boston days. The old chieftain decided it would take many false victories over his son's weakness before he could totally win back the boy with the keen wit and farsighted soul who had fallen prey to the city so many years before.

Because of his temperament, reasonable and jocular, Waban found himself supervising the Taquonk preparations with characteristic gusto. He kept count of the days until his first meeting with the white woman his favorite, Wakwa, thought so remarkable.

* * * *

Most of the hunters were encamped on a high ridge far to the interior of the Massachuseuck grounds. For days they had stalked bear and finally found several who still gorged on late berries. The bear hunt was to precede the drive for the deer, and spirits were merry around the fires as the young sachim and his companion loped into camp. The men were pleased to be starting the rich haul they expected from their late fall hunt.

Assuming he would, as usual, take the lead part in the bear kill, Wakwa stripped and made for the pots of paint.

"Will you not save some of the red and white for me, men?"

One man offered him the dregs of two vessels and a half-hearted smile.

378

"Brother bear will see no one to run after. There is nothing left!"

Conversation ceased and the band of hunters avoided Wakwa's eyes. He sat thoughtfully, drawing a weave of bright lines up his legs.

"What is our number of iron-tipped arrows?" Wakwa asked while Awepu painted white gulls across his shoulders and outstretched arms.

Mosq took the count and came with the total of their deadliest points, but stood dumbly, Wakwa's feather headdress crushed under his arm.

"Mosq! Are you in mourning because the bear who is to die and you share a name in common? I come into camp and the laughter stops? Go we not for bear today, men?"

"Wakwa." Awepu turned the sachim by his freshly painted shoulders toward White Cat, standing near Wuttah Mauo.

The young captain, his body covered with a brilliant network of red and yellow designs, stepped forward. "Sachim! We have chosen another man to run before the bear."

Wakwa stared at White Cat, then broke into a hearty laugh.

The other hunters crowded around their leader, relaxing at the ease with which he received the news.

Wakwa tied on his breechcloth. "Who is this man, eh, White Cat? Is he faster than am I? Is his voice stronger than mine? You have found someone with more experience in finding and luring the bear?"

White Cat stayed stiffly unresponsive to Wakwa's tease.

"Come, brother. You and the men have chosen someone more pretty than the Black Fox? Is this new man so strong and beautiful the she-bear would run after him for a mate!" Wakwa clapped his hands and all the men laughed.

Wuttah Mauo, warmly dressed, not taking part in the hunt, did not laugh.

"It must be the swiftest, the strongest, the most tested man, to seduce the bear into the ring of arrows. Every fall of the leaf it is me. Because I have two wives now, you think I am worn out?" Wakwa reached for the headdress but Mosq backed away.

"White Cat, tell him before he bursts," Wuttah Mauo yawned.

For the first time Wakwa took offense at his cousin's disrespect. "King Willie, is it you who will keep pace with the bear?"

Wuttah Mauo closed his eyes, deciding against retaliation in front of the men, knowing his father would blame him for any unbecoming squabble.

"Sachim. It is simple." Wuttah Mauo talked as he walked toward Wakwa. "No one questions you are still the most agile. Since the feast is in your honor, we all agree it is your place to run before the bear." Wuttah Mauo touched his cousin's shoulder in a conciliatory way, then chanced a sarcasm. "I wish you would. But the powwaw saith you shall not make the run." Wuttah Mauo returned to the leafy bed under the tree and prepared to sleep.

Wakwa sorted this mystifying information.

White Cat folded his arms decisively. "It is I will make the run."

"You! Ha! I see. We have adorned ourselves for your burial rites. Have you ever done it? Why do we not simply let Awepu shoot him down with a musket ball and save the mess of paint and feathers? White Cat, we would not lose you! You will miss me playing the lyre at the feast." Wakwa snorted at the neophyte.

"It is to please Pequawus I will make the run."

"My father has hobbled me?"

"He and the taupowaw agree there shall be no bear near you at the time of celebration. You are free to hunt him all other times."

White Cat was suddenly aware, as he stood in a crosscurrent of glances between Wakwa, himself, and the men, that he was in a delicate position over the insignificant bear hunt. He had received his first lights on the difficulties of balancing power. He sensed this chance to serve his guardian would ever remain a sore spot with Pequawus' only son.

White Cat had come under the protection of Pequawus a common child without exact kinship ties, neither owned nor disowned by anyone. Because of his indefinite status, he could never aspire to leadership. He was most content listening to Pequawus, a willing disciple learning his perspectives and priorities. White Cat was fond of the sagamore, but had kept an imposed distance from Wakwa, who was so preoccupied with foreign people and pursuits. Since his inclusion in the affairs of the household of Silent Fox, White Cat had begun to flirt with ambition.

Wakwa swallowed the decision about the hunt, knowing his father's bitter memories of another bear, at another feast, that had robbed him of his wife and Wakwa of a mother. He took the headdress from Mosq and settled it over White Cat's elaborately dressed hair.

"My father is growing old. I must grant him his whim." Wakwa sighed. "White Cat, draw our brother bear into the widest space you can find. Stay close enough to let him see you, but not so close he takes a bite. We will do the rest and you will earn his skin for your mother." Wakwa reached for an arrow case and joined the other hunters.

The bears spotted in previous days, two females and a short, burly male, declined to come to water early in the afternoon. With so many details of his wedding left to settle, barred from the glamour of the hunt, Wakwa's ennui was complete as he waited in the dull, chill weather.

His regret at leaving his lyre at the lodge made him smile at the subtle influence of his white kin. There was fingering to practice. His mind active with annoyance, his body idle, he could see Dr. Mac's rationale for making his flute his constant companion. Wakwa became beguiled by a daydream experiment, projecting himself into the next autumn's hunt, tempting the bear out of hiding with mellisonant Bach. Substituting his knee for his lyre, his fingers pressed out the exercise Gil had rehearsed with him. He became conscious of Awepu's curious look.

"Flush him out!" Wakwa barked to White Cat. "That is your job!"

But the restive bear could already be seen approaching the stream. White Cat's unimpressive teasing arrow pierced the bear's foot, then broke loose. Wakwa was reminded of Awepu's son Tamoccon, who always found Mosq shining among the other constellations before anyone else at the summer remove to the forest for prayer. With silent understanding, the other hunters gave Wakwa the place at the end of the long ellipse which cordoned off the bear's escape.

Wakwa climbed a tree at this pivotal position, Awepu behind it with his favorite musket ready for an emergency. Inevitably the screams of the beleaguered bear came, coupled with the loud taunting of White Cat as he ran ably down the path, just out of reach of the heavy claws.

From his perch Wakwa noted the unseasonable vitality of the animal, his hide already burdened by several arrows. He saw White Cat's surprise when he whirled to judge the distance between himself and the beast. He laughed at the spurt White Cat put on, discovering the bear's closeness.

The bear responded with a courageous run at the fast-disappearing bundle of noise and feathers. Then White Cat faced a decision at the forking of the main route. Wakwa watched his fatal hesitation, his stumble over a large tree root, and the scramble out of the wider path into the narrower. Wakwa refused to judge White Cat's mistake as cowardice. Perhaps he would dupe the fast-running animal and come back out on the wider way at better advantage.

The band of hunters slowed the bear's progress slightly with a barrage of arrows from both sides. Tenaciously, the near-sighted animal sought his enemy along the main way, then picked up the new direction of the scent and veered through the undergrowth, gaining on the man. White Cat, who had been forced to come back to re-signal for the bear's attention, cursed the small path which frustrated his speed.

The hunters were cut off from a clear view of their target by the veil of close-growing trees. The blunder had left White Cat unprotected.

It was then that Awepu's musket ball ripped the intervening leaves and broke through the bear's shoulder. The angry animal kept on after the loathsome sight of White Cat's waving arms.

"The head! The head!" Awepu chided himself, his teeth biting the plug of his powder horn.

"That skin is ruined, cousin," Wakwa said coolly as he dropped to the ground.

Bottled in by undergrowth, White Cat screamed in mental anguish and physical agony and leaped to the safety of a maple bough as the bear's claw came away with a chunk of meat from the runner's calf. Blind arrows flew into the thicket, the hunters hooting to distract the beast from his lust for vengeance on White Cat.

"Paukunnawaw!" A legato growl, sounding another word for bear, made the harried animal whirl, confused by the scent of another man so close to him.

The hunters stilled their attack in deference to Wakwa.

Moans sounded from the bear's foaming mouth, and he flailed at the form that courted him close.

Staying toward the animal's uninjured side, to bore his message home to his tribesmen, Wakwa captivated the bear with the fascinating movements of his head and torso. His enticement was strong enough to cause the bear to pivot one full circle. Aroused, the bear at last rose to his full height and swiped at Wakwa's evasive body with his good claw. While the other men held their breaths, the animal advanced, meeting the flirtatious two-legged creature on his own terms.

Wakwa shrieked and reared back, letting his hatchet fly, splitting open the bear's skull. It dropped under the shower of its own blood.

Hunters filtered onto the path, mumbling their impressions to one another.

Awepu apologetically rammed his bayonet into the carcass. "For Pequawus, dear friend."

"What is another hole, Awepu?" Wakwa retrieved his weapon and held Awepu around his shoulders. "It is not a pretty kill. Be happy Tamoccon was not here."

Several of the men broke their arrows out of reverence, offering the valuable iron points to their sachim, Silent Fox. All others followed suit.

Wakwa accepted them, then tossed his knife into the bark of the tree that sequestered the suffering White Cat.

"Come, brother. You and I will skin our bear."

Chapter 53

Rain came but did not douse the enthusiasm struck by this dramatic beginning to the big deer drive. And while the men were occupied killing and hauling the meat home, the women set up a fresh camp closer to the river, removed from the summer fleas.

Elizabeth happily draped bark over a new wetuomemese as her body's cycle returned to its former rhythm. Each day there was the sound of singing through the wind as the hunters brought in their catch.

In the cool, dry bluster of late October, when her stay in the female hut was over, Elizabeth escaped from the activity in her big lodge to walk and bathe in the company of her son.

Noh-annoosu had grown handsome and heavy for a child of five weeks, and when he was not nursing or eating the powdered corn his mother mixed with her milk, he was raising his green-brown eyes above the side of his wicker basket to regard his world or sleeping his tremulous but healthy sleep. This late afternoon found him resting soundly in his basket hanging from a willow, breathing in the smoky fragrance of the forest and forming dreams to sounds of the deep water of the pond where his mother glided, rinsing her hair of herbal liquid.

Her body was restored to its former slimness except for the weight of her milk-filled breasts. This day, already having conquered the physical manifestations of Noh-annoosu's birth, Elizabeth was seeking to purge herself of the last year's emotional heat. In the rosy stillness of the autumn afternoon she washed away the fatigue of her wait for the birth and the bitter remembrance of her near ruination from overwork a few months before. She sought to dull the continuing pain of eternal separation from her parents in the cold, clear water, fearing the life coming to her in the lodges of the Ninnuock.

Her skin shaved, clean, and cool, she practiced the strokes her husband had taught her, propelling herself smoothly in the water like the slender branch just separated from the mother tree.

She rolled over and was blinded by the sun and smiled at its warmth on her flat stomach. She floated free, her hair spreading on the surface in a pattern of brown lace. From the low dell where she swam she saw the saplings that mounted to the sky as guards of her soul, ever fresh and changing, stronger with age.

The strummings of the wings of small birds and their magnified shrieks brought her head around to make sure of the safety of the son who was always with her. Daily he wove himself into her being, extending the threads of his possibilities in a mad spider's embroidery, ever more intricate in overlay of mysterious design. She straightened and stood to judge the firmness of the band supporting the cradle, could not determine what had excited the birds, and gladly walked back to a deeper level. Then she heard the pop of a chestnut on water and was encircled by the silver rings it caused. She abandoned herself to the pond, wrapped in the security of the fluid demarcation, and splashed and sank and surfaced in a seethe of bubbles. Satisfied sounds escaped her, filling the wooded basin with an echoing, "Ah!"

Knowledge that at the end of her reverie lay a lodge full of people, packing and sorting, transferring her works and solitude into the noise and company of another race of people, made Elizabeth fight the chill of the infant night breeze and swim toward the middle of the pond again.

Now other chestnuts dropped around her, breaking the patterns of the wind-rustled water. She knew, as the birds had, she was no longer alone. She walked toward the basket, keeping her body well-submerged, not from fear but from a guarded self-sufficiency.

"Committamus!" Wakwa called "wife" into the hollow, but Elizabeth could not trace the source of the enveloping sound.

Then she saw his big form appear on the rocks at the deepest side and bravely started for the spot, happy to open her privacy to his presence. She caught the foot he dangled in the water.

"Come in! Come in! Wild one!" she coaxed. But Wakwa drew back, offering apologies for interrupting her enjoyment.

"I do not believe you are sorry, husband, else you would not have used me for a target. Come, come in."

"It is cold." Wakwa leaned down and gathered her wet hair up to himself. "Thou art a wild thing thyself, Elizabeth, at last."

"I hope I grow so. You smell a beast. Come swim with me!"

"No. They wait for me at the sweathouse. The hunt is over. I am tired from carrying a moose."

"Poor moose!"

"I came only because Gilbert and Qunneke grew concerned." She tried to pull away.

"You have been long absent they say." Wakwa ran the fingers of his free hand under her chin. She tossed her head to get free.

"Let go my hair! I will freeze if I do not swim."

Wakwa laughed and held her there, knotting her hair onto his fingers.

Elizabeth clung to the stones and kicked her legs for warmth. "So, you all ensnare me at my last hour of freedom. And why must you go into pesuponk filthy? Can you not sweat with a few layers of dirt removed?"

"The sun is past where I told them it would be. Oh! I will swim you to the shore." Wakwa stood and sprang up in an arc from the ledge, disappeared under the water, and brought up a spindle of foam as he surfaced.

He joined his wife in long, easy strokes, working horizontally toward their sleeping infant. Wakwa watched Elizabeth's movements and noted with gladness the absence of girlishness as she used a sidestroke with pendulous grace, adjusting to her heavy breasts with the new gravity that elongated all her movements since the birth of their son.

She stood, waist-deep, her toes squeezing the sandy bottom, but did not advance to the cradle. Wakwa surfaced from an underwater fillip and wrapped her moist body from behind with his arms.

"It will be well." He shyly kissed the hair at the nape of her neck. "Let us return here every Taquonk, until this smooth skin dries like the fall leaf and you and I blow away into dust, and wait the deep snow."

Elizabeth felt fear behind his tentative touch but, swept along by his poetry, concentrated on the view she had of the long grass half obscuring the basket.

"He is like Moses in the bulrushes this afternoon, my Silent Fox."

386

Taller, Wakwa could clearly see the basket, backed by the darkening rise of the hills behind it.

"Oo. The man from your Bible who walked far. Our papoos. He does not seem afraid to drift in the air above the grass with Massachusetts behind him."

"You give the word some meaning?"

"Kayaskwa, woman from another shore, the meaning gives the word! Massachusetts is the place you see. It betokens the blue hills floating back and back as viewed from the ocean. Moses in the bulrushes. So! Moses Massachusetts."

"Moses of the blue hills!" The mother skidded her fingers across the face of the water, tossing a benediction of spray in the child's direction.

"Elizabeth." Wakwa shivered. "Moses Bluehill will be his English name."

"Yes! Wakwa! I like that! How fitting. I think father would have liked it." She hugged him. "Everyone will like it. Moses Bluehill. Dr. Mac will be so pleased. He feels on more solid ground with a name from the Testament."

"Moses. Pequawus will like it." Wakwa sounded the name to himself, greatly satisfied at this inspiration.

Elizabeth dipped beneath the surface and did not hear. She circled his legs, the whiteness of her skin making lights underneath the water. She bobbed up and seized his waist and pulled him down to his knees.

"Elizabeth, I am late and you play. Take Moses Bluehill home before they call him Moses Bluenose."

She responded by swimming into deeper water so that as Wakwa walked behind her the water reached his breast. With a deep breath, she submerged and held his body with her hands, running her lips across his lower back and side, gasping fresh air as she concluded one full ring of kisses.

"Elizabeth? Know you what you do?" Wakwa held her up, the water too deep for her to stand.

For her answer she dipped down once more, toiling to descend low enough to see his legs beneath the water. His skin in the liquid light was a glowing green and she was moved to caress him, then, needing air, allowed her body to press against him as she rose and breathed a dozen feet from where he stood.

Wakwa put his head under water, then whipped back his hair

and did not move as Elizabeth glided back to him. She swam an arm's length away, a placid smile on her face.

"Yea, Elizabeth?" Wakwa was desirous yet hesitant.

"Yea, husband."

"You will do this?" Never having known a woman after she had given birth, unfamiliarity and tenderness bound him in.

"Shall you let the pool turn to ice?" She came and wrapped her legs around him and he swam with her like a mother bear with a cub.

"Take thou me to thyself?"

"I do receive you. Be not remote." She reassured him in whispers, repeating the touch of her hand between his legs, receiving the response she sought, loving the growth she felt in her palm.

Wakwa, tall as he was, no longer had any footing and threw her high from himself and called, "Swim then, or you shall be all in my power."

Unwisely, she sped toward the center of the pond and after the spurt floundered in the deep water. She spluttered to Wakwa who was swimming slowly toward her, feeling no need to pursue her in a hurry. She swallowed water but laughed through her choking as he reached her.

Now he held her body in his turn, sweeping her back toward the flat and sandy bank. Wakwa lay on his side, half in the water, not wishing to hurt her with an embrace, her breasts hard with milk unreleased for hours. He painted her bosom with a soothing mixture of wet sand and silt, letting it slide smoothly between his fingers onto her skin. The husband touched the new mother's body reverently from face to thighs with the plane of his fingers, closing off her ready opening with his palm, still doubting the wisdom of what seemed to him to be too speedy a renewal of their married life.

"I am cleansed of the birth, of the wetuomemese, of all the bitterness I have caused within myself. Lies not Moses healthy and pure just here above us? Wherefore do you fear to traverse the recess consecrated to thee?"

The words poured over Wakwa's harried spirit like melodic wine and he turned aside the ancient custom of long waiting, touched, and slipped into the velvet sheath of her body to be bound in the security of her affection. His movement's gentle-

388

ness changed with the warmth that shot through him, though the sun left the sky. Increasingly freer, stronger thrusts of his body pushed her to the edge of the water where her hair was buried in the bright earth of the bank.

Sound ceased. The vision of a bluebird in the dusk, screeching noiseless messages to the coming night, sustained the sensations they felt at each motion. The bird flew on and Wakwa tumbled between Elizabeth's breasts after his fiery release, not moving until her arms came heavily around his neck, and the trembling that he felt through her came from cold, not inner heat.

Noise returned and Elizabeth listened to the voices of the water, the dry leaves, and the small nocturnal animals, growing in intensity with her discovery of new space within herself Wakwa had seemed to fill. She felt the birth of their son had increased the comfort of Wakwa's exceptional phallic touch, which always mended her breakages of spirit.

Their child's cooing forced them to hurry another rinsing, the pool gone black for lack of light. Wakwa stopped Elizabeth as she dressed and he kissed her, marveling, "I have a wife."

"Two." Elizabeth admitted Tame Deer into the sanctity of their attachment, and the look of gratitude Wakwa gave her dwarfed all her private struggles of the past twelve months.

The baby was wet and tearful, and while the mother tended and nursed him in the shelter of her heavy blanket Wakwa dried and combed her hair.

Elizabeth insisted on carrying Moses slung at her side while Wakwa led her through the darkening evening. When they began to see smoke from the lodge Wakwa seized the sling and held its weight off her shoulder, kissing her mouth for the last time in her state of obscurity and privacy. The embrace ended as they heard Gil's sprightly guitar at the edge of the trees, meant to guide Elizabeth home.

She would not move toward the sound. "There are things no one will tell me. New things from Sweetwood you all think me too weak to bear."

"Kayaskwa, if there is danger you shall be told." Wakwa took her hand and smiled. "Now it is Taquonk."

* * * *

The minister of Sweetwood closed his bedroom curtains to the setting sun that same autumn day. He lit a candle and reread the second draft of a note to Prue. He crossed out a word and copied the message again, then blackened his scraps over the single flame.

This colorless girl had saved him from maniacal depression over Beth's loss. He blessed Prudence Hanson for that service. He prayed for her daily because of her convoluted charity to him. But the minister scratched her from his life like the unnecessary word.

He chewed his finger as he read the letter a third time. His words must say nothing, and all. His own future depended upon the scrupulous keeping of his agreement with Gilbert Worth. He did not fear the guileless gentleman, but his unpredictable temper. To provoke him into making a case before the Session was no less dangerous than shooting a bullet into his own temple.

Annanias Hudson relived his tumble from his code of virtue, studying the bland expressions he hoped would carry meaning only to Prue. Feeling deeply the dreary emotional residue of their brief romance, Hudson had to work hard to make sure he had hidden their complicity, bound up their mutual injury, and had left himself unfettered at the closing.

"I am like the boy who falls from the line at snap-the-whip," Annanias punished himself. "Wiping off the dirt and getting nothing out of all this excitement but bruises."

He surveyed his room as he left to post the letter. The respectable Oriental rug Worth had called dowdy, the stout bed newly hung with warm velvet for the fall, his mahogany secretary replete with little drawers and cubbyholes, and the carved highboy for Beth, in the alcove, offered no comfort now that he had learned how undesirable it was to use them alone.

Annanias wet his shoe in the evening afterglow, walking through a mirror-like puddle in the rutted road. He checked his steps as he had his writing.

His position's privilege did not allow him privacy. To bring the letter to the general mail at Bearing's Tavern would invite raised eyebrows from Isaac and interference from Nathan Hanson. Prue's father fetched his own mail. He thought of Bottle's shop. The old Indian, Jack, would be the man to get this note to Prue. But even though he was close-mouthed, he was not to be trusted with the folded paper containing four crisp notes of Pennsylvania currency.

Busily bedding birds mocked his indecision as he stood lost in the dusk. And then a smile filled the lower portion of his face as a flash of his old brilliance surfaced.

With the dark coming swiftly, Annanias Hudson began the climb to Dowland Farm to pay a call on the disillusioned housekeeper, Mrs. Winke.

* * * *

Mrs. Winke went about her errand with the good sense that had shown so clearly when she had scalded Gilbert Worth's peach tree insects. She packed up a bag of cotton lace she made during her long evenings spent in the stately desolation of the Dowland house, depending on the selling of it to secure a private moment with Prue. She drove the cart alone, following the girl's route of household errands to the village. The Hanson cart with parcels and driver passed on its way home, but Prue was not in it. Finally, at mid-morning, Winke met her en route to the shoemaker's.

Prudence Hanson was wise enough to cover the importance of the note by buying the matron's lace. Her disposition and a summer of secrecy also gave her the control to wait Winke's lagging descent of the hill before running to the shed for a secluded place to read.

A sober, smoking Wuttah Mauo waited early, and Prue tossed the bundle of lace near him in annoyance. With her back to him, she broke the seal of the long-hoped-for letter. She moved her lips as she read:

> "My dear Mistress Hanson, With the concern I bear all my congregation, I proffer you help in the difficulty you undergo which has come to my attention. . . ."

Color left Prue's face, the letter's tone revealing its import before her eyes reached the words.

> "Out of my modest private funds, I am able to provide
> a place for you, of your choosing, to board during this
> time of ill health. . . ."

"Ill health!" she whispered, pushing her eyes across the short
lines of Annanias' plain script.

> "Rest and peace should restore you to Sweetwood to
> your most attentive family, or help you to choose a more
> satisfying life elsewhere. Remember, Prudence, you are,
> as ever, in my prayers.
>
> > Your servant,
> > Reverend Hudson"

She sat looking toward the closed door, enduring the cool
assault of Hudson's words. She had not expected this. She read
the note again, suffusing its rejection of her with the affection
she desired.

"Remember, Prudence, you are, as ever, in my prayers." "As
ever . . ." Those words keyed her hopes.

But the truth was simple. No minister could marry and be
father to a seven-month babe. It was the hundred-pound notes
sticking to Prue's perspiring hands that sealed her understanding. Reverend Hudson bought at bargain rates. She was bitter
that Annanias was denying his child for less than half the
amount Charles Dowland had offered for mere news of Beth.
Prue tucked the money away in her sleeve.

"You spend money on such trash!" Wuttah Mauo called, ri-
fling the bag of trimmings.

"I add an extra breadth to my skirts this winter." Prue was
gloomy.

"You should buy you some rouge."

"Won't you shut up?" Prue stuffed the letter into her skirt
pocket.

"Say not this to me, little witch!" Wuttah Mauo pinched her
cheeks pink.

She leaned her face against his wrist. "You wouldn't have a
horse, my chum?"

Wuttah Mauo unhooked her clothes and ran a string of lace
around her like a measure, the creases in his cheeks deepening
with the slightest of smiles.

She pulled away. "Leave me alone!"

"Poor little bitch, do not struggle. I will help you."

"Why should you help me?" Prue's glance was toward the left as she tried to piece together a solution to her immediate problem. To expose Annanias would crush any hope she had of redeeming their relationship. Some way she must leave Sweetwood, preserve herself, and grasp at his sympathies from afar.

Wuttah Mauo watched her deliberate as he filled the storage room with the aroma from his pipe. He did not scorn this farmer's daughter. Unlike Elizabeth, Prue had not lost faith in her race, nor did she suck at his people to fill her life with new meaning.

He knew Prue's problem. His own was to restore something of his security and respect in the otan.

The People did not understand the courage it had taken for him to face and to beat back at the specter of gold, the obstacle to their happiness. While Wakwa niggled with Locke over the prices of skins and was satisfied with his fifty or sixty pounds a year, Wuttah Mauo gambled high stakes with the tough adventurers who circulated metal money between Europe and America. He felt pride in the memories of their stripped purses littering the tables after he would show them his hand. Once, living a year on the proceeds of two wild nights and days of their ridiculous cards, Wuttah Mauo had had time to hear the death knell of his people in the Sunday church bells that aggravated his hangovers.

The People were fools, still believing their destiny remained within the bug-ridden forests. Poor People. They would all end up at Patty's Feather. And so must this mouse-colored girl he believed carried his child.

Gilbert Worth's sharp estimation of his character was faulted more as the days passed and Prue's middle swelled. Wuttah Mauo flirted with the hope that his own issue would make a proper foil to Noh-annoosu.

"Why should I not help?" Weeping Heart asked.

"What can you do for me, Willie?"

"I could win you a Rhode Island pacer this afternoon, but there is not much gaming in your tiny town, girl. I may ask your father if he needs a few ditches dug."

"You stay away from there! I've enough trouble with him already. He'd pay you with buckshot."

393

Wuttah Mauo uncorked the bottle Jack had brought him, disgusted that his contacts with whites were always a cheap imitation of Wakwa's. He drank and made Prue drink. "How else am I going to come by the money to get you out? Are we going to walk the distance to Boston, and you getting bigger each time I see you!" he growled.

"How can we go anywhere?"

"We are here!"

"That is different. . . . Here . . . no one sees. . . . I mean . . . what goes on here is no one's business."

"Yes? And is not your small problem growing into open sight? Should we not buy a cart, steal one if we must?"

"That is all I need!" She was exasperated. "Pa angry with me and then to go stealin' carts and ride off next to . . ."

Wuttah Mauo turned slowly on her.

She flushed under the stare which forced her to continue, no longer needing artificial color. "You know it better than I, Willie, you're an Indian," she mumbled.

Wuttah Mauo's stomach tightened in the familiar way, but for the first time his shoulders pained under the weight of racial insult. "So is the child you carry!"

Prue was amazed. The truth of her situation crowded her mouth but the mistaken man kept speaking.

"Do you think I wish to live with you? Take you for my sweet white bride? You make me laugh with your stupidness. I want that baby. You can go to hell!"

"You want it?" Prue was incredulous.

"I do you a favor? I do not mind. You will do me one, eh? If it is a boy, I take it. A girl like you is no use to me."

Prudence plumped onto the floor. Annanias Hudson's son—fat, pink, and jolly—crowned with feathers danced before her eyes, and she coughed out her momentary glee at such stabbing revenge.

Wuttah Mauo put out his pipe. "And if you would not ride next to me you may pull the cart, but you will come to Boston. From somewhere I will get me horse and money. I will even stand your company until you drop my son from you. Then you may go become the very queen of Beacon Hill for all I care."

Prue swung happily from the man's neck, her mind leaping past his petulance toward this astonishing solution. "I have money!" she announced grandly, throwing the notes into the air. She was fraudulently accepting asylum and planned to use his knowledge of the city to protect her private aims. But gaiety washed out her guilt. "Four hundred pounds! Shall I enter my confinement on King's Road then!"

"From where? From where?" And the man so wary of gold bent to rescue the money, as surprised with this turn in his luck as Prudence was with hers.

She avoided answer and Wuttah Mauo threw a dainty noose he had been making, catching her as he used to snare deer. He pulled it tight and urged her toward him. "You will not talk to me now you are a rich woman?"

"Stop that! You will split my lace! I need it! And don't think to use my cash to slide out of your gambling debts."

"You will get your money."

"I want it back now!" Her face was red as she thought of her unrewarded patience with Annanias. "I won't be lied to anymore!"

Mercilessly, Weeping Heart wound her breast and shoulders with the strand, tying her arms back, binding her like a carcass, glutting his hurt over her bigotry. "Little by little, Prudence, you will get the good of it. I have made me no debts here in the forest." The man bit her face with warped enjoyment, reminding her of the purpose of their meeting.

She leaned against his chest, dizzy from the baby and her new doubts about Annanias. "I want to go now. Oh! Do not touch me." Constricted by the lace, she tried in vain to refuse his possessive caress where the minister's baby rested. "Not there!"

Wuttah Mauo undid the fragile knots, pressing himself against her, easily able to overcome her resistance. But he took pity on the young woman he thought carried his child. "Take care, little white witch!" he whispered as he slid the bolt from its cradle and sent her on her way.

The sachim's eldest son drank and slept through the day. He did not walk home until hours past sunset when the knife edge of the first quarter moon slit the western sky.

He had slept off the alcohol and was left hungry not for food, but for some sincere attachment. His lonely forty-year-old heart laughed. A beautiful woman, willing to raise his mixed-blood son, might come to him as easily as the money padding his pocket.

Chapter 54

The solemnization of the union between Wakwa Manunnappu and Elizabeth Dowland was to take place on the last Sunday of October, forty days after Noh-annoosu's birth.

Early on the Friday before, Matthew and a retinue of servants mounted the hill from the river with the sun. In full display of his status as freeman, the black man had put aside his servant's baize for a new suit of blue-gray wool and a turban of striped India silk.

Strung behind him, in two wheeled carts, were carefully chosen laborers from Gil's farm, bringing beef and apples, and great pots of raspberry sherbet entombed in ice, from Cooke. An itinerant artist down from French Canada, hired in Boston to record the important moments of the feast, shared the space with the chilly confection. He justified his fee by promising to help Matthew concoct the marinade for the meat and even to turn the spit when he was not busy with his chalks and pencils.

Matthew negotiated efficiently with Awepu, the steward of this special Taquonk, and quickly settled Gil's workers into the huts provided by his Indian hosts. He had been under strain about what his treatment would be in the society of red-skinned people. Observing he would be treated with an attitude between disinterest and respect, Matthew shed his fine coat for his old leather apron and began reducing two sides of beef to suitable size to be marinated in crocks. While he wielded his cleaver and kitchen knife, his assistants rubbed the fruit to a red-brown burnish and arranged it in long wicker trays, and Louis Plant chopped pounds of carrots, garlic, onions, celery, and peppercorns.

Waban came after prayer, his guards around him, to watch Matthew's expertise. Sweat seeped from under his colorful bandana in reaction to the sachim's scrutiny, but Worth's houseman made a pretty show severing bone and flesh with surgeon's skill. His perfectionism drew applause, and Waban rewarded him with an obsidian blade.

While Matthew admired its carved handle and tested its edge, Plant's artistic eye wandered from his culinary chore to the loose line of big men against the light sky. The Frenchman draped his necklace of garlic over Matthew's shoulder and approached Waban with his book and pencils and a courtly bow.

The first picture of the feast became a record of its preparation, the strong faces of seven Massachuseuck alight as Matthew threw a clove of garlic and split it in midair with his new knife.

The dancing pavilion, scaled twenty feet high and two hundred feet long, was lifted by the young men that day, and its decoration was the work of the wives. They wrapped its straight poles with firethorn berries and wintergreen and tied gray clouds of gooseberries into place with beaded ribbons. Rich mannotaubana covered two walls, but two sides were left open this year to afford the overflow of guests a view of Nuppohwunau's charity dance and the gifts from the new saunks and her family which would be displayed there.

The gambling arbor went up as well, but it stayed naked of its drapery of wampum, not to be added until the day after Wakwa's wedding.

Strawberry bread, kettles of honey-sweetened cranberries, and the succotash boiled fragrance into the air. Old women and girls plucked turkeys, pheasants, and wild geese while the men constructed aisles of spits for the munificent supply of meat.

Tamoccon and Sequan were sent to the river to gather reeds for the wedding ceremony. The two most perfect were to be exchanged by Silent Fox and his young wife.

Tame Deer delegated the honor of their painting to Awepu's wife, Meadow-in-the-night, since she had been so delayed in her own progress on the two long mats that would provide a flawless carpet for the wedding couple to Waban's sachimmaacommock. Wolf-of-the-mist-He-hopes' arrival at the corn harvest had interrupted the pattern of her life.

Among the honored at the feast, Tame Deer's duties did not include helping with the cooking this year. But inside her own house she was quietly preparing a delicacy meant only for the sachimmauog and the uncle of Elizabeth Dowland.

The tender muzzle of Wakwa's and Awepu's moose, brought in the last day of the hunt, was being spiced and roasted. Careful of her standards as a cook, Tame Deer watched with concentration when she happened upon Matthew and Louis adding olive oil, brandy, and splashes of bright red wine to the crocks of beef.

Trusting in Gilbert Worth, Tame Deer decided she would taste some of this meal when it was cooked, but could not conscience the use of hot spirits in food. She had seen the effect of liquor on Wuttah Mauo. She was convinced that yellow-haired Gilbert would fare better on moose's nose.

****

When the air was cold enough the next night to drive each family inside its wetu, Wakwa Manunnappu arrived in advance of the English party. He was to spend the night apart from Elizabeth and see her in front of his uncle's house in the morning as if for the first time, making his promises to her in the hearing of all his kin and tribe. It was with boyish happiness that he hugged Tame Deer and examined his newly finished clothes.

"I saw no one, Qunneke, but felt five hundred eyes like cat's claws in my back as I crossed the camp. They are not supposed to see Elizabeth and she is not far behind."

"They are happy for you! I may lie on my own belly in the grass to glimpse of Hanna Worth! Now, go to Waban and come back with a mind made up to rest or you shall fly up into the air like a stray feather. You look like you have been smoking jimson."

Wakwa caught her and kissed her freely and the happy wife did not object.

"Take care, or I will lock you away for ten sleeps or so until it wears off!" Tame Deer shooed him toward the door as the sound of horses and the voices of the sentries relaying messages from the river brought them to the present.

Wakwa slipped a tall feather into his headband, mustered a serious look, and left his house. His first wife could hear his chuckle until he went through his uncle's door.

A party of five cantered toward the rings of round houses. They invaded, hooded and cloaked, looking threatening in the dark, but the guards greeted Gil Worth with enthusiasm. There were Gil, Hanna, Stirling, his wife, Ann, and his son, Israel. Behind them were women of Wakwa's tribe bearing the boxes of clothes, the gifts Elizabeth had sewn, and her belongings from the lodge. The last woman carried the new chair by Samuel Spinney bound over her shoulders.

The central circle was filled at once with helping hands as the encumbered English people struggled to dismount. Gil winced with worry as a stranger took his small, portable harp and guitar from his paternal grasp. He retained his lute defensively, helping his wife from her gray.

Awepu came to greet them and was startled by the phantom look of Hanna's velvet riding mask. Before she could remove the silver mouthpiece which held it on, Stirling said, "Disreputable-lookin' bunch o' vagabonds we are!"

"Father!" Israel disapproved, walking close to his mother toward the open curtain of Waban's house. Waban's many fires gave a glow to the interior and Israel muttered to Mrs. Stirling, "It's like the portal to the Inferno, Mother."

The old woman quivered and Dr. Mac snapped, "Shutoop, son! Half of these gargantuas speak King's English, don't ye know!"

Gil was familiar by now with the large house and its many rooms branching off at right angles, and he went without direction to where the three sachimmauog waited to greet them. But this was no hasty council drawn on a moment's notice. The sight of the three leaders seated among their full complement of advisors, the powwaw, and Waban's wife, all decked in the rich refinements of native dress, subdued the Englishman in his heather wools.

The seriousness of this cultural cross sent tremors of uncertainty through him, and Charles Dowland's legitimate fears whispered in the fire's hiss.

Waban, enthroned on a white bearskin, regarded these English people with warm attentiveness. He had met them under the sad circumstances of Dowland's death the winter before, and thought it for the good of everyone that he reintroduce his family and the sagamores. His old wife observed her guests from a place behind him.

Gil followed Waban's lead and presented his own party with a description of each, saving Hanna for last.

She was lost in the aura of the curved walls, the scents, the hangings, and the presence, everywhere, of the trophies of Waban's youthful hunts. When she heard Gil speak her name she started forward automatically, as if being presented to an assembly at a manor house. With her chin properly drawn in, her neck straight and stiff, she moved toward Waban, executed a graceful curtsy, and rose, her cloak swirling tightly around her like a closing flower.

"Good evening, Sachim!" Her voice was pleasing and her smile perfect.

"Cowaunkamish, wife of Gilbert Worth!" Waban was charmed.

But the longer Hanna stood in front of him, staring into his lively old eyes, the more she wished Elizabeth were there for her to lean on for courage and the more she became aware of the presence of Waban's two sons. Nuppohwunau's laconic good will and Wuttah Mauo's intent dissatisfaction banked their father's face like splinters of his own personality.

Waban reached his hand up toward her and Hanna accepted it, the formality of her stance melting at the friendly gesture. She held his plump fingers with the grip of anxiety, telling him through her muscular stress all the concern she had for the welfare of her brother's daughter.

Another hand, lean and long, crossed in front of the old sachim and Hanna reached for it as well and put it to her cheek. From where he sat, Wakwa reassured her as Hanna's tears wet his knuckles.

"Elizabeth is safe, wife of Gilbert Worth!"

The voice he trusted swept away Gil's agony of last-minute doubts and he sealed the tableau of Hanna's communication with the Indians in his soul, relieved by the solidarity of family ties that would soon surround his niece.

"With a government of Englishwomen many unnecessary words with our white brothers could be avoided." Pequawus cast a rare smile on the young sister of Charles Dowland.

Hanna's mind cleared, knowing that somehow she had made herself understood.

* * * *

The plan had come to fruition. To become one in the privacy of the wood, to explain their state, and, finally, to live among the Indians had been Beth's proposal to Wakwa. She stood now in the doorway to her uncle's temporary lodging, the darkness behind her, her self-inflicted exile forever ended. She shouldered her new state as she entered the wetu.

Everyone went to sleep for the night without delay. It was Hanna who listened to the hum of community living and woke repeatedly, bothered by unaskable questions about her niece's new life. She was happy to respond to Matthew's call to wake, which came in the cold before day.

Sparrow screamed as the black man freely picked his way among the boxes, attempting to fix a place for his master's toilette. Elizabeth soothed the maid, and the baby woke and wailed for milk. Hanna listened to directions to the area the town used for waste and washing. Gil hid under the fur, refusing like a boy all Matthew's pleas to rise and begin the day.

"Nissese! Pesuponk begins! The first boat has crossed the river!" Awepu's voice rose over the din.

"Wetomp! Give me but a moment." Gil was up and poked his head out into the darkness.

"Sun woh kuppeegwhitteamwoo?" Awepu ran his hands over his face.

"Friend, if I'm to shave first I will miss this event."

"Gilbert, I worry not that the sun will wait for thee. But we are to emerge cleansed, with the powwaw's words in our ears. You must remove the hair or wear it to the feast!"

"Wouldn't Hanna love that! I'd best shave, Awepu."

"Nuppohwunau will take you across."

"And the doctor?"

"He is already on the river, most anxious for the steam. It is his son who doth refuse to come." Awepu held out two breechcloths to Gil. "We must be running into the water when the morning star is rivaled by the sun." He left for his canoe.

"That Israel's a cocky buck!" Gil's remark was met by a brushful of foam as he turned toward the inside.

Matthew sat his master down and shaved the area around his lips before permitting Gil to call to Hanna, "Ana, it is not right. This red-headed freshman Israel must oblige Waban or it looks not so well for Elizabeth."

Matthew worked down Gil's throat from his upraised chin.

Hanna stopped near them on her way out with Elizabeth. "Then, Nissese, you must go and bring him."

402

Gil strained away from the razor's edge. "Even if his papa cannot make him do it?"

"The sachimmauog look not to Dr. Mac for authority."

"The old Dowland starch, eh? If I practice your look, will that get him?"

"Do it any way, dear, but do it." Hanna deserted him for the pre-dawn air.

Matthew was cutting gold stubs from around Gil's ears when Nuppohwunau called. Only the servant's deft reaction to Gil's swerve saved the master from a razor slice.

"Enter, Nuppohwunau!"

There was no reply.

"Nuppohwunau, come in!"

"Art ready, Gilbert Worth?"

"Matthew, can you not finish? Nuppohwunau, I am ready."

Matthew was unsatisfied with the job he had done in the unsteady light. He daubed Gil's face with foam again for touch-up.

The sachim's son opened the flap of straw and broke into laughter at the sight of his important English relative blotted with white soap. "I have always wished to see you remove the hair from here." Nuppohwunau drew a line on his face where Gil's moustache had been.

"Why come you not in, Nuppohwunau?"

Again there was silence.

Matthew forcibly turned Gil's head back for finishing touches.

"Moody Matthew has cut my moustache all off, but I will grow it back for you before this week is out if you will dance for my harp today." Gil beguiled the Indian from reticence.

Nuppohwunau allowed his smile to seal the bargain. The expression did not change as he unleashed his concern. "My father will be saddened if all your party be not at the sweat-house. Waban hath persuaded the taupowaw much over this marriage." He winced as Matthew slapped a cooling lotion onto Gil's cheeks.

Gil checked his face in a hand mirror. "Go, Matthew, and bring young Stirling before we push off." He unbuttoned the cuffs of his nightshirt.

Matthew continued to polish the straight razor. "Think you, Master Worth, he would come with such as I?"

"Matthew!"

Matthew turned his back, knowing the persuasiveness of his master's eyes. "Frenchie and I must see to the meat."

"Damn it, Matthew. Save your cheek for privacy." Gil knew his request was unfair, but Matthew's independence grated on him. "Are you going?"

"I will go with you, sir."

Neither his servant nor his host, who still refused to enter the warmth of the house, left him any choice. Gil plunged into the black morning, trembling with cold and undiplomatic ire. His thin gown batting the new breeze, Gil stood waiting for the boy to come out of the Stirling wetu.

Israel came, dressed in traveling clothes. The two white men stood glaring at each other until Gil stuck out his hand with the small apron in it.

"Put this on, young fellow. Important folk await your presence."

"I refuse to go." Adamant, Israel's chin quivered.

"Refuse?" Gil became aware that Matthew and Nuppohwunau had caught up to him. He looked at the purpling sky and softened in his approach. "Be a good fellow and try to understand. We are guests here. Should not a guest accommodate the host in thanks for his hospitality? Even a Presbyterian is not so clean he can avoid a bath before he dresses for a wedding."

Israel did not reciprocate the humor. "Sir! I am not dressed for a wedding. I am going home when the sun is up."

"Who is on the viol then, may I ask?" Gil saw his breath frost the air. "Do not think, young man, to be self-indulgent when the feelings of so many people are at stake."

"Feelings? People? Mr. Worth! You are reputed to be intelligent. Even Father respects you, but I wonder at your involvement with these savages."

"Israel!" Gil glanced at Nuppohwunau, hoping his imperfect understanding of the language had muted this remark.

"Are we captives here? Must I partake of secret ceremonies I do not choose to share in?"

"Secret . . . ? Ah! I see. We have transported our theology to the woods. Bend a bit, sir! There is sacrifice poured into this little soiree would rival the crucifixion!"

"I know thy reputation, you curioso!" Israel sneered. "Life is all one great party to you."

"You pup! We are not here to dissect my beliefs, but to honor a union, be it in one religion or another. Do it not for your father, nor me, nor even your own self-respect, but for my poor niece who needs as good a start as can be. Do you not understand, the native people are rooted in sanctity to the very air we breathe? Show some fellowship! Leave your textbooks behind for a day."

At the word *fellowship* Nuppohwunau extended his hand to the red-haired youth.

Israel recoiled. "Wiser men than I have said it. 'There can be no fellowship between the religion of God and of the Devil!' "

Gil pushed in front of the insulted Nuppohwunau, his testy persuasion yielding to command. "You sound not like the son of J. Macmillan Stirling to me! Put this thing on and come or I shall have you dragged by that outlandish crop of hair!"

Israel squared off his bulky frame. "No torture could induce me to your wildman's rites in nakedness."

Gil doomed the boy's argument by giving his own nightshirt a pull, scattering buttons in all directions. He ripped the garment off in his vehemence, exposing himself, the wiry gold hair on his body glowing in the light of Nuppohwunau's torch. He fumbled with the other doeskin apron.

"One ties the string at back, thus, be he a man, Israel Stirling!"

Israel's resistance liquefied in shock. "Never," he whimpered.

"Strip him, Matthew. Unmarried men can just as well go without, sunna matta, Nuppohwunau?"

"Yea, Gilbert Worth! The sky will wait no longer. I shall ready my canoe."

Matthew had less trouble obeying Gil's second order of the morning. But the Stirling boy was raw of bone as he was of temper and even powerful Matthew had to work hard to disengage him from his coat.

"Blackamoor! What are ye doin'?" Ann Stirling had come.

"Good morrow, Mrs. Stirling." Gil saluted.

"Gilbert, are ye behind this horrible scuffle?"

"We are only trying to take our old Israel for a ride in a canoe!"

"But . . . the lad does no' swim!" The woman stared at Gil's attire.

"Halloah, Israel! Hiding behind the skirts of your Christian scruples when all the time you were afraid!" Gil had himself a hearty laugh, then snapped, "There are good swimmers enough here to save an hundred like you."

Israel hung his head, his freckles showing in the increasing light. "It is not that!"

The mother looked from one to the other, then settled her glance on her son. "Undress an' follow along wi' some pluck."

* * * *

A score of men were packed into the little room when the trio shed its aprons and entered. The place of honor opposite the door had been reserved for Gil. He coughed as he picked his way over to Wakwa among the patient, smoking men.

Wakwa dropped his hand onto Gil's knee in acknowledgment of his arrival, but his gaze was inward and his eyes downcast as he awaited the taupowaw's message meant for him.

Nuppohwunau settled Israel securely between himself and Dr. Mac, and the powwaw rose to lay an alder branch across the glowing stones and sprinkle it with water. As fragrant steam circulated upward, refreshing the sweating bodies, the Indian priest began to speak.

Gil sensed the priest hastening his remarks due to his and Israel's lateness. Yet the soothing sounds of the still unfamiliar Narragansett tongue fused him in comradeship with the rows of legs and torsos and muscled shoulders. He knew that Massachuseuck men had gathered in several places on both sides of the river for pesuponk, but the luminaries of the feast were assembled in Wakwa's cave. His eyes glided from Waban's round stomach to the lines framing Wuttah Mauo's mouth, to the ghostly paleness of the Scots, the perceptive languor of Awepu, and the aloof intelligence of Pequawus. His attention wavered as he descended into speculation of what this coming dawn would have held for himself if, twelve months before, he had discovered his niece in this same cave.

Next to Gil, Wakwa let his face sink into his palms, remembering Elizabeth's first visit to the sweathouse and their swim. The powwaw's voice washed over him and he absorbed the speaker's premonitions of the heavy price selfishness would exact from those who indulged in its delights. Wakwa's pensiveness did not lessen when the old man's insights subsided into silence and grunts of acquiescence came from behind puffs of sweet smoke.

Gil did not like the mood the unintelligible words had provoked. Wakwa and his father looked drained, not energized. He chaffed through the wise man's chant, impractical argumentativeness battling with his gentlemanliness, urging him to demand outright what had been said.

Almost in answer to the Englishman's unguarded expression, the powwaw drew the first sachim to himself. Finally, Waban leaned away from his whispers and translated a message for the foreigners present.

" 'Those that merely live upon the face of the earth cannot trust, nor know, nor be treated kindly by her. Those who would love the mother must be lost in her, possessed by her, buried inside of her and be reborn through her to know the sweetness of her milk. Remember, through all your days, we gather here because an English maiden is thus filled with love and trust. The best has combined with the best, and fruit has blossomed and fallen into the arms of this tribe. Elizabeth, the mother, will nourish her son, feeding all through him, and Wakwa, the father, will protect all his people, protecting Wolf-of-the-mist-He-hopes.' "

Equanimity returned. Supplied with a goal he could live with, Wakwa embraced the taupowaw.

Twenty conversing men erupted into the flush of day, the upper rim of the sun's disc piercing the only cloud in the sky.

* * * *

Elizabeth sat in the eye of the preparations, enjoying Sam Spinney's cherry inlaid rocker while Moses took his milk. She reached out to receive Sequan, who had slipped into the wetu behind Sparrow, returning from an errand to Qunneke's house.

But the child would not come close to Elizabeth today. She

had met her father's second wife many times in the hunting lodge since Noh-annoosu's birth and had treated her with shy adoration. Believing "Zabeth," as she pronounced her name, to be the swan, the shining creature her father had depicted months ago, Sequan allowed herself to be charmed by English words and the magical white hands that had produced the poppet. In the world of negligees, caps, powder, the linear order of square boxes, and Priscilla's makeshift vanity table, Sequan was less sure of herself and backed away, directly into Hanna.

Their joint discomfort and secret fear forged an instant bond between Hanna Worth and Tame Deer's daughter. They assumed Elizabeth's place in the new rocking chair and shared the thrill of Sequan's first experience of furniture.

The Indian and the English maids were drawn to the peaceful scene, watching the prettily painted child gently moving her hands over the glossy silk of Hanna's underskirt, the English lady singing a tailor's song of tippets, tea, and mice. Priscilla saw the charm of the pastel mural on Sequan's innocent roundness. Sparrow admired the symmetry of Hanna's simple coif, her cleanness, and her powder-dusted skin.

In silent self-assertion the maids interrupted Elizabeth at her recitation of a speech for the ceremony.

"Nut-annogkinum, Elizabeth?"

"Matta. No paint, Sparrow."

"Mistress Beth, will you not consider powder?"

"Priscilla!" Elizabeth laughingly examined her face in the standing mirror Gil had carted in. "Do I look ill or loathsome?"

"Close up you are charming, though a bit blue under the eyes." Hanna was up and interested. "From far away you will be nothing but a pale blur. Give just a bit more, dear. Let us fuss over you!"

Sparrow had already gone for Tame Deer.

Hanna and Qunneke met, painlessly, at the door, their mutual curiosity waylaid in their rush. They trained their concentration on Elizabeth.

Joining their individual arts, the women sought to produce a surface flawlessness to match their estimation of the bride's interior nature. After preparatory creams and powder, Priscilla tore a page off the new Spanish vermilion and rouged the bride's cheeks. Hanna darkened her lashes, then held Elizabeth's head still while Tame Deer applied a fine line of black across her lids.

"How unfair!" Elizabeth ran to the mirror, worried. "Was I not good enough before? You are turning me into bisque! How imperfect Wakwa will judge me when I must take this off!"

"Elizabeth! Apsh!" Tame Deer commanded.

"What is she saying to you?" Hanna whispered defensively.

"Sit, thou." Elizabeth answered her aunt.

"Apsh," Hanna seconded, and her niece sat.

Qunneke moved a wisp of feather dipped in red to outline the second wife's lips.

"Marvelous!" Hanna seized Qunneke's wrist. "Will you do that to me?"

It was then that they searched each other's faces, while Priscilla rouged in the outline.

Qunneke had arrived nearly ready for the brief ceremony, wrapped in a skirt of red fox and a chemise of the bodkin cloth of gold and silk thread Hanna had brought from Boston. She saw the Englishwomen in their house robes and gave a quiet order to Sparrow to dash the fire and clear away the smoke for the gowning.

The Indian women watched as Priscilla hooked up the long stays and Hanna secured the philomot hose, the rose-gray color of dead leaves, with the embroidered garters. Elizabeth stepped into thin silk slippers, philomot and silver-striped, tied with silver bows.

Tame Deer sighed as the underslip of pinked alemode was covered by the hooped petticoat, showing salmon-colored roses when light caught in the folds of the brocade.

The matching kincob stomacher fit flat and tight against Elizabeth's front, and the girl winked her appreciation to Qunneke.

Hanna settled two breadths of Palestine gauze over the petticoat for a short sheer overskirt. She motioned the women close as she proudly explained the material's gossamer striping, achieved by the hand separation of several threads from the weave at regular intervals. A single silver thread tipped the pinked edges.

"Such a ruin it will be when Noh-annoosu cries to be fed and

I am occupied with the solemnities. My front will be all stained with milk," Elizabeth said to the mirror.

Hanna was unbelieving. "Do you mean, Beth, it comes . . . without . . . any pull?"

"I think, Aunt, it makes as good a reason as any to marry first and then to bear the babe." The mother-bride was whiter than her powder.

It took Priscilla's genius for the practical to pick up the baby and hold him to Elizabeth to nurse again. Noh-annoosu's surprised mother stood helplessly cooperative.

Padding of linen and doeskin was stitched inside the bodice before they all stood back to admire their work.

"Brides of the best ton will not touch a veil," Hanna said and handed Tame Deer a set of combs and brushes.

After an hour, Elizabeth struggled up from the overturned pail where they had seated her. The white ribbons she had made were wound through her hair, braided into a narrow spiral forming a high crown at the top of her head. Qunneke secured the whole with Wakwa's silver pins.

They quietly withdrew, leaving her standing, unseeing as a stone.

* * * *

" 'Full nakedness! All joys are due to thee. . . .' " Gil burst through the doorway of the now-hushed lodge. "Dear wife, are we alone? I am drunk with the place! We shall winter here! What a breakfast we have all had at the expense of Weeping Heart's labor. Mountains of fruit and fish, sassafras tea and camaraderie!"

"Gilbert, cover yourself. Priscilla is dressing in the next room."

"Ana! How beautiful you are. What extraordinary taste you have." Gil drank in the sight of his wife in a sky blue lutestring gown splashed with watercolor primroses, violets, and daisies. "Kiss me once! Sustain me until tonight." Gil rested his fingertips on the soft silk at her bosom.

Hanna held herself away from his intoxicated embrace.

"Gil. Beth is afraid."

In the wave of panic that cut short his exuberance, instead of

Hanna's contours beneath his hands Gil saw the stones of the sweathouse that he had not overturned in his search for his niece.

Discussion was quashed as Elizabeth came through the door sideways in deference to the width of her skirt. She approached her uncle with the vial of needles he had given her the year before.

"I would wear it this day, dear Uncle. Pin it on? At last I am gowned for a wedding."

Gil secured the silver case at her breast and kissed her lips. "Fair dove! Would you walk back this day through the trees? You know I will walk with you."

"Uncle Gil, you are perfect. Thank you." She smiled palely. "If father had once told me that in regard to Annanias, would I have begun all this?"

"This is Wakwa's doing, not your father's nor . . . anyone else's." He squelched her rhetorical question.

"I like to think that. It is magical. Once you cross the pines, they close behind you. There is no going back. I am planted here. Settled. I must spread new roots. I hear a note at night plucked of air. It never fades but vibrates and sustains. Its tension is its voice. It is me! I cannot change my tune. My note is set. If it be so, well and good. Now Moses has a voice."

"You should write such things, child. Pitiful parrot I am can but recite, not make, poetry."

"No one recites as do you. Tell me some now?"

"I am late. A shame, Beth, you did not hear me a moment ago. It is only you and I can abide that bounder Donne. See how pale he makes your aunt? Father sky, as your husband would say, is beaming close to noon. Would it not be more proper if I went out there dressed?"

"No!" Elizabeth touched her throat. "No! I had made a ruff out of feathers and I have misplaced it!"

"We will find it." Hanna rushed off with her.

Not long after, Matthew came in and found Gil nearly dressed. "Master, I am sorry."

"Let it go, man. Only help me with these buckles."

Matthew closed a pair of diamond rosettes at the knees of Gil's breeches. "The barge is finally here, sir."

"You have checked all against the list?" Gil submerged his excitement in efficiency.

"Each thing is as you asked, Mr. Worth."

"The coat?"

"I have brought it to Mistress Beth's tall lord." Matthew bound Gil's hair into a tail with a black satin bow to keep it from touching his coat collar.

"Matthew, stay close to me today."

"Light and shadow, Master Worth."

"Matthew, that is better poetry than Donne's." Hanna brought her husband his cravat.

"Odd-looking thing." Gil examined the slim piece of white satin.

"Show more respect, please. That 'odd-looking thing' cost eight pounds."

"Hanna! Eight pounds for a neckpiece! An old-fashioned stock would have done as well. The French are a wretched people! Eight pound sterling? Beth could have made it for two straws!"

Hanna struggled to secure the stylish tie. "How do you rail over eight pounds for a cravat when you willingly spend thousands upon thousands to make this wedding?"

"I never rail over money, Ana. But eight pounds! Incredible!" Gil settled the tie on his ruffled shirt front. "White on white. Can't hardly see the thing. Perhaps it is for the best. In any case I will reveal to Waban the ultimate extravagance."

"Not with the cravat!" The wife brought out a rich felt hat, black with a slightly upturned brim in the style of a country gentleman. It was crowned by two great ostrich plumes, dyed green to match Gil's eyes.

"I will not! Hanna, darling. What were you thinking of? Among these people I will draw laughter. Feathers hold more meaning for them than peacock decoration."

"You are worse than Beth." Hanna froze in disappointment. "You started all this. We could simply have come and had a good time in calico! Now you choose to be seen by all these Indians like a woodsman, with your natural hair showing. Why, even the man who made your shoes wears his gray peruke in the shop!"

412

"And would your brother, Charles, have worn a wig to please the very king?"

"You dare bring him up to me today?"

"Hanna, I think you know I am talking of headgear, not in-laws." Gil sought to cool her flare-up.

The tense woman forced some control. "At least try the hat on!"

Gil obeyed, wondering what besides the strain of the wedding flurry had spoiled Hanna's mood. He studied the effect of the hat. "Well, I will carry it. Mayhap we will warm one to the other."

"You and I must try that as well." Hanna sounded sour.

Silence settled outside the house, and the couple stood unavoidably close in the semi-darkness, their misunderstanding left unsettled.

The moment broke with the sweet harmony of young men's voices singing a love song.

Priscilla flew in from the back room, a swirl of daffodil damask. "Mistress, I have forgot your rouge!"

"There is no time!" Hanna passed the glass in horror on her way toward the doorway, where Mosq now stood holding aside the matting.

But Gil pulled Hanna close before releasing her to Awepu, waiting just outside. "What need hath the rose for rouge? How I shall know thee tonight!" He kissed her with Elizabeth and the household looking on.

Hanna's blushing face caused the buoyancy of rewarded expectation in the three hundred watching people as she obeyed Awepu's guiding gesture and gracefully walked over the flowered matting toward the inner circle where the three sachimmauog waited.

Chapter 55

The day that had dawned close to freezing warmed enough for Elizabeth to leave behind the velvet whisk that would have covered her neck and shoulders. The impact of yellow autumn light flattened her vision as she stepped onto the woven carpet, waiting for Sparrow to carry Noh-annoosu to where her aunt stood. She saw selectively in the mellow brightness as the north wind spun dry leaves as high as her line of sight. Her eyes took in only Wakwa, his back to the river, his body the buffer between her and the rushing cold that tangled his long cloak of fringe up into his headdress.

She bore the walk toward him, her hand balanced on her uncle's well-tailored sleeve, hearing small sounds from the old tanning hut where Wakwa had stood blocking her exit so many months before.

There was a second of giddy independence after her uncle's swift farewell kiss as the transfer of her guardianship happened. She gave herself into Wakwa's warm hand grasp, accepting the richness and the poverty of the primal existence they would pass to their son as his legacy.

Wakwa seized both her hands, astounded at the transformation of her candid handsomeness into the fragile perfection of English style. He almost touched her necklace of white swan's feathers, the link between what he knew of her and what he saw.

Her own awe of his hunter's crown of antler points hung all around with ermine tails, the whiteness and delicacy of his doeskins lavish with the beaded history of his triumphs, and the whipping leather fringe cut as fine as tassels, dropping from his shoulders to his ankles, obscured her memories of his straightforward charity.

Gilbert Worth dropped back to his wife's side, breaking his exquisite pairing with his niece. Almost more than Elizabeth he attracted the collective eye of the assembled Massachuseuck. The sun glanced off his person and he impressed them, seemingly spun of gold, commanding an audible response to his splendor and lack of vanity.

He held his hat at the hilt of his sword, a gentleman from among American settlers, ecstatic at ceding his land back to red hands.

The sheen of his light hair, his gleaming coat and breeches of buff-colored satin, the diamond buckles topping his cream silk hose, the gold and green thread flowers embroidered onto his waistcoat of snowy larredo, belied the fear that passed through him as he listened to the blended sounds of Indianne unnontoowaonk and English.

"I told you you should have worn your hat," Hanna greeted him, studying the effect of Wakwa's headdress.

Too fascinated with the ceremony for repartee, Gil watched the couple exchange the painted reeds, symbolic of the endurance of their union. He thought Waban was genuinely tender when he placed Elizabeth and Wakwa in front of himself and the taupowaw. The headman said in Indian and in English, "Weetoomau, he marries her, carrieth the meaning, he takes her to his house to dwell . . ." and then Waban smiled, "but their dwelling is from before now and always within one another."

"Beth's won him," Gil ruminated to Hanna. "It is well we've dressed."

Elizabeth's voice rang out with Ninnuock words learned from Awepu, surprising the tribal assembly with her answer to a question from Waban.

"Waban hath seen beyond the kincob, Gil," Hanna whispered as Elizabeth repeated the vow in English for the Worths' sake.

"With glad heart I subject myself to Qunneke, the first wife of my husband. To her I shall defer in all things, like grass underfoot, and follow her counsel as doth the hare the whispers of the wind. I will labor to close the circle of our harmony, as the throstle weaveth round her nest."

Qunneke extended her hands briefly, according to form, but Elizabeth was not content with symbol. She left the path of mats, knelt, and kissed the hands. Qunneke objected, pulling the second wife up. Elizabeth caught her around the neck and rested on her breast. Qunneke could not refuse this embrace and her arms came around Charles Dowland's daughter.

"I see how the Corsican blood will defer, Hanna."

But Gil's wife ignored his goading, occupied with a private victory, kin to Elizabeth's affectionate mastery. The sister-

415

wives' fortunate affinity absorbed Hanna less than their contrasts.

The English lady felt the tall woman emanated a vigorous beauty that Elizabeth's lily grace could never duplicate. Tame Deer's black hair, wound with her own blue wedding beads, hung down in a solitary braid over a shawl of the mulberry blend of silk and wool Gil had chosen by letter through Hanna. Qunneke's arms parted this simple garment at its trim of silver orrice, and Hanna, turning her attention to Gil's face, could not blame him for the admiration he showed Wakwa's Indian wife.

She recalled how she had fought off Tame Deer's influence in Elizabeth's lodge, and now felt ashamed of the fussy tiers of silken fallals ruffling her own arms and the old-fashioned drape at the back of her gown, tossing uncontrollably away from her hooped skirt.

This pretty fabric caught Tame Deer's eye, and for the second time that day each woman looked behind the mask of the other.

There was no mistaking that when Qunneke brought Elizabeth back to Wakwa, although his expression was steady, his face was wet with tears. Gil interpreted this display above sentimentality about his wives' friendship. In fact, he pitied the Indian for the precarious bliss that was his as a result of his skill in bridging the gulf between his culture and European civilization. Wary of the effect the American colonial disdain and fear of native people would have on Wakwa's nature, Gil saw him as the man among them with the loneliest battle in his private life, no matter how full his house grew with wives and children.

But Wakwa visualized the wavering picture of his wives, Gilbert Worth, and the meadow of spectators in conjunction with the ripe beauty of the day. Sun meeting the wind stirred scent from the dry vegetation, the last vivid leaves caught in the finery they wore, aromas of roasting meat culminated private hungers and seemed the fulfillment of this season of his manhood. Like smoke, as it disappeared in air, or the point of space that vanished at the end of a deer path he had sought to touch as a boy but never did, this day satisfied him to bursting and tears came. He was exhausted with the potential and futility of his future. He foresaw people like himself and Gilbert Worth dying a natural death like the leaves, leaving the world a place of dead wood

416

and stolid evergreens. But touched by the legend of the black fox, whose name he bore, bitterness was not part of his insight.

"Nunnaumon! Muckquashim-ouwan-Noh-annoosu. Among his mother's people he shall be called Moses Bluehill!" Wakwa's voice turned Elizabeth scarlet as he owned his son.

She brought the baby to Waban and the crying child was passed from hand to hand in the crescent of sagamores.

"Nunnaumon wunnaumonuh! The son of my son!" Pequawus returned Moses to Elizabeth himself. "He hath the Dowland eye!"

The daughter-in-law had no time to defend herself. Sparrow swept the child away and Elizabeth's petticoat was crushed against Wakwa's legs as he held her close. Dancers wound a vociferous circle around the pair.

From his perspective Gil saw the couple as one form, Wakwa's headdress and tall body and Elizabeth's flaring hoop blending into the high crest and neck, full back and tail, of a swan.

"Where to begin? Where to begin?" Plant waved his artist's gear in frustration.

"Begin right there." Gil urged him through the ring of dancers with the tip of his sword.

Wakwa felt how cold Elizabeth was and broke their pose to bend and whisper, "I have the means to make thee warm. Shall we go with Waban to the place of the gifts?"

"I know you have the means, Sachim! Pray must we take Waban with us?"

Wakwa laughed, scandalized, catching the old man's attention.

"This is bewitchment, little Saunks. Never have I seen Wakwa Manunnappu throw back his head to laugh since he has been a man."

Elizabeth and Waban walked at the head of the party toward the pavilion where her handiwork had been hung.

"I am young to look at you, Elizabeth. Wakwa tells me how you are like water, turbulent but quenching. I find you a powwaw's charm, sent to keep me sachim for an hundred more winters!"

He was so approachable Elizabeth slipped her arm through his and marveled that he was Wakwa's uncle and not his father.

The place was turned into a bazaar. Families of the tribe thronged into the open-air hall, studying and touching Elizabeth's unique work.

Waban was impressed by the quilt she had made his household, its motif of setting suns, orange, green, purple, and red satin, stuffed with down and backed with soft melton.

A crowd grew around her gift to Wakwa's father, the silver webbing of tree shadows on snow. So flattered he refused to speak, Pequawus listened to Dr. Mac describe the hauling of Elizabeth's treadle wheel down the deerpath for the spinning of the thread. Elizabeth revealed the significance of the appliqué of satin branches to the tall grayed man, and for the moment he succumbed to her sincerity as he saw his place in her mind between her own father and her son.

He touched her cheek. "I begin to see what my son found and desired not to lose. I would not call thee 'Kayaskwa' as doth he, but 'Mamunappeht,' Spider-who-weaveth-silver-webs." Pequawus ran his hand across the metallic netting.

"Shan't I ever wind one about you?" Elizabeth was stubborn.

"And so she looks this day, thin as a thread, me Bonnie!" Dr. Mac roughly held her to him in grandfatherly embrace.

She fingered his new neckcloth trimmed in purple galloon, taking his rich dress for her wedding as a compliment to Wakwa. "Thank you, dear Dr. Mac. Where is Israel today? I want to thank him for coming."

"About. About. Tha' lad's always dull at a party. Too young for the social life. Am I right, Sagamore?"

Stirling and Pequawus launched into a discussion of sons as Elizabeth, handicapped by her four-foot hoop in the packed hall, began the effort of looking for Israel.

She turned onto the sight of Wakwa and a beautiful Massachuseuck woman, apparently conversing about the coat with the wolf sleeves. She watched his lovely teeth show with his smiles and pushed back the image of them grinding up the raw deermeat the night she had finished sewing the coat. Unwillingly, she learned much about his expansive nature, watching his enjoyment of the crowd.

"That is Panther Eye, white Saunks!" Wuttah Mauo grinned and disappeared among the milling guests.

The youngest sachim broke away from his ward and immediately a path cleared for him. There was humor in his eyes when he found himself face to face with Elizabeth.

"Nummittamus. My wife." He weighed her arms down with the coat he had ordered from Thomas Kirke.

Elizabeth gazed at the mass of fur. "Wakwa!"

The generous circular coat, which he put on her himself, was not wide enough for the circumference of her skirts and it hung behind in a luxuriant black train. He turned up the silk-lined hood and Elizabeth buried her hands in the sheen of the fur bordering her face.

The uncomplimentary tone of Wuttah Mauo's expression, "white Saunks," returned to her, and the English girl declined to touch the gorgeous gift further in front of the people. She smiled her gratitude to her husband, thinking of something appropriate to say. But she rebelled at enforced composure and hugged the man. "Oh, come! I have waited so long to see you wear the coat I made for you!"

Wakwa and Elizabeth stayed together until the celebration moved from the pavilion, and Worth's fruit wine was broken out, and everyone of every age sat drinking and chatting under the sky.

＊＊＊＊

Gil felt Beth's absence from the area reserved for his household and the winnaytue, the men of estimation, and their families. He very much wanted her in her old place, and for the first time he realized she could be next to him only as a visitor. She had been absorbed into the Massachuseuck family, and Gil felt the foreigner. His deserted look was answered by Sequan.

"Zabeth! Zabeth! Zabeth kah Qunneke!" The child pointed to her mother and Elizabeth making their way to the Worths' wetu.

"Gilbert, they are after the long glass to admire themselves." Wakwa looked lovingly at the pair in coat and cape.

But pain had begun in Gil, and he turned away from the sight of Wakwa's wives without comment. "Tell the people the giving is not over. All that good food must wait, nephew." He left Wakwa and went to find his houseman.

"Now, Matthew, and quietly. And where in hell is Plant?"

"Cooking." The black man pointed to the artist, who was seeking out Panther Eye for a portrait.

Gil slapped Grandee's quarters and Matthew rode out of camp.

In the second hour of the special afternoon the people sat patiently on the plain, adjusting to a day of stretched traditions as delicately as they had handled Elizabeth's stitchery.

By the time Panther Eye's features had begun to take shape in red chalk, Matthew's turban could be seen inching over the line of the western palisade. The pounding that rose up to the high meadow was no longer from the hooves of one horse. The houseman let out a singsong call and the crowd stood, craning to see the approaching spectacle.

Matthew guided a line of horses by a lead of woven ribbons and paced their advance with the flimsy cords from a gallop at the top of the hill to a walk as they neared the populated plain.

Hanna and Wakwa stared together at the magnificent animals prancing at the edge of the camp. Gil brushed by on his way to present the horses, and Hanna said, looking at the back of his stylish coat, "That is a hopeless poet, Silent Fox!"

They were faced by a quintet of British hunters, blended with alchemist's fervor by Thomas Kirke. Bypassing hot Arabian blood, he had developed larger-boned, steady-tempered horses, Celtic and Norwegian stock, suited for rough weather and terrain. Kirke had created not workhorses but tall, powerful hunters with a tinge of the middle ages showing in their voluminous manes and tails.

Gil cut the ribbon wedding the lead pair and walked them to Wakwa and Elizabeth. "One black and one chestnut, ordered to match your hair."

"It is too much, Nissese!" Wakwa tested the black, running his hands over the neck and immense chest and through the mane that fell from poll to forearm. Without leverage, he pulled himself onto the stallion's bare back and spun with the rearing horse. He howled his delight, whipped by mane and fringe and fur, enjoying a horse that could fittingly bear his weight and stature.

Elizabeth fondled the lowered muzzle of her filly. "She is sweet, Uncle Gil."

420

"Yea, little Beth, a mountain of sugar candy. It will take you half the day to comb her tail."

Waban thought this was an unusual white man. He did not impose useless trinkets on them but had provided them a flexible livelihood. Worth had turned crass gold into flight from enemies, power in peaceful times.

Waban made a reverential nod in accepting two duns for himself and Qunneke. "You give new life to the tribe, Gilbert Worth. You, too, are a father."

Flushed from Waban's compliment, Gil made his way toward Wuttah Mauo.

The man was standing apart, watching the progression of the gift, hoping that the dazzling white stallion would be his. He began to count imagined profits from breeding and selling its offspring. His need to help Prue had been handsomely answered.

"You are extravagant, English Uncle!" His voice was a mixture of relief and embarrassment.

"Beyond your wildest dreams, my disconsolate friend." The unsuspecting Gil spoke low, leading the cream-colored horse to Waban's first son. "This horse only shall ne'er breed. I paid good gold to have him gelded in Dublin before the voyage."

"Gelded!" Weeping Heart went gray.

"But fast he can run, and far. I lay odds you will need him."

Disappointed laughter carved deeper lines into Wuttah Mauo's face. "Nut-jishantam! I hate you, Gilbert Worth! For this spite you will pay and pay again!"

"If Silent Fox were angry with me, I would be afraid. See you keep the account between us straight, Weeping Heart. By your receiving this gift we might teach each other something valuable, your opinion of the future being so low."

To answer the people's demand, Wuttah Mauo joined Wakwa in a race, his mind working as the horses opened up, their tails fanning out behind like evening cloaks.

Awepu stood next to Gil, watching. "I do not feel Charles Dowland at the feast."

"This is not his kind of affair," Gil said archly. "Let our brother rest, Awepu. He will return in more sober times to watch over his daughter."

"Join us, Gilbert. Your speech grows pretty."

"A tempting invitation. But I would be troublesome to you. Awepu? You like my bay?"

"Oo, Gilbert. He is more good a horse, I think, than all these together."

"Grandee's to be a papa come planting time. The foal is yours."

Wuttah Mauo's shouting interrupted Awepu's astounded thanks.

"He said my name, Awepu!" Gil was puzzled.

"Nux. He says you wish to address the people. Do you?"

"I?"

"He says you wish to tell them what you think of him and them and their customs."

"Not today!"

"Gilbert?"

"Damned clever." Gil gathered himself. "He knows I am not that sort. Dowland was the man with a homily at the ready."

"They want you to talk to them. They sit." Awepu went for Matthew.

Committed, Gil drew out his handkerchief from a kid-lined pocket and blotted his face.

Wakwa slid from his horse and made his way to Gil. "Go gently, Gilbert Worth. I do not know why my cousin has said this. But thy words will nourish the people like honey, whatever thou shalt say."

"I depend on thee, Silent Fox, to translate my ramblings into something memorable for all these good souls."

They walked together up a rise to where Matthew waited with Gil's horse.

"Well done, my man." Gil placed his thin black shoe in Matthew's waiting hands, glad to mount his horse on strategically high ground.

Plant wrested the plumed hat from Hanna. "Tilt it, Monsieur, à droite!"

Gil rode off alone, a little sick in his stomach. He urged Grandee to climb a gray shelf of granite. "This is too perfect, old boy! Let us hope Louis Plant is worth his money, and watching now!"

Gil searched his library shelves in his mind, desperate for an

422

adequate quote, unable to phrase anything original. Wakwa stationed himself at the rear of the crowd. When Gil raised his eyes to the faces of the Ninnuock, Wakwa was in his line of sight and Gil filled with confidence.

"Sachimmauog! Netompauog! Many thousands of years ago, a great man of my race talked of a glorious age in his land called Greece. . . ."

The translation flowed over the expectant men and women, their spokesman's familiar voice giving veracity to a new story from the beautiful stranger before them.

"My brother, Hesiod, talked of times that once did exist for white men, as now and always before they have existed for you! His memory of his people describes what I see before me today:

'They lived as if they were gods,
Their hearts free from all sorrow. . . .
When they died it was as if they fell asleep. . . .
The fruitful grainland yielded its harvest to them
of its own accord
While they, at their pleasure
Quietly looked after their works, in the midst of
good things. . . .' "

A rustle of approval passed through the tribe and Gil exposed his hair to the sun and walked his horse to where he had started. Hands reached up to touch him and he patted the bolder ones that clung to his foot or leg.

He dismounted and returned the hat to Hanna. "I trust we made good use of one another. It for a perch, I for a think cap?"

Wakwa rode up. "Uncle, I did not change one word. If my league against the English is not agreed to this winter, you have my promise Elizabeth and I leave for Virginia." The men embraced while the crowd dispersed to serve the food. "But if we go not to eat, I fear my bride will be a widow."

Wuttah Mauo pushed them apart. "And have you, Gilbert Worth, like the sorcerer you are, also trained the new horses to stay out of the corn?"

"Alas, Weeping Heart, they are English beasts, by nature poking their noses everywhere at the most inconvenient times."

Wuttah Mauo stalked away, not feeling the cold gust that

423

whipped the silk shirt Elizabeth had made him. Gil trembled at his own boldness, taking pleasure in his antagonism.

"What comes between you two now?" Wakwa trotted after his cousin to conciliate.

* * * *

While groups reclined about fires enjoying trays of meat and fruit, sweet sauces and succotash, Israel Stirling sulked behind his father's round house. All he had seen from the dawn pesuponk through the wedding ceremony and Gilbert Worth's address left him confused about himself. Israel tended his trumpet, unable to solve his own troubles.

No one was prepared for its blast as he let it peal a Purcell sonata from his hidden place. It was the loudest apology he could make, and Israel blew, blinded by his effort, aching to redeem his self-assurance. Unconscious of the moment when the wedding guests discovered him, he stood puzzled what to do with the trumpetless adagio. He saw his father and Gilbert Worth running for their instruments, gulping the last of their dinner, and he experienced the sweetness of ensemble as they joined in under his solo.

But it was Israel's trumpet that fired the senses of the listeners as it expanded and continued and pushed out the last unrelenting, elongated note of the ending, causing the shout, "Anue! Anue!" as the people craved for more of the sound that reluctantly sailed away.

Music never stopped on this day which had evolved with the complexity of a fugue. Divergent faces and costumes played in counterpoint to the varied foods of the native and colonial culture and diffused, one into the other, like the pink sherbet melting in the sun. It was what a wedding should be.

And for Gilbert Worth the dulcet sounds of each instrument he played were the wringing-out of each hope and aspiration that had led him there. He peeled off his confining coat and led a willing quartet in gentle chaconne and minuet, fascinating his large audience with the plucking of his fingers on the thirty-six shining wire strings of his little harp.

The doctor's virtuosity acquired in Gil's sunny sitting room, Israel's grim determination to meet any challenge the connoisseur set, and Wakwa's obliging performance of his simplified parts arranged to suit the measure of his technique, drew all the hundreds who watched into the baroque.

The French tunes, the Viennese, courtly Telemann, and Leipzig Bach distilled into Vivaldi's G Major Concerto.

And then, like the unfurling of a banner of silk on a breeze, Nuppohwunau started to dance. This man, whose name meant He-who-hath-wings, was two bodies, his feet digging the music's primitive cadence into the dirt, while his torso and arms moved with the Italian melody.

Gil stood with his lute and played the allegro directly to him, and Hanna and the People, sensing the need for bass support, pounded the rhythm into willing palms.

And with the clapping, and the strings and the dancer's moving feet, there came a minute of community in the New England sun that Louis Plant was helpless to reproduce.

Such satisfactions surrounded each activity of the day, mellowing even the Ninnuock judgment of the fascinating impropriety of mixed dancing when Waban lifted this taboo.

Gilbert Worth and Hanna smiled fully at one another, poised under scrutiny as they moved together in delicate flirtatious gesture in their buff and blue clothing, like the sand meeting the sea. And the afternoon waned.

＊＊＊＊

"Husband, I am quite satisfied where I am!" Elizabeth objected as Wakwa ushered her into his house. "Wherefore must I leave my own party? I was listening! Does it not set a flame in here when you listen to Mac's flute far away in the dusk?"

"It is most beautiful, but you must come."

"Must?"

Wakwa drew the curtain closed. "Kayaskwa, we are expected to be alone for now."

"I have fallen out of the habit of doing what is expected."

"The young men will come to sing. I will turn them away with wampum. They will return to sing more, and I will fill their hands again. And so the custom goes."

"Custom, custom! I was deep in conversation with Meadow-in-the-night. Talking of quilts and such with her and Awepu.

She wishes to learn! Mayhap weave! It has been so long since I have done such things with a friend! Why must I come when you call and stay closed in here? Who expects us to be alone? Root silliness! We have a child, twelve pounds, to bear witness we have been alone before this!"

Wakwa sat. "Kayaskwa, I never thought to obey this small and lovely rule twice in my life." He defeated her.

The old struggle between duty and desire deepened her voice.

"It is ill-omened I should make a quarrel my first minute in your house."

"You are tired. See. See what I have built for thee!" He pulled her toward the new section of his house.

The great auxiliary room was shaped into an ellipse, its fire at its heart. Her baskets from the hunting lodge were stacked in copious disorder, and new mats painted white, blue, and brown lined the walls. On her low bed, transported from the forest, was Qunneke's welcoming gift, a slender beaverskin dress, tanned black, painted with bright concentric circles on the right side.

"Qunneke sees thee as my sun." Wakwa hung back, watching Elizabeth discover her surprises.

Against the arced west wall, under a flap open to the early stars, Elizabeth found a new quilting frame, his lover's gift to her. The four flat poles of maple wood were carved with foxes and birds and rubbed to a satin smoothness for the French calicoes and India stuffs she delighted in. They were made to fit square at the corners, drilled at intervals with notches so that as she turned the poles in, progressing toward the center of her work, the frame would stay square, manageable by one person.

"Art ready then, to live with me, nummittamus? Remove this." Wakwa searched the back of Elizabeth's gown, in vain, for fastenings.

"My Fox, how it will break my heart to leave here when we move to the valley for the winter. It is a place out of dreams!" She apologized with a kiss.

"Why should you leave your house behind, little wife? It will be carried and remade in an afternoon." He watched her unwind the ties at the front of her bodice and undo its tiny points.

For the first time he saw a woman in stays. He winced for her as his large hands struggled to unclose the hooks and eyes.

"It will be far easier to break and remake our house than

426

undress thee out of these! How did you smile all the day, so enclosed?"

Air slid through his teeth when he saw the red indentations in her flesh made by the whalebone. He massaged the tender skin and his hands strayed from her ribs to her breasts.

"Take the bottom away. I cannot come near!"

"That, my Sachim, may just be the purpose of the hoop."

"The English!"

A chorus of male voices struck up, and her hands closed on his and stilled them.

Wakwa leaned on a leather trunk and watched her lift the overskirt of gauze above her head. She collapsed the petticoat with one pull of a ribbon.

"The English!" She grinned at him.

He held her fragile shoe, now torn at the instep, ignoring the summons from outside. Wooden rattles shook angrily, but the man was not disturbed. It was the slight laughter of the singers that pulled him away from her.

When Wakwa appeared against the light of his own fire, respectful silence fell, but as soon as the bribe was paid the tease began again. It was louder than before.

"Wait. I want to see!" Wakwa called, forced back to the door, anxious to reach Elizabeth before she dressed in the skins.

Three times he bought off the marriage choir. Then he threatened, with good humor, to lay a fine on them if they did not search out another groom to bother. He turned, too late. His young wife was dressed.

They rested together on her bed while Wakwa painstakingly pulled the silver pins from her hair.

* * * *

The wind, blowing all day from the north, had turned late autumn mildness into the dampness before rain. Stars were covered over in the quiet moments as dusk broke into dark, and the otan cleared away the remains of one celebration and lit fires for the harvest feast. Elizabeth Dowland sat with Wakwa and Qunneke in the sachimmaacommock.

The husband took a hand of each wife. "Cowwetuck. Let us sleep."

Elizabeth touched Qunneke on her shoulder in parting and

fled toward her part of the house, pausing at the passageway. "I should not have let the maids off for the evening." She smiled. "Moses is fretting." Then shyly, "Take time together."

The child, Sequan, battled sleep, lulled by her parents' conversation, disturbed by Elizabeth's look as she turned into her chamber. The little girl hid her face against the pillow Elizabeth had made for her and wondered if someday there would be another baby and a third wife to keep it.

The laughter and rumble of the River Peoples congregating for the next day's Taquonk feast pressed against the tired family.

"I wish it were quieter for Elizabeth's sake." Qunneke gave in to a yawn. "She is unfamiliar with the sounds of so many."

"The noise is to her good, dear wife. She will think of it instead of more troublesome things." Wakwa was concerned more about Tame Deer's feelings with Elizabeth in the house. "Have you any other wish?"

"Go in to her. She is waiting."

"I think I am unwanted! I have no place to put my mat! Each of you bids me stay with the other!" Wakwa meant nothing by his light remark.

But Qunneke moved aside, shamed. Sequan scurried away to join Elizabeth as her father drew Tame Deer near again.

"Wakwa, you must be with her on your wedding night."

"It is a wedding for us three!" And Wakwa's resolve to refrain from seeking out Tame Deer drifted out of the house with the smoke.

"The wishes of a girl I have, yet do not have."

"You grow better?" Wakwa gave her time, stroking the skin of her face, her throat, her breasts, her arms and legs, anyplace untouched by the shield of her hair.

"Soon you are going away. . . . Oh, Wakwa! I should be round with your second son when you return."

"I do not need that of you!"

And without stop, Tame Deer shook her head, denying the man access to her confusion.

The first drops of rain marked their pattern on the roof as Wakwa sat with his fingers around her ankle, as unwilling to break this thin connection as his Indian wife was unable to accept a stronger one.

Qunneke looked around at the sound of Gilbert Worth's voice as he passed by in the increasing rain.

"Good, our Uncle Gilbert in buckskin, playing like a youth." Wakwa caught her eyes.

But Moses cried aloud again, overwrought from his day of being fondled by too many hands. Tame Deer ran to relieve the work of the white wife.

"My poor Wakwa," Qunneke consoled as she came back to him with his baby in her arms. "Elizabeth is asleep."

He went and saw his bride, her arm wound around Sequan like a child with a doll, her young face contorting at the shouts from the center of camp. He left for a solitary ride on his new horse.

As Wakwa had assured Qunneke, the boisterous party did not delay Elizabeth's sleep. She closed her eyes, remembering the brave meeting of cultures during the day, and waited for Wakwa. Sequan filled her arms instead.

Loud sounds and the unexpected sweep of rain dissolved for dozing Elizabeth into dreams of a misted morning. As she sank into slumber, outside sounds became forest birds shrieking with jungle shrillness, suffocating the sound of two paddles on the river. Elizabeth navigated at the front of the canoe, Wakwa supplying power from behind. Tame Deer sat between them, Wolf-of-the-mist on her back, Sequan snuggled between her knees.

Silver and dark green grew into a landscape. They were, the household of three and the two children, safe from eyes, from tongues and law. The narrow boat slipped past a tease of whitewater and a cleavage in the tall bank grass displaying a pearly meadow where Thomas Kirke's horses grazed.

The whir of an emerald drake's wing blurred the sound of the first arrow splitting through the grass into the flesh of Wakwa's left shoulder. The suddenness of red spilling and his shout brought the wives' horrified eyes around. His paddle raced backward on the current from where he dropped it, as he rose, fighting shock, looking for his enemy.

Unaided, Elizabeth brought them to the bank. She raced across moist grass, her bare feet remaining dry, leaving behind the moans of Qunneke, huddled over Silent Fox.

429

"Brun!" She sang for her filly, and the horse made a low reverence, lying in the grass like a trained Lipizzaner inviting her to mount.

Armed with nothing but hatred of the unknown attacker, Elizabeth stopped in a grayed thicket seeking a direction. And in the raucous patter of the birds, the slide of wet leaves against one another, and her own fierce breath, Elizabeth heard the hiss of him.

On his belly, in the slender reeds on the western bank, fixing another arrow against his bowstring, Annanias lay, chiding himself for missing Wakwa's heart. This fatter, healthier Annanias filled Elizabeth with fear, but Brun's forelegs extended like the neck of Worth's music stand, and the distance between the assassin and the wife closed in a step.

Hudson gazed with cordiality, admiring her body's outline in her trousers and fine shirt. His cherubic smile took up all her vision. From his lips, which separated without stiffness, as if he would say mild things, came softly voiced bitter reproach.

> " 'I know your rising and sitting,
>   your going and coming,
>   and your raging against me.' "

Annanias kissed her hand. His touch was clammy death and the bride pulled away from his eccentric gesture. The black-coated man seized her wrists, forced her by her arms to keep her face down beside his, and interspersed kisses with the Biblical phrases that bloated him.

> " 'Because you have raged against me
>   and your arrogance has come to my ears,
> Therefore I will put my hook into your nose,
>   and my bridle to your lips,
> And I will cause you to return by the way
>   by which you came. . . .' "

"Wherefrom do you learn to shoot with arrows!" Beth's mouth formed a challenge but there was no sound.

Annanias turned and let an arrow fly. It struck something soft.

"Ah! Beth!" Annanias' smile was truly content.

430

Elizabeth slapped his mouth. Her horse, one with her body, kicked out.

Annanias doubled up, twisting his face around, showing her she had hurt him. But on the plane of his face Elizabeth saw Wakwa's wound streaming, and she laughed at Hudson's distress.

The horse reared and sent an unshod hoof glancing off Annanias' temple.

" 'I will cause you to return,' " Hudson insisted, nursing his head, " 'by the way by which you came.' "

The horse Gilbert Worth had supplied to ease her burdens kicked as Elizabeth answered Annanias. Proudly she pulled Isaiah, her favorite prophet, from disuse.

" 'Woe to you, despoiler, though you have not been
despoiled!' "

Annanias was kicked over onto his back.

" 'When you have made an end of despoiling,
you will be despoiled!' "

Annanias' face was without shape. And the filly pounded and stamped and broke what was base and strangulating in the life that Elizabeth had left.

To see his conquered corpse was spring water in July. Inside himself, below his heart, at the center of his body, the minister must have known guilt to submit so tamely. Yet his obsessive grasping did not cease until his crushed hand lay at his side.

Elizabeth rode out of the dream into darkness and silence.

She was jostled by Sequan curling tighter into her wool blanket, and she awoke, displaced in the new room. Half her wedding night had slipped underneath her fears. She felt moving air about her and was still excited from her vision but turned by habit to check her child.

"Moses!" She searched Noh-annoosu's empty cradle in panic.

"Elizabeth!" Wakwa's unexpected voice brought sweat to her face.

"Qunneke has him." Wakwa signaled her from his couch of pillows to come to sit with him.

"To wake and find him gone!" Her dream blacked out and she

431

surrounded Wakwa with her arms. "I feel as if I have slept for days! Why do you sit so far away and not lie down to rest?"

"Strange events, weddings. The guests feast and dance like swans at a mating, and we can hardly move."

"Our wedding makes much to ponder, Fox."

"Sigh not!" His caress was stiff. "It is done. Wilt rub my back?"

When her warm touch was withheld, Wakwa twisted around and took her face between two fingers. "Muddy water, your eyes. What is it, Elizabeth? Are you afraid to be here with Qunneke?"

"I am afraid of something."

"You do not like my going north?"

"It is not just that. I do not like your going with things unsettled here with Annanias."

Hudson's name was never mentioned between them, and Wakwa pulled away, surprised.

"Your uncle and I are watching him."

"I know that. But tonight I feel him all around me."

"Elizabeth! I am here."

"In this you and Uncle Gil treat me like a child. You hide his doings from me, when I should help myself. I think I should go to him and make him go away."

"Aquie. Enough."

"But Wakwa, is it not best? It will be trouble enough for me to go back among English folk when we are in Virginia."

"If we go to Virginia!"

"Wherever we are, have you thought that he might follow me? Sue me for breach of contract? You would have to study quickly to win that case for me. Today's solemnities, my love, are no marriage anywhere but in the woods."

Wakwa spoke softly. "And do you think, Elizabeth, the Snake still wishes you, knowing to whom you give your love?"

"I believe had I a skin of scales and spines for hair, and Beelzebub for a lover, he would take me back. . . ." And the pictures from her dream returned and she held onto Wakwa. "He would take me back by the way by which I came!" Hudson's words became her own as recollection grew stronger.

"My wife!" Wakwa gathered her hair away from her moist forehead. "Still he haunts thee?"

432

"I see myself killing him."

"Kayaskwa! How you make me worry when you grow so strong like a hunted animal! Be patient." A sound came into his throat and he covered her trembling mouth with tiny kisses. "Summer is not so far away. Give him time to keep his bargain. We will outlast his vengeance together."

"And if he is not gone by then? You will let me settle it?"

"We will settle it together. Ah! Woman!" Wakwa groaned with satisfaction then as she laid him gently down and began to massage his back. "Spend not thy time in worry over him. You must help Tame Deer while I am gone."

"I will work hard for her." Elizabeth sat astride his buttocks and leaned her weight against the tension in his shoulders, not knowing why she was so relieved to find his skin unmarked.

"Qunneke needs other help than that. She needs your guidance."

"It is I must come under her wing! Feeling unwise as I do tonight, what shall I teach Tame Deer?" Elizabeth ceased rubbing and sat quietly beside him while he tried to frame an answer.

Finally, his voice tense and embarrassed, he revealed, "She is holding Moses now. Why? But tonight she talked of another child to me."

"Wakwa!" Elizabeth breathed fast and her smile came and went as she saw the circle of their friendship closing its trinity of parts. At that moment she felt how much easier it was to give out hate than love, and she put aside thoughts of Sweetwood and caused herself to say out of her will, "I am glad."

"Be not glad. Ever it is only talk." He hid his face against a hunched shoulder, warding off the pain of memory. "Without meaning it, she leads me. I follow . . . and die a little each time she turns cold." His eyes moved to Sequan, the flower of his early married hopes, and he despaired for her mother. "I cannot move that woman."

Elizabeth began to knead his muscles again, not thinking of herself.

"Nor," came his muffled voice, "will I be brought to stud, like one of your uncle's horses, every four years! Elizabeth, she and I must fall apart when I return if she cannot change before." He watched the child he was so loath to lose. "Teach her, words or no. Bind up this house, little Kayaskwa!"

She worked over him for a while, empowered by his bidding to influence their home for good. With capable fingers she untwisted the tautness built by the growing complexity of their life.

It was at last the moment to embrace her fate, not slave-like, but with decisive liberty. The man was leaving for an unspecified time and she must survive his absence. Her removal from her natural surroundings, her relationship with the children and Tame Deer, the submergence of the primacy of herself, built heat into her massage.

There was no need to vie with him as she rubbed in rhythm with her thoughts. Her being did not require victories over his dominance, but reciprocation of strength. Just as the earth changed color under the varied light from the sky, she must respond to the needs that poured from him to her.

And the shadow of her bride-weed fell away like an outgrown skin. She was determined not to shield herself from her troubles but to receive them and to allow experience to softly configure her personality, just as the dust covered the stones.

"Sepsish!" he pleaded.

She lay down beside the man as he had asked. They slept next to Sequan, three of them together.

At the beginning of day she awoke with his hand on her breast. She had forgotten Sequan's presence and, half dreaming, settled on Silent Fox with the delicacy of down. They kissed, bodies humid, even in the fireless chill. Her feet warmed the soles of his own. And enfolded, as his long legs came around her, she kissed the beauty of the concave arc joining his neck and shoulder.

"Sequan!" Her eyes widened.

The child unraveled herself from her blanket.

"She was asleep!" Wakwa moaned and heedlessly slid into the body of his wife.

Sequan ventured a fresh morning smile, asking admittance to their closeness.

Not knowing what else to do, Elizabeth wrapped her arm around her husband's daughter and kept her close against them both.

434

Wakwa's enforced stillness brought a sweet taste to his mouth, and he whispered, "Go to baby Moses, Sequan!"

"Moses!" The conscientious girl padded into the other room.

Alone, Wakwa hurried against the largeness of Elizabeth's milk-filled breasts.

"Moses sleeps!" The girl was back.

"Mauataunamoke!"

Sequan obeyed with alacrity, proud that her father would trust her to throw sticks into the faded fire.

"She will see!" Elizabeth buried a languid giggle against Wakwa's breast.

He pulled their robe up over her shoulders. "There is nothing to see." And the man began to search out the zenith of his love for his wife.

And there was nothing to see. Filled with purpose, Elizabeth restrained the man, pressing her hands against his torso to stay his aggression, lifting from him responsibility for their culmination. It was with a few slow and tender circles of her hips she informed Wakwa that he was unguardedly loved.

And still they lay as his body rained appreciation into hers. She moved down onto the mat, fitting against his side, invisible except for the small white round of her shoulder.

"Zabeth?" the child asked after her.

The happy man rolled his eyes to the light spot at his left.

Then the daughter began a game with the second mother, peeping over the wall the man made between them, until a summons came from Tame Deer.

Alone again, Wakwa hovered over this wife, then bent to her with his kiss.

"Nosh!" Sequan dashed back. "The headman of the . . . the . . ."

"Oh!" he groaned. "The Nipmuc is here!" And he laughed in glorious vexation from work and love.

Elizabeth caught her moccasins from him and they bundled into thick rugs and escaped through the back door to go to wash. They screamed from cold and woke their neighbors.

The two figures hurried toward the stream, past twined roots as the swans from Great Pond departed for the south on the eddy-wind in such numbers they blackened the sky.

But Elizabeth ran the straight path clearer in vision than she had been since the day she left Sweetwood behind.

She trusted in the value of this marriage, this family, as firmly as she believed in the return of the swans and spring.

Bibliographical Note

Among the many materials I have consulted to substantiate historical detail, the most supportive were the following:

A Key into the Language of America, by Roger Williams, 1643, Fifth Edition, 1936.

Natick Dictionary, by James Hammond Trumbull, 1903.

Mourt's Relation, Journal of the Pilgrims at Plymouth, 1622.

Salt Rivers of the Massachusetts Shore, by Henry F. Howe, 1951.

The Harp, by Roslyn Rensch, 1950.

Cottage Economy, by William Cobbett, 1833.

The Farmer's Instructer (sic), Volumes I and II, by J. Bull Esq., 1859.

New Voyages to North America, by Baron de Lahontan, 1703.

The New Indians, by Stan Steiner, 1968.

The Indian and the White Man, edited by Wilcomb E. Washburn, 1964.

John Long's Voyages and Travels, 1768–1788, edited by Milo M. Quaife, 1922.

Colonial Times on Buzzards Bay, by W. R. Bliss, 1888.

Who's the Savage, by David R. Wrone and Russell S. Nelson, Jr., 1973.

"It seemed to them" (nineteenth-century European philologists) "impossible that languages so perfect in their systems and so carefully precise in their adaptations of those systems could maintain their integrity among tribes of savages who had no system of writing."

—Edward Everett Hale, 1901
from the Introduction to the *Natick Dictionary*

Glossary

All native American words used in this book are of Algonquian stock, represented mainly in the Narragansett dialect. All spellings are taken from *A Key into the Languages of America,* by Roger Williams, 1643, and *Natick Dictionary,* by James Hammond Trumbull, 1903, using English orthography, approximating actual Indian pronunciation. The asterisk marks proto-Algonquian words found in *Contributions to Anthropology, Linguistics I,* National Museum of Canada, Bulletin 214, Series No. 78, Ottawa, 1967.

ahtomp. bow
annóosu. hope
ánue. more
apsh. sit thou
aquíe. leave off
asco wequassunnúmmis. good morrow
askuttaaquompsìn. how do you
askùg. a snake
asnpaumpmaûntam. I am very well

438

aspaumpmáuntam commíttamus. how doth your wife
awêpu. a calm

cowàmmaunsh. I love you
cowaúnkamish. my service to thee
cowequetúmmus. I beseech you
cowwêtuck. let us sleep
cuquénamish. I pray your favor

enàtch kéên anawáyean. thy will shall be law

hawúnshech. farewell

Indianne unnontoowaonk. the Indian language

kah. and
Kautántowwìt. the great southwest god
*kayaskwa. the herring gull
keén. you
kenaumon. thy son
kíhtuckquaw. a virgin marriageable
kusseh. behold

mamunappeht. spider
Manìt. God
Manitto. God
Manittóo. "A God!" one who excels in wisdom, strength, valor, God-
     filled
Manittówock. gods, superior beings
mannotaúbana. embroidered hangings
manunnappu. he remains quiet or patient, he sits patiently
Massachusêuck. a small Nation or tribe in Massachusetts
matta. no, not
máttapsh. sit
mauataúnamoke. mend the fire
mauataunamútta. let us mend the fire
mâuo. weep, cry, bewail
miâwene. a meeting
míchachunk. the soul

micúckaskeete-nokannáwi. meadow-in-the-night

mockussínchass. shoes

mosq. the bear

muckquashím. wolf

nanwunoodsquaosue mittamwossis. a whorish woman

nasuck. my husband

neechau. she is in labor

neèn. I

neen-kuttánnum-ous. I will help you

neesintuh. lie thou with me

neesneéchick. twenty

neesneéchick nab naquìt. twenty-one

neetu. he is born

netasûog. cattle

netompaûog. my friends

nétop. friend

nickómmo. a feast

Ninnuock. the People; the natives of America

Nipmuc. a tribe from southern New England

nissesè. my uncle

noh. he; she; him; her

nókace. my mother

nonantum. I give blessing

nosénemuck. he is my son-in-law

nòsh. my father

nowaûtam. I understand

npunnowwáumen. I must go to my traps

nummíttamus. my wife

nunnaumon. my son

nunnaumon wunnaumonuh. my son's son

núnnowa. harvest time

nuppohwunau. he-who-hath-wings

nutahtomp. my bow

nut-annogkinum. I paint

nut-jishantam. I hate you

nutonkqs. kinswoman

nux. yea; yes

okásu. a mother
okummes. aunt
oô. yes
osacóntuck. a haddock-like fish
otàn. a town
ouwán. mist

papoòs. an infant
paukúnnawaw. a bear
péisses. a small child
peeyàush. come hither
péquawus. a gray fox
pésuponk. a sweat hut
pigsuck. swine
powwáw. a priest; holy man
puttuckquapuonk. a gambling arbor

qunnèke. a doe

sáchim. "he who has mastery"; one who governs
sachimmaacómmock. large house of a headman
sâchimmauog. leaders; governors
sachimaûonk. a governed place
saunks. wife of the headman
sepsish. lie down
séquan. the spring
sohquttahhash. boiled kernels of corn
Squáuanit. the women's god
squàws. a woman
sukauhock. black shell money
sunna matta. is it not so
sunnúckhig. a falling trap
sun woh kuppeegwhitteamwoo. will you be shaved

tamóccon. a flood
taquònk. fall of leaf, autumn
taubot mequaun namêan. I thank you for your kind remembrance
taúpowaw. a wise speaker
tawhitch. why; wherefore

441

toh kittinnoowam. what do you say
touohkomuk. forest
touchkomukque puppinashim. wild beast

uppaquóntup. bass head
uppéshau. to burst forth into bloom

waban. the wind
*wakwa. fox
wampum. white shell money
wéetóomau. he marries her
wetomp. dear friend
wetompauog. dear friends
wêtu. a round house
wetuomémese. a little house for women
winnaytue. a man of estimation
wonqussis. a red fox
woskehhuwaen. one who hurts
wússese. an uncle
wunnegan. beautiful
wuttáhimneash. strawberries
wuttámmagon. a pipe
wuttàh mâuo. weeping heart

yeu. this